"Which house model do you like best?" Brady asked.

He glanced at Abby. "Come on. Stop worrying and get happy. This is supposed to be the part where you get all excited and make me feel like a hero."

Her mouth lifted slightly at his silliness, and he felt better.

"I love that one," she said, pointing at the plans.

"The country cottage?" He'd chosen that one for her the minute he'd seen it. It was simple and charming. Like her. "Look at the interior plan, too. We can change it if you like, but it's perfect for your daughter's needs."

She looked up at him with those soft brown eyes. His chest expanded. She liked it. She liked it a lot. He realized then that he'd been overanxious about this home makeover, afraid she'd regret letting him barge into her life and turn it upside down.

"You think of everything, don't you?" she said, smiling.

That was the reaction he'd been looking for.

Linda Goodnight, a *New York Times* bestselling author and winner of a RITA® Award in inspirational fiction, has appeared on the Christian bestseller list. Her novels have been translated into more than a dozen languages. Active in orphan ministry, Linda enjoys writing fiction that carries a message of hope in a sometimes dark world. She and her husband live in Oklahoma. Visit her website, lindagoodnight.com, for more information.

Lois Richer loves traveling, swimming and quilting, but mostly she loves writing stories that show God's boundless love for His precious children. As she says, "His love never changes or gives up. It's always waiting for me. My stories feature imperfect characters learning that love doesn't mean attaining perfection. Love is about keeping on keeping on." You can contact Lois via email, loisricher@gmail.com, or on Facebook (loisricherauthor).

The Christmas Family

New York Times Bestselling Author

Linda Goodnight

&

Her Christmas Family Wish

Lois Richer

LOVE INSPIRED

INSPIRATIONAL ROMANCE

LOVE INSPIRED®

INSPIRATIONAL ROMANCE

Recycling programs for this product may not exist in your area.

ISBN-13: 978-1-335-42504-1

The Christmas Family and Her Christmas Family Wish

Copyright © 2021 by Harlequin Books S.A.

The Christmas Family
First published in 2015. This edition published in 2021.
Copyright © 2015 by Linda Goodnight

Her Christmas Family Wish
First published in 2016. This edition published in 2021.
Copyright © 2016 by Lois M. Richer

This edition published by arrangement with Harlequin Books S.A.

For questions and comments about the quality of this book, please contact us at CustomerService@Harlequin.com.

Love Inspired
22 Adelaide St. West, 40th Floor
Toronto, Ontario M5H 4E3, Canada
www.LoveInspired.com

Printed in U.S.A.

CONTENTS

THE CHRISTMAS FAMILY

Linda Goodnight

For my Aunt Edith, last of the Porter dynasty.
Ninety looks good on you! Thank you
for always being proud of me. Love you, dear lady.

For everyone to whom much is given,
from him much will be required.
—*Luke* 12:48

Chapter One

Brady Buchanon had planned his escape well. Three more minutes and he was out of here for the day.

He hurriedly tossed his tools into the back of the work truck, eager to be gone. Man, he loved this time of year! Cool, crisp and clear weather, and Christmas practically dripped from the trees.

He clicked the locks on his royal blue F-350, waited for Dawg, his faithful mutt to leap into the seat and was about to climb inside himself when his father, owner of Buchanon Built Construction Company and, by all rights, Brady's boss, stepped out into the late November day.

"Brady, hold up."

Not fast enough. Brady blew out a resigned breath. He leaned a hand on the truck top and waited, though not at all patiently.

"Been meaning to talk to you about something."

"Sure. What's up?"

"This makeover thing you do every Christmas, better cancel this year."

The request sailed right over Brady's head. "Too late. I already have the recipient lined up."

Dan Buchanon, his salt-and-pepper hair hidden under a Buchanon Built ball cap, scratched at the side of his neck. "You've made the announcement?"

"On my way there now. Dad, you should see this house. It's bad, but Buchanon Built can make it shine." Donating a home makeover for one needy family each Christmas was Brady's favorite event of the year, and the publicity was great for business, an important consideration to his father.

"I appreciate the sentiment, son, and in years past didn't mind the lost time and expense but not this year. We need all hands on deck."

"I can work it out. Don't worry. Buchanon projects won't suffer. The guys who volunteer can work on the makeover on their downtime or when things are slow."

But Dan was shaking his head. "With all the work on the schedule and the slowdowns we've encountered, you don't have time for charity. *We* don't have time for charity. Jaylee just told me you still don't have a plumber lined up for the Edwards project."

"I'm working on it."

Irritation flashed on Dan's face. "And you want to pull off six paying jobs for a freebie? Forget it, Brady. Forget it. And fix the plumber problem today. No more delays. No more excuses."

Brady's blood heated. He held his temper in check better these days, but no one worked him up like his dad. And vice versa. "I'm doing my best."

His father's thick jaw clenched. "I don't want your best. I want the problem solved."

"It's not as if I haven't tried." Leaving the truck door

open and the dog in the seat, Brady pushed away from the vehicle to face his father. He spread his hands in a plea. "Be reasonable, Dad." Like that was going to happen in this lifetime. "Jack Taylor had a heart attack. The man can't work." And the plumbing problem had nothing to do with Brady's home makeover.

"Then get someone else."

Brady didn't believe in kicking a man when he was down. "Jack's business needs the work. And he's the best plumber around."

"And *we* need to bring this project in on time or lose a boatload of money. The vandals have thrown us behind on everything and now subcontractors decide not to show up. Buchanon Construction was built on dependability and speed. If Jack can't work, find someone who can. Spend your time on business, not on some feel-good Christmas project."

Brady stifled an angry retort. He had places to go and much more enjoyable things to do tonight than get into another fight with his father. A plumber who'd had a heart attack didn't "decide" not to work. The choice was out of the man's hands.

"I'll talk to Jack's wife first thing in the morning." Mary Taylor was busting tail trying to keep the small plumbing business going while taking care of her ailing husband. Good plumbing temps were hard to come by. He should know. He'd called plenty, though telling that to his father was a waste of good clean Texas air.

"Tomorrow isn't good enough." Dan stacked his hands on his hips for emphasis. "I want plumbers on the job site by six in the morning to fix the problem." He jabbed a finger toward Brady. "See her now. Tonight. And don't take no for an answer. Understood?"

Brady took a step back, fuming, his back teeth tight enough to crack.

"Right. Sure. The job will get done." Brady always did the job, but his father seldom noticed progress. He only noticed the problems.

As if his demands were law—which they sort of were—Dan spun away and slammed the office door behind him. The sound reverberated in the formerly pleasant evening.

Adrenaline jacked to ninety, Brady dragged a frustrated hand down his face. Another minute and he would have been gone. Another minute and he could have gone through an entire work shift without letting his father get under his skin.

He was six inches taller and fifty pounds heavier than Dan Buchanon and had been the foreman at Buchanon Built since graduating Texas Tech eight years ago, but his father still managed to make him feel as insignificant as sawdust.

Brady turned back to the truck, where Dawg sat behind the wheel as if he was about to drive away. The comical picture erased some of Brady's frustration. "You driving?"

"Can't. He doesn't have a license."

Brady pivoted toward the voice. Dawson, one of Brady's three brothers and the dimpled twin to Sawyer, ambled around the end of the warehouse, tool belt bouncing against his hip like a gunslinger.

"Don't let Dad ruin your day. He's been in a meeting with Marilyn Tenbears for the last hour and a half."

"That explains it."

Marilyn Tenbears owned a strip of woods along Gratitude Creek that Dad was determined to purchase. Marilyn was just as determined to either get rich from the sale or keep the land.

"He thinks I should shelve the makeover."

Dawson unhooked his tool belt. "I heard. But weren't you planning to tell the recipient tonight that her home had been chosen for the remodel?"

"Still am. In fact, I'm heading over there now. Want to come along?"

"You're still going to do it?"

"That's the plan."

Dawson cast a concerned glance toward the office door. "What about Dad? How will you get this past him?"

"I'll think of something. He'll come around."

"He doesn't like his orders to be ignored."

"Dad never likes anything I do, but I get the work done."

"That's because Buchanon Built has flourished with you as foreman in a way it never could with Dad in the role. He was too harsh with subcontractors."

Brady huffed. "No kidding? Dad? Harsh?"

The brothers exchanged a chuckle.

"Hop in, Dawson, my man." Brady popped a palm against the roof of his truck and slid into the driver's seat. "Santa Claus is about to do his thing."

"What about the plumber?"

"I'll worry about him later."

With an amused shake of his head, Dawson shucked his tool belt and climbed into the big Ford with his brother, relegated Dawg to the backseat, and slammed the door. "No wonder you and Dad butt heads. Who is this year's beneficiary of a Buchanon Built makeover?"

"Abby Webster. You know who she is. She works at the Buttered Biscuit."

"Yeah." Dawson turned an interested face toward Brady. "I know who you mean. Good waitress, all business and not too smiley or talkative but remembers exactly how I like my eggs and coffee." He put the edge of his hand at nose level. "Up to here, pretty tall with long brown hair she wears in a ponytail over her shoulder. Right?"

Brady glanced from the road to his brother. "Tall? She's not tall."

"Compared to you she's not tall. Compared to other women she is."

Brady conceded a truth he had to live with and really didn't mind all that much. He was some kind of genetic throwback to his giant Celtic ancestors, both in looks and size. Even his rust-brown hair, which he clipped short, was out of sync with the rest of the family. Dawson, on the other hand, was so black-hair-and-blue-eyed pretty, he belonged on the cover of a magazine. Not that Brady would tell his manly little brother he thought he was pretty.

"Did you know she has a little girl with some kind of handicap?"

"Like I said, Abby Webster's not much of a talker. Brings my food and skitters away." From the backseat, the dog poked a cold nose in Dawson's neck. Dawson gave him a gentle shove. "Stay in the back, fella."

"Wait until you see this place, Dawson." The enthusiasm Brady had for the Christmas project bubbled up inside him. "Abby and her little girl need this makeover badly. The house is run-down, shingles missing, windows cracked, no handicap accessibility. She's going to be thrilled."

"How do you find out this stuff?"

"I ask. I look." Truth was, he drove all over town looking at houses. "People tell me."

"That's because they know you're a soft touch like Mom."

"To whom much is given, much is required."

"That's Mom's favorite verse."

"Yeah, well, she's right. Giving back is the right thing to do, and it feels pretty good, too, especially at Christmas." And nothing made him feel as worthwhile and as necessary to the planet, especially after a run-in with his critical father. "I'm not backing out no matter what Dad thinks."

"What if he pulls the powerful Buchanon rug out from under the project? You need the company to make this happen."

Brady hadn't had time to think that far, but he couldn't deny the possibility. When Dad was crossed, he could be a tough customer.

But Brady had made up his mind. One way or the other, Abby Webster was getting a home makeover. And he couldn't wait to see how happy she was when she heard the news.

Gabriel's Crossing, Texas, was the kind of place where few people crossed the railroad tracks into "that" part of town unless they lived there.

Abby Webster and her daughter lived there.

Legs aching from the twelve-hour shift at the Buttered Biscuit and delighted to be heading home, Abby encouraged her exhausted old CR-V to travel the distance from the Huckleberry Play School to the sagging house on Cedar Corner. Anyone could find her house without the number—something that had been missing far longer than Abby had lived there. Hers was the house with duct tape over a crack in the front window and the cheery crayon drawings of blue and red angels hanging next to the crack. Her four-year-old had a thing for colorful angels.

Abby parked in the driveway, a strip of blacktop with dead grass poking through the cracks. "Out you go, jelly fingers."

Her daughter, the joy of her life, giggled from her car seat. "I'm hungry."

"Imagine that, Lila Webster is hungry." Abby hopped out of the car and went around to the other side. She opened the door and unbuckled her daughter's seat belt. "How about a peanut butter and broccoli sandwich?"

"Ew, Mommy."

Smiling into her child's chocolate-colored eyes, Abby lifted the four-year-old into her arms, thankful Lila was still small. Hopefully, by the time Lila was too big to carry, they could afford a house with the space for her special equipment. Or just maybe Lila would be walking on her own without a walker or wheelchair. Such possibilities existed and Abby would never give up hope that the mild function in her child's spinal cord would continue to develop.

"Okay, then, maybe macaroni and raisins?"

Lila cocked her head, a tiny frown between dark eyebrows as she considered the combination. Then, her face lit with enthusiasm, she said, "Okay!"

Marveling at the precious gift of her child, Abby juggled Lila and her keys to unlock the front door and bump it open with her hip. Raising a child with special needs wasn't easy, but Lila's undaunted spirit and joy in living made everything worthwhile. What other child would react with such pleasure to a meal of macaroni and raisins?

"Were you a good girl at school today?"

"Ycth."

"Did Gerry say mean things to you?"

"He was nice."

Abby breathed a sigh of relief. Some kids didn't understand why Lila was different. While most didn't seem to mind that Lila wore braces and didn't walk normally, some were downright cruel at times.

Dropping her keys on the table, Abby set her daughter on the love seat with the ever-present crayons and paper and went to the kitchen to create another macaroni masterpiece.

The pasta was on to boil when Lila called, "Somebody's here, Mom. In a big, big car."

Abby heard the rumble of an engine and identified the big, big car as most likely a truck. Hmm. She hadn't ordered anything through UPS.

"Not expecting guests." She went to the side window and peeked out at the graying evening. A bright blue pickup had pulled into the driveway behind her Honda. "Who in the world is that?"

Lila, busy with another of her art projects, didn't look up. "I don't know. Maybe Santa Claus."

Abby smiled, though the statement squeezed her chest. This year was the first time Lila was old enough to really get into the idea of Santa Claus, but Lila's medical expenses kept their small budget strained to the breaking point. Lila wouldn't notice the small size of the Christmas gifts under the tree, but her mother would.

"Too early for Santa, so I don't know who…" Her voice dwindled away as two gorgeous males exited the gleaming blue truck and sauntered up her drive. They looked familiar and they had to be brothers. Though one was half a foot taller than the other, their strides matched and they swung their arms with identical confidence as though the world was their oyster. With looks like those, it probably was.

"Oh, my." As they came closer, she recognized them. Buchanons, two of the four sear-your-eyeballs-gorgeous brothers.

Abby opened the front door as the men stepped upon her wooden porch. A weak board groaned and she held her breath, hoping they wouldn't fall through.

"I don't have home owners' insurance," she blurted.

The taller one with swimming-pool eyes tilted his head. She wished she could remember his name. "Ma'am?"

"The porch," she managed, feeling stupider by the minute as her brain refused to work but her mouth kept going. "Some of the boards are weak. You're big. Don't fall through."

Both men dipped their heads to stare at the porch and then exchanged glances. "Needs work."

"Don't I know it," Abby said.

She stood in the doorway, blocking the entrance and wishing they'd state their business. Buchanons didn't exactly hang out on this side of town and they were letting out expensive heat.

"That's what we want to talk to you about."

"My porch?" Abby poked a finger into her breastbone and then flung out her hand. "Sorry, I can't afford to hire anyone right now."

"Oh, no, that's not why we're here," said Mr. Swimming-Pool Eyes. "I'm Brady Buchanon and this is my brother, Dawson. Buchanon Built Construction."

Brady and Dawson. She could never remember one brother from the other, only that all four were heart-throbs. She did, however, remember their routine orders at the diner.

Two gorgeous men on her doorstep was not the norm and she was pedaling fast to figure out why they were here. She pointed to Dawson. "Eggs over easy. And you—" Her finger went to Brady. "French toast and large milk but occasionally the house special."

A killer smile split Brady Buchanon's face. "You're making me hungry."

"Hazard of the job. I equate everyone in Gabriel's Crossing with their most common order at the café." Which, now that she thought about it, wasn't too flattering.

"May we come in for a minute?" Brady asked. "We'd like to talk to you about something."

"Oh. Well, sure, I guess so." She stepped to one side. "Come on in. Just be careful—"

Brady gave her another of those swoon-worthy grins. "We'll try not to break the floor."

"I'm sorry, I didn't mean that as insult. It's just this house is—"

He waved her off. "Don't worry about it. I'm a big boy."

"You certainly are." A hot blush raced up her neck and heated her cheeks. Her mouth was out of control tonight. At five-nine, she was unused to having men tower over her. And Brady Buchanon definitely towered. "Have a seat. That little sprite on the couch is Lila."

Lila had been staring at the men with the wide-eyed curiosity of a preschooler.

"Pretty picture," Brady said as he lowered his oversize frame onto the faded blue sofa next to Lila. Dawson took the only chair in the room, leaving Abby to perch on the other side of Lila. The couch was fuller than it had ever been.

"I'm making a kiss-mas twee. See? That's an angel."

Brady studied the crayon drawing earnestly. "Almost as pretty as you."

"Want to color with me?"

If the man had a heart, those brown eyes would melt it.

"Maybe next time, okay? Do you mind if I talk to your mommy for a few minutes?"

Lila shrugged and scribbled a little harder on her kiss-mas tree. "Okay."

Brady gazed over the top of Lila's head at Abby. "I don't know if you're familiar with my family's business, Buchanon Built Construction—"

"I am." Was he joking? The Buchanons practically owned Gabriel's Crossing. You couldn't live in this town without seeing one of their white trucks with the big blue logo or passing a sign that announced a Buchanon Built home.

"Great. Every year our company offers a home makeover to someone in town."

"I've heard about that. Last year, you remodeled Ted Bickford's house and built an addition to make room for all their children."

Ted and Teresa were kid magnets who had adopted

six and fostered as many more on any given day. The people were saints.

Brady beamed as though she'd awarded him the jackpot prize. "That's right. We did. Nice family."

But what did that have to do with her? "Excuse me a sec, will you? I have macaroni on the stove." And she hoped it hadn't boiled to mush.

"I like macaroni," Lila said, looking up. "With raisins."

Abby laughed a little as she hurried the few steps to the kitchen to drain the pasta. The kitchen-dining area was small, a throwback to the days when microwaves and dishwashers were unheard-of. "Lila would eat rocks if I added macaroni."

She turned to reenter the living room only to discover that Brady had followed and now blocked the narrow doorway, as large and intimidating and every bit as beautiful as some mythological warrior. Her pulse did a double step.

Whoa, what was that all about?

"My niece and nephew are the same way." He stepped aside, letting her pass, a movement that brought them in very close contact. Her shoulder brushed his arm. He smelled good, like new wood and Eternity cologne. "Mom cooks T-bone steaks and the kids want macaroni."

Disconcerted by the highly unusual skitter of pulse and the hum of blood in her veins, Abby hurried back to the couch. Brady followed, but not before he'd casually leaned in to the kitchen and had a look around.

What was he doing? If she didn't know him by reputation, she'd think he was casing the place for robbery. Or worse.

"Macaroni rocks the world, right, Lila?" said Dawson, whom she'd dubbed the thoughtful one long ago at the café.

"Uh-huh." Lila went right back to coloring. This time the angel was yellow.

"Now, as I was saying," Brady said, retaking his place at the end of the couch. He leaned forward, startling blue eyes holding hers and his big hands clasped in front of him. "We offer a home makeover every Christmas. This year, we'd like to remodel *your* house. Merry Christmas, Abby."

His big white smile was dazzling, and she understood he expected her to be thrilled.

She wasn't. She was embarrassed. Mortified. Humiliation heated her cheeks to chili-pepper status.

She had flashbacks to pitying teachers dragging used shoes and coats from school closets.

Her back stiffened. "That's very nice of you, but no. I couldn't accept."

Brady's smile disappeared. "No?"

"No. But thank you for the offer." She stood, expecting him to leave.

The brothers exchanged looks. They were good at that. Must be some kind of sibling symbiosis, although she wouldn't know. Being a street kid who had never even known her mother, Abby had grown up alone, mostly in group homes. Not that she minded so much now that she was an independent adult. What doesn't kill you makes you stronger. She was happy on her own. Truly, she was. She had Lila and a job and this house. She most definitely was not a charity case.

And the fact that she'd all but swooned over the handsome Buchanon brothers humiliated her even more. Men like them didn't look twice at a girl like her.

Even her ears were burning now. She wanted to dissolve right into the floor of her run-down, makeover-worthy old house.

"If you're worried we would interfere with your everyday living, we won't. We'll work out a schedule that fits yours."

Abby swallowed, her pride throbbing like an ingrown toenail. The house needed repairs but she'd get to them eventually without becoming the object of someone's pity. "Lila and I are doing fine the way we are."

"If you're worried about the money, this is a gift. No charge."

Which made it even worse. "I pay my own way, Mr. Buchanon."

Brady stared at her as if her brain was as loose as the boards on her porch. Finally, he nodded and slowly rose.

"Sorry to have bothered you." He looked so disappointed she almost caved and said yes. In fact, if her pride wasn't so insulted, she would agree anyway, just to see him smile again.

"No bother. I'm sure there are others far needier than Lila and I."

The brothers did that glancing thing again. Brady took a business card from his pocket and handed it to her. "In case you change your mind, my number is on here. Call me anytime."

"Thanks." Her smile was brittle. "See you at the Buttered Biscuit."

"Mister," Lila said, though it sounded more like "misser."

"I drawed this for you." She offered the yellow angel to him. "Hang it on your window."

His face softened. "It's beautiful. Thank you, Lila."

Lila beamed at him, pleased with herself and proud of her scrawling, four-year-old jumble of lines, circles and color.

Some of the starch went out of Abby's spine at the exchange between her small child and the giant man who accepted the drawing as if it was as valuable as a van Gogh.

Brady Buchanon was a nice guy. A guy who could easily get to her.

All the more reason to refuse his offer.

Chapter Two

"That was different," Dawson said as the brothers joined Dawg back inside the pickup.

Different didn't even come close to explaining the past ten minutes.

Stunned to numbness, Brady leaned over the steering wheel and stared at Abby Webster's house. The paint was peeling, the porch sagged—at least to his expert eye—and a dozen or more shingles were missing from the roof. The inside was as retro as any he'd seen in a while. A child like Lila would never be able to maneuver a wheelchair or a walker through those narrow doors and hallways.

"No one's ever turned us down before."

"Kind of painful, wasn't it?" Dawson gave an exaggerated shudder.

"Why? I don't get it?" Brady flopped back against the seat cushion. "The house is in sad repair and she needs us. She *needs* us."

"Getting a little overwrought, aren't you, brother? Wounded pride, maybe?"

"Yeah!" Brady cranked the engine, listened to the

rumble and put the shifter in gear. "She's supposed to be thrilled."

"Wonder why she refused. Do you think she actually doesn't see the problems?"

"Nah, it's not that. She was upset, not oblivious. The problem is, I don't know what button we pushed to fix it, but she was offended."

"The little girl was cute, huh?"

"Adorable." The truck bumped across the railroad tracks. The sun was in midset, shooting orange fingers through a purple sky. "Did you notice her artwork all over the walls?"

"Couldn't miss it. The mom's not too bad, either."

Brady gave him a hard look. "What's that supposed to mean?"

"They need this remodel. Maybe you could turn on the Buchanon charm."

Brady snorted. "No."

"You haven't dated anyone since Kiley and that was months ago."

"Not interested. I'm a builder, not a Romeo." Never mind the strange sensation that had tingled up his arms when Abby brushed past him in the kitchen. Or the weird, *weird* heat in his chest when Lila gave him her angel drawing. "You're the man about town. You ask her out."

"The Christmas makeover is your project." Dawson's wide shoulders lifted in a shrug. "We can always find another recipient. That side of town has plenty of candidates."

"Yeah, I suppose you're right. Plan B." But Abby and her little girl needed the remodel more than anyone else he'd considered. Lila, especially, according to his sources at the day care, suffered from the lack of special-needs accessories in her home. He wanted to do *that* makeover.

The next morning Brady awakened hungry. Nothing unusual about that, but this morning he decided to eat breakfast at the Buttered Biscuit. Call him stubborn or perverse, but he wasn't ready to give up on Miss Abby Webster. If a little of his presence reminded her of how much she needed him and what a good guy he was, all the better.

The drive to the café took a few minutes. He'd built his house, or rather half of it, on the edge of town not far from the river in a copse of bald cypress and red oak. As he liked to say, his home was a work in progress. The lower floor was finished and the rest evolved in squeezed-out hours and minutes. All of the Buchanon kids except Quinn had, over time, acquired a Buchanon Built home.

Older brother Quinn was, himself, a work in progress, still trying to pull his act together after a life-altering accident, though most of the family thought ten years was enough time for anyone. Forgiving Jake Hamilton, the cause of the accident, had made a difference, but Quinn had a ways to go.

Brady turned the lock on his front door and whistled his way out into the cool morning with Dawg at his heel.

As he drove into town and down First Street to the café, gray fog crawled along the ground in mysterious wisps and wiggles.

"Sit tight, pal, and I'll bring you a sausage patty." Brady gave Dawg a pat and rolled the window down enough for the animal to stick his nose out if the mood struck. Dawg, accustomed to waiting for his master, put his chin on his paws and went to sleep.

Breakfast smells hit Brady full in the olfactory glands the minute he entered the café. His stomach reacted with wild abandon.

As usual this early in the morning, the café was jammed and the clatter of conversations mixed with the clink of plates and the cook's voice calling "order up!"

An old-time diner-style café that served up home cooking and comfort food, the Buttered Biscuit was the place to be for good eats and all the latest and greatest in Gabriel's Crossing news.

Brady greeted friends and acquaintances as he made his way to a table still cluttered with someone else's empty plates and took a seat.

Jan, the owner and baker of the fluffiest biscuits in Texas, whipped past. "Get that in a sec, Brady."

"No rush." Which wasn't technically true. He was always in a rush these days.

Two other waitresses were on duty, all of them moving at Mach speed to fill cups and deliver plates. Abby Webster, pad in hand, took orders two tables away. She looked up, spotted Brady and hesitated as if she didn't want to see him.

Too bad.

She had kept him up late trying to figure out why anyone would refuse a free home makeover from the best builders in the area. The least she could do was bring him a cup of coffee.

She whipped toward him and he noticed her as he never had before, though he ate at the diner fairly often. Probably because, as Dawson said, she was all business. The other waitresses smiled and bantered with the customers—he noticed *them*—but Abby simply worked. He wondered, randomly, if she did anything for fun.

"French toast and milk?" she asked. Her cheekbones were tipped in pink.

"Sure. And the strongest cup of coffee you have." Coffee, like her eyes. Dark and shiny and able to deliver a jolt.

She didn't offer a joke, as Jan would have, by asking him if he'd been out all night partying or some other sass-mouthed comment she was known for. Abby simply scribbled his order, grabbed a pile of plates and sailed away.

He watched her move through the customers, topping off coffee and delivering checks as she made her way to the kitchen with his order.

She was actually kind of pretty, a truth that surprised him this morning. Mink-colored hair that gleamed over one shoulder, huge dark eyes framed by thick, arching eyebrows and a wide, full mouth. On anyone else, the large features would be too much, but they looked good on her.

"What are you staring at, big brother?" Dawson pulled out the chair opposite him. Sawyer, the other twin, joined him on the right.

Brady ignored the question. "What are you two doing here?"

"Same as you. Too lazy to cook breakfast. Have you been able to locate a plumber for the Edwards job?"

Brady slapped the heel of one hand to his forehead. "Ah, man, I forgot."

He'd been so keyed up after the strange meeting with Abby he'd not given the plumber another thought until this moment.

"Dad's not going to be happy."

"I'll find someone." But not before the already-passed deadline of six o'clock. "Any ideas."

"A couple. You might call Richie Clonts up in Idabel."

"Good idea."

"Give Charity a call. She'll know his number."

Charity was their oldest sister, a powerhouse real estate agent with a steel-trap mind and a list of contacts a mile long.

He fished his cell phone from his hip pocket, got the number from his sister and called the plumber. Five minutes later, he hung up a happier man. "Richie can send someone tomorrow. Dad wanted someone today, but tomorrow is better than nothing."

Abby appeared with his coffee in a thick white mug and took orders from the twins.

"You're pretty busy," Sawyer said, saying the obvious with a toothy smile. Brady's younger brothers, especially Sawyer, were always scoping the field for ladies.

"Slammed, but it's letting up."

"Still have my phone number?" Brady asked.

Her gaze flicked his direction. She got pink again. "Haven't you chosen someone else?"

"I'd rather give you time to think about the offer."

"Why?"

The question caught Brady off guard, but he said, "I like your little girl and I can give her something she needs."

A look, almost of panic, flamed in Abby's eyes. Again, Brady wondered what her problem was.

"Lila and I are okay, but thanks. Anything else on these orders?"

The twins lifted their fingers off the table in an identical gesture. "We're good."

And Abby whirled away, leaving the Buchanon brothers staring after her.

"Stubborn," Brady muttered as he reached for the steaming cup.

"Embarrassed," Dawson said. "Did you see how she blushed?" Intuitive and empathetic, Dawson was the brother who always noticed things like that.

"Nah," Sawyer said, and laughed. "She was overwhelmed by my charm. Girls always turn pink in my studly presence."

His brothers hooted.

"Dawg's more charming than you."

"Prettier, too."

"Aw, thanks, guys." Sawyer hung his head in mock offense.

"Kidding aside, do you think we embarrassed her?" Brady asked.

"What's this *we* business? You're the guilty party."

The concept gave Brady pause. He'd never purposely embarrass someone, but maybe Dawson was right. Maybe Abby somehow mistook his intentions. Maybe she thought he was putting her down.

Man, he'd never considered such a thing.

"I think I should talk to her again, show her the possibilities."

The twins exchanged looks. "Can't take no for an answer, can you, Brady?"

Never had. Never would. Not when someone needed him, and he was convinced Abby and Lila needed his help.

Before he left, Brady slid a twenty-dollar bill under his plate.

* * *

He'd left her twenty dollars. Abby didn't know whether to be pathetically grateful or even more humiliated than she'd been last night.

"Wow, girlfriend, you must have been on your game this morning. Twenty bucks," Charla Patterson, one of the other waitresses and Abby's friend said as she helped clear the Buchanon table. "Have you caught the eye of one of Gabriel's Crossing's most eligible bachelors?"

Abby shook her head at the ridiculous notion. "Like that would ever happen."

"Hey, don't sell yourself short. You have lots to offer."

"Tell that to Warren." She'd trusted her ex-boyfriend, a man who'd promised love and marriage but bolted when he learned the child Abby carried would be special-needs. Now, she only felt loathing for the man who had never once laid eyes on his beautiful daughter.

"Warren was a user. It's time for you to stop beating yourself up over him and move on."

"I'm not beating myself up. I'm glad he's out of our lives."

"And I'm thankful for that. I never liked the guy, even though I still think you should force him to pay child support. You could use the money."

"No way. I don't want him involved with Lila any more than he wants to be. He doesn't deserve to be part of her life. Him or his lovely wife." She sounded bitter and didn't want to be. But his cruel rejection had stabbed deep and left her uncertain and bruised.

"There are good guys out there, hon. Guys like Brady Buchanon. His cute twin brothers, too."

A funny little twitter went off in Abby's belly. She

clattered a fork onto a plate and ignored the feeling. "I have Lila. She's all I need."

"So why did Brady leave such a fat tip this morning?"

"Not because he's after me, that's for sure." She forced a laugh, surprised to be bothered by that truth. "Remember how the Buchanons give away a home makeover every Christmas?"

"Sure. The makeover is a big deal. A really big deal." Charla slapped a bleach rag against the tabletop as her eyes widened. "You don't mean—"

"Brady offered it to me."

"Abby! That's amazing. Congratulations. No one deserves a new home more than you."

"I turned him down."

"What? Are you out of your mind?"

"I don't need their help, Char. I can take care of my daughter and my house and my *life* without anyone."

"Oh, Abby." Charla looked at her with sympathy. Dishes rattled as they stacked them on the cart. "Sometimes you're too independent for your own good. Warren really did a number on you."

Warren wasn't the only one though, admittedly, he'd been the latest in bad decisions that had come back to bite her. Abby was smart enough to know her background made her wary. Nobody did something for nothing. Stick your heart out there and it would get tromped. Every time. If trying to fit into a family and failing at age thirteen hadn't proved that, Warren had.

Big, beautiful Brady Buchanon would have to find someone else to feel sorry for.

She stuck his twenty dollars into her pocket and debated on giving it back.

* * *

Lila's play school telephoned an hour before Abby's shift ended.

"For you, Abby," Jan called, holding her hand over the mouthpiece. "Christina at the play school."

The café was in the lull shortly before dinner hour and Abby was in the middle of filling and wiping down saltshakers. She recapped the latest one and went to the phone.

"Sorry," she said to Jan. "I'm out of minutes for my phone." But with Christmas coming, she was holding off on the purchase as long as possible.

"You know I don't care when it's important." Her boss, a sturdy, energetic woman with close-cropped blond waves, winked. "Lila's always important."

"Thanks, Jan." Her boss was good to her so Abby never wanted to take advantage. She took the phone and said, "Hello."

A minute later she hung up. "Jan, Lila had a bathroom accident at school. I really have to go over there, but I'll come back as soon as I take care of her."

Jan glanced around the quiet café. "Charla and I can handle it for an hour until Mercy gets here. Get Lila and go on home. Tell her accidents happen to everyone."

But they happened to Lila more than most. While her potty training had progressed to a good schedule considering the nerve damage below the waist, on occasion she had an accident.

Abby didn't know whether to be grateful for her boss's understanding or worried. She needed the hour on her paycheck, but Lila came first. "I'll see you at five-thirty in the morning then?"

"Deal." Jan waved her off.

The streets of Gabriel's Crossing bustled with Christmas preparations. City workers in cherry pickers were draping strands of green lighted garland from one side of First Street to the other. In the center of each garland was a huge green wreath with artificial candles and a big red bow.

Just looking at the decorations going up everywhere filled her with excited dread. She loved seeing Lila's excitement but wished she could give her more. Lila didn't even have grandparents or other relatives to spoil her and buy her things.

But that was okay. They didn't need anyone else. They had each other.

She swung by the house to pick up a change of clothes and reached Huckleberry Play School soon thereafter.

Greeted by Christina, the owner/operator of the day care where Lila had gone for the past year, Abby fretted. One of the rules of this facility was that children had to be potty trained. The staff accommodated Lila's special needs in other ways, but this was a rule for all children, not just Lila.

"I'm really sorry about this, Christina. Lila's been doing so well."

"She has. Don't worry about it this time, but if she regresses, we'll need to talk again."

"I understand." Truly she did, but this was the only preschool in town that accommodated Abby's long hours and odd work days. Plus, Lila loved it here. Abby wasn't sure what she would do if she had to find another placement.

"Lila is waiting in my office," Christina said. "She was very upset."

Abby hurried to the office and found her red-eyed

daughter sitting with her small legs dangling from an adult chair. Chin on her chest, mouth tilted down, Lila was the picture of dejection.

Abby's heart broke at the sight. Her chest clutched as she gathered her child into her arms. "Hey, jelly fingers. Mom's here, and I brought your favorite outfit to change into."

"My jammies?" Lila asked hopefully.

Around a lump in her throat, Abby managed a chuckle. "We'll get into those after a bath at home. Okay? For now, how about your pink princess set?"

Lila sniffed, long and shuddery, and nodded her head.

Abby gathered her child into her arms and carried her to the bathroom to change, and then they headed home.

The usually chatty Lila said little in the car, though Abby tried to start distracting conversations about Christmas.

"Lila," Abby said, as they pulled into the blacktop drive and parked. "Accidents happen. Miss Jan said to remind you of that. You're doing great, and I'm proud of you."

"Will I ever be big like other kids?"

Unexpected tears jammed the back of Abby's nose and throat. She'd been dealing with the effects of Lila's mild spina bifida for years, but, instead of getting easier as Lila grew old enough to notice the world around her, the task became harder.

"You will always be the most awesome Lila in the world."

For now, this was enough to bring the faintest glimmer of a smile to her daughter's face. But how long before a nonanswer was not enough?

Heart heavy, Abby gathered her child into her arms

and started to the house. As she stepped up on the porch, keys in one hand and Lila on her hip, the board she'd warned Brady Buchanon about gave way.

Her foot caught in the broken board and Abby struggled to maintain her balance. Struggled and failed. Instinctively trying to protect Lila, she twisted to the left and tumbled onto the porch in a heap. She lost her grip, and Lila hit the wooden porch and started to cry.

"Are you hurt? Oh, baby. You're okay. You're okay." In a panic, Abby scrambled to her feet and pulled Lila into her arms, searching for blood or bruises. With her nerve impairment, Lila didn't always know when she was injured.

Once she was certain no real emergency existed, Abby opened the door and carried Lila inside the living room. Both of them were shaking. She had never dropped her daughter. Never.

Lila curled up on the couch and sniveled. This hadn't been her best day.

Abby scooted onto the couch beside her daughter and laid her head against Lila's. "I'm sorry, baby. Do you hurt anyplace?"

"Uh-uh. Can I have a drink?" The usually sunny child sounded so small and pitiful Abby wanted to cry.

"Sure, you can." Abby pushed off the couch and went into the kitchen, adrenaline still pumping from the scare. "Stupid board. Stupid old house. Stupid, stupid, stupid."

As she railed against the accident, she opened the cabinet for a glass, and another chip of paint fell from the overpainted wood.

She needed a new house. A place that wasn't a danger to Lila.

Abby leaned her forehead against the cabinet and

fought off the surge of pride. Brady Buchanon's voice played in her memory. He could give Lila something she needed.

As hard as it would be for Abby to accept charity again, this wasn't about her. This was about doing the right thing for Lila.

She dug in her pocket and pulled out the card with the blue Buchanon Built logo and Brady's number, and resigned herself to a little more humiliation.

Chapter Three

"You have to be kidding me?" Grimly, Brady leaned a shoulder against one unfinished wall of gypsum board, his cell phone pressed against his ear. He gripped the device as if he wanted to strangle someone. Which he did. "When did this happen?"

He listened as his father railed against yet another act of vandalism against one of the company's building sites. No one could figure out why Buchanon Built was being targeted, but someone seemed to know when a home-in-progress would be devoid of workers.

"I'll sleep here if I have to, but this project is not going to be damaged." Brady shuddered at the thought. They'd chunked thousands into this showplace along Crystal Ridge. A break-in could set them back for months and cost them more than the insurance could cover.

His father ranted, growing louder by the minute, as if the situation was entirely Brady's fault.

"Right. I hear you, Dad. Call Leroy at the police station. He knows about the others."

When he tapped the End key a few minutes later, his blood boiled and his finger trembled. What a lousy day.

The trenchers had hit an electric cable and downed all the power in the Huckleberry Creek addition. A frame carpenter had been taken to the ER with appendicitis. Dad was furious over the lack of a plumber on the Edwards house. And now this. Another Buchanon Built home damaged by thugs.

He ran a hand over the top of his head and debated on a trip to the damaged site or staying with this project for the remainder of the day. Not much he could do over there until the police had made another useless investigation. Dad was already there and mad enough to spit nails faster and harder than an air gun.

Here was preferable at the moment.

From the back room, a table saw revved up in a high-pitched wail. The twins were on it, trimming out the bedrooms in a unique routered design created specifically for this house by the Buchanon brain trust.

His phone vibrated again. Brady groaned. Loudly. *Please. Not more trouble.*

"Hello," he growled into the mouthpiece, daring the caller to give him one more bit of bad news.

No one said anything for a couple of seconds, and then a very hesitant female voice asked, "Is this Brady Buchanon?"

A pleasant voice, sweet and warm and womanly.

Nice. But who?

His brain played mental gymnastics as he softened his reply, "Yes, this is Brady. May I ask who's calling?"

"Abby Webster. Have I caught you at a bad time?"

He almost laughed. She didn't know the half of it. "Not at all. What can I do for you, Abby? Maybe a little remodel work?"

He couldn't help it. He was born to be pushy when

he wanted something. She'd probably turn him down again, but he had to try.

"Actually—" there was that hesitation again "—yes."

The word hummed through the cyberspace connecting them. She'd said yes?

"You changed your mind? May I ask why?" A smile lit his insides, erasing some of the lousy, lousy events of the day. Teasing, he said, "Was it my charm, or my pretty brothers? Or maybe the double order of French toast?"

He didn't—wouldn't—mention the tip.

She sighed out a weary breath. "Blame it on my front porch. I fell through."

Brady's shoulders tensed. "Are you hurt?"

"No, but I had Lila in my arms. She wasn't hurt either, but she could have been." Her words faded in an anguished breath.

Brady got her meaning. She didn't particularly want the makeover, but for Lila she'd take it. He didn't care what her reasons were. In the end, she'd be delighted with the results, and Lila would be better off while he got to play Santa. A win-win in his book any day of the week.

Already feeling vastly better, he said, "Let's get together tonight and talk this over. I'll come by after work."

"Well, I—guess that would be okay."

"Do you and Lila like barbecue?"

"What? Yes, we love it, but you don't need to bring food."

Brady laughed. "Abby, I'm a big boy. I gotta have food, and so do you." Even though he couldn't recall a time when he'd brought food for a prospective client. That was his sister's domain. "What time works best?"

After a few more useless protests against him doing anything nice for her, she named the time and they ended the call.

His mood much elevated, he slid his cell phone into his back pocket and gave a soft whistle. "Quitting time, Dawg."

The canine, sprawled in a corner of the great room like an ornament befitting the massive fireplace, lifted his brindled body from the bare concrete floor and gave his fur a hardy shake.

"We're going to Abby Webster's, and I might let you say hello. What do ya think about that?"

Dawg trotted to the door and looked back expectantly.

The dog was weird that way. He seemed to know what Brady was talking about most of the time. "Hold on a minute. I have to tell the other guys."

Feeling unusually chipper, considering the problems of the day, Brady cleaned up his mess and secured his tools before talking to the twins.

"Another break-in," he said as he entered what would be the master bedroom. At the moment, sawdust covered the floor, along with a stack of clean-smelling lumber. Smack in the middle of the room stood a table saw and one of his brothers in plastic safety goggles. "Dad called."

Sawyer pushed the goggles atop his black hair and tilted his chin toward the unfinished ceiling in a pained groan. "That must have been fun."

"Loved it," Brady answered wryly. "You boys about ready to call it a night?" He rubbed his hands together. "I've got places to go and things to do."

Dawson, on his haunches fitting trim, pushed to a stand. "You seem in a seriously good mood for someone who's been talking to Dad about vandalism. Don't tell me you have a date."

"Nah, nothing like that." Although he was taking food and going to see a woman, the reason had nothing to do with a date. It was all about the project, not the woman. "Dad's not the only caller. Get this. Abby Webster changed her mind. The makeover is on!" He pumped a fist.

A grin deepened the single dimple in Dawson's cheek. "Yeah? That's terrific. When do we start?"

"I'm headed over there later tonight to work out plans. This should be the best makeover ever."

The twins exchanged looks.

Brady pointed two index fingers, one at each brother. "Don't start that. Abby's not the only single-mom makeover we've done."

Dawson held up both palms. "Hey, I'm with you. I was over there, remember. Nobody in town needs this remodel more than Abby and her little girl."

"Yeah, the little girl," Brady said. "She's the kicker."

Sawyer spiked an eyebrow in his usual tease. "And the mom's no slouch."

No, Brady thought, surprising himself. No, she wasn't.

Abby's nerves jittered as she opened the door for Brady Buchanon. He came inside, bringing with him the scent of hot, spicy barbecue.

"I can tell what's in that sack," she said as he handed it over. "The smell is fabulous."

"Danny makes the best barbecue in this part of Texas."

She knew, though budget constraints had meant she

hadn't eaten any of it in a long time. Eating out was a luxury reserved for Lila's clinic visits when they really had no choice.

"You didn't have to bring dinner."

Brady shrugged. "It's just food."

Lila, who was lying on her belly on the rug sorting through a bag of magnetic shapes, held one up.

"This is a wetangle," she said.

"Rectangle," Abby corrected, unsure if Brady would understand Lila's developing speech.

"I see that." The big man went to his haunches beside her daughter. "Do you know any of the others?"

"Yes." And she named off the circle, square and heart, making her mama proud.

"I brought you something." From inside his jacket he took a small, stuffed animal. "I hope you like dogs."

"A puppy!" Lila's eyes lit up as Abby's suddenly filled with unexpected tears. "Mama, look. A puppy. I love him."

Abby wanted to protest the unnecessary gift, but how could she when it had made Lila so happy?

"Brady," she simply said, shaking her head. Why had he done that? They weren't friends or relatives. They barely knew each other.

Brady ignored her protest. He was, she noticed again, good at that.

"I have a dog outside in my truck," he said to her beaming daughter. "Want to see him?"

Lila's eyes grew wide. "A real one?"

"As real as can be."

"What's his name?"

"Dawg."

With an odd hitch beneath her ribs, Abby listened to

the easy conversation between her child and the giant man. Lila, accustomed to doctors and technicians and physical therapists, rarely met a stranger, but it was the man who bothered Abby. He couldn't be for real. She knew that for a fact. People were nice in the beginning but after a while, they'd disappoint you.

Someday Lila would learn those things the hard way, a truth that made Abby ache. But today Lila was an innocent, trusting child clearly fascinated by the idea of a real dog, something she'd never had.

"Does he like little girls?" Lila asked.

"Crazy for them."

"Will he jump on me?"

"Not if I tell him to be good."

"I want to pet him." In total trust, Lila reached her arms up toward Brady. "Let's go."

"Do you mind?" he said, rather belatedly to Abby.

Abby scoffed softly. Even if she minded, he'd put her in an impossible situation. "You don't have to do that."

"I want to."

She wanted to ask why he'd bother when he'd come to discuss the remodel, but instead she said, "Go ahead. She loves animals, especially dogs."

Those mesmerizing blue eyes sparkled. "I gathered that by her reaction to the stuffed one." To Lila, he said, "Come on, little one. Up you go."

He dwarfed her child, this huge man with the handsome face and stunning eyes, but he was as gentle as a whisper as he lifted Lila into his arms.

A big, big man. Her tiny, precious girl.

Something tender moved inside Abby.

She whipped away to open the door, but Brady with

his long stride beat her there and easily maneuvered both the door and the child.

"Watch that board," she warned, suddenly scared that his superior size would send him plummeting with Lila as she had done.

"Got it." He stepped over the opening.

Abby walked alongside, aware of Brady Buchanon in the most uncomfortable way. His kindness bewildered her. Not once since his arrival had he mentioned the makeover. Or the fact that she was the Buchanon charity case for the year.

The twenty-dollar bill was in her back pocket. She should return it, remind him that she didn't want his pity or his charity and that she was only accepting the makeover for Lila's sake. Even that stuck in her craw like a dry slice of toast. *She* wanted to provide for her daughter.

As they approached the blue pickup, a large brindle-colored dog with soulful golden eyes and a sweet expression stuck his head out the open driver's-side window.

"He thinks he can drive," Brady said, eliciting a giggle from Lila. "You can pet him. He's a big sap. He'll love it."

Lila placed a tentative hand on the dog's wide head. When he didn't move, only looked at her with those sweet eyes, she ruffled his ears. "Can he come out and play?"

"Sure. Open the door for him, will you, Abby?" He said the words casually, and she could see he felt comfortable with people in a way she didn't. But then, the Buchanons were a large family.

She opened the truck door, and the dog named Dawg leaped gracefully to the ground and stared up at his owner as if waiting for commands.

"Sit down, Dawg. This is Lila and Abby. Friends. Be good now."

The dog flopped on his rear, long tail bumping the ground with comical eagerness. Brady went down on the balls of his feet in front of the animal with Lila on one khaki-clad knee. Abby watched as Dawg behaved like a gentleman while Lila petted him.

"He likes me," Lila said.

"He sure does. Hold your hand out like this." Brady took Lila's tiny hand and turned it palm up. "Now say, 'Dawg, shake.'"

Lila did as Brady asked. When Dawg carefully plopped a furry paw into her palm, her giggle sent happy chills down Abby's spine.

"He did it! Mommy, Dawg shaked my hand."

"Is he always this well behaved?" Abby asked.

"Pretty much. I take him on the job with me." Brady hitched a shoulder. "Basically take him everywhere. He has to behave or be stuck at home alone."

"Do you let him inside the house?"

"Sure. He sleeps at the end of my bed."

Okay, that was too much information. She didn't want to imagine a sleep-rumpled Brady in baggy pajama pants. He was a builder, here to do a job.

"Mama, can he come inside? Dawg can sit by me. I'll show him my shapes."

Abby hesitated. To Brady, she said, "Should I let him?"

"Up to you, but he won't be a problem. I can promise you that."

Promises. She knew how those worked.

"I suppose it's all right this once. What kind of dog is he?"

"Anyone's guess. Some boxer, shepherd, Lab. Who knows? I got him from the shelter, but we don't care, do we, pal? We're all mutts in our way." With one final pat on the dog's head, Brady rose with Lila. The dog trotted along behind as they returned to the house.

Abby was keenly aware of the man who gently put her daughter on the floor mat, commanded the dog to behave and followed Abby into the kitchen.

Uncomfortable and uncertain, she asked, "Do you want to talk while we eat? Or after?"

This was not a social call. He'd surely want to do his business and move on. The Buchanons were busy people, involved in many segments of Gabriel's Crossing life.

"Might as well eat while the barbecue and fries are hot. Talk can happen anytime."

Though her kitchen-dining space was minuscule and made smaller by the invasion of a man the size of some mythological warrior, Brady made himself at home. He opened cabinets, found plates and knives, and generally embarrassed her.

"I can do this," she said, grabbing the utensils from him.

"Many hands make light work." He grinned. "That's according to my Grandfather Buchanon who started the construction company. Having a bunch of grandsons made work easier for him."

She quickly set out the dishes and food, going a little mushy to discover a foam container of macaroni in the bag.

He'd remembered Lila's love of all things macaroni? Who was this guy?

"I'll get the little one," he said, and ducked his head beneath the doorway as he went into the living room.

During their meal, Brady talked about everything but the makeover. He drew her out, asking questions about her work, Lila's school, Christmas and all things Gabriel's Crossing. He told her a funny story about his sisters and a skunk, and Abby found herself relating funny experiences from the café. Then they shared a laugh about the ongoing feud between Hoss Hanover, town mayor, and Flo Dubois, a former Vegas showgirl now in her seventies and still as sassy and ornery as ever.

Once or twice, she even forgot he was here on a charitable mission.

By the time the messy barbecue was demolished, the nervous butterflies in her stomach had subsided. Brady might be big but he wasn't nearly as scary as she'd thought.

"Well," he said, pushing his plate aside. "That was good. Now my brain can work. Let's talk makeover."

She held up a finger. "First, you have to know something. I'm only doing this because of Lila."

He aimed those swimming-pool eyes at her. "Understood. Now, let's get down to basics. I'll do a walk-through and make notes of what needs done. Then, we'll talk about it. I want your input, your ideas, what you want and need. I have people on my team who know all about special-needs construction. They'll be in on the planning, too, but basically this project is my baby. Mine and yours."

She was feeling a little overwhelmed. "I don't even know what to say."

"No need to say anything. I'll bring by appliance catalogs, color charts, carpet samples and that kind of thing for you to look at." He flashed a smile. "That's where you come in."

Carpet? Appliances? "I didn't expect all that."

In truth, she hadn't expected anything, but this...this. She was starting to get excited. Not good. Not good at all. Excitement preceded disappointment.

As usual, Brady paid her no mind. He took a note-pad from his jacket hanging on the back of a chair. "If it's all right, I'll inspect the structure first, get a basic idea of what we'll need to do, and we'll go from there."

"Sure. I'll just... Can I follow you around?"

He chuckled. "It's your house."

Leaving Lila to watch a *Veggie Tales* with Dawg sprawled adoringly at her side, Abby joined the builder. As they did the walk-through, she saw the house in a new light, from a stranger's viewpoint, and shame trick-led into her stomach.

He must think she was a sorry excuse for a mother, raising her special-needs daughter in a run-down house with nothing more than a safety bar beside the bathtub.

"I installed that myself," she said, half in self-de-fense. She didn't want him judging her. She tried. And for now, she could carry Lila. "I was planning to add more as she grows."

"You did great." But he jotted all kinds of notes on that pad of his as he inspected plumbing under the sinks and thumped his big fist against walls. She cringed at the last, concerned he'd go right through.

"We could create a bathroom here specifically for her. Put a walk-in shower there," he said. "Big enough to accommodate her walker or a wheelchair. Add some bench seating, lower the sink and commode so she can access them herself."

The ideas made Abby's heart soar and her eyes water. "That would be wonderful. I don't know how to thank you."

"No thanks needed. Gotta make things right for the little princess." He winked. "Dawg said so."

She smiled, grateful to him for making light of a humiliating situation. For her, anyway.

They moved through the house and her brain spun as he discussed removing walls, widening halls and re-arranging the interior of the house for more space and flow.

Hope, that sneaky weed, sprouted up inside her chest. His ideas were wonderful, beautiful, a dream come true. He was amazing, kind and funny, and Abby found herself looking forward to the days and hours he'd spend in her house making it better.

Though the decision had come slowly, like Cinderella preparing for the ball, she now wanted this makeover badly. For Lila's sake. Brady really could give her child what she needed.

When they entered her bedroom, Abby was thankful she'd made the bed and tidied up before his arrival. She lingered in the doorway, a little disconcerted to have him in her private space. But she'd have to get used to that, she supposed. He was a builder; he didn't think anything about it.

Brady pointed to the ceiling and exterior wall. "Some leakage in here."

"Only when it rains." She tried to sound chipper, but Brady frowned and her stomach dipped. "Will that be a problem?"

"Depends." He walked across to the window and the wooden floor groaned. He paused, bounced a little and frowned again. "Where's your crawl space? Lots of weak spots in the flooring. I'd better have a look at the joists before we get too far into this."

She didn't know a joist from a joust, but she knew where the crawl space was, though she couldn't imagine a man his size crawling under her house. "You'll get dirty."

Humor brightened his face. "I'm in construction. We get a little dirty."

"Yes, but you're the owner."

"A hands-on owner. Dad insisted we know the business from the ground up. Literally." He rotated his wide shoulders and looked down at his large body. "Though nowadays I usually send someone smaller under the houses."

"I fixed a broken pipe last winter. I could go under there and tell you what I see."

"Don't worry. I got it. Be right back."

"You'll need a flashlight."

"In my truck."

He headed outside while she checked on Lila and Dawg, and then started on kitchen cleanup. She heard him clang on a pipe with something metal, so she knew he'd somehow squeezed into the small space.

He was gone for quite a while and when he came inside, he didn't look happy.

Putting away the last dish, she dried her hands, worry niggling.

"You have spiderwebs—"

His chin dipped toward his shoulder. "Where?"

"Your hair. Bend down." Without thinking anything of it, she dusted the cobwebs from his russet hair and the back of his shirt. The action felt intimate somehow, and she finished quickly.

"Sorry. I thought I knocked them off outside."

A little dust on the floor was the least of her concerns. "What's the verdict?"

"Not what I'd hoped. Or expected."

"What does that mean?"

"Sit down. Let's talk a minute." He motioned to the table.

They'd been talking for two hours, but she pulled out a chair and sat. He did the same. A knot formed in her belly. Something was wrong.

"I have bad news, Abby." Brady pinched the top of his lip, drew in a deep breath and blew it out in a hearty gust. "Your house is not salvageable. I can't do the remodel."

Chapter Four

Abby had known it was too good to be true. She shouldn't be disappointed. But she was. Which was exactly what she got for getting her hopes up. She knew better.

"Is it that bad?" Sure, the old house leaked and was draftier than a barn, but she and Lila lived in reasonable comfort. Except when it rained. Or the north wind blew.

"Bad enough that it isn't cost-effective to remodel."

"Okay." She nodded once. She'd been let down before. At least she hadn't started dreaming and planning too much. Maybe a little when he'd mentioned color charts and carpet samples.

She put on her best fake smile and stood. "Thank you for trying. I appreciate the thought and your time, and I'm sure you'll have no problem finding someone else for your Christmas makeover. It's a wonderful thing you do."

Brady titled his head and lifted his index finger. "Whoa, wait a second. I didn't say I was giving up. Buchanons never give up."

"But if you can't repair the problems—"

"There's always a way." He twitched a shoulder. "We can start fresh, build new."

"What?" She slithered back onto the chair, more than a little stunned. Was he serious? Build new?

"Makeovers come in many forms. Remodel. Brand-new. In your situation, we'll shoot for new. We can bulldoze this house and build exactly what you want in its place."

Abby refused to acknowledge the sudden, thrilling anticipation frolicking in her belly. What he asked was impossible. Completely impossible. Even though the property was hers to do with as she pleased, she had no place else to go. Bulldozing to build new was out of the question! "I don't think so, Brady."

"Why not? I can build bigger, better and more efficient from the ground up, a house exactly the way you want it. With all the bells and whistles and lots of pretty things for Lila."

Oh, he was cruel, dangling that carrot in front of her. For a fleeting moment the image of a perfect little cottage with fresh paint and matching shutters surrounded by colorful flowers flashed through her mind. A dream home for her and Lila. A place that would assist Lila to develop her strengths rather than inhibit her.

Then reality, that cruel beast, came roaring back. Some things just weren't possible. "Thank you, but it won't work."

"Sure it will," he said with the confidence only a successful man with an easy upbringing would display. "Starting fresh is the perfect solution."

He clearly hadn't been kicked in the teeth very many times, and he had no understanding of a person without alternatives, with no place to go, no one but herself to lean on. "This place may not look like much to you, Brady, but this is our home. There's nothing perfect about tearing it down. We live here."

"You can live somewhere else temporarily. It won't be long. My crews work fast."

She wanted to accept his offer so badly her throat ached from holding back a shout of *Yes!*

"I can't," she said instead. "Please understand, as much as I appreciate the offer, I like my home the way it is." And frogs had wings. "Lila and I are fine right here."

She wasn't about to admit that she had nowhere else to go, no money for another monthly payment on a rental and no relatives to impose upon.

He tilted back in his chair and pinched his upper lip. He had a habit of doing that, she noticed, when things weren't going his way. He breathed in through his nose and out through his mouth in a puff of frustration. His blue eyes, laser bright, dimmed the slightest amount.

"You're saying no?" He seemed incredulous as if only an idiot would turn down a brand-new house, and she wasn't going to explain the circumstances to change his assessment. It was bad enough he pitied her living conditions; she sure didn't want him to know the rest.

"Yes." From the living room, she heard Lila giggle and fought off a surge of longing. Her baby deserved better.

She stood again and this time Brady stood with her, towering over her. There was something comforting about a nice man who could make her feel small and feminine.

Teeth clamped tight against the bizarre emotions Brady Buchanon elicited, she led the way into the living room.

Dawg was lying with his nose on Lila's lap. Her tiny hand rested on his wide head as they both watched cartoons. The dog lifted his eyes toward his master. Brady nudged his chin toward the door. "Time to go, boy."

Slowly, Dawg stretched to his feet.

"Oh," Lila said, and wrapped her arms around the animal's neck.

"Brady and Dawg have to leave now, Lila. Tell them bye."

Lila looked as if her best friend forever was abandoning her. She gave Dawg one final squeeze. "Bye, Dawg. Bye, Mr. Brady."

Brady, whose jaw was tight, as if he held back a hearty temper, softened. He gave one of Lila's twin ponytails a gentle tug. "Bye now, little one."

Stiffly Abby opened the front door, eager now for him to leave so she could forget this had happened, forget she'd almost let herself dream. "Thank you for the barbecue."

She didn't know if she was making the right choice or not, but for her, refusal was the only choice.

"So how's the home makeover going?" Dawson asked as he plopped down next to Brady on the couch at Mom's house the next Sunday afternoon.

"It's not." Brady stuck his hand in the chip bowl and filled his paw with Fritos and tossed one to Dawg.

"No?" Sawyer joined the pair in the family room waiting for the NFL game to come on. From the kitchen came smells of hot Ro*Tel cheese dip and homemade chili as the seven siblings gathered for the weekly after-church hangout and football frenzy. "Why not?"

"Abby changed her mind." Brady was, he had to

admit, pretty steamed about that little turn of events. What kind of woman turned down a new house when she could obviously use it, especially when her kid had needs that weren't being addressed by her current residence? And the way she'd refused, without so much as a reason, irritated him.

"I thought she was on board." Dawson crunched down on a chip. "What did you do?"

"You think this is my fault?" Like the fiasco on the Crystal Ridge building site. According to Dad, Brady should have foreseen the decorative-rock mix-up. Now he had an entire fireplace to demolish and start all over, as if deadlines weren't tight enough. Even the church service, where he usually found some peace, hadn't eased the stress tightening the back of his shoulders. This deal with Abby was the straw that broke the camel's back.

He glared at his twin brothers—first Sawyer and then Dawson had blamed him for the problem. If steam wasn't coming out of his ears, he'd be surprised. He'd enjoyed that barbecue supper with Abby Webster and her little girl. Maybe that's what bugged him most. He'd liked her. He thought she liked him.

Dawson raised both hands in surrender. "You'll hear no blame from me. I only meant, what's going on? Why did she back out?"

"Who knows? Abby Webster is the strangest, most stubborn woman I've ever encountered."

Dawson gave him a long look. "I thought you liked her."

"Yeah, well, the feeling wasn't mutual, I guess. She showed me the door."

"So, what did she say?"

"Just that she couldn't. It wouldn't work."

"Couldn't what? What wouldn't work?" Sawyer, the mirror twin to Dawson, stretched his long legs out on the floor next to the sofa. By the time the game started there would be Buchanons all over the room. Brady was happy he'd gotten here first to grab a seat on the couch, but he usually ended up on the floor with Dawg.

He had a quick flash of Dawg on the floor of Abby's house with Lila, the angel-drawing charmer. He'd seen her pink ankle braces and the walker she used for balance. Abby's house, with the crooked floors and raised thresholds, was a hazard to Lila. He really wanted to do that makeover for the little girl.

"Long story short, the house is a wreck. Joist rotted, leaks everywhere, bad plumbing. There's so much wrong, I wouldn't spend a dime to remodel it."

"Then you're the one who backed out," Dawson said. "I knew I should have gone with you."

"No." Brady frowned at a Frito and then at his brother. "I offered a new house instead of the remodel. Raze the old one, build from the ground up. It's only a matter of time until she'll have no choice but to move." He'd never built from ground up before on one of his makeovers, but why not?

Dawson turned a bewildered face in his direction. "She turned down a new house?"

"Flat. No reason. Just no."

"That *is* weird."

"See?" He pointed a Frito. "I told you."

"Her little girl sure is cute. Kind of gets you right here." Dawson tapped his chest with a fist. "I thought Abby would go for it for her sake."

"Yeah." Brady popped the chip in his mouth and considered going to the kitchen for the Ro*Tel dip. "Pretty adorable kid."

"A kid who needs a handicap-accessible house."

"I don't get it," Sawyer said. He dragged a throw pillow from the sofa and shoved it under his dark head. "Why would the mom refuse? Makes no sense."

"Take it from the top, Brady," Dawson said. "What exactly went down? She was on board before you mentioned the rebuild. When did things go sour?"

Brady related the conversation, trying his best to remember the exact point when Abby backed away. "It was the demolition. She said it would never work. After that—" He drew a finger across his throat. "The project was dead."

"Hmm." Dawson pushed back against the cushions of Mom's enormous gray sectional. His Dallas Cowboys jersey stretched across his lean, toned chest. Like all the Buchanon brothers, he'd played college football and was still a fanatic about the game. "She said it wouldn't work? Wonder what she meant by that? What wouldn't work?"

Brady's shoulders hitched. "You got me. I promised a fast rebuild so she wouldn't have to live elsewhere very long."

Dawson snapped his fingers and leaned forward. "Could that be the problem?"

"What? She didn't believe we could work that fast?"

"No. The living-elsewhere part."

"I don't know what you mean."

"I get it." Sawyer sat up and thumped the pillow with his fist. "Maybe she doesn't have another place to live. Or maybe money for the rent, even for a few months, would be prohibitive. A waitress doesn't make much money, and with the little girl's special needs..."

"True, but they could stay with relatives," Dawson said.

Brady shook his head. "According to my sources, she doesn't have any. Grew up in foster care, I think, and her little girl's father skipped out on her before Lila was born. It's just Abby and Lila against the world, which was part of the reason I chose them."

"That poor girl." Karen Buchanon breezed into the room bearing hot cheese dip. Behind her was Brady's adored younger sister, Allison, a peanut of a woman with dark, flippy hair. Her fiancé, Jake Hamilton, once an outcast in the Buchanon household, would show up at some point in the afternoon after checking on his cattle and his grandmother.

"I never considered her living arrangements, but that could be the problem," Brady admitted. "Maybe she has nowhere to go."

"And no spare money for a rental, even a cheap one." Dawson took both hands, rotated his head and popped his neck. "Crick," he said to no one in particular.

Brady arched an eyebrow. "You don't get much cheaper than her house."

"But it's hers."

"I wonder why she didn't simply tell me she had no place else to live during the rebuild. If that's the case."

"Oh, Brady." His mother stood behind Dawson and began kneading his shoulders. "If the girl has any pride at all, which she clearly does, she wouldn't tell you such a thing. No one wants to be pitied."

Brady opened his mouth and then closed it again,

the salty taste of chips making him thirsty. "You think that's her problem?"

"Makes sense to me," Dawson said, settling into his mother's massage with his eyes closed. "Though it's your problem, not hers."

"Ditto," said Sawyer.

Brady had always been surrounded by a huge family, sometimes to the point of smothering. He couldn't fathom anyone being completely alone, but if Abby Webster had no one but her four-year-old daughter, she was a pretty amazing woman. Really amazing. She'd bought a house, such as it was, and balanced a job with the needs of her special child. Lila was clearly loved and well cared for.

"I guess I embarrassed her."

"No doubt about it." His mom left Dawson's side to pat Brady's shoulder. "But you meant well, honey."

Brady put his big paw over her hand. "Thanks, Mom. Any ideas of how to fix it?"

"Fix it? No. But I might have an idea of how to get her out of that house so you can build her a new one. Dad won't mind."

"If it involves Dad, forget it. He's against the project this year."

"I heard." She smiled. "But you're going to do it anyway, aren't you?"

"If I can convince Abby to let me."

"Good." She tugged at her pressed slacks and perched on the arm of an easy chair. "Abby's excited about the makeover. She wants it, son."

"How do you know this?"

"Jan, Abby's boss, talked to me at the BPW meeting." Mom was president of the local chapter of Business and

Professional Women. "She was thrilled for Abby. She also told me what a hard worker Abby is and how well she takes care of her little girl. According to Jan, no one deserves your makeover any more than Abby and Lila Webster. That's why I'm willing to step in and help out."

Brady looked at his mother in awe. "Is there anything in this town you don't know?"

Her eyes crinkled. "Not much."

Sawyer snorted. Dawson just smiled. Allison found an empty space next to Sawyer, curled her little feet beneath her and reached for the dip.

"Yeah, well, that still doesn't solve the problem. I can't move her in with me." Though the thought didn't exactly repulse him. Dawg would be thrilled.

"But *I* can move her in with *me*."

Four sets of sibling eyes turned to their mother. She pushed back a lock of tidy blond hair, a cat's smile on her lips.

"Since you kids built your own places, Dad and I ramble around in this big old, empty house. We've got the room. Abby needs a temporary place to stay, and a child always makes Christmas season more fun. So why not?"

"You'd do that?" Brady didn't know why he was asking. Of course, she'd do it. In the past, she'd mothered a number of foreign-exchange students along with her brood of seven. And that didn't count the handfuls of friends and relatives who'd lived temporarily in the Buchanon house, including Jake, Allison's fiancé. Mom loved having the house filled with people.

"I think it's a great idea." This from Allison.

Brady, for all the hope suddenly surging through his veins, had his doubts. Mom might be on board, but what would Abby think? The Buchanons were strangers to her, and the family didn't know Abby like he knew Abby. She was stubborn, prideful, independent to a fault. Pretty, too, he'd noticed, though why his thoughts had gone in that direction he couldn't fathom. "I don't know. Think she'll go for it?"

Mom arched one eyebrow and reached for a chip. "There's only one way to find out."

"Someone here to see you, Abby. Take a break."

Abby slid a tray of dishes onto the sink in the back of the diner and turned toward her boss. The noon rush had passed but there was still plenty to do. "Who is it?"

"Karen Buchanon."

"*Karen* Buchanon?" If Jan had said Brady, she wouldn't have been surprised. In fact, she'd probably have gotten that jittery wiggle in her stomach, a totally stupid reaction to a man she barely knew. But he was a good guy who could cause Prince Charming fantasies even in a hard nut like her. She also felt a little guilty for upsetting him. He'd offered an act of kindness and she'd shot him down.

Yesterday, he'd come into the Buttered Biscuit with a big grin and a crazy invitation for her and Lila to temporarily move in with his parents while he built her brand-new house. Even though her heart had leaped at the offer, he could not have been serious. Well intentioned, yes. Serious, no way.

She didn't know the Buchanons. They didn't know her. Things like that didn't happen except in movies. And how had he known a decent place to live was her primary reason for rejecting the makeover?

Five minutes later, as she sat across an open table from the blonde and lovely Buchanon matriarch, she learned how serious Brady had been. "Mrs. Buchanon, please don't take this the wrong way, but why? Why would you open your home to a complete stranger?"

"My family has been tremendously blessed, and we believe that caring about others is not only a directive from the Lord but it makes us happier people. We love to give. Brady's gifts are in his ability to build, and he loves giving away a Buchanon Built home at Christmas. He plans for it and looks forward to it all year."

Abby fidgeted with the saltshaker, realized what she was doing and shoved it back to the side of the table. Brady had hinted that the Buchanons were devout Christians, but so were lots of people in Texas and none of them gave away houses. At least none that she knew about. "There are other people in Gabriel's Crossing who could use a makeover."

"My son's heart is the biggest part of him and, as I'm sure you've noticed, that's saying a lot. When Brady sets his sights on something, he's a bulldog."

"But why me?"

"It's the way Brady's made. He picked you and you're it." She folded her hands atop the table. "I do know this. He was taken with your little girl. He told the family about her, showed us the angel she drew him and even hung it on his refrigerator."

A piece of pride chipped away. "He did?"

Karen nodded. "'An angel from an angel,' he said. Now, we're all anxious to meet her. She must be amazing."

"Oh, she is. Lila is the kindest, funniest, smartest, most resilient—" She caught herself and laughed, self-conscious and sure her warm face glowed pink. "Sorry.

I get a little carried away about my daughter. She's everything to me."

"Then do this for her, Abby. Let Brady build your house. Give that amazing daughter of yours a new home for Christmas. And give us the pleasure of knowing your special little girl."

Unbidden tears welled in Abby's eyes. Buchanons didn't play fair.

Karen leaned forward. "I respect your pride. I even admire it, but say yes for your daughter's sake. We'll make the transition as easy as possible. My girls and I will help you pack, and the boys can have you moved in a single day. There's plenty of storage at the company warehouse for your extra things."

Abby wasn't about to admit she didn't have much extra sitting around. Her pride was aching as it was, and her cynical inner voice was screaming in her ear. *No one does something for nothing.* If she went along with this, she had to remember that.

"You really are serious?"

"Absolutely. You'd be doing us a favor." Karen waved a hand and a diamond flashed, another reminder of the chasm between Abby Webster and the Buchanons. "Our house is too big with the kids gone. Imagine, a house that has raised seven kids and welcomed an endless array of their friends. A house of noise and activity and energy. Now, the place is too quiet all the time. Frankly, it's lonely without the laughter of children."

"Lila is special-needs."

"No worries about that. We added accessibility when Dan's father moved in with us after his stroke. She can move around most of the house without a problem. We'll make sure Lila has whatever she needs."

"I meant she's not like other children and never will be. Potty training is still ongoing. She uses a walker and braces but still crawls at times. We have therapy exercises every night and activities to encourage independence. Living with a spina bifida child can be a challenge, and some people are put off by her differences."

Karen sat back, her serene brown eyes locked on Abby's. "Honey, God made us all with special needs. Some are simply more apparent than others. Lila will find welcome at my house. More than welcome. I promise you."

Buchanons were good at tossing out promises. She couldn't help wonder if they'd keep them.

Abby pulled the napkin holder toward her and straightened the narrow sheets in the dispenser. The back side needed a refill.

A few afternoon coffee drinkers sat at the counter talking politics, and at a side table near the window where he could keep a watchful eye, police deputy Leroy was having his pie break. Apple à la mode. The smell of cinnamon reminded her of the coming holidays. Jan would want them to decorate the café soon.

Wouldn't it be wonderful to have a beautiful new home to decorate?

She was fidgeting, scared to say yes and knowing she'd be a fool to turn down the best offer she'd ever had. How many people had a chance like this to give their child a custom-built, handicap-accessible home, free of added payments? Certainly not someone like her, who could barely stretch her paycheck to the end of each month.

"This is kind of overwhelming," she admitted.

"If it would make you feel better, come to the house for dinner tonight, get acquainted, see the house and then decide. You and Lila will have your own private space. We won't crowd you."

"I'd expect to help with the chores." The gesture was pure self-preservation.

"And I'd take you up on that." Karen's mouth curved. "What time do you get off work?"

"Six."

"Dinner at seven, then? Is that too early?"

"No. Seven is perfect."

"Here's the address." Karen scribbled on the back of a Buchanon Built business card and pushed it across the table.

Abby knew where they lived. Gabriel's Crossing wasn't that big. She stared at the address and wrung her hands. "Are you sure about this?"

Karen laughed as she picked up her handbag and scooted back her chair. "Abby, you fret too much. See you at seven."

Chapter Five

Abby and Lila moved in the next Saturday. Or rather, three Buchanon males, minus the older brother, Quinn, along with Jake Hamilton, all in pickup trucks, roared into her front yard at eight o'clock to do the heavy lifting.

She'd worked frantically all week, staying up late each night after work to pack her belongings into boxes. When Karen had called to set a date for packing, she was surprised that Abby was finished. A girl had to keep control of something!

The truth was, she was letting herself get too excited about the project, and Lila was over the moon. The night they'd gone to dinner at the Buchanon house, she'd suffered a longing so deep, she'd lain awake later wondering what it would have been like to have grown up in that house with Karen and Dan Buchanon. Wondering what it would be like for Lila to have grandparents like them to dote on her.

Brady had come for dinner, too, and turned her mushy by the sweet way he interacted with her little girl. Though Dan Buchanon wasn't as effusive as his wife and son, he'd been kind to Lila, who could charm the quills off a porcupine.

"Let the games begin." Brady, looking too good for words, leaped from his truck cab with Dawg right behind and rubbed his hands together with glee. The rest of the men piled out of their vehicles and started tossing around furniture like dollhouse toys.

Abby had a moment of misgiving. She was developing a killer crush on Brady Buchanon, a feeling she would have to keep under wraps. The Websters from the wrong side of the tracks were not in the same league with the prominent, successful Buchanons. She and Lila were a project, a charity case. She needed to keep that front and center in her thinking. A crush was normal. Anything more was off-limits.

As it was, Brady slapped her a high five as he entered the house and headed straight for Lila, whose big brown eyes were wider than saucers. Abby understood. She was feeling a little overwhelmed herself.

"There she is," he exclaimed. "Princess Lila." He scooped the little one up into his big arms. "Look here, boys. Meet Lila. She's the best angel drawer this side of the Red River."

Lila's face glowed with the attention. "Did you bring Dawg?"

"Sure, I did. He's outside, though. Didn't want him underfoot while we work. Want to hang out with him?"

Abby came alongside the pair as the Buchanon twins ducked into Lila's bedroom to begin the move. The jitters started up again. This was really happening. "I'll take her outside to play, so she won't be in the way."

Brady didn't relinquish his hold on Lila. "You could

take her over to the folks' if you want to. We'll be back and forth."

"No." She shook her head. There was something wonderful about being here, watching them work with the knowledge of what was to come. "I'd rather stay if it's okay. I'll keep Lila out of the way."

"Sure. No problem. Whatever you want. Just don't want her to get bumped or stepped on." His cell phone chirped. She took Lila from his arms so he could answer. Jake, the cowboy who'd won Allison Buchanon's heart, drifted by with a stack of boxes marked "kitchen." The twins, Dawson and Sawyer, shuffled past with Lila's dresser.

"Hey, Dad. What's up?" Brady turned slightly and Abby stepped back to give him some privacy. "Yes. I told you about the substitution on the Jefferson house, remember? It can't be helped. The supplier is out of that particular color."

The voice on the other end grew loud enough that Abby could tell he wasn't happy. Brady's mouth tensed. "Whatever you think, Dad. I'll give him a call Monday morning." More loud conversation from the caller and then Brady said, "All right. I'll get in touch with him today if he's available. Some contractors actually take off on weekends."

He listened a bit longer before hanging up.

"Trouble?" she asked.

"Nothing to worry about." But his light had dimmed and his jaw was tight.

"If you're needed at work…" She gazed around at the activity churning through her house. When the Buchanons started something, they didn't waste time. "This can wait."

"To Dad, work never ends." He winked, but she could see his father had rankled him. "That's where the two of us differ. I take off on Saturdays."

"You call this taking off?"

"This is the fun stuff." He tugged at one of Lila's dog's ears. "I'd better get with it before the others have all the fun without me."

He left them then to help Jake maneuver the refrigerator onto a two-wheel dolly.

By noon, most her belongings had been transferred to storage at the Buchanon Warehouse on the outskirts of town, and her personal items were stacked in cardboard boxes in a spacious bedroom at the Buchanon house.

She stood in the doorway between her room and the adjoining room that would be Lila's. Living with strangers was no big deal to her. She'd done it most of her life. But the Buchanon home felt different than the foster homes she'd bounced in and out of as a teenager. Or maybe she simply wanted it to be different.

The suite off the garage at the back of the house was an addition built for Brady's grandfather and a nighttime caregiver, used now for guests. The house was enormous, at least to her eyes, a sprawling two-story with two living spaces, two dining spaces and more bedrooms than she'd had time to count, all lovingly decorated, as befitted a home builder. And yet, the house felt lived in and comfortable. The night she'd come for dinner, she'd made up her mind to accept Karen's offer the moment she'd walked in the door and Lila had said, "Mommy, it's a castle."

Indeed, the Buchanon home was a castle, and though Abby was embarrassed to accept the help, she wanted her daughter to feel like a princess, at least for a little while.

* * *

Brady was feeling pretty good. He'd managed to get his father off his back on Monday morning and the demo bulldozers were on the job at Abby's house by early afternoon. He was too busy with the Huckleberry Creek addition to stop by until after work, but he'd called in some favors to clear the utilities and unhook lines and power, and wrangled the permits out of town hall in record time, thanks to his perfectionist baby sister, Jaylee, who could cut through red tape like a blowtorch. She was office manager to Allison's financial wizardry, two cogs in the mighty Buchanon wheel who kept things turning. Quinn was the grumpy, reluctant architect; the twins computer designed and trimmed out the houses; and Brady served as chief operating officer who could do it all if need be. Charity handled the real estate and Mom designed the landscapes. Though they employed subcontractors, they remained a family operation where every member played a crucial part. But Dad was the big boss. The big tough boss who saw the problems instead of successes.

The ongoing vandalism on Buchanon Built job sites had them all on edge. The police had yet to come up with a suspect, though nearly a year had passed since the problems began. Trouble didn't happen often, only enough to make them crazy when they let down their guard. Insurance had covered the destruction, but nothing made up for the lost time. Dad had put up a reward for information leading to an arrest but, so far, no takers.

At the row of under-construction homes along Huckleberry Creek, Brady walked through the first nearly finished house, satisfied that they were on schedule. Then he made his way across a wide packed-dirt space that would soon be sodded with grass to house number two. The electrician's van parked on the red dirt yard and ladders leaned against the house indicated work in progress. Brady breathed a sigh of relief. The electrical contractor hadn't been sure he'd be here today. One less thing for Dad to complain about.

He stepped into the structure, smelled the familiar scent of sawdust and drywall mud, Dawg at his heel. An electrician toted a huge reel of cable down the hallway. His assistant poked his head down from the attic and said hello to Brady, then disappeared again.

Brady spoke briefly to the contractor, watched them work for a while and, satisfied everything was going as planned, headed back to his truck. Dad had taken on too many simultaneous projects, at least in Brady's opinion, but he was juggling them all. Something would have to give for him to spend the time on the home makeover, but he'd figure it out. This was the highlight of his year every Christmas and this one seemed even more special than the others.

He didn't question that enthusiasm. Lila and Abby got to him. He liked them, adored Lila and was even starting to enjoy working his way around Abby's defenses. His mother had opened his eyes there. Lacking a family to lean on, Abby had erected a wall of self-sufficiency buttressed with ferocious pride, a wall she didn't need with the Buchanons around, though she probably didn't know that yet.

She was going to love her new home. He'd make sure.

Figuring ten minutes wouldn't make or break him, he drove across the railroad tracks to check on the Cedar Corner demolition. He'd invited Abby to watch, but she'd had to work.

By this time tomorrow, the landscape would be level and ready to start anew. Foundation work could begin immediately. The excitement of a new project all his own revved his engine.

With dust flying amid the dozer's roar, Brady stepped out of his truck to watch the big machine operate.

His father called twice, once to grumble about the substitute plumber he'd hired and once with the good news that the special-order Italian marble had arrived. Jaylee and Charity each texted him a couple of times, and he made eight calls to confirm subcontractors, or subs as he called them, or to line up volunteers for Abby's house, though he planned to do a lot of the work himself. So far, the response had been heartening. His Christmas makeovers were gaining in popularity. Each year, the local newspaper ran a big article, listing all the companies that donated time or materials. Last year, they'd run several, including interviews with the recipients. All of the publicity made his father and the donors happy.

A car pulled alongside his pickup and Abby got out, a hand over her open mouth.

Brady grinned. Watching a demolition was pretty spectacular.

He jogged over to her side. Above the loud engine he shouted, "I thought you had to work."

She crossed her arms over a white button-up sweater. Beneath she wore a Buttered Biscuit T-shirt, though why he'd notice such a thing baffled him.

"I only have an hour. I took a late lunch break so I could take a look."

"Well, what do you think?"

"My house. Oh." Her big brown eyes looked even

bigger as she stood in the dust and chill and watched the big machine.

"Is that a good *oh* or a bad *oh*?"

"It's so…permanent."

Were those tears in her eyes?

Alarm pushed Brady into action. "Are you okay? You're not upset, are you?"

"No. Oh, no. This is going to be wonderful."

"Then why the tears?"

"Oh, I'm being sentimental." She patted at her cheeks. "This was the first home that was truly mine."

He studied her features, suddenly seeing the dilapidated old house in a new light. No wonder she'd struggled to let go. As a child of the system, she'd never had a permanent home before.

"You did good, Abby," he said gently, touched. "Real good."

She found a wobbly smile. "Lila and I made a lot of memories here."

Feeling tender, he looped an arm around her shoulders the way he'd do with one of his sisters. "Memories are good. You'll make more in the new place, a home where Lila can grow up and grow strong."

She nodded. "And become independent."

He dipped his head to look at her, saw the hope and longing in her espresso eyes. "Will she?"

"The therapists are always telling me I have to encourage her do more for herself, but it's hard when she can't maneuver the walker farther than the living room. Having a home where she can move more freely, a house with rails and ramps, a lower sink and toilet, will make a world of difference."

Brady's chest expanded. This was why he'd started the Christmas makeovers. There was no feeling as good as this one.

"I have some house plans for you to look at. Mind if I come by later?"

"I get to choose?"

Was she kidding? "Sure. I want you to be happy with the results. It's your house."

She twisted her face toward his and suddenly they were chin to forehead close, and Brady realized his arm was still comfortably wrapped around her shoulders. Nice.

She stared up at him for two beats and must have come to the same realization because she slowly, carefully, edged away. Brady's arm dropped to his side. Abby crossed hers.

He cleared his throat and looked back toward the dozer. The house was now a dusty pile of rubble, and a pair of dump trucks had backed to the site, ready to load up and haul away.

"So, do you want to look at the plans or not?" He sounded gruff and didn't mean to.

"If that's all right with you."

"I wouldn't have asked if it wasn't. My laptop is in the truck if you'd rather take a look now instead of later."

A breeze blew her ponytail across her cheek. She brushed it away. "I have to get back to work."

She backed up two steps, pivoted and walked away. When she reached her car, she turned back. "Brady."

He stuck his hands in his jacket pockets. "Yeah?"

"Thank you."

He dipped his head. "See you later."

After her car chugged down the potholed street, Brady stood in the gray November afternoon strangely discombobulated, and he couldn't for the life of him figure out why.

All afternoon Abby thought of that weird moment when she'd become too aware of Brady's arm around her. He'd meant nothing by it. It was a casual thing. Something he did naturally. He was a man comfortable in his own skin, comfortable with other people, but in that one little moment, his touch had seemed personal. And she'd wanted it to be.

My, but his eyes were blue. And he smelled good even after a busy day on the job.

While she'd served customers and listened to Charla, Jan and Fran the cook discuss the town's Christmas parade and the possibility of opening the Buttered Biscuit afterward for pie and coffee, Brady kept intruding on her thoughts.

She was finally distracted when the bell over the door tinkled and Flo Dubois pranced in on mile-high legs. In tan high-heeled knee boots and cheetah-print leggings, the former Las Vegas showgirl, now in her seventies, retained a flair for the dramatic. Flo stiffened like a cat when she spotted Mayor Hanover perched at the counter reading the newspaper. She marched right up to him and slapped her hand on the paper. The mayor didn't even jump.

He sighed, pushed at his glasses and looked up. "I knew that was you. Could smell the stench of perfume the minute you ripped the door open."

Flo sniffed. "A real man would appreciate it. Which means you don't."

The dozen other customers in the diner quieted, their attention on the mayor and Flo. Abby bussed a suddenly emptied table and wasn't a bit ashamed to have her ears tuned to the entertaining feud. The pair butted heads at least once a week.

"Eau de funeral home," the mayor said. "Flowers and formaldehyde."

Flo rolled her eyes. "New one, Hoss. I suppose you got your nickname from the back end of the equine?"

The mayor sighed. "What do you want now, Flo?"

She smiled a little too sweetly. "So kind of you to ask. As a member of the voting public and a concerned citizen, I want to register a complaint about the trash on Fenton Street and request that something be done about it ASAP. The stink is drawing rats. Which invade homes. Freda Pendleton killed two with a shovel in her front yard."

"Freda did?"

"She did. Bless her heart, and her ninety years old with that awful arthritis having to do such a thing while the mayor is sitting around eating pie. It's a disgrace and a health hazard."

"Couldn't we discuss this in my office?"

"We could if you weren't in here stuffing your face. Funny how I always know where to find you."

He tsked and lifted his fork. "Jealous. Have a bite. It might sweeten you up."

She recoiled as if the fork was a lethal weapon. "I haven't updated my shots."

"Too late. The rabies has already affected your brain. Mouth foaming shall commence. Oh, too late. It already has."

She gave an annoyed huff and flounced. "Are you going to address the situation or not?"

"I'll see what I can do if you promise not to call me for at least a week."

"Promises, my dear mayor, are so pedestrian. Like you." She tossed a mustard-colored scarf over one shoulder, spun on her heel and pranced out as if making an exit in the grand finale at Caesars Palace.

The rest of the time until Abby's shift ended, everyone chattered and chuckled about the latest installment in the continuing saga of Flo and Hoss. Abby and Charla thought they were hilarious. Fran worried about them. But Jan shocked everyone by claiming they were secretly in love and all their gibes were nothing more than a mating ritual.

By the time she'd picked up Lila from day care and headed to the Buchanon house, Abby had put the incident with Brady out of her mind. Mostly.

Nightly dinner with Karen and Dan, which she'd not considered when she'd agreed to camp at their house, was a bonus even if a little on the uncomfortable side at first. The food was far superior to anything she scratched together after work. Karen was a great cook and Abby watched every move she made to learn from her. She'd never known what to do with herbs and seasonings and Karen tossed them around with skill and abandon.

The mealtime prayer had also come as a surprise but Abby kind of liked it, though she knew next to nothing about religion. Only one of her foster families had taken her to church before child services had moved her elsewhere. All she'd learned was the sweetly comforting song, "Jesus Loves Me," which she sometimes sang to Lila. She'd considered attending church for her daughter's sake, but with her work schedule, she'd found Sunday mornings a perfect time to sleep in. The prayer, though, was nice and she felt soothed by Karen's words of faith and grace.

Tonight, the addition of Brady, considering her errant thoughts this afternoon, was both pleasure and discomfort. Sitting on one side of Lila while she sat on the other, he was his usual relaxed self, talking business with his dad, asking his mother about one of his siblings and playing with Lila. She must have imagined that personal moment when he'd looked into her eyes and time had stopped. For her at least. Not for him. Who was she kidding? He'd barely spoken to her since his arrival.

"Will Quinn be here on Sunday?" Brady asked his mother.

Karen frowned down at her chicken piccata, a dish Abby had never heard of until tonight. From all indications, Lila loved the lemony flavor and buttered noodles as much as she did.

"I invited him," Karen said.

"You're worried." Brady's big hands stilled as he looked at his mother.

"I am. Since he moved out of here and into that cabin along the river, he's become more reclusive than he was after the accident."

"I thought he'd put that behind him."

"How can he?" Dan spoke up, his expression hard. "Just because he admitted his culpability in the shooting doesn't mean he isn't permanently handicapped."

At the word *handicapped*, Karen's eyes cut to Lila. Abby carefully put her fork aside. From gossip in the diner she knew the story. Quinn Buchanon had been shot in a hunting accident and the shooter, Jake Hamilton, had been ostracized for years until Quinn had forgiven him and admitted he'd been drinking that day, too. The problem remained, though, that Quinn's professional football career ended on that bloody morning when his throwing arm was forever damaged.

"Dan," Karen said.

"Didn't mean anything by it." He winked at Lila, who beamed, clueless to the undertones about handicaps. Abby wished it could always remain so. "I'm worried about Quinn, too. He does his job at the office, but then he holes up in that cabin like a hermit."

"I tried talking to him," Karen said. "He claims nothing is wrong."

Dan reached for another hot roll. "You don't believe him, do you?"

"Of course not. I know my children." Furrows formed in Karen's forehead, puckering her tidy blond eyebrows. Abby felt awkward at being privy to such a private family conversation, but the Buchanons seemed not to care that she heard. Even successful Christian families like the Buchanons, she saw, had problems. That surprised her, too. She thought Christians had to be perfect.

When dinner ended, Brady helped the women clear the table before heeding his father's call into the living room. Abby organized Lila on a mat with her puzzles in one corner of the kitchen while she assisted with the cleanup. She tried to maintain a low profile and keep Lila out of the Buchanons' way as much as she could. In foster care she'd learned that the less a family noticed her, the longer she got to stay.

Dawg, relegated to the patio during dinner, scratched at the door and whined. Karen let him in. He settled next to Lila without fanfare.

"You don't have to help with cleanup, Abby. You

must be worn out from work and you still have Lila's exercises."

"This was part of the deal, remember? I'm okay. Really, and Lila will put off her exercises as long as she can, right, jelly fingers?"

Lila beamed and held up a brown puzzle piece. "Mama, does this piece go there?" She pointed to a spot on the puzzle, clearly an animal, though Abby didn't say so.

"Try and see."

Her face a study in concentration, Lila turned the piece around and around before sliding it into place. "It fits! It's a dog, Mommy, like Dawg."

Dawg put his head in her lap, golden eyes adoring.

"I think you have a friend." Abby retrieved a dishtowel from the cupboard and began drying the dishes too large for the dishwasher.

"He is rather taken with her, isn't he?" Karen's look was amused. "I heard you had an interesting episode today with Mayor Hanover and Flo Dubois."

Abby chuckled. "Oh, that." But before she could rehash the story, raised voices came from the living room.

"I won't put up with slack at the office," she heard Dan say. "None. No concession."

She froze, suddenly wishing she'd made her escape to the bedroom. Conflict stressed her out.

"Buchanon Built has never suffered because of this project. It won't this year, either, Dad. Frankly, I don't know why you're so dead set against something that generates great PR for the company."

Humiliation flushed hot through Abby's body. They were talking about *her*, about the home makeover.

Karen, busy polishing a stainless-steel pot, frowned

toward the doorway and clanged the pot onto the counter to cover the conversation. "Don't pay them any mind, Abby. They butt heads all the time."

She'd noticed. But this time the argument was about her.

Chapter Six

"Your dad doesn't want you to build my house."

Abby's blunt statement turned Brady's attention from the stack of floor plans to her face. He could read the hurt and confusion, the embarrassment she tried to hide behind directness.

His temper flared and he battled it down, back teeth tight. No use Abby taking the brunt of his ongoing conflict with his father. Tact was never Dad's strong suit. He should keep his mouth shut.

He and Abby were alone in the breakfast room, thanks to Mom, who'd taken Lila into the family room to watch TV.

"What gave you that idea?"

"I heard." She put her hand over the plans he'd opened on the bar. "I don't know what to do, Brady. My house is gone or I'd walk away from the makeover. The last thing I want is to cause problems for you and your family."

"Stop. Whoa. You are not causing problems. No way. Dad would not want you to think that. I'm sorry if you overheard our discussion, but this is a business issue, a problem between him and me. You have nothing at all to do with it."

"Are you sure?"

He leaned back, looked up at the ceiling and huffed out a breath. Not exactly. Since truth was his method of operation in all things, he admitted, "In the beginning, Dad was against this year's Christmas project. He's usually gung ho, but we've had a rash of vandalism along with the usual problems of running a construction company. Contractors fall behind. Supplies don't come in. Weather delays." He lifted his hands. "Stuff happens. It's the nature of the beast, all of which is my responsibility as chief of operations."

"I've heard about the vandalism. People talk about it at the diner." He saw her glance with longing at the plans.

"Yeah. A real pain in the neck."

"No clues about who's behind it?"

"Nothing that's panned out. We're praying that someone has seen something and will step up with information, but a year has passed and here we are."

He pushed a page of house photos toward her. He had more opened on the laptop if these didn't suit, but they were plans he'd worked with before and could build quickly even with customization.

"Which do you like best? Come on. Stop worrying and get happy. This is supposed to be the part where you get all excited and make me feel like a hero."

Her mouth lifted slightly at his silliness and he felt better. He was still ticked at his father, but that was nothing new.

"I love that one."

"The country cottage?" He'd chosen that one for her

the minute he'd seen it. The tidy facade with covered porch, railing, a single dormer and lots of sunny windows was simple and charming. Like her. "Look at the interior plan, too. We can change it around if you like, but the flow is perfect for a walker or a wheelchair. No stairs or ledges. Wide hallways. Lots of storage and cupboards, a safe room and garage."

She studied the plan while he explained each designation and the extras he would add to accommodate Lila's needs. He had a few other extras in mind for Abby, but he was saving those to surprise her.

When he finished, she looked up at him with those soft brown eyes. His chest expanded. She liked it. She liked it a lot. He realized then that he'd been overanxious about this home makeover, afraid she'd regret letting him barge into her life and turn it upside down.

"A safe room, too?"

"This is tornado country. Gotta keep the princess safe. We can add more square footage if you prefer, but the plan has adequate space without making your insurance or utilities too high. I'm thinking cost-effective over the long haul."

"You think of everything, don't you?"

He grinned. "Keep saying things like that and I'll build you the Taj Mahal."

"Who needs the Taj Mahal when this is a dream house, perfect for Lila and me?" She shook her head in wonder. "Is this really going to happen?"

That's the reaction he'd been looking for. "Want to show the princess?"

"She's already so excited she has trouble going to sleep."

"I promised her a princess room."

"She told me. This morning she asked if it was finished yet."

They laughed together in warm affection for the little girl, and once more Brady had the weirdest longing to put his arm around Abby.

"I hope you told her a house takes a little longer than that. If the weather holds so we can complete the exterior and work inside within the next couple of weeks, we're aiming for sixty days, give or take."

Abby looked at him in awe. "That fast?"

"Many hands make light work, remember? We may need longer. Things happen."

"I won't complain no matter how long it takes."

"A Christmas makeover needs to be in progress during the holidays and if we can get close to the finish before New Year's, all the better. The footing crew starts tomorrow morning."

"Tomorrow? Oh, my. I'm overwhelmed. And thrilled. I don't know what to say. None of this seems real."

"Believe it, Abby. It's happening."

Abby was amazed by how soon the house's frame went up and the walls began to take shape. Each day the hours at the diner seemed to creep past before she could rush to the building site to observe the progress. She'd started dreaming, an irresistible by-product. Jan and Charla had gotten in on the excitement by bringing magazines and discussing colors and decor. Brady's mother also fueled the excitement by taking Abby window-shopping the next Saturday afternoon. She didn't have the heart to admit she had no money for extras. Dreaming was fun and she'd almost forgotten how.

Today, when she and Lila arrived, the job site was

quiet, completely empty for the first time. Except for a cat sunning on the neighbor's porch with one eye tweaked toward the cardinal hopping around the cluttered lawn, nothing was moving. Yesterday the woman across the street had come over for a look, though because of a language barrier, she and Abby mostly exchanged smiles and charades. Even though Mrs. Herrara seemed genuinely happy for Abby and Lila, the encounter made Abby realize how much a new home would change the look of this tired neighborhood. Sometimes she felt downright guilty for her good fortune.

Often Brady was here when she arrived. When he wasn't, like today, she suffered a twinge of disappointment, quickly scotched, though Lila was much more vocal.

"Where's Bwady and Dawg?" the four-year-old asked as she peered eagerly through the back car window from her car seat. "Where's his twuck?"

Abby unbuckled her daughter's seat belt. "He must be working somewhere else today."

"But I want to show him my papers." Lila's bottom lip puffed out. "I made him a new picture."

She made him a new picture every single day, and every single day Brady accepted the latest offering as if it was the first and best he'd ever seen.

"Sorry." Stepping carefully around the stacks of lumber debris and packages of shingles that hadn't been here yesterday, Abby and Lila entered the structure. With all the building material around, she carried her child instead of pushing her in the stroller as she did in other situations.

The house was nothing but a frame of concrete and golden wood, but her pulse jumped that she could make out the room divisions. "Look, baby, this is the living room and that will be the kitchen."

"Where's my room?"

"Let's go look." Moving through the space, Lila on her hip, her feet made scratchy sounds against the raw concrete slab as she identified the bedrooms to the left. "One of these will be yours. You can choose which one."

The child blinked in disappointment. "It's not a princess room."

Abby laughed. "Not yet, but it will be."

"And that's a promise." The male voice turned her around. At the sight of Brady, tall and broad, grinning at them from the doorway, her heart leaped with pleasure. "Hi."

"Bwady!" Lila's greeting was much more effusive. She waggled her slender arms and Brady swooped her into his. She giggled.

"Hey, squirt. What's shaking?"

"I made you a picture."

"You did? For me?"

There he went again.

Lila beamed. "And guess what?"

"What?" Brady made his eyes wide.

"We had cookies today. Tara bringed them."

"No," he said in mock awe. "What kind?"

"White ones." She nodded in glee. "With chips."

"You're making me hungry. What are your mom and my mom cooking for dinner tonight? I might have to come over."

"I don't know."

He nuzzled her ear, made her giggle and filled Abby with a longing she didn't want. Lila didn't have a man in her life. No dad. No grandpa. No uncles. Abby felt guilty to let her child down in such a fundamentally simple way, though there was nothing she could do to change her empty family tree.

She turned away from the tender sight of big man and tiny girl, arms crossed over her jacket. The weather was cold today, a warning that Mother Nature could interfere with construction anytime she wanted.

"The twins are headed this way. We'll make some progress tonight."

She turned back. "But you've worked all day."

He shrugged. "Is that a problem?"

She supposed not, but if he could do double duty, why couldn't she? "If you'll show me what to do, I'll help."

"Nah, we got this."

Her shoulders tightened. "Sweat equity, Brady. I want to. In fact, I insist."

Brady studied her for several seconds and she could see the wheels turning behind his blue, blue eyes. Foolishly, she wondered how many women had gone gaga over those thick-lashed eyes?

"There are always odds and ends a layman can do, but why not wait until we're working inside. Evenings get pretty cool."

"They aren't going to get warmer."

"Once the house is enclosed, the weather won't be a factor."

"What are you working on tonight?"

"Decking." He pointed upward at the empty space where a roof would be. "Sheets of plywood for the roof base. We should be able to knock that out tonight."

"I can use a hammer. I fixed the shingles on the old house." She didn't add how nervous heights made her or how her stomach dipped anytime she stood on a ladder. A girl did what a girl had to do.

"We've put up decking so often we're really fast."

"In other words, I'll be in the way?"

He squeezed her upper arm between his finger and thumb, a gentle touch. "Give us another week or two to get the rough work finished. After that, there'll be plenty for you to do."

Though she didn't want him to know he was winning or how relieved she was not to get on the roof, she nodded. "Okay, that makes sense."

Car doors slammed and Brady looked through the framing toward the lawn. "Sawyer and Dawson are here."

"My cue to leave. Your mother will be wondering where we are." Her cell, as usual, was out of minutes.

She took Lila from him and headed toward the exit.

"Go feed the princess."

She glanced over one shoulder. "What about you?"

"I'll grab something later."

He was planning to work half the night on an empty stomach?

Abby thought about his words until she reached the car. He'd told her once before he required plenty of fuel for that big body of his. She may not be able to help with the house just yet, but she could definitely help with food.

Brady heard her pull up, recognizing the car by the engine clatter. Like her former home, the car was nearing the end of its long life.

From his spot on top of the house, he saw Abby's dome light illuminate, saw her hop out of the car. In the shadowy glow of halogen floodlights he'd set up in the front yard, she waved. "Are you guys hungry?"

Dawson, nail gun rat-a-tatting, stopped nailing long enough to call, "You brought food?"

"From your mom's kitchen."

"I'm starving." To his brothers, Dawson said, "You?" Both men nodded.

In seconds, the three had cast aside their tools and descended the ladder.

"You didn't have to do this," Brady said. His belly growled at the smells coming out of his mom's picnic basket. "I could have grabbed a sandwich when I got home."

Abby had tossed on a coat, a parka that had seen better days, but the red color turned her dark hair to ebony in the dim lighting.

She hoisted the basket and said, "Delivering plates is what I do. I'm pretty good at it."

He frowned. "You don't have to wait on us like a servant."

Sawyer elbowed him. "Lighten up, brother. She brought food. Mama's food."

Dawson rubbed his hands together. "What are we having?"

"Roast pork tenderloin, new potatoes and green beans. Chocolate cake for dessert."

All three men moaned in appreciation. "Bring it on!"

The temperature had dropped with the sun, so they piled into the back of the company work van and sat among tools and compressors. Brady was accustomed to eating wherever he could on a job site, but this time he found a mostly clean drop cloth and spread it in the open space between a table saw and several five-gallon buckets.

"Elegant," Dawson said, teasing as he settled on one of the buckets.

Brady shot him a glower. "There's a lady present. We don't have to be slobs."

Dawson and Sawyer traded amused glances. Brady knew they had some kind of silent twin communication thing going on. They always had. But this time, the glances went from him and Abby to each other. Then Sawyer gave a nod and they both twitched an eyebrow.

Were they talking about him? And Abby? Brady wouldn't ask now, but he *would* ask.

"Where's the princess?" He took the plate Abby offered and parked his big body on the drop cloth.

"Asleep in the backseat. It's nearing her bedtime, so the drive did her in."

He glanced toward the car, parked a short distance behind the van. "Is she okay out there?"

"Snug and warm, but I'll be checking on her."

"You could have left her with Mom."

"I wouldn't impose like that. It's enough that your parents are giving us a place to stay. I don't expect free babysitting service. With my work schedule and day care, I like to have Lila with me as much as possible anyway." From a thermos, she poured cups of coffee and passed them around. "How are things coming?"

"Decking's almost finished. Then the moisture barrier. That goes on fast. If this good weather holds, we'll make some serious progress this weekend."

"Exciting."

"Isn't it?" He liked hearing her say that. "Feel free to watch anytime."

"And help."

He jabbed a piece of tenderloin. He admired her spunk, her determination, and if assisting with the house would make her feel better, he'd find some little task for her to do. Something easy and not too taxing. She worked hard enough as it was.

"So you said. Are you working at the diner this weekend?"

"I'm off the next three days. Tomorrow Lila has her appointments."

"With the doctor?" He paused, fork in midbite. "Is she okay?"

"The usual. Therapists, doctors. The plan of action for the next six months." Abby ran a finger over the rim of her mug. "She'll have a blood draw and other tests. Those are not fun."

"Yeah, I guess not. I'll pray she handles it okay." He offered a smile. "That both of you do."

As though she didn't know how to respond, Abby blinked at the declaration. Hadn't anyone ever prayed for her before?

"Oh…well…thanks."

He hadn't intended to make her uncomfortable, but apparently faith was an area where he'd have to walk softly and pray hard.

"Did you see the picture she gave me today?"

Abby shook her head. "Another angel?"

"A pink angel with wings…and a walker."

"Oh. Oh, my baby." Abby's expression melted, and Brady fought the urge to draw her into a hug. The last time he'd put his arm around her, something weird had happened. With his workload, he didn't need weird in his life right now.

He tapped his heart. "Yeah. Got me right there. What a little champ."

"She's a trouper. No matter what the therapists ask her to do, she perseveres. I wish her life could be easier. She's such a great kid with a terrific attitude and sunny personality. I worry the obstacles of spina bifida will eventually beat her down."

She worried a lot. He'd seen that as he'd gotten to know her better. He didn't like that she worried so much, though in her situation raising a child alone, especially a child with unending medical needs, who could blame her?

He stopped short of asking about Lila's father. Too personal. With his temper he might have to punch someone and he hadn't done that since he'd fully committed his life to Christ. Not that his temper had suddenly disappeared. He was simply better at handling it.

Once again, he resisted the urge to touch her, jabbing at a green bean instead. "She can't fail. She's got you for a mother."

Suddenly, her eyes got all shiny as if she was going to cry. She turned aside and scrambled to her feet. "I should take a peek at her. Be right back."

She hopped out of the van and slammed the door before he could react.

Brady stared at the closed door. "I didn't mean to upset her."

"I don't think you did." Sawyer made a humming noise. "I like her, too."

"Not the way Brady does, I hope," Dawson said. "I wouldn't want your pretty face getting smashed up."

Brady chewed a buttery potato, swallowed and

growled at his dimpled brother. "What are you two muttering about?"

"You and Abby sound pretty cozy. I think you completely forgot about Sawyer and me."

He had. "Don't be stupid."

Sawyer laughed and whacked him on the shoulder. "Go ahead and finish your dinner, old man. Dawson and I can nail those last couple of sheets on before we hit the road."

Brady stared at his half-finished plate. How had they eaten so fast and he had so much left? Had he really been that engrossed in the conversation with Abby? "I'll be up in a minute."

"Take your time."

He tossed back the rest of his coffee, zipped his jacket and followed his brothers back up on the roof. Time was a commodity he couldn't waste.

Chapter Seven

Abby's usually dependable, ancient Honda wouldn't start.

Shivering against the early-morning chill, Abby ground the starter. After a few sluggish chugs, the thing clicked twice and went silent.

"Battery," she muttered. Or starter or alternator or... something. She didn't have time for this today, not with the hospital an hour away and Lila's appointments at nine.

"Mommy, are we going?" Lila, bundled in her car seat in back, peered out from a pink hood.

"I hope so." With shoulders slumped, Abby stared at the windshield while she tried to figure out her next move. The Buchanons had already left for work, not that she would have asked. As she contemplated going back inside to phone a mechanic, a big blue Ford rumbled up behind her.

Brady hopped out and came to the window. His breath blew vapor into the chill. "I thought you might already be gone."

"I would have been if my car would start."

His eyebrows came together in a frown. "Pop the hood."

She did. He poked his head inside the workings of the Honda. "Crank it."

She did. A few clicks later, he slammed the hood and came around. "Probably your battery. This time of year, a weak one gives it up on the first cold morning. I could give you a jump, but I don't think it's a good idea for you to drive that far until a mechanic has a look."

"I have to."

"No, you don't. I'll take you. Hop in the truck. I'll get the princess."

Abby was already shaking her head. "No, Brady. Thank you for the offer, but we'll be gone most of the day. You're too busy for that."

"A man who's too busy to help a friend is too busy." He opened Lila's door and reached inside, unhooked the car seat and lifted Lila, seat and all, out into the morning. She giggled and patted his face.

Abby sighed. As usual, she didn't have much choice. Coordinating all of Lila's appointments in one day required extra time and effort from the doctors and therapists. Canceling was not a good option.

"Do you always get your way?" she asked, making one last attempt.

He already had Lila in the crew cab, buckled in with paper and markers and a new coloring book in hand. "Time's wasting."

Suffering deeper feelings of obligation, Abby grabbed Lila's backpack and climbed into the cab.

Brady pulled onto the highway and headed toward the regional medical clinic an hour away. Abby was right. He didn't have time for this. But he wasn't about to tell her that. She had enough trouble accepting a simple act of kindness. For some reason, she couldn't get it through her head that friends helped friends. It was the Buchanon way.

He'd made a few calls from his truck's Bluetooth, rearranged some appointments and let the office know he was out of pocket for the day. He was sorry about making the calls in front of Abby because she'd slumped farther into her seat with each one.

"I've caused you too much trouble," she said when he completed the final call.

"Don't worry about it." The rest he could manage on his smartphone while he waited at the hospital.

"Why did you come by this morning anyway? Or are you just especially unlucky?" She had her arms crossed, a sign she was uncomfortable. He wanted to change that but didn't know how.

"Mom asked me to drop off a coloring book for Lila on the long ride."

"Your mother is incredibly thoughtful. So are you."

He lifted his fingers from the steering wheel, ignoring the compliment. "What's the itinerary today?"

She went through a litany of doctors, tests, therapists and meetings. "Sometimes we stay on schedule, sometimes not. I'm hoping this time will go fast."

"I've never known anyone with spina bifida before." He glanced in the rearview. "Is it okay to talk about it in front of her?"

Abby nodded. "I'm careful with what I say, but she knows even though she's still too young to understand what the diagnosis means for her future. This is her normal."

Her normal. The truth pinched him. Lila had never known any way other than her physical impairment. But someday, when she was older, she'd notice the things other kids did that she couldn't.

He glimpsed the mirror again, saw Lila's eyes drooping. In a minute, she'd be fast asleep. He kept his voice low just the same. "What *does* the future hold?"

Abby hitched one shoulder. "No one can predict. We were fortunate that the spinal cord opening was down low on her spine and not on the outside. Because of that, she has greater nerve development than most spina bifida patients. But still, some kids with her exact diagnosis never walk and some don't seem to have any disability at all." She lifted her palms. "Every child with a neural-tube defect is different."

Neural tube defect. She was talking over his head. His degree was in business, not medicine. "You talk like a doctor."

"I've lived and breathed her diagnosis for a long time, Brady. I had to educate myself for her sake. The more I know, the more I can help her."

Chalk another one up for Abby Webster. Impressive woman. "What causes spina bifida? Or is it one of those mysteries?"

"No one knows for certain." She lowered her eyes and fidgeted with her thumbnail. "There are risk factors, like low levels of folic acid in the mother."

He glanced toward the highway and back to her. "You feel responsible?"

"That I might have done something to hurt my baby? I'd never heard of folic acid before I had Lila, but if I'd taken it, she'd probably be fine. Now, she struggles to walk, struggles with toilet training. She can't even climb a playground slide. Everything is a struggle for her. She's endured four surgeries and will likely have more." She blinked shiny eyes. "Of course, I feel guilty."

Brady reached across the bucket seat to squeeze Abby's hand. "Don't. Lila's blessed to have you."

"I'm the one who's blessed," she said softly, and then turned her face toward the passenger window and the miles of yellowing grass and piney woods.

The cab grew silent, and deep in thought, Brady clicked on the radio. He had a feeling he was about to get a life lesson from one sunny, tough little girl with something called spina bifida…and her equally strong mother.

The following Sunday, Abby attended church with the Buchanons, the day she'd spent with Brady at the hospital heavy on her mind and heart. The truth was, she'd thought of little else, of his compassion, his consideration and the way he'd dumped his schedule to drive them. She wasn't accustomed to anyone going out of his way for her. As nice as it was, she questioned his motives. Why would he do that? What would he want in return?

Whatever the price, Brady's company had been worth it. He'd made the usually grueling day almost enjoyable. Lila, determined to be brave in front of her hero, had basked in his attentions and sailed through most of her tests with a smile.

Today was Abby's first time attending church in years and she'd come mostly to please Karen. How could she refuse after all they'd done for her? Seeing Brady again was an added bonus.

The Buchanons, she discovered with amusement, required two pews. The only one missing was Dan who'd decided to work today, and Abby found herself wedged between Karen and Brady. Brady cleaned up really well, as if he wasn't already good-looking enough. In dark slacks, white shirt and a blue tie that matched his eyes, he looked as good as he smelled, which was delicious.

All during the worship service, while the music director led them in songs she didn't know, Brady shared his hymnal. He had a pleasant voice and she mouthed the words to hear him better.

And if the image of this giant man holding her baby girl on the slide at McDonald's played in her head, she couldn't help it.

After a woman made announcements, the pastor spoke. Abby was prepared to be bored, but the message was surprisingly simple and relevant, and she found herself listening with interest. He spoke of a father's love for his child, something she didn't know anything about, but when he spoke of the breakdown in families that damage the father-child relationship, she knew exactly what he meant.

"Some of your earthly fathers may have been absent or they may have disappointed you or hurt you or let you down too many times to trust them," he said. "But God is a Father you can depend on. He is a compassionate and merciful Father who wants to be there for you always, to heal your hurts and guide your steps every day of your life." The minister lifted his hands, palms up as if holding something in each. "The choice to be a greatly loved child of God is yours. The Father waits with arms outstretched."

Abby got a lump in her throat when he said the last. She'd never had a father's embrace and remembered movies in which the child ran into her father's arms for a hug. Sometimes she fantasized about being that child.

Would her daughter feel the same someday?

Surrounded by Buchanons and with Brady's arm brushing hers, Abby couldn't help dreaming of a father and a family for her little girl.

At the end of the service while the piano played softly, the minister asked if anyone needed prayer. She recalled Brady's offer to pray for Lila and her. Prayer. She'd given it little thought. Did praying really do anything?

So many questions and feelings swirled inside as she left the church and got into the car with Karen for the trip home.

"Did you enjoy the service?" Karen asked from her spot behind the steering wheel.

"I think so."

Karen laughed before sobering. "Was something wrong?"

She turned in the seat. "It all seems too good to be true."

"What does?"

"A loving Father who forgives you for all the rotten things you've done and never stops loving you. Why would He do that?"

"That's where Jesus comes in, honey. The Father loved us so much He allowed His son to die in our place. If He was willing to do that, His love must be pretty big."

"It sounds like a fairy tale."

Karen was quiet for a moment before saying, "I grew up without a father, too, Abby."

"I didn't know that."

"My dad died in an oil field accident when I was three." Karen clicked on the signal light and turned at the stoplight. "I struggled to comprehend a father who could love me, a father who wasn't absent, but once I became a child of the King, oh, honey, I can't tell you what a huge hole in my soul Jesus has filled."

"Did you grow up around Christians?"

"No, I didn't. My mom hated God because she blamed Him for the loss of my dad. I was scared of God, afraid He'd kill me or someone else I loved." She pulled the car into the garage and stopped. "I was terribly wrong. That's not who God is, Abby. God is for us, not against us."

Abby said nothing but she absorbed Karen's words to ponder. She'd always thought of God, when she thought of Him at all, as an invisible being who didn't care, like her earthly father. Or if He noticed her at all, it was to pass judgment on her misbehavior. *God will get you*, she'd heard people say.

She exited the car, unstrapped Lila. Karen came around to her side, house keys in hand.

"Thank you," Abby said.

Karen cocked her head. "For?"

"Answering my dumb questions."

"Questions are never dumb. Ask me anything, anytime." She unlocked the door and pushed it open. "Smell that soup. Is that delicious or what?"

"Is everyone coming over for dinner?" Abby shifted Lila to her opposite hip, trying to pretend she wasn't asking specifically about Brady.

"I'm hungry, Mama."

"You're always hungry, jelly fingers."

Karen opened the pantry and handed out a pack of gummy fruits. "Will these hold you until dinner?"

"Yummy!"

"What do you say?"

"Thank you vewy, vewy much."

The mothers exchanged smiles.

"The whole gang will show up before the day is over. The Cowboys don't play until tomorrow night, but my bunch will gather for anything that involves the three F's—family, food and football." On chunky heels, Karen tapped over the tile to peer in the oven. "I hope you like noisy crowds."

She worked in a diner. It couldn't be any noisier or more crowded than the noon rush.

She was wrong.

Sunday afternoon proved to the wildest, noisiest time Abby had witnessed in years. The four Buchanon males, their three sisters, kids she'd never seen and couldn't remember, and a couple of extra guys, including Jake Hamilton, roamed through the kitchen and living areas in friendly arguments about Fantasy Football teams while stuffing their faces. Everyone brought something. Pizza, buffalo wings, chips, dips, and a huge veggie and fruit tray contributed by one of the sisters, Jaylee, the only one who seemed concerned about carbs or processed foods and who made a point of reminding her brothers that chips and dip would clog the arteries and lead to a sure death. The men were not in the least deterred.

They all talked at once, hooting and laughing at the TV or something one of them said. Abby's head swam from the sheer energy of the group.

And Brady. She couldn't keep her eyes off him.

"It's a party. It's a party!" Lila said, and giggled when Brady pointed his big index finger at her and winked.

"Sure it is, squirt. Come here and I'll teach you about football. All you need to know is that the linebacker is the man!"

Lila pulled her walker as close as she could to her adored Bwady. So many legs sprawled across the floor, she couldn't maneuver through. Sawyer, the closest to her, saw the dilemma and shouted, "Handoff."

He scooped her up in his strong carpenter's hands, lifted her high over his head and passed her to Dawson, who handed her to Brady. Lila's giggle rang out, sweet and joyous.

"You boys," Charity said with a head shake.

"Again, again," Lila cried.

"Lila," Abby said. "Don't be a pest."

"Sowwy." She hung her head.

"Hey, no sad faces." Brady tugged gently on one of her twin ponytails, grinning. "Santa Claus might be watching."

"Really?" Lila perked up and glanced around the room. "Mommy, guess what?"

"What?" Abby leaned against the doorway between kitchen and family room, smiling at her daughter's pleasure and at the sweetness of her interaction with Brady.

The need for family pulled at her.

"Santa Claus is coming."

"Won't be long."

"Tomorrow?"

"Not that soon. Thanksgiving comes first."

Karen poked her head into the room. "Is everyone going to be here on Thanksgiving? Jake, did you remember to invite your grandmother?"

Jake waved one hand. "Done. She said she'd pencil it

on her social calendar but if the governor called, she'd have to cancel."

They all chuckled. Granny Pat, best friend to Flo Dubois, was as sassy as her friend, though her health had deteriorated in recent years and, like Lila, she used a walker for mobility.

Allison, lounging close to her cowboy, patted the opposite side of the couch. "Come sit down, Abby, if you can tolerate my brothers. There's room."

Abby did as she asked, pleased to be included. She didn't say much, but she smiled a lot and laughed at the interactions between the siblings. She listened to their snatches of conversation, both teasing and serious, if listening was possible when everyone talked at once and the big screen blared. They were wonderful, happy, loving, a family like she'd never witnessed before. A hot balloon of emotion expanded in her chest, a chasm of need so deep and wide as to make her eyes misty.

She blinked away the moisture.

Being with the Buchanons was both overwhelming and fulfilling. And if she found herself focused more on Brady and listening to him talk, it was because she knew him best. That was all. This silly schoolgirl crush would subside when the house was finished. She knew better than to let that kind of emotion get out of hand.

At halftime of the game between Arizona and Denver, the five males trotted into the backyard to throw a worn football around while the women discussed the upcoming Thanksgiving meal and Black Friday shopping.

Brady's father still had not returned from work, and Abby found it interesting that he was the only Buchanon not fully committed to church and Sundays off.

After a bit, the men swarmed into the kitchen like a biblical plague to gorge on more food and claim victory.

Brady, sipping Coke from a can, reached for a slice of apple. His cell phone jangled. He stuffed the apple in his mouth, set the Coke aside and answered.

"Dad, what's up?" he said, around the bite of apple. "Yeah, yeah, everyone's here. Why don't you knock off work and come home for the second half? It's a pretty good game."

Whatever Dan replied erased Brady's cheerful expression. His next words were too low for Abby to hear, but they were short and crisply spoken.

He tapped the screen and rang off, staring down at the phone for a couple of seconds.

"What is it, son?" Karen asked. "Not another break-in."

"No." He blew out a sigh. "Dad thinks he needs my input."

"Can't it wait until tomorrow?"

"Apparently not." He pocketed the cell.

"Want us to come along?" Dawson asked. He popped open a bag of tortilla chips.

"Nah. I got this." Brady play-punched his brother's arm. "Keep the party going. I shall return."

The afternoon wasn't as much fun after he left.

Thanksgiving proved to be a bigger, noisier version of Sunday afternoons. Abby worried about intruding on a family event and worried even more about Lila being in the way, particularly when Dan was home. Even though Brady's dad was cordial, he made her nervous. She'd heard his harsh tone with Brady and she didn't like it.

But when Thanksgiving Thursday arrived, she and

Lila weren't the only non–family members invited to the Buchanon feast. Several men and women Abby had seen on the construction site joined Jake and Pat Hamilton and a half dozen unfamiliar kids who ran in and out of the house with Dawg.

Inside the kitchen, Abby helped the others organize the enormous number of casseroles and desserts while Brady and Dan carved up two turkeys and a ham, joking about who was the best carver and chuckling over Samurai warrior jokes from a TV show. Abby watched, puzzled and intrigued that two men who could be at odds one day were clearly having a good time together.

The inner workings of a big family, particularly this one, bewildered her.

Lila tried to keep up with the other children on her walker but failed and ended up standing at the patio door watching the game of tag. The sight made Abby's heart heavy. Without being obvious, Abby observed her daughter, all the while wondering what she could do to make up for Lila's lack of playmates. She was never one to ask for special privileges or attention, even for Lila.

Brady's niece, Amber, pressed her face against the glass of the patio doors. She was a cute thing, blond as her mother with a tilted nose and blue eyes. Her gaze lit on Lila and she grinned, showing an empty space where her front teeth had been. She slid open the glass door, letting in a waft of cold air and said to Lila, "I brought my dolls. Want to play with me?"

Abby's heavy heart lifted even as tears of gratitude stung her eyes.

Lila's face lit up. "Okay."

Amber shed her jacket, letting it drag behind her as

she took two steps toward the living room, then turned to watch Lila's progress. "I'll wait for you."

Abby's chest squeezed with gratitude as Charity's little girl patiently strolled alongside the walker, one hand on Lila's back as if to assist. Lila, her face set in concentration and determination, maneuvered across the room and down the hall.

Abby caught Charity's eye over the bar piled with food. "Your little girl has a kind heart. You should be proud."

"I am." Charity's smile was soft as her gaze followed the two girls. "Her daddy and I live for moments like this. Lila is a sweetheart, too. She's easy to like."

Pleasure ballooned inside. "Thank you."

Charity moved a chocolate pie to the dessert table and reached for a coconut cream with sky-high meringue. "What's the latest report on your house? Brady seems supercharged this year about the project."

Supercharged. "Isn't he always?"

Charity chuckled. "Oh, sure. He's a regular Santa at Christmas, the big teddy bear, but I don't know, he seems more excited about your house for some reason."

"Probably because he's building from the ground up instead of remodeling." It couldn't be anything else. "We're in the dry now, as he calls it. I'm impressed at how fast his crew can build."

"They are pretty impressive." She leaned closer. "Dawson thinks Brady has his eye on you."

Heat flushed Abby's neck. She opened a drawer in search of a serving spoon. "Dawson likes to kid around."

Guys like Brady Buchanon didn't look twice at girls from the wrong side of the tracks except when that particular girl was his latest charity project.

Charity tilted her head, eyebrows knit together. "Brady's a good guy. Don't you like him?"

Like him? She was smitten with all six-and-a-half feet of him. "He's been very kind to us."

Before Charity could embarrass her more, Dan's voice boomed across the room. "Listen up, folks. Heads bowed. We're going to say grace and let the games begin."

After a round of *shh*, silence fell on the house like a curtain and Dan spoke a simple prayer.

"Thank You, Heavenly Father, for this incredible feast you've provided. Thank You, too, that this family could once more gather as a whole to celebrate this day, and thank You, Father, for our blessings of this year and for the guests who've come to share those blessings. Through Jesus we pray. Amen."

It was simple, heartfelt and as foreign to Abby as this Thanksgiving dinner. The only big holiday meals she'd attended had been held by social services for foster kids. They were nice, but not like this, not family.

"Buffet style, y'all." Karen circled a finger around the tables and counters of food. "Everything is organized by type. Salads there. Meats here. Side dishes and casseroles over here. Grab a plate and help yourself."

The long dining table filled in minutes and the overflow sat at the bar and at a pair of folding tables stretched as far as the family room. Succulent scents floated into Abby's senses as she filled Lila's plate and sat her daughter in a booster chair at one of the folding tables dubbed the kids' table. She didn't know what was wrong with her today, but she got teary when Amber and another little girl parked on each side of Lila and stared to chatter.

"Looks like you've been demoted," Brady said as his big body maneuvered through the crowd of plate fillers.

Abby blinked away the unusual tears. She wasn't a crier—life had taught her that crying didn't do a bit of good and often made things worse—but, lately, her emotions were too close to the surface.

"I'm glad. She's having fun with the girls today. Your niece is a sweetie."

He reached around her for a chunk of turkey and a bigger chunk of ham. "Aren't you going to eat?"

"If you leave me any of that turkey." Her sassy answer caught her off guard. She was not one to joke around, even at the diner. These lighthearted Buchanons were having a strange effect on her.

Brady stabbed another piece of turkey and dropped it on her plate. "There you go. How about some stuffing?"

She took the spoon from him. "I'm a big girl, but this piece of turkey is enough for a week."

He grinned and jerked his head toward the table. "Fill 'er up. I'll save you a seat."

He would? Pulse thrumming a little erratically, Abby helped herself to the abundant meal. Brady topped his plate with two steaming hot rolls and moved away. She took her time, trying to get a handle on the emotion dancing around in her chest. Brady meant nothing by the saved seat. He was being hospitable, friendly, making a stranger feel welcome. She really needed to stop overreacting to kindness just as she needed to get a handle on this stupid crush.

When her plate was filled, she avoided looking toward Brady's table, choosing instead an empty chair next to Jaylee. When she saw the tiny amount of food on the woman's plate, she regretted her decision. Svelte and diet-conscious Jaylee made her feel like an Amazon. A gluttonous Amazon.

But sitting with a thin, beautiful Buchanon was better than making a fool of herself by chasing after the handsome giant Buchanon. They passed the meal in pleasant conversation, mostly about the town's upcoming Christmas parade and chocolate festival and tomorrow's Black Friday sales ads.

"Do you want to go with us, Abby?" Jaylee dipped her fork into a tiny portion of cranberry salad.

The invitation caught Abby off guard. "Oh, no thank you. I don't think so."

"You don't know what you're missing. We have a blast and find a lot of bargains in the process."

"Charity maps out a plan." Allison leaned around her fiancé, her fork filled with baked-potato casserole. "Then the four of us split up, using our cell phones to text or pix a bargain we find."

"It's so much fun," Jaylee said. "Afterward, we meet up for a late breakfast and share our treasures. A real girls' day out."

"Exhausting and exhilarating, especially when one of us snags a limited-supply item. You should hear the squealing, in text format, of course." A piece of pumpkin pie in hand, Karen had stopped at their table. She smiled at the last statement. "We'd love to have you come along."

It did sound fun, but her budget couldn't manage much this year and she didn't want to embarrass herself in a group of free spenders.

Abby reached for her tea glass. "You're nice to ask, but I'll be working at the house tomorrow."

Now that the house was enclosed, she spent every

extra minute there. Often Brady or the twins were the only ones working and she'd quickly learned to run a sander and a nail gun.

"I don't blame you one bit, Abby," Karen said. "A new house is even more fun than a wild spree with the Buchanon girls. Let us know if there is anything in the ads we can pick up for you."

"I—haven't had a chance to look." She hadn't planned to look. Looking led to longing.

"What does Lila want for Christmas?" Allison glanced toward the little girls.

"We really haven't talked about it. We're both too excited about the house. That's our Christmas present this year."

Her statement moved the conversation to the makeover, which made Abby about as uncomfortable as the topic of Christmas presents. She was thrilled over the house, truly she was, but being the focus of the Buchanons' altruism at the dinner table drove home the fact that she and Lila were a charity case, not family like the rest.

Later that afternoon, when guests had departed and only the family remained, Karen stepped in front of the television with an announcement. "Who's going to help put up the tree?"

When Abby glanced at Allison, she explained, "Thanksgiving evening is our traditional day to put up the decorations."

"That's because she has all of us corralled," Sawyer said, grinning.

"You got that right. Sawyer, you and Dawson can start on the outside lights," Karen ordered like a general.

"Brady and Dan, if you'll get the tree out of storage, the girls and I will find the decorations."

"What about us, Nana? We want to help?" This from Amber, who bounced up and down in excitement at the mention of a Christmas tree.

"You, my little sugarplum," Karen said, tapping Amber's pert nose, "along with your brother and Lila will be my very special helpers. Brady, turn the channel to Sounds of the Season."

The men groaned good-naturedly. "Mom and her Christmas music." To Abby, Quinn said, "Prepare to be driven crazy for the next few weeks."

Karen's laughter rang out. "Don't complain. Santa is watching."

Dawson looped an arm over his mother's shoulders much the way Brady had once done to Abby. Casual. Affectionate. "She used to torture us with that dire warning when we were kids."

"Yeah," Sawyer said. "If Dawson and I got in a disagreement, which might have happened pretty often, we were doomed to nothing but twigs in our stockings and no visit from Saint Nick."

"It worked, didn't it?" Karen patted her son on the very flat belly. "You boys were good as gold from Thanksgiving until Christmas."

"After that, the deal was off." Dawson feigned a punch at his twin. "Hammer time."

"We weren't as bad as Brady," Sawyer said. "He had to hold his temper for an entire month even when we pestered him and snitched his stuff without permission."

Brady pointed at his brother. "You knew I couldn't retaliate."

"Exactly. Santa Claus was watching." Sawyer's grin spread across his face. "We thought you might explode."

Amidst the good-natured family reminisces, the tall, artificial pine went up in the family room. The Buchanons pulled her in, handing her ornaments to hang and asking her opinion. Lila helped Amber place small golden bells on the lower branches and no one seemed to mind the uneven clumps of bells and empty spaces the girls created. With a thick ache in her chest, Abby watched her child be swept into the wonder and warmth of a big family.

The longing grew to such intensity that when the room was darkened and the tree twinkled merrily, Abby slipped away to the new house with Lila. Being with the Buchanons too much caused her to dream of things she'd never had and never would.

Chapter Eight

❧

Abby had ditched him.

The next day, as Brady pulled into the home make-over site, his ego still smarted from yesterday's dinner. She'd rejected his offer to sit together even though he'd saved her a chair next to his, an act that had brought comments from his brothers, especially when she'd chosen to sit with his sisters, instead. And during the time they'd put up the lights and tree, she'd not said one word to him. Not one.

He'd thought they were… He wasn't sure what they were. Friends, at least. On the cold, gray day he'd driven her and Lila to the medical center, a subtle shift had occurred in their relationship. At least for him.

He thought about that day a lot. He'd never imagined the amount of tests and exams one small child would have to endure. Lila had cried a couple of times and Brady had wanted to hit something. Instead, he'd given her piggyback rides up and down the corridor, made her giggle and promised lunch at her favorite eating place.

But the real kicker had been afterward. Instead of heading home, they'd visited the pediatric wing, where

Lila had dragged her walker from room to room to distribute her brand of cheer and hand-drawn angel cards to sick kids. As if she didn't have problems of her own.

Abby was a great mother, as strong and resilient as her daughter, and he'd admired the way she interacted with the medical team, absorbing advice and adding her own. He'd seen the tears she hid from her daughter. They'd ripped him in half.

So, yeah. When he considered that day, along with the time they spent on the house and the family gatherings, he thought Abby liked him. They talked and laughed over silly things at the building site, shared a love of country music, polished wood, fried cherry pies. They were friends, weren't they?

Okay, he got the message. He hadn't meant anything romantic when he'd invited her sit with him anyway. At least, he didn't think so. He simply hadn't wanted her to feel alone and out of place in the sometimes overwhelming Buchanon household. He'd had girlfriends who'd felt that way.

At the thought of girlfriends, he paused. Abby was not a girlfriend although they spent a lot of time together. Especially lately, since she'd become as much a crew member as some of his professional volunteers. He liked her, wouldn't mind hanging out more, and he got this little hum of energy under his skin whenever he saw her.

Having her and Lila present during the tree decorating had given an extra zing to the family tradition. And maybe he'd glanced her way a few too many times. Her look of wonder and pleasure had matched that of the children, and she'd hummed along with Mom's Christmas carols.

So yeah, he wouldn't mind getting cozy with Abby Webster. She, apparently, was not on the same page.

She was, however, inside the house when he turned the knob and stepped inside. They were insulating and he could hear her dragging fiberglass batting across the concrete, alone except for Lila. He'd balked at first about having a toddler on the job site, but Abby insisted. So, after the heating unit had gone live, he'd cleared out a space in one of the soon-to-be bedrooms, where Lila could play safely while the adults worked.

And, man, did Abby work. She'd stand on her feet for ten hours at the diner and then show up on the job immediately after and labor until midnight. She had to be exhausted but if she was, she wouldn't let anyone know. She just kept on working.

A man had to admire a woman like her.

"Hey," he said, entering the master bedroom. Abby stood on a stepladder pressing insulation into the spaces between the two-by-sixes.

Her head swiveled toward him. She tugged down the yellow particle mask he'd insisted she wear. "Hey, yourself."

"I see you remembered your safety glasses."

She made a face, her dark eyes even more enormous behind the plastic goggles. "My big mean boss threatened to fire me if I didn't wear them."

"He's a slave driver." With a smile, he leaned a shoulder against the open door facing. "Where'd you run off to yesterday?"

One minute they'd been decorating the tree and the next she and Lila were gone. Even Dad had noticed the departure and wondered if someone had upset her.

"Take a look at the master bathroom."

He stuck his head inside the adjoining space. "Did you do all that by yourself?"

Her smile was bright. She always lit up like Gabriel's Crossing's Christmas tree whenever he paid her a compliment. "Will you check to see if everything is done right?"

"We thought you might be upset about something."

"Why would you think that?"

"You left early. Kind of abruptly. We wondered." Actually, he'd wondered more than anyone.

"We loved yesterday. Really. I am simply too excited about the house to stay away."

Okay, that made sense. His mood elevated as he stepped into the other room and flipped on the light. Pink batting lined the walls in a tight configuration. He walked around the room, tugged on the batting here and there, checked the rough-in electric outlets for a tight fit.

She must have stayed half the night to finish this alone. And yesterday was Thanksgiving, a day to kick back. Except for Abby. He should have known she'd come here.

He returned to the master bedroom. "Great job, Ab. You're hired."

She beamed again and he got a weird swoopy feeling in his belly.

"I'd better say hello to the princess before I get started."

Abby replaced her mask, hauled up the dangling roll of insulation and went back to work.

After a few minutes with Lila, who seemed masterful at entertaining herself with angel drawings, Brady meandered through the house, checking and double-checking as he read through the calendar on his cell phone. He shot a group text to volunteers, then ordered the engineered hardwood flooring. He wrangled for a better deal but still winced at the final price increase.

"Sorry, Brady, it's the best I can do this year."

"Thanks anyway, Dale. Something's better than nothing." But he hung up discouraged. Getting material donations had been tougher this year. Tight economy. Rising prices. He was already dipping into his own account on this project, something he seldom had to do this early in the game. But Abby and Lila were worth it.

He headed back into the master bedroom, where Abby worked with her back to him. He stood in the doorway watching her. She was perfect for a guy like him. Brady's brain snagged on the word. Perfect height, he'd meant. She was slim with long legs and shapely arms that could reach high up on a wall to secure the batting. Her mink hair was pulled back in its usual ponytail and he wondered what she'd look like with all that dark hair falling around her shoulders.

She shoved a piece of batting against a two-by-six but quickly jerked her hand away, muttering, "Ouch."

"Splinter?" Brady pushed off the door and crossed the room.

She backed down the ladder, shaking her finger. "Got any tweezers?"

He arched an eyebrow. Seriously? Tweezers? Here?

"Let me see."

"I can get it."

"Don't be stubborn." He pulled her hand into his. Her fingers were long and slim but dwarfed in his big mitt. A sliver of pine was embedded beneath one of her nails. "That's a good one. Hold still, I think I can get it."

He moved into her personal space, a necessity under

the circumstances, though one that made him more aware of her. As if he wasn't already struggling in that department. Warmth emanated from her, but her fingertips were cool. Feminine and soft.

Brady swallowed, forcing himself to concentrate on the splinter. He nabbed a protruding piece of wood and tugged. He felt her tense. "Sorry."

"Did you get it?" Big brown eyes lifted to his.

"Done." Quickly, he dropped her hand and took a step back. He didn't know what his problem was with this lady. "You okay?"

She shook her hand up and down. "Better, thanks. It'll be all right when it quits stinging. I thought you had to work on a paying job today. The Huckleberry Creek addition, right?"

"This is Thanksgiving weekend. Subcontractors don't want to work. I knocked off a few hours early."

"Won't your dad be upset that you're here instead of there?"

"Don't worry about my dad, okay?" Ever since she'd overheard his father's complaints about a nonpaying job, she'd been anxious.

"It bothers me when he gripes at you."

"I'm used to it." He forced a grin. "Arguing is our love language."

She started back up the ladder. "Seriously, Brady, why is he so hard on you?"

"Beats me. Conflicting personality types, I suppose." He'd always wondered why Dad picked at him but not the others. "He got worse after Quinn's injury."

He didn't know why he'd brought that up.

She paused on the third rung and turned toward him. "That's interesting. Do you know why?"

He had his suspicions. Dad had always favored Quinn, bragged about him in the coffee shops and ridden high on the wings of his son's success. After the accident, he was stuck with watching his second-best son play football. Brady never measured up to Quinn.

"Quinn was the smart one, the talented one. After he got hurt—" Brady frowned. "I don't know. This is a bad subject."

"He hurts your feelings, doesn't he?"

She was getting too close to the truth. Brady was the overgrown kid who had to work harder for his grades and to make the team. For Quinn, everything came easy. Quinn made Dad proud. Brady didn't. End of story.

Abby's dark eyes peered down at him. With a seriousness that clutched at his gut, she said, "No one is better than you, Brady. And no house is more important than your relationship with your father. Not mine or anyone's."

He heard what she didn't say, but for all their quarrels, Brady knew Dan loved him and was there for him. Abby had never known a father's love.

"Dad and I will be okay, Abby. He'll come around. Don't worry about us." That was *his* job. He slapped the metal ladder, eager to change the subject. "Come on. Get busy, woman. Let's get this insulation installed so we can start the drywall. We've got a house to build!"

His statement brought a smile. Splinter forgotten, she gazed at him a moment longer before she took up the batting again and went to work. He watched her climb, admired her long legs and her work ethic, and then laughed at himself for the combined thought.

Toting a roll of batting to the opposite wall, Brady

got busy, his mind humming with Abby Webster and a tangled version of "Jingle Bells."

Christmas makeovers were awesome. And this one might be the best of all. No use stressing over Dad today.

Every bone in Abby's body ached. She'd worked until after midnight last night and gotten up at dawn to start again. As accustomed to long hours and hard work as she was, construction challenged a new set of muscles. A new kind of fatigue.

But she would not complain. Not when Brady worked long hours, too, and tolerated his father's bad moods to give her and Lila this beautiful home.

"Time to close up shop," Brady said from behind her.

"Let me finish this one wall." They'd completed the first bedroom and moved on to another. She glanced at her watch. "I can't believe it's already this late."

Time had flown while they'd worked together, making small talk and banter. "We've accomplished a lot, but the princess needs to go home to bed."

"She's probably asleep on her play mat."

"She is. Or she was when I last checked." He walked across the space to her ladder. "The other princess needs rest, too. Come on down. You're tired. You barely stopped to wolf down that plate of leftovers I brought, and now your eyes are glazing over."

"But this wall—"

"Will be here tomorrow."

She brushed a weary hand over the top of her hair. "But I can't finish the job until after work. I'm at the diner tomorrow."

He frowned up at her. "What time?"

"Six."

Something hot flared behind his electric-blue eyes, a flash of lighting. "Why didn't you tell me that before? Get down from there now. You're going home."

If she hadn't been so tired, she'd have told him to take a flying leap. Instead, she accepted the command for what it was—concern—and climbed down. "I'll get Lila and head home."

"*I'll* get Lila. You go to the car."

Instead, she followed him into Lila's play space. Lila was fast asleep on her mat, a blanket tucked around her neck. "Did you cover her up?"

Brady frowned again. "Sure."

Something sweet and warm turned over beneath her rib cage. The man made her crush worse every day.

"Thank you." She carried Lila's walker but left her toys in the room for tomorrow.

Brady gently lifted Abby's daughter, taking care to keep the blanket snug around her. He nodded toward the exit. "Go ahead. I'll lock up after you leave."

Abby led the way to the car, opened the back door and stood aside for Brady to lower Lila into her car seat. He dwarfed the small car and had to duck low but completed the task like a pro. As her daughter snuggled deeper into the car seat without ever opening her eyes, Brady snapped her seat belt. Then, as Abby watched, he leaned in and kissed her baby on the forehead.

"Sweet dreams, princess," he whispered.

Everything inside Abby melted.

Brady maneuvered his big body out of the backseat and closed the door softly with a single shove of one giant hand. Lila didn't stir.

When Abby started around to the driver's side, he followed, opening the door for her. He was a well-mannered Texan, doing what a gentleman did. He couldn't realize how he was affecting her.

She stood in the open door with him on the opposite side. The dome light cast a straw-colored glow into the darkness though Brady's height hid his face in the shadows above the car.

"You did a great job today." His voice was deep and soft.

She crossed her arms against the chill and his charm. "So did you."

"If we weren't so busy—" he started to say but seemed to change his mind.

Her heart skipped a beat. "What?"

He glanced toward the house and then back to her. "It's cold. You should get home."

She hesitated a second before sliding into the driver's seat. "Good night, Brady, and thank you."

"See you tomorrow." He leaned in and touched her cheek. "Sweet dreams to you, too. You deserve them."

Thankfully, he slammed the door and stepped away before she could find her voice. Her chest ached with feelings she didn't want and couldn't afford to feel.

She lifted her hand and drove away. In her rearview mirror, he stood in the cold moonlight watching her leave. The giant man with the bigger heart.

"Oh, Brady."

Either she was very, very tired or her heart was in a world of trouble.

Chapter Nine

Brady didn't like to shop, but on this particularly cold Friday morning he'd been out and about on other business and walked past Wonder World, a local store with a little bit of everything. In the Christmas window display, a fold-and-play art studio complete with easel and neon-orange stool caught his eye. The little princess liked to draw and color. He'd been wondering what to get her for Christmas. Voilà. Problem solved.

Abby would say he shouldn't have, but she would relent. She was a soft touch with Lila.

He bought the item and had it gift wrapped by Mary Hill, the store owner who also happened to be Mayor Hanover's daughter.

"Is this for Amber?" she asked.

"No." He frowned. "You think Amber would like one, too?"

"Sure, she would. Little girls love to draw and paint."

Awesome. Two birds with one stone. He never knew what to get his little niece. Boys, like his nephew, were easy. Girls, a puzzle. Generally, he relied on one of his sisters. This, however, got him completely off the hook.

Abby wouldn't be miffed because he'd also shopped for Amber. He loved it when a plan came together.

"Got another?"

Mary chuckled. "Want it wrapped, too?"

"Yes, ma'am."

As she worked, twirling ribbons and creating something beautiful with paper, she asked. "So who's the other lucky little girl? One of your Christmas projects?"

The question was asked in all kindness, but something about the term didn't sit right with Brady. Lila wasn't a project. Maybe she'd begun that way, but now…

"A friend's little girl," he said.

"Ooh, a friend." Mary, his mother's childhood friend and a woman he'd known all his life, raised her eyebrows. "Has someone captured the heart of one of Gabriel's Crossing's elusive Buchanon bachelors?"

He laughed and, without answering, took his packages and left. But her question swirled around inside his head the rest of the day.

He stopped at the appliance store and then the paint and lumber companies, making selections and gathering samples. Some were for Huckleberry Creek but most, he had to admit, were for Abby's house. He'd promised to let her choose and today was as good as any.

With his errands complete, he drove from project to project, making sure subs were in place and things were going smoothly. He did a bit of troubleshooting, rescheduled a couple of subs and wrangled with a vendor over delivery dates. Then he stopped by the Buchanon Built offices to check mail and work with Quinn on plans for a new construction job Dad had taken on. An addition to a local business.

Brady and Quinn were both miffed about the added

work. They'd not planned for anything more until spring, when the current buildings would be finished. But, as always, Dad was the boss and expected Brady and the others to make the project happen. All the projects.

His father arrived, annoyed by a mistake made on the McGruder house.

"I thought you had that under control," he said to Brady.

"I spoke with Perry last week. He seemed to know the buyer wanted a heat pump instead of a furnace."

"Well, apparently he didn't know. And now we've got a furnace to pay for and replace."

Brady's heart sank. Delays and mistakes were costly in both time and money. Both issues irritated Dan more than anything other than the mysterious vandalism. "I'll get together with Perry and see what we can do."

"That house has to come in on time, Brady. It's already sold and the buyer is paying extra to move in before Christmas. Unless you get off your duff, your halfhearted attitude is going to jeopardize the deal."

Temper flared. Brady could feel his face and neck heating up like a long day in the Texas sun. "There's nothing halfhearted going on, Dad, but I can't be everywhere. You're killing us with your demands."

"My demands wouldn't be that hard if you'd keep your mind on business."

He stiffened. So that was where his father was heading. "I thought we had this resolved. You like Abby and Lila. You agreed they deserve a home makeover."

"Liking them has nothing to do with business. Fix the problem, Brady. I don't care what you have to do." Dan spun on his work boots and stalked off, slamming the outer door hard enough to rattle the metal building.

Brady ground his back teeth. He'd fix it. He always did.

At five, the other Buchanons closed the office and left. Quinn, on his way out, said, "Go home and forget this for a while, Brady. You're taking things too seriously."

"Easy for you to say. Dad's not on your back."

"All work and no play," Jaylee added with a flip of her long hair. "I have a date. You should try it sometime."

"Right. Like I have time for dates."

"I can think of someone who might be interested."

"No more setups with your friends. The last one approached stalker status."

Quinn clapped him on the shoulder. "I don't think she meant one of her friends, Brady. I think she meant one of yours."

He didn't have to ask who they meant.

With a grunt, he turned and went back to work.

He stayed at the office later than usual that evening, jockeying schedules and procuring the missing heat pump. The problem remained, though, that Perry couldn't return to install the unit for several days and another heat-and-air company wouldn't touch someone else's half-finished job. Unless he could figure out another scenario, the project was doomed to fall behind.

At seven, discouraged and rubbing the knot on his shoulder, he and Dawg knocked off for the day. He started home, changed his mind and drove across the railroad tracks to Cedar Corner. Abby's car was in the driveway.

"All work and no play." She was as bad as him.

He parked the truck and hopped out. The air had a sharp bite tonight, stinging when he sucked in air. The night was moonless, but a pale lemon light seeped from the sidelights of the red front door, a fancier entry than he usually put in his Christmas makeovers. In others he'd used a less expensive, utilitarian door, but this one had caught his eye and seemed right for Abby.

Dawg, eager to hang out with Lila, loped to the front porch and waited patiently, his tail thumping.

When they entered, Dawg sniffed the concrete before trotting down the hall toward Lila's playroom. Brady followed the sound of country music to find Abby in the future laundry room sweeping trash into a heap. The old radio he carried onto building sites pumped out Carrie Underwood. Plumbing fixtures protruded from the walls, reminding him of the heat pump and the discussion with his dad.

Not happy thoughts. He turned his attention to the woman.

In hoodie, jeans and athletic shoes, with her hair in a ponytail, she looked about sixteen.

"How old are you?" he blurted without thinking.

"Twenty-eight." Her smile was quizzical. "That's a strange question. How old are you?"

"Thirty-three and feeling every minute of a hundred thirty-three." He held the dustpan while she swept the dirt onto the tray.

"Bad day?" She took the pan from him and leaned the broom in a corner.

Brady's past few hours rode his shoulders like a two-hundred-pound gorilla. "I'm tired, I'm hungry and I've had a lousy day. Let's go somewhere and cheer me up."

"What?" She blinked rapidly, puzzled and maybe a little amused.

He reached for her hand and tugged. "Come on. I'm serious. Forget about the house for one night."

"I—I'm at a standstill anyway. I don't know what else to do at this point. That's why I was sweeping."

"A few guys are scheduled to hang rock tomorrow night. Once the drywall is up, things go fast. There will be plenty to do." He tugged again. "Come on."

She gazed around the kitchen uncertain. "Well…"

"If it will make you feel productive, I have samples in the truck and we can pick out tile and paint colors over dinner and maybe watch some mindless TV."

He didn't know where the invitation came from. It was one of those spontaneous things, completely unplanned, but he wasn't backing down.

"TV? Where?"

"My house. We'll throw some steaks on the grill, nuke a couple of potatoes, toss a salad." The idea improved by the minute.

"Your house?"

"Is that a problem?"

"No… I—"

"I want you to see the cabinet stain I used. Golden oak. I think you'll like it in your kitchen, too." Actually, the stain was a last-minute thought to convince her, but he warmed to the idea of impressing her with his handiwork. He'd built that house from ground up, as far as he'd gotten, and he loved every rock and board.

"Well… I guess it would be okay. If you're sure you want to."

Nothing sounded better right now. "I'll get the princess."

"I'll follow you in my car so you don't have to drive back here."

"Better ride with me."

"Why?"

"Do you know where I live?"

"No, but you can tell me. I follow directions well."

She did, indeed. As a helper on the project, she was a gem. He was, however, concerned that she'd get lost on the windy river roads. Lots of people did, but they had cell phones. Hers never seemed to be working.

"I'm on the outside of town, a little off the beaten track near the river."

"Oh." She seemed to be debating something.

"I'll bring you back here whenever you're ready."

"If you're sure it's not too much trouble."

He wished she'd stop staying that.

They drove over the railroad tracks and through town, down the T-shaped main street with satellite radio playing a mix of country's top forty and country Christmas. Overhead, long strings of multicolored Christmas bulbs cast rainbow reflections on the pavement.

"Pwetty, Mommy," Lila said from the backseat of Brady's SuperCrew cab. Next to her, Dawg sat like a human being with his nose pressed against the window.

Abby shifted in the passenger seat, caught Brady's smile in the dash-light glow and answered with one of her own. "Real pretty."

She didn't know what had come over Brady tonight and she'd almost refused his invitation. Being alone with him would be torturous given her crazy feelings though, admittedly, a pleasant kind of torture.

Years ago, she'd thought the same about Lila's father. Spending time with Warren and feeling loved had outweighed her good sense, though she'd learned soon enough that he was like everyone else in her life. His love was nothing but empty words with no depth, and when the going got tough, he was gone. No one kept her around for long.

Troubled by such morose thoughts when she had so much to be grateful for and the normally upbeat Brady had clearly suffered through a rotten day, Abby said, "What happened? Problems with your dad?"

"Partly." He turned down the radio volume and cut short a Blake Shelton song. "Today was one of those days when things went wrong and I let the pressure get to me."

They drove past the Buttered Biscuit. Except for the string of white icicle lights shining around the front window, the diner was dark and quiet, the norm in a town that closed up early even during the holidays.

"I think you handle pressure extremely well. I'm amazed at how you juggle construction sites, contractors, vendors, work on my house and all the other things you do that I don't even know about."

"Doesn't leave much time for a social life, as my siblings so kindly reminded me today."

Abby blinked. Social life? As in dating? "Was that why you invited me to dinner at your house? To get your siblings off your back?"

"What?" He glanced from the wheel to her, scowling. "No!"

"Then why, Brady?"

"Because I'm hungry and I don't want to eat alone. Because we have samples to look at. Because—" He shook his head. "Will you stop questioning my motives?"

Was that what she was doing? She'd been suspicious of others' motives from the time she was old enough to know everyone had an agenda and those agendas were primarily for their own benefit. If Brady was different, she'd be very surprised.

"I'm sorry. You've had a rough day and I'm making it worse. You can take me back to my car if you're sick of me already."

"Stop assuming I don't want to spend time with you."

She wanted to ask what he meant but bit her tongue, instead. She'd come along to cheer him up, not to aggravate him more. But the thought that he actually wanted to be with her made her feel suspicious rather than complimented. How pathetic was that?

She leaned back in the seat and looked out at the passing town, silent. Brady turned the radio up again.

At the stoplight, he took a left past the IGA and followed the winding road through a residential area that eventually opened into wooded countryside. After a few miles, when the pickup turned down a dark, empty country lane, Abby leaned forward to peer into the darkness.

"I can't see a house anywhere."

His teeth flashed. "You will."

Past a cove of leafless trees, bright security lights suddenly lit the darkness and shone on a large two-story structure with shadowy landscaped evergreens. From what she could see, the house was built of river rock and timber with wraparound balconies up top and a chimney reaching high into the darkness.

"Brady," she breathed. "This is beautiful."

"Better in daylight." But she heard pride in his voice. "A work in progress. The lower level is basically complete. The upper story, not so much."

"When do you have time to work on it?"

"Ah, here and there."

He pulled the truck to a stop and they went inside. Lila, who had somehow managed to remain awake, said, "I like your house, Bwady. And guess what?"

"What?"

"It's big like you."

Abby flushed in embarrassment. "Lila!"

Brady laughed. "It's big like me on purpose. And has plenty of room for a certain little girl to wheel around." He put her walker on the hardwood floor. "Go ahead. Explore. Dawg knows the way." To Abby, he said, "Want to look around?"

"I do, but you're starved. I heard your stomach growling on the way out here. Steaks on the grill first. Tour second."

He raised his palm in a high five. "You genius woman."

Companionably, they worked together in the gorgeous golden wood and rock kitchen, both rustic and modern and a testament to Brady's eye for detail and his building skill.

When the simple meal was ready, they gathered at the table situated to the left of the granite-topped bar and near a wall of windows that looked toward the river. Dawg parked his behind on the polished hardwood next to Brady and stared hopefully at the sizzling beef steaks.

Mealtime prayer had become a comforting routine, and when Brady stretched his hands toward her and Lila, she put hers in his and closed her eyes. Not surprisingly, his palm was hard and callused. She liked the manly feel of his skin, a reminder that, regardless of her height and large bone structure, Brady was all male and she was female.

"Amen," Lila said at the end of a prayer Abby hadn't

heard. She'd been too focused on the man, a fact that shamed her. She hoped God wouldn't hold that against her.

"Mommy, can we do this at our new house?"

"Do what, baby?" Abby unfolded her napkin and spread it in her lap.

"Hold hands and pway."

Brady turned a quizzical expression toward Abby.

"We never said grace at meals before," she said. "This is new to us."

"Prayer is ingrained in the Buchanons. A habit formed in childhood." He sliced into his steak with a knife and fork. "In my wilder days, prayer and church became rote and meaningless. Things I did to keep my parents off my case. Dumb on my part."

"You had wilder days?" Abby speared the steaming baked potato and swirled her fork in the butter-laced sour cream.

"Oh, yeah. Bad temper. Fights."

"Anyone who would fight with you has a death wish."

He laughed. "Another reason I had to get my temper and myself under control. I didn't want to hurt anyone. Football gave me an outlet for the aggression, but it took a relationship with God to really set me straight. Not that I'm perfect by a long shot. Just ask my family."

He was close enough to perfect for her. Maybe too perfect. She had started to trust him, depend on him and like him too much. She was falling for the big beautiful lug. Falling like a rock from the top of Mount Everest. The fall was exhilarating. The crash landing was going to kill her.

Chapter Ten

Brady was hyperaware of Abby tonight for reasons he didn't examine. She looked relaxed and pretty seated next to him on the leather sectional as they sorted through the tub of full-size tile samples. He liked seeing her smile and loved hearing her laugh, so he told wild stories about his childhood with six siblings. He'd brought other dates here once or twice but couldn't remember a time when an evening had been this enjoyable.

Quinn was right. All work and no play was taking a toll. Tonight he felt happier and more relaxed than he had in several weeks. Even Dad couldn't rattle him after that steak dinner and an hour or two alone with Abby in his favorite place.

At the opposite end of the sofa, Lila was propped like a princess on a stack of pillows with her hands behind her head, the stuffed toy he'd given her snuggled close and Dawg curled on the floor next to her, snout on paws. Lila had snuggled down with a blanket and Abby predicted she'd be asleep before the first cartoon ended.

He'd set her up on his Netflix account with a show Abby said she loved. A family of pigs frolicked across the screen, mindless TV as he'd promised Abby, though Lila was enchanted. Every once in a while, the little girl giggled and his heart squeezed. She was something special.

"It must have been crazy fun," Abby said in response to one of his tales.

"Completely nuts, as you can tell by Sunday afternoon. There was always something going on, someone to play with or harass—" he grinned, remembering "—as we boys often did to our sisters and each other. What about you? Any wild childhood antics?"

"You don't even want to know the answer to that."

"Sure I do. Come on. I've confessed that I terrorized my sisters on a regular basis. It can't be worse than that."

"I was in foster care, remember? Group homes can be crazy at times." Her smile was wry and a little sad. "Not always fun crazy, either."

He sobered. He'd forgotten that her childhood was vastly different from his own. She didn't talk much about herself but curiosity got the better of him. He wanted to know her. Not only her obvious struggles with money and medical care. Everything.

"What was that like, Abby? Growing up without parents. It had to be really difficult."

"Time has a way of softening the edges, but yes, it was hard having no family, no stable place to belong." She bent to the box at her feet and took out two tiles, examining each with care. "Special occasions were the worst."

No one to celebrate her birthday or attend school functions. No rowdy bunch in the stands to cheer her graduation.

"Do you remember any of your birth relatives?"

"Not really. I was told my grandmother turned me over to social services after my mother died when I was around Lila's age. Or as one social worker so kindly put it, she dumped me like a stray cat and never looked back."

Ouch. Brutal. "You weren't ever adopted?"

"Apparently, I wasn't the most appealing kid. Big feet, gangly, somber." She shrugged. "Not a sunny doll face like Lila. When I was thirteen a family *almost* adopted me, but things didn't work out."

Her casual acceptance of rejection twisted like a knife in the gut. Something that brutal had left scars, he was sure of it, though she covered them well. "What about your father?"

"He was never in the picture." She glanced toward her daughter. As she'd predicted, Lila's eyes were closed and her chest rose in rhythmic sleep, the pig family not enough to keep her awake. "He was a deadbeat dad who left my mother pregnant and disappeared. Like Lila's. I hate that I did the same thing to my own child. Someday she'll realize she has no dad and it will hurt her. I never meant for that to happen."

He'd wondered about the man she'd loved enough to have a child with. "What happened to him?"

She sighed, crossed her arms in that signal of discomfort she always used when she was uncertain. It made his chest ache to know that she was.

He scooted closer but didn't touch her—the temptation was strong, but he wasn't sure she wanted that from him.

"You don't have to tell me if it upsets you."

"I loved him, if that's what you're asking. He said he

loved me, too, and I had visions of the family I'd always wanted and someone who would stay forever."

"But he didn't."

"Deep inside I knew it couldn't last. Nothing ever does. Still, when Warren couldn't deal with Lila's diagnosis, I was crushed. We fought for three days, but when he realized I was going to have this baby with or without him, he moved out. I haven't seen him since."

Warren. Somewhere out there was a complete jerk who called himself a man. A jerk who had walked away from his own sick baby. A jerk who'd broken Abby's already wounded heart and left her to deal with a frightening diagnosis all on her own. Alone, the way she'd always been.

Brady's temper flared. He clenched his fists, glad he didn't know where to find the creep. He was tempted to do some serious face pounding.

"His loss."

"Excuse me?"

"A beautiful woman like you. A sweet little princess like Lila. The man is an idiot." He tugged her arms apart and slid his hands down to hold hers. "You're somebody special, Abby. Don't let other people's failures convince you otherwise."

She shook her head, the dark ponytail swishing against the leather coach. Brody caught the tail in his fingers and rubbed the silk, again wishing to see her hair loose and long. Someday he'd slide the band from her hair and run his hands through the warm, heavy silk.

Someday.

"You've had a lot of letdowns in your life," he murmured, feeling tender and protective.

"Life is hard. It's the way things are."

"They don't have to be." When her soft espresso eyes snagged on his as if she longed to believe him, he couldn't resist saying, "Life is good, too. There are people who care about you." *People like me.*

They were close and he watched her black pupils dilate as he leaned nearer. He had the wild urge to kiss her and realized he'd wanted to kiss her for a long time. But beyond the obvious romantic feelings filling up his chest, he wanted to hold her and promise to be more than Warren or the dozen foster homes she'd drifted through in search of love and acceptance.

He trembled with the need to wipe away all her loss and hurt. He slid his arms around her and tugged her closer. Her stiff body slowly melted into him. She fit as if she belonged there, not like some women who were so tiny he feared crushing them. Perfect.

Her soft breath warmed his ear and he might have brushed her hair with his lips.

She rested against him with a deep sigh as if she'd needed this. It occurred to him that no one had held Abby in a long time. She had no shoulder to lean on. No family to carry her through life's inevitable hard times. No one to hold her when she cried. No one to tend to her when she was sick.

He snugged her closer, kissed her hair again and made a vow. Abby needed him and he would be there for her. He'd be the one person in her life who wouldn't let her down.

Brady almost made her believe in the impossible.

Abby didn't know whether to run or grab hold and pray that the ride didn't end in disaster.

The next day at the diner, her thoughts were stuck on

the evening with Brady as she slid plates of roast beef onto table six. The noon rush was on and the Buttered Biscuit was filled with businesspeople popping in for a hearty meal. The hot smell of grilled burgers mingled with the scent of fresh coffee and warm apple pie.

Every time the bell over the door jingled and cold air wafted inside, her heart leaped and she glanced up, hoping to see Brady.

Last night had touched her deeply. Snuggled in Brady's arms, they'd talked of heartaches and hard times, life and faith and each other.

She didn't want to fall in love with Brady. But she figured it was too late to turn back the tide. He was all the good things she'd ever dreamed of in a man.

And he scared her out of her mind.

When he'd driven her back to the car and followed her home, she'd felt more protected than she'd ever felt in her life. She, a tall Amazon of a woman, didn't need protection, but knowing Brady cared enough to give it anyway fed a hungry spot in her soul.

He'd carried the sleeping Lila into his parents' home as if Abby hadn't done the task hundreds of time. She'd never had a partner in caring for Lila. She'd heard the adage that you don't miss what you've never had, but that wasn't true. Brady's kindness showed her what she and Lila were missing.

"Abby, order up!" Fran leaned through the server's window and looked at her with curiosity.

Aware she'd been in a fog thinking about Brady, she hurried to the window. "Sorry."

"Where is your head today, girl? Is Lila sick?"

"No, no. I'm sorry. Tired, I guess."

She should be tired but she wasn't. Not really. Brady

Buchanon filled her head the way his big body filled a room. Completely.

He'd kissed her last night. Her. Awkward Abby from the wrong side of the tracks.

He'd been standing in the doorway to his parents' garage, the entry she used to access her rooms without disturbing the Buchanons. She'd switched on the light and followed him to the door, though she couldn't say why. The hour was later than either of them had planned, but their conversation had gone on and on until the Milky Way streaked the sky.

"Thank you for dinner," she had said. "And for everything."

"Thanks for cheering me up."

She scoffed softly, amused. "If my whining cheers you up, you're a sick puppy."

His mouth curved. "You never whine. That's part of your charm. But you do cheer me up." He touched her cheek. "You."

While she absorbed the compliment like a thirsty camel, he leaned closer, his face serious, his eyes holding hers captive. "Good night, Abby."

"Good night." But she didn't step away from his touch, a touch that became a caress. The rough calluses of his manly hand stroked the softness of her face and sent pleasant chills through her.

Like a marble in a tin can, her heart rattled against her rib cage. When Brady leaned closer, mingling his breath with hers, the soft smile still on his perfect lips, her pulse went ballistic.

His mouth touched hers in a gentle, warm, heart-stopping kiss. Abby didn't notice or care about the late hour or the fatigue in her shoulders as time spun out through the garage and into the star-sprinkled night. Filled with a silken emotion, a gossamer thread of hope and pleasure she could ill afford to nurture, she kept her fists tight at her sides, afraid she'd throw herself against him and do something stupid.

When he stepped back, still holding her face with the tips of his strong fingers, his expression was serious. They stared into each other's eyes long enough for Abby to drown in his swimming-pool eyes before he dropped his hold. Then she watched him walk away, start his truck and drive into the darkness.

She'd awakened this morning wondering if it had all been a beautiful dream.

The bell over the diner door jingled and she looked up, aware that she was, once again, woolgathering instead of waiting tables.

Charla sailed past, balancing three dinner plates and slowing long enough to whisper, "It's not Brady. But you are so going to tell me what's going on with you two."

Heat rushed up Abby's cheeks. Thankfully, her skin was dark enough to cover her embarrassment.

"Charla," she hissed. "Hush. Nothing is going on."

But she couldn't keep her focus off the jingling bell and the diner doorway. For the rest of the day, she watched. Brady never came.

After work she drove to the building site. No one was there. The drywall team hadn't arrived and no progress had been made. With no work to do on the house, she and Lila ran some errands and headed to the Buchanon house for dinner.

Dan was in a dour mood at the table and even Lila's perkiness hadn't cheered the man, a rare turn of events for the charmer. When Karen asked what was wrong, he'd said, "Trouble on the McGruder site."

"Vandals?"

Dan braced his hands against the table and breathed out a harsh gust.

"We've gone more than a month without any trouble and now it has to happen on a nearly completed project with an incentive to finish early." He scowled at his dinner plate. "Sometimes I think someone knows exactly which properties are the most important to us. We had to pull a drywall crew from another job to repair the wall damage, a job that will also fall behind schedule."

So that explained Brady's absence and the missing drywall. Even though the reasons meant her house was behind schedule, she felt better. Brady wasn't avoiding her.

Karen passed Abby a bowl of green salad, her concerned focus on her husband. "What does Leroy say?"

"The police in this town are worthless, Karen. A year of trouble on Buchanon Built projects, and they don't have a clue."

"They're running shorthanded, honey. You know that. Ever since Beau was in the car accident and Frankie moved to Dallas to get married."

Dan reached across the table to squeeze her hand. "You're right, as usual. What would I do without you?" He took a deep breath as if purposely calming himself and his hard face softened as he glanced at Abby. "This woman keeps my head on straight. I'm a fortunate man."

Karen patted his forearm. "You work hard. Problems like this are frustrating. But the stress will make you sick if you let it and I don't want you sick. I worry about you, Dan. You need to slow down."

Abby watched the exchange of affectionate concern with interest and a nearly constant longing in the pit of her stomach. A couple who had weathered many life storms, raised a large family and built a business still loved and needed each other.

Such relationships were possible. She knew they were. But were they possible for someone like her?

Two days passed and, though she drove to the home makeover each evening after work, no progress had been made and she'd barely spoken to Brady. She understood. Truly, she did. Brady was busy troubleshooting. The drywall crew was busy with repairs on the ransacked property. She didn't expect them to drop paying work to build her house. She also didn't want to impose on the Buchanons any longer than necessary.

She was stuck. She didn't want to ask the Buchanons about the delay and appear demanding, but she couldn't live on their charity forever. Brady didn't call or visit and she missed him.

"He's busy. Really busy," she told Lila, who wanted to know when Bwady was coming to see her.

The fact that she'd still not spoken to him since the night of the kiss activated a host of insecurities. Like school-yard bullies, they bunched together to torment her. Maybe he regretted the impulsive, too-tired-to-think-straight action. Maybe he was glad for the extra work. Maybe he was avoiding her.

Common sense said none of that was true, but the bullies kept right on pounding away.

Gritty eyed from lack of sleep, Brady measured a sheet of gypsum for the McGruder repair. His drywall guys were working as fast as they could, but they weren't fast enough. Every experienced hand was needed. That meant him and any of the other Buchanons who could spare a minute. Subcontractors were exactly that. Subs. Though they were willing to work a little extra, Buchanon Built problems were not theirs to worry about. They went home to their families at six o'clock.

The Buchanons, on the other hand, had more to lose and pushed on. The whole family was exhausted, especially him and the twins who built trim for one job during the day and had replaced kicked-in cabinets and defaced trim here for the past two nights. The vandalism had escalated on this house and parts of the damage looked as if someone had taken an ax to the finish.

Escalated. He didn't like that word or the thought that whoever held a grudge against Buchanon Built might continue to go unchecked and do something worse.

He hadn't slept more than four hours a night this week and Dad was running about the same. They'd butted heads so many times today Brady refused to answer his father's calls. When he was tired, his temper was harder to control. He hated the failing and prayed about it plenty. The prayers must help because he wasn't in jail.

He paused to rub a hand over the back of his aching neck.

"Hey, Brady." Dawson stood in the doorway leading into the kitchen, tool bag low on his hip and nail gun in one hand. "We're knocking off for the night. You should do the same."

"Not yet."

"Go home. Get some rest." Dawson's dimples were nowhere to be seen. His normally happy blue eyes were lined with fatigue.

"Go ahead. I'll lock up when I finish this last piece."

Dawson stepped into the garage and grabbed hold of the drywall sheet. "Let's do this, then. We both need sleep."

Grateful, Brady hoisted the board and led the way through the kitchen, where Sawyer was cleaning up. The leftie twin, powdery sawdust covering his clothes, looked as worn as his brother.

"We're going to knock this one out and head home," Dawson said as they passed, toting the drywall.

"Even Brady?"

"So he says."

Sawyer scooped a handful of nails into a box and followed his brothers. To Brady he said, "You're worried about finishing Abby's house?"

He was worried about way more than that where Abby was concerned. She must think he was as much a jerk as her ex. Not only had he kissed her and disappeared, he'd made promises he wasn't keeping. He wanted time to explore this thing with Abby, and he wanted her house finished. But every day he fell further behind on the project he loved most, a job that was joy, not work. Repairing the McGruder house, however, was hard, irritating, frustrating work.

"My focus is this site right now."

"Understood." Sawyer braced the plasterboard while Brady and Dawson nailed it in place. They'd had to cut out this entire wall, thanks to sheer destructiveness. "Christmas is only a few weeks away."

Brady scowled, a nervous knot in his belly. "Yeah."

"You're doing the best you can, Brady. Abby understands."

Did she? People had let her down all her life. He'd

wanted to be the one who didn't, the hero she could lean on. He wanted to help her, make her life easier and better, and, yeah, he wanted to be with her. That one kiss had rocked his world, stirred him up worse than a blender.

He slammed the hammer one last time to set the nail head. "Got this, boys. See you tomorrow."

"You're going home, right?"

"Absolutely."

After his brothers drove away, Brady locked the doors, drove home long enough to shower, eat, feed his dog and collect his sleeping bag. He hadn't lied. He'd come home.

Then he and Dawg headed back to the McGruder house for the night.

Chapter Eleven

"Brady spent the night at the McGruder place again."

Abby overheard Karen and Dan talking as she entered the kitchen for a cup of morning coffee.

"He's doing what's necessary, Karen. It's his job as COO to make sure the job sites are safe, protected and on schedule."

Karen's usually serene expression darkened. "My son is human, too, Dan. You push him too hard."

"You think I push him too hard? I push everyone hard. Hard work is the way I've built a successful business, and someday the boys will appreciate my effort."

Karen handed her husband a cup of coffee, and, though she said nothing, her lips were tight.

Abby was considering slipping back down the hall when Karen spotted her. "Come on in, Abby. Don't mind us. We're all on edge these days."

"I wish there was something I could do." She was part of the reason they were behind, a fact that made her feel terrible.

Karen's expression relaxed into a smile. "Having you and Lila here cheers us up. Are you at the diner today?"

Abby poured herself a cup of coffee and shook her head. "My day off. I was hoping to work on the house but—" She stopped, sorry she'd said a word. They had enough stress. "But the house can wait as long as you don't get tired of us in your way."

"No worry about that."

Dan went to the door and Karen followed, tiptoeing up for a murmur of conversation and a goodbye kiss. Abby turned away discreetly to give them a moment. As old as they were and even when they disagreed, the Buchanons still seemed in love. She could hardly fathom that kind of commitment.

After Dan left, Karen turned with a smile on her face. All trace of irritation was gone. "When you're finished with breakfast, would you mind running an errand for me? I'll keep an eye on Lila."

"I'd be happy to." Very happy. She felt like deadweight and jumped at any chance to be of help.

"Terrific. Brady will work all day without eating unless I force the issue. A man can't put in that much physical labor without fuel, so I'll fix him a hearty breakfast and you can run it over to him."

Abby's pulse did a stutter step. "Oh, okay."

Karen pulled a carton of eggs out of the fridge. "You sound unsure. Is there a problem with Brady?"

"No. Of course not. No problem at all." Unless she counted the little problem of her heart.

On the drive to the McGruder property, a gorgeous new residence Brady had proudly shown her a few weeks ago, Abby thought about what she would say and how she would behave when she saw him again. Should she give him a hug? Peck him on the cheek? Or pretend the tender moment in the garage that had sent her dreams spinning hadn't happened at all?

By the time she arrived at the job site, her hands shook and her belly jittered. She was a mess, behaving like a teenager. Wishing she'd brought Lila to break the ice, she took three deep breaths and carried the insulated bag of food into the house.

As she stepped inside, a chalky smell greeted her. White drop cloths covered the already carpeted and hardwood floors, and masking paper protected the windows and undamaged wood. The custom showplace had almost been finished, and her stomach sickened to think of the time spent and the hard work that now had to be redone. Whoever was damaging Buchanon Built properties had a serious ax to grind.

The house was silent but as she started down the hall in search of Brady, Dawg came out of the would-be den, stretching his long brindled legs.

"Hey boy, where's your master?" She rubbed his ears before looking into the den.

Brady, all six-and-a-half feet of him, lay sprawled in a sleeping bag, his eyes closed. She stood in the doorway and looked her fill. Even in sleep, fatigue lines edged his mouth and spoked around his eyes. A slight furrow wrinkled his brow. He was still the handsomest man she'd ever seen, but he was too exhausted to even hear her come inside.

And the front door had been unlocked.

Not wanting to startle him, she knelt at his side and set the fragrant insulated bag above his head. She longed to touch his face in the same gentle manner as he'd touched hers and to lean in and kiss him awake. She wondered how he'd react to such a bold action from awkward Abby the Amazon, as classmates had called her.

Before she could think too much, she placed her warm fingertips against his cheek. Overnight stubble made his skin scratchy in a good kind of way.

"Brady," she murmured.

Bright blue eyes flew open, full of confusion. He sat up abruptly, ready to battle any vandals who'd trespassed. When he realized it was her, his face changed and the look in his eyes softened. He seemed both happy and relieved that it was her.

"The front door was unlocked."

He stretched, shuddering. Heat pumped efficiently through the house but the plastic-covered floor was cool. "What time is it?"

"Eight."

"Man." He shoved aside the sleeping bag. "I let Dawg out earlier and afterward I lay down again for a minute." He made a sheepish grimace. "A minute turned into a couple of hours."

"Your mother said you're sleeping here every night."

"Got to. I can't take any chance of letting the vandals do any more damage. Although I kind of wish they'd show up again while I'm here, so I could nail them to the wall once and for all." His fists flexed as he gazed around the room. Brady Buchanon would be a formidable enemy. "This house must come in under schedule, and I have a week to make that happen."

"Can you do it?"

He sighed and scrubbed a hand over scratchy whiskers. "I hope so. I think so."

The vandalism wasn't his fault. He was a busy man, working as hard and fast as he could. Maybe too hard.

His dad pushed him. Expectations were high all around. Everyone wanted a piece of Brady's time, including her. It was a wonder he didn't have an ulcer.

She set the insulated bag in front of him. "Eat. Your mom sent breakfast."

"I love that woman." He unzipped the bag. "Want some? I'll share."

She shook her head. "I've already eaten."

While he devoured the plate of sausage, eggs and toast, Dawg roamed in for a bite.

"Your kibble's in the garage," Brady said, but he tossed the dog a sausage patty anyway.

Abby sat cross-legged on the floor beside him. "So what's the plan for today?"

"Hopefully, the drywall crew will finish up here and move on to Huckleberry Creek." He crunched a bite of toast and chewed. "We haven't forgotten your house, Abby."

"You can't do everything. I understand that my house won't be finished anytime soon, certainly not by Christmas. I'm okay with that." She swallowed, hoping to sound convincing. "Really, I am. I never expected to have a new home in the first place."

"We'll get there." But she heard the doubt and concern in his voice.

"If the house is never finished, I'll get by. I always have." She hunched her shoulders inside the snug red jacket. Brady was under intense pressure and she was part of the reason. "There are some furnished apartments on Osage Street. I'll look at one today. The price sounded right and if I move there, I can get out of your parents' way. Then you won't feel so pressured."

Her budget would scream, but she'd saved money living with the Buchanons and she could add another day at the diner. Maybe two.

"You'll do no such thing." He pointed a fork at her, frowning. "You stay put. They want you there. So do I."

She wanted to believe him so badly. "You do?"

Did she sound as pitiful and needy as she feared?

Brady set aside his plate, dragged a napkin across his lips and scooted around to face her. "I hope you know the answer to that, Abby."

Her pulse started that craziness again, a wild hope thrumming through her bloodstream faster than flood water down the Red River.

He took her hand, stroking the tops of her fingers. "I bulldozed your home, and I promised you a new one in its place. I'd be a sorry excuse for a builder and a lousy friend to leave you stranded. I plan to bring this project in on time no matter what I have to do."

Abby's raging heart slowly descended back to earth. It was all about the Christmas makeover for Brady. It wasn't about the pair of them or the sweet kiss they'd shared, a kiss she'd read more into than he'd intended. It wasn't about the fact that she was in love with him. Brady's focus was her house and his Christmas project, not her. She was only Abby, the foster kid, the charity case.

Abby was acting strange.

Brady had noticed the way she'd gone quiet before hurrying away as soon as he'd finished breakfast. The drywall crew had arrived as she'd left so he'd had no more opportunity to question her. He would, though— if he ever found an extra minute.

"Hey, Brady." Dell, the best drywall man in this part

of Texas, came into the kitchen where Brady was putting hardware on the cabinet doors. "We'll be out of here by noon if you want to call in the painters."

"Thanks, Dell. You're a lifesaver." The screwdriver whirred as he finished a knob. "I can't tell you how much I appreciate the effort your crew put in on this."

"Christmas is coming and Buchanon paychecks always cash."

They both laughed. He knew what Dell was saying. "Yeah, but you went above and beyond this time around."

"You, too." Dell scratched a patch of drywall mud on his arm. "Sorry about that waitress's house. Are she and her little girl going to be okay until we can get there?"

"They're okay." He'd see to it. "Abby's not a complainer."

She'd touched him with her offer to move into one of the awful apartments on Osage. Touched and scared him. He wanted to keep her close. She and Lila both needed and deserved the Buchanon family Christmas experience. They would love it. And he wanted her there, too. Abby was special, like her daughter, but in a different way. He hadn't liked a woman as much in a long time.

Dell disappeared and Brady took out his cell to inform the painters. He knew a couple of guys willing to add some extra hours. Christmastime was good for that. Everyone needed a little extra money for the holidays.

He'd no more than hung up when his phone vibrated and an unfamiliar number flashed on caller ID. Relieved not to see his father's name, he answered.

When the call ended, he was in a daze. Slowly, he

slid the smartphone into his pocket and looked heavenward. "Thank you."

This call truly was the answer to his prayers.

Later that afternoon, Dawson sauntered into the McGruder house carrying a bag that smelled suspiciously like burgers. Brady glanced at his watch. A long time had passed since his sweet wake-up breakfast with Abby.

Dawg suddenly appeared from nowhere and raised his nose in the air.

"You look…better," Dawson said, shoving the bag against Brady's happy-dancing belly. "What happened? Santa Claus come early?"

"I think he may have."

Dawson's dimple flashed. "Been sniffing too much sawdust, brother? Burgers aren't that big of a deal."

Brady laughed, his mood significantly elevated. "The burger counts, but no, that's not the reason. Wait till I tell you the news."

"Talk while I work. I want this trim up and finished today."

"You and me both, bro." He extracted the burger, paper crinkling and took a giant bite. The burst of dill pickles and mustard stung his taste buds in a good way. He tossed a French fry toward Dawg. The mutt caught it in midair and dispatched the potato in one gulp.

Dawson strapped on his tool belt and sauntered out to the garage, where sawhorses were set up next to the table saw. Brady followed, eager to share his news with someone.

A pile of trim lined one wall. Dawson took up a board and began to measure. The tape made a high-pitched whir and snapped shut before he hung it back on his tool belt.

As he aligned the trim on the saw guides, the dimpled twin glanced at Brady through safety goggles. "So what's up?"

"TV Ten wants to do a feel-good Christmas piece on Abby's home makeover."

"Nice. Dad will be happy. He loves free publicity."

"A TV spot might get him off my case for a while."

"Can't be a bad thing."

Dawson activated the saw and Brady chewed while the machine screeched. The burger was nearly gone. He'd been hungrier than he'd realized.

"I don't think you get it, Dawson," he said. "This program is more than getting Dad off my case. Not that I wouldn't love that little gift in my Christmas stocking."

Dawson hefted the trim and blew off the sawdust. "What, then?"

"I'm behind on Abby's house."

"I know that. We're behind on everything."

"I'm over budget, too, and Dad is not friendly with the purse strings this year."

"So?"

"If worded correctly, the TV spot could bring in donors, volunteers, people who are looking to do something good for someone else at Christmas while getting a little promo for themselves."

Dawson headed back into the house with Brady trailing behind. He stuffed the rest of the burger in his face and grabbed his nail gun from the counter as he passed.

His brother aligned the mitered corners, holding the trim in place while Brady shot in the nails.

"What did Abby say about being on television?" Dawson asked. "She's a quiet person. Proud, too, remember?"

Brady frowned. He remembered, but this was different. If the TV feature went as he hoped, she'd be the big winner. And he wouldn't have to worry about her crazy idea of moving out of his parents' house before Christmas.

"I haven't told her yet, but she'll be thrilled. I'm sure of it."

Abby was not thrilled. She was mortified.

Her heart sank and her face heated as Brady told her with much enthusiasm that the local television station wanted to film a Christmas feature about her, Lila, and the Buchanon Built Home Makeover.

"The public clamors for this kind of story, especially at Christmas," Brady was saying as they walked through her unfinished house with Lila alongside in her walker and Dawg trailing behind. "According to the reporter— Marvella Mayes—a feature at this time of year will generate the kind of positive publicity that brings volunteers and donors out of the woodwork. If we want to finish the house sooner rather than later, we'll need all the help we can get."

Abby recognized the name. Marvella Mayes was a sharp African-American reporter with a genuine way about her who specialized in tear-jerker stories. Normally, Abby wouldn't miss one of the reporter's features, but she cringed at the idea of *being* one of the features.

"Would I have to be on TV or can you do it all?"

"Me? Why would they want my ugly mug when they can have this." Brady scooped Lila into his arms. "Look at this face." He gently squeezed her daughter's cheeks between his thumb and pinky until her lips pooched out. "Who wouldn't love a face like that?"

Lila scrunched up her nose, crossed her eyes and stuck out her tongue. Brady tickled her under the chin and Lila wiggled against him, giggling madly.

"A star in the making," Brady declared, and Lila giggled harder. "Hollywood, here we come."

"Over my dead body." But Abby couldn't help smiling at the exchange. "Really, Brady, I think you should do the interview. I'd be awful in front of a camera. I don't even like to have my picture taken. You're a natural with people."

"You and the princess will slay the dragon and win hearts all over Texoma. It's a win-win deal."

She couldn't quite see the win-win he obviously visualized. She hated the idea. Hated being the object of pity. Her stomach churned with painful memories of being exactly that too many times.

Abby gnawed the inside of her cheek, battling the sense of obligation to the Buchanons, especially to Brady, against her need to stand on her own two feet.

Brady seemed convinced this was the way to go and the thing to do. She didn't want to disappoint him. After all, in the end, she and Lila would have a beautiful new home because of his generosity.

Given the stress he was under, refusing ranked right up there with spitting in his face. Accepting meant the real possibility of public humiliation.

Abby breathed in the smell of new wood. All around lay the unfinished brainchild and handiwork of a man with good intentions. Now, his good intentions weren't enough. He needed help.

Screwing up her courage and swallowing a boatload

of screaming, crying anxiety, she made a decision. If a TV spot would help Brady and the Buchanons, she owed it to them to at least try.

"I'll be awful."

Brady eased Lila back to her walker and slung a friendly arm around Abby's neck, pulling her against his side. "You'll do it?"

"If you promise to do most of the talking."

"Deal!" He kissed her on the forehead with a loud smack. "This interview is the answer to our prayers, Abby, and we'll have a blast. You won't regret this."

She already did.

Chapter Twelve

The morning of the scheduled interview Abby's stomach threatened revolt. She skipped breakfast and started getting ready hours before the taping.

When the tape aired tomorrow night at six and ten, everyone at the diner would be watching. Given Brady's enthusiastic promotion, the whole town and all of Texoma land could very well watch Abby Webster make a fool of herself.

"It's important to Brady," she whispered to the bathroom mirror. Her face was pale and she thought she might throw up. She couldn't imagine how much worse the actual interview would be. "Help me, Jesus."

The words came unexpectedly. She stared back at her surprised and puzzled eyes. She'd been going to church, praying with the Buchanons, but those things had been for them. Little by little, she must have absorbed their faith, because today she wanted the prayer to be real for her, from an anxious heart to God above.

She closed her eyes as hot tears pushed at the backs of her eyelids. Not tears of fear or embarrassment but of a tender tugging deep in her spirit.

Scared and nervous and feeling terribly alone, she whispered, "I've never known You before, Jesus, but I want to."

You'll never be alone again. The thought came out of nowhere and she knew it wasn't hers.

The room suddenly seemed brighter and her unruly insides settled. If that was Jesus, she wanted Him around all the time.

This interview wasn't about her. The ultimate purpose was to give Lila a healthier, more accessible home. She wanted that with all her heart. The interview also promised a means of giving back to the generous people who'd made the dream house possible. A short television interview was the least she could do.

"I can do this," she said, though her voice shook again at the thought of cameras.

She dressed Lila in an outfit she'd intended for Christmas, a fluffy red dress with ruffles and a white sash that looked amazing with Lila's dark brown hair and eyes. She combed and curled the wavy hair, and finished it off with a red side bow, smiling proudly as Lila toddled off with her walker to show her finery to Karen and Dan. Her baby was beautiful.

At the reporter's request, Abby wore jeans and a sweatshirt to appear as if she was working on the house. Which she would be. Considering her limited wardrobe, she was relieved, but she'd pressed a crease into the faded jeans and scrubbed her tennis shoes with an old toothbrush. She'd do her best not to look like a poverty-stricken, homeless bum even if she was one.

As she debated between leaving her hair down and her usual ponytail, a knock sounded at the door. Her heart leaped into her throat and nearly choked her.

"Just breathe. God is with you," she murmured to the mirror, borrowing the words Karen had spoken earlier. This time she knew they were true.

To the door, she called, "One minute." Sleeking her twice-washed hair into a tail, she secured it with an elastic band and hurried to the door. Brady stood in the hallway.

"Ready?"

Panic stung through her veins. So much for her calm. "Is it time?"

"Just about. The princess looks like a…princess." He beamed his thousand-watt smile. "And you, you're perfect. The two of you are going to be awesome."

She blew out a nervous breath. *God is with me. I'm not alone.* And followed Brady to his truck.

The next night Brady gathered with the entire Buchanon clan around the television at his parents' house to watch the interview. Abby tried to beg off, but Brady had snagged her hand and dragged her into the living room. She'd been extremely nervous during the interview, and if he'd known how white her face would get and that her hands would tremble, he'd never have asked her to do it. But she had, and admiration had filled his chest for the way she'd persevered. Even better and sweeter, she'd turned the focus on him and Buchanon Built, grasping every opportunity to make them look good.

Abby was something special.

A couple of times during the taping she'd floundered, but he'd stepped in to explain his passion for Christmas and the home-makeover process, the remaining work to be done and the need for volunteers. Marvella, as she'd promised, plugged Buchanon Built and opened the door for donations and experienced workers. He prayed they would be successful.

"Come on now," he said to Abby. "You don't want to miss Lila's debut. She charmed the socks off that camera crew."

It was true. Lila, in her walker and fluffy red dress, became the focus of the feature. With childlike poise and delight at being the center of attention, she'd pulled her walker through the unfinished house, describing every detail she could remember. Especially the details about the princess room Bwady was building for her.

Brady couldn't have been more pleased with the results. This was going to work. He was certain of it.

As they gathered, the clan helped themselves to bowls of steaming beef stew and thick slices of corn bread before settling in front of the television. Abby, he noticed, didn't eat a thing.

When the news came on, Abby grimaced and huddled inside her crossed arms. Lila, seated on Dan's lap, pointed at the TV and said, "There's that nice lady."

When a close-up shot of Lila came into view, tongue between her teeth as she concentrated on moving the walker, the little girl squealed and clapped. "It's me. It's me. Guess what, Mommy? I'm in the TV."

Abby's smile was wan. "Shh. Let's listen."

"I'm recording." Dan winked at Lila. "She'll be able to watch it all she wants. I'll make a DVD for you to keep."

Under her breath, barely loud enough for Brady to hear, Abby said, "Oh, great. Eternal evidence."

Brady chuckled and hooked a finger on to the pinky pressed to her side. It was ice-cold.

A hush fell over the room as the interview continued.

Brady glanced at his father and was pleased to see him nodding, a gleam in his eyes. For once, maybe his father approved of something he'd done.

Abby was more nervous now than she'd been this morning, and she'd nearly fainted then. Suddenly, her oversize face appeared on the screen. She covered her eyes, but her voice went right on speaking in a Texas twang that couldn't be hers. Did she really sound like that?

She peeked through her fingers and, sure enough, it was her, although her normally tan face was pale and she had licked her lips too often. They'd been as dry as her throat.

The shot moved to Brady, who explained about the project and his love of Christmas. That part she enjoyed. His good looks could sell ice in Antarctica.

He paraphrased a Bible verse. "'To whom much is given, much is required.' Our family and business has been blessed so we want to give back to our community. What better way to show Christ's love during the holidays than to give someone a new home, especially someone as deserving as Abby and her daughter?"

The interviewer turned to her. She hated this part. Hated it. She'd even prayed this section would be edited out.

"Abby," Marvella said, "I understand you grew up in foster care. Can you tell us a little about that and how your difficult childhood affects your desire to be the recipient of Brady's Christmas project?"

Abby cringed as the interview continued. She'd swallowed her pride and the nasty taste in the back of her throat to answer, but she couldn't quite get past feeling diminished. She was nothing. A project.

When the feature ended, a jubilant Buchanon clan talked at once, high fives all around.

"Great job, Brady." Dan said. "Brilliant the way you worked in the reward for information on the vandalism."

"Maybe we'll get some takers."

Abby focused on Brady's wide grin. She'd done the interview for him and he was happy. Good enough. Her embarrassment would pass. It always had—though every episode left a small, throbbing scar.

The next week was crazy. By Monday morning Brady juggled a glut of volunteers and donations for Abby's house with his usual overload of work. Relieved more than he'd thought possible not to let Abby down, especially after he'd convinced her to submit to the interview, he'd purchased Dawg two extra sausage patties at the diner while he'd gone over the list of offers with an overwhelmed Abby.

The appliance store donated top-of-the-line kitchen appliances in exchange for the publicity Brady had promised for those who stepped up to the plate. The furniture store offered Abby a gift certificate to choose a living room suite. An individual donated princess furniture, and the latest and best accessibility tools for Lila. Lumber and hardware stores vied with each other to give fixtures, flooring, paint and supplies.

By Friday, Brady's Christmas spirit returned in force even though he was snowed under. It was a good kind of busy as he coordinated work at the makeover—now charging full speed ahead—and directed the Buchanon Built projects. The McGruder house came in on time, a major accomplishment that he credited to diligence and plenty of prayer. He could finally sleep in his own bed, knowing the owner had taken possession. Best of all, Mom told him that Abby, in her quiet, private way, had committed her life to the Lord.

Friday afternoon he popped into the Buttered Biscuit for a late lunch and a little time with Abby. A man had to eat and he liked company. Hers. So he timed his meal to coincide with her afternoon break.

With the noon rush over, she was sweeping the floor while Charla and Jan polished tables and replenished condiments. Stenciled snowflakes decorated the front windows and a miniature tree blinked beside the cash register. Two pie eaters sat at the counter below dangling ornaments while the Spencer sisters shared a table next to the door, a pile of shopping bags and wrapped gifts at their feet. Brady lifted a hand in greeting—he'd dated Shannon for a time—though his attention was riveted on a dark-haired waitress with a shy smile and a red Santa hat.

The swoopy feeling he attributed only to Abby stole his breath.

"Break time, Abby." Jan leaned over an empty table, scrubbing away. Her necklace of tiny Christmas lights blinked a rainbow against the damp table. "Grab some lunch while you can."

Abby glanced around the half-empty room, then parked the broom in the corner and came in his direction.

"I like your hat." He touched the jingle bell on top with his index finger and they both grinned at the tinny tinkle.

"Jan's big on celebrating the season."

The other employees wore them, too. "I'm good with that. The bigger the better."

"I noticed." Her smile widened. "What would you like for lunch?"

"Whatever's ready."

"Today's special. Meat loaf and mashed potatoes."

"Perfect."

"Jan baked cherry pie this morning."

"I knew today was going to be a good one."

She whisked away, returning in minutes with his food and a plate for herself. While they ate he filled her in on the latest progress on the house.

"The plumbers are there to set the new fixtures."

"I can't believe how fast things have gone this week."

"Many hands make light work. But trust me, we have plenty left to do."

"I have errands to run after work but as soon as I can, I'll be there to do my part."

"No one could ever call you a slacker."

She beamed as if he'd paid her the world's best compliment. "You either, Mr. Buchanon. I think you border on workaholic."

The comment set him back. Him? Like his dad? No way.

He chewed the homey meat loaf, considering. This year had been exceptional. He didn't always maintain this kind of manic schedule. Did he? But then, didn't his siblings regularly tease him with the all-work-and-no-play joke?

"Your house isn't work. It's fun. Christmas projects are what I do for a hobby."

"Looks like work to me. What do you actually do to relax?"

He laughed and leaned back in his chair to study the queen of workaholic. "I could ask you the same. When did you last do something for fun?"

"I—" She opened her mouth, closed it, opened it again. "Lila and I came to your house for steaks and watched TV."

"That was too long ago. We should do it again." And again and again. "Tomorrow night is the Christmas parade and chocolate festival. Let's do it. You and me and Lila."

Yeah. He hadn't come in here to ask her out, but why not? He'd been wanting to spend time with her that had nothing to do with her house, and he never missed Gabriel's Crossing Christmas events, especially the parade.

"I was already planning to go. Lila's riding on the church float."

He knew that. The little princess had nearly levitated with excitement at participating in the Christmas parade.

An awful thought struck him in the gut. Like a sledgehammer.

"Are you going with someone else?" And if she was, who was the creep and why hadn't he known she was seeing another guy?

"No. I'd thought about asking Charla but she already has plans."

Hurray for Charla.

"We'll go together. Me and you. Afterward, we'll grab the princess and head to the chocolate festival." He aimed a forkful of cherry pie at her. "What do you say?"

Soft espresso-colored eyes gazed at him as if he must have an ulterior motive. He did. Her. Did he have to spell it out for her? Me Tarzan. You Jane. Let's go to the parade together.

"Okay."

Brady blinked. Twice. Had she said yes without an argument? Without an explanation?

"Sweet."

Life kept getting better and better.

He popped a bite of cherry pie into his mouth. Sweet, indeed.

Abby parked her Honda in the lot outside Lila's day care. The car needed an oil change and she added that to her to-do list, stressing about the cost in light of the fast-approaching holiday. The new battery had set her back a little.

She'd put some toys and clothes on layaway for her daughter, but she desperately wanted to give gifts to the hospitable Buchanons as well as put money in the offering plate at church. God was being so good to her. She needed to give back.

Being a new Christian at Christmas was pretty special. She felt a new appreciation and kinship to the holiday that had been missing before. Funny how easily the change had come, as if her spirit had been waiting all this time for her to acknowledge the need for Christ.

This newfound relationship was something else she owed to the Buchanons. Her IOU list was growing longer by the day. They were good people. Giving to others was as much a part of them as the construction business. They'd never intentionally make her feel obligated but, of course, she did.

Exiting the car, she pulled her puffy red jacket closer against the north wind and started across the gravel parking lot. Cold stung her ears and nose. Her eyes watered. She hoped the arctic front moved on through before tomorrow night's parade.

She was still shocked that Brady had asked her to go with him. Not as his latest charitable act but as a date. A real date.

She'd been in a great mood all the rest of the day. When she'd told Charla, her friend had said, "Girl, Brady Buchanon has had his pretty blue eyes on you for a long time. You better grab that man. He's a keeper."

Grab him. As if she could.

She stepped inside Huckleberry Play School, where she was greeted by children's voices and activities. Brightly colored Mother Goose murals filled the walls along with child-made Christmas crafts and ornaments. Lila had brought home a star made of glued craft sticks and silver glitter to add to the Buchanon tree.

Christina came out of her office. "Hi, Abby. Could we talk a minute before you pick up Lila?"

"Sure." Curious, she followed the owner inside the office. She'd paid her bill, hadn't she?

"Have a seat," Christina said as she settled behind a cluttered desk and folded her hands on top. "Lila had another accident today."

"Oh." Abby's hand flew to her lips. "Why didn't you call me?"

"We took care of her with the extra clothes in her locker, but, Abby, this is the second time this week. The fourth time this month. The teachers are maintaining her schedule, but it's not working."

"I'm so sorry. I—"

"I'm sorry, too. Really sorry. Lila is a wonderful little girl and we adore her, but if I make an exception to the rules for her, I'll have to do the same for everyone.

This is a play school for toilet-trained children. Parents expect that. So do my employees."

"Have there been complaints?"

"Yes." Christina sucked in a deep breath. "Please understand that I'm in a bad position here and feel I have no other choice but to ask you to find another day care for Lila."

Abby's happy bubble burst. Another day care she could trust with her child? At a price she could afford that could accommodate her long hours? Where? She pressed her lips together, stung and worried.

Christina leaned forward, her kind face full of compassion and regret. Abby didn't blame the day-care owner. She'd known the rules when she had enrolled her daughter, and Christina had looked the other way more than once.

"You're paid up until Christmas. After that…"

Abby nodded and rose, her back stiff. "I understand."

Stomach heavy as if she'd swallowed a brick, she collected Lila and started to leave. Christina followed her to the door. "I'm really sorry, Abby."

Abby didn't answer. She couldn't with the tears burning at the back of her throat. Rejection of herself she could deal with. Rejection for her sweet, sunny, innocent daughter ripped her apart.

Sorry didn't begin to cover it.

Chapter Thirteen

"Everything all right?" Brady took Abby's gloved hand as they walked back to First Street from the church parking lot where the children riding the float had gathered. Charity, who taught Sunday school and was riding with the children, had taken charge of a very excited Lila.

"I'm fine. Why?"

"Just a feeling I have." Abby was always quiet but since he'd picked her and Lila up at the family home, she'd barely said a dozen words. Was it something he'd said or done? Had she come with him out of a sense of obligation and now regretted the decision? "You were deep in thought last night, too, but I figured you were concentrating on the house."

"I was." Her boot heels made tapping sounds on the sidewalk. He fit his steps to hers, pleased at how well they fit. Did she notice it, too? "I'm still in awe of all that's been done."

Okay. He could accept that. Her mind was on the makeover. Still, she didn't seem as animated as he'd expected and he couldn't shake the feeling that she was upset.

"Construction is going well. I'm hopeful—" He stopped there, not wanting to promise something he couldn't deliver. "Colder tonight than I'd expected."

Perfect for snuggling. He didn't say that, either. He was content with her close to his side and her hand in his.

"Last year we were too hot."

"The guys in Santa suits nearly melted." He chuckled. "Christmas weather in Texas is unpredictable."

The tall, hovering streetlights illuminated the chilly night in long, finger-shaped shadows of silver. Residential homes added a glow with their Christmas lights and yard art, including a bell-ringing inflatable Santa and a waving Frosty. Down the street, the high school marching band warmed up with "Deck the Halls."

Other couples walked toward the parade route and snatches of conversation danced on the crisp air. Brady's breath puffed vapor as he considered the woman at his side. She reminded him of his sister's cat, soft and quiet but mysterious. Abby kept her feelings close to the vest. Buchanons weren't very good at that.

"Want some hot chocolate?" he asked when they passed an open coffee shop. "Or popcorn? The cheerleaders have a popper set up next to the courthouse."

"I smell it," she said, and lifted her nose to the fragrant air. "Maybe after the parade."

Brady chose the tall courthouse steps as their spot to watch the event. A crowd had already gathered, including friends and business acquaintances and any number of people who frequented the diner. Brady figured he knew practically everyone in Gabriel's Crossing, at least by name. Events such as this were perfect opportunities to say hello.

From the south end of First Street, a police siren

wailed to announce the parade's beginning. Police Chief Leroy in his shined-up cruiser crept by and waved. Behind him came the ambulance and fire trucks with Sparky the fire dog riding up top, a bandanna around his neck. Abby made a cute squeak of excitement. Brady gazed down at her with a smile. Her cheeks glowed and her brown eyes danced. Whatever had been bothering her was washed away in the simple pleasure of a hometown Christmas parade. Good. He wanted her to enjoy tonight.

The emergency vehicles wailed on past and Abby laughingly covered her ears. Teasing, Brady added his giant paws to the sides of her head and they both laughed as he dwarfed her.

Behind the sirens marched the American Legion Color Guard and the high school band, followed by a dozen floats decorated in simple poster-board and crepe-paper designs and lit by Christmas strands attached to the sides of flatbed trailers. Some participants sang carols. Others waved or tossed candy into the crowd. Children scurried for the peppermint and Tootsie Roll treats.

Christmas spirit was tangible and Brady felt it to the tips of his very cold toes.

"There she is." Abby bounced up and down, pointing. "Look, Brady. She's coming."

Brady had watched Gabriel's Crossing parades his entire life and participated in many. This year an employee drove a Buchanon company truck and the employees' kids, dressed as elves, tossed mini Buchanon Built Frisbees into the crowd. He'd always enjoyed this event to kick off the countdown to Christmas, but this year was even better as he watched Abby watch Lila.

The love she showed for her little girl moved him. He

could fall for a woman like her, a woman who shared his passion for family.

Taking her by the shoulders, Brady maneuvered them closer to the street to be sure Lila could spot them. Standing taller than most, he figured she'd notice him first.

"Bwady! Mommy!"

Lila's gold tinsel halo wobbled above her head and glistened in the reflection of the white lights dancing around the float. Dressed in a white angel costume, her dark hair curled around her shoulders and her cheeks pink with joy above a glowing smile, she fit the part. She perched in her wheelchair at the head of the nativity scene, waving her tiny hand at everyone. Other church children filled the parts of the Holy family. Behind them, a small choir sang "Silent Night."

The sweet scene reminded him of all that was good about Christmas, about the ultimate gift God had given to the world. It reminded him, too, that he cared deeply for the little angel on the float. Her biological father was a fool for tossing her aside. He never wanted Lila hurt by that abandonment, but she would be and there was nothing he could do to stop it.

"She's gorgeous," he murmured against Abby's hair.

Abby raised shining eyes to his and he couldn't help saying, "So are you."

Abby's full, beautiful mouth fell open in what he hoped was pleasant surprise. They were in a crowd in the middle of a parade, but Brady dipped his head and touched her lips with his. Her breath was warm; her lips were cold.

"You need warming up," he murmured, and pulled her closer.

Abby didn't object. In fact, when he slid his arm around her waist, she returned the favor.

Side by side, snuggled close against the cold, they watched her daughter, the child he'd come to love ferociously, slowly move on down the street. The church float was replaced by a marching Boy Scout troop and then the local dance school in red-and-white fur, tap-dancing to a boom-box version of "Santa Claus Is Coming to Town."

Abby shivered and Brady moved to cradle her inside his coat and block the wind. He felt cozy and comfortable, as if he and Abby belonged together this way.

When the parade ended with a very jolly Saint Nick *ho-ho-ho*ing from a horse-drawn sleigh, Abby turned in his arms, smiling. "That was wonderful."

"Best ever," he said, close enough to consider kissing her again, but he refrained. He rocked her back and forth, grinning into her happy face. The crowd began to disperse, but he wanted to stay right here with Abby in his arms and not a care in the world. No business pressing. No calls from Dad. Nothing and no one but him and Abby enjoying each other in the spirit of Christmas.

He could get used to this.

Abby put a hand to his chest. "We have to go get Lila."

She was right. They did. With a regretful sigh, Brady led the way down the street. "Chocolate Festival?"

"Oh, yeah."

He laughed. "I thought so. Hot chocolate and all the goodies."

They collected the overexcited four-year-old from the church parking lot, placing her in the wheelchair for easier travel along the streets. Stores stayed open late on parade night and Brady wheeled Lila close to window displays. Unlike his niece and nephew, who wanted everything under the sun for Christmas, Lila asked for nothing, not even the kitchen play set that made her say, "Ooh, Mommy, look." She broke his heart.

"How about that hot chocolate?" Abby said in what was an obvious attempt to distract Lila from the expensive toy.

"Hot chocolate coming up. Hang on tight." He performed a wheelie with the chair and set off down the street, earning a giggle that tickled his chest. But even as the conversation turned to chocolate, Brady didn't forget about the kitchen play set.

"I've never seen this much chocolate in my life."

The community center had been transformed into the most delicious-smelling place on earth. Abby stared around the huge hall at tables and tables of treats, all of them following the chocolate theme in some way. Gift baskets, candy treats, cakes, pies, boxes of dipped fruits and nuts were for sale along with individual bite-size offerings. She never attended this event. The goodies were not only too tempting but an unnecessary expense.

"Indulge. I have a running tab with the head chocolate guru."

She bumped his side. "Silly."

"Serious. Check it out." He nudged his chin toward the cash register and a robust blonde woman in a red-and-white striped apron and gold-framed glasses. "Aunt Debbie. Mom's sister. She makes a bundle for the Arts Council on this event. Dad claims she makes the most off him."

"Your dad does like his desserts."

"So do his sons, but the chocolate also makes terrific gifts for vendors and contractors. And Aunt Debbie knows it." He lifted a hand and waved at his aunt, grinning. "See how her eyes lit up? It's not because she adores her nephew. It's my wallet that makes her happy. That woman's a barracuda for the Arts Council."

Abby grinned and cocked her head. "I thought she was the guru."

"Guru, barracuda. I could think of other names, including chocolate queen. Wait until you taste her lava bites. Come on." He tugged her hand onto the wheelchair handle and put his on top. "Let's say hello and see if we can finagle a sample or two."

Abby fell in step beside her daughter, acutely aware of Brady's hand over hers. She couldn't help wondering if he was being Brady the nice guy, the giver who loved Christmas, or if his attention was really for her, Abby the woman, not Abby the project.

Did he have any idea what he was doing to her?

She was crazy in love with him, the man with a heart as big as his body. Crazy was probably the key word.

"Brady!" His aunt came around the counter to give him a hug. "Loved the TV interview. Brilliant on your part, I'd say. How's it working?"

"Great so far."

"Any takers on the reward?"

"No."

She patted his arm. "Don't give up. Someone knows something and the truth will eventually come out."

"I hope it happens before they destroy anything else."

"So do I, honey." Debbie stepped back as if assessing the woman with Brady. "You must be Abby."

"Oh, sorry," Brady said. "I thought the two of you had probably met."

"Not yet, but I'd say it's time."

"Oh, because of the home makeover," Abby said. Of course. That must be what Debbie meant. "Brady's been very kind to us."

"Kind." Debbie's eyes sparkled. "Yes, I imagine so, but from the looks of you two, I'd say kindness wasn't the only thing."

Abby's pulse stuttered. Really? Was she serious?

Floundering, Abby glanced at Brady and found his electric-blue eyes on her. A swarm of emotions buzzed inside her. Confusion. Longing. Hope. And most of all, an overpowering love.

Oh, but she hadn't meant to love him. Hadn't wanted to ever love anyone again. Love hurt too much.

Lila's voice broke the tension. "Are you the chocolate queen?"

Debbie laughed and adjusted her glasses. "I guess I am. Would you like a sample?"

"Yes, please!" Lila clapped her hands in delight and the moment passed, though Abby couldn't get Debbie's remark out of her head.

Armed with a bakery box, they roamed the festival, sampling goodies. Jostling friends and neighbors, Brady shared warm greetings and banter with practically everyone. With him at her side, Abby felt a part of the town in a way she never had before. He was a magnet, not only because of his superior size but because of his friendliness.

Abby realized how seldom she'd done more than say hello to people she didn't know. At the diner, she knew the names and food choices of the regulars, but she never took the time to know them the way Brady did.

No wonder she was lonely.

"Give me two boxes of mixed truffles," Brady said to the man behind the table. To Abby, he said, "Want a few boxes for the other women at the diner? Jan, Charla, Fran?"

"Oh, I—" She frowned. She'd love to give something this lovely and extravagant to her friends, but the expense worried her. "Last year Lila and I baked cookies."

"Great idea, too, but you're pretty tied up at the house this year." He took one of the white-capped truffles and waved it under her nose. "Running tab, remember? Buy everything that appeals to you. The money goes to a good cause."

A good cause. Like her? "Well—"

Brady said to the clerk. "Four more boxes, please."

"Brady!"

He laughed. "Stop fussing. This is supposed to be fun."

Fun to him. Misery to her. She was a beggar.

But her coworkers would adore the truffles, and she and Lila *were* occupied this year with the house.

"Mommy," Lila said, tugging at her coat sleeve. "There's my teacher." Stretching up high to be noticed, she waved her little arm in excitement. "Miss Christina!"

Across the room, Christina somehow heard the small, childish voice and turned, waving. When her gaze landed on Abby, she smiled, then turned back to the rows of chocolate.

"I love my teacher," Lila said.

The reminder cut Abby to the bone. How was she

going to break the news to her child that she was no longer wanted at Christina's day care?

"Hey, why the long face? Did I do something wrong?" Brady dipped down to look in her eyes. "Are you mad about the truffles? You don't have to take them if you hate the idea."

She put a hand on his arm to stop the flow of worry. "The truffles are great. They'll love them."

"Then what happened? One minute you're laughing and the next you look as if your dog died."

"Nothing. Really." She pretended to study the array of cheesecakes. Her day-care issues were not his problem.

Brady put his fingertips against her back and leaned in. "You sure?"

She forced a smile. "Positive."

An older gentleman in an electric wheelchair pulled alongside and spoke to Lila. "Didn't I see this pretty little girl on television?"

Lila's face wreathed in pleasure. "My mommy, too. And Bwady. At our new house."

"How ya doin', J.D.?" Brady asked, offering a hand to shake. "Abby, you know J.D., don't you?"

"Hi, J.D. We've missed you at the diner lately." Southwestern omelet, Abby thought, with lots of *picante*. How pathetic that his order was the only thing she'd ever discussed with the man.

"Had a hospital stay, but I'm up and going again now." Thin as a rake with the bony arms and fingers to match, J.D. battled the aftereffects of a stroke.

"Glad to hear it," Brady said. "Anything you need?"

"Nah, nah, you've done enough for us." J.D. turned his focus to Abby and Lila. "You ladies are very fortunate to have Brady in your corner. He does wonders for this town."

"Now, J.D.," Brady started, shaking his head.

The old man waved a boney hand. "I keep my ear to the ground. I know what's going on."

Brady sidestepped the compliment, but Abby caught the drift.

Like many others past and present, she was his project. Once the house was finished, he'd move on to the next needy soul.

She had to be smart, to guard her heart—what was left of it. She was no longer a lonely teenager wishing for a Prince Charming. She was a grown woman with a child. And not a thing to offer anyone.

Oh, but the sneaky Christmas spirit made her dream of things she shouldn't.

Chapter Fourteen

Santa Claus didn't have anything on him.

Brady loaded a wrapped box containing the kitchen play set into the back of his truck along with a half-dozen other gifts. Dawg looked at him through the back glass as if he knew who the toys were for.

"A kid needs Christmas presents," Brady said to the affable canine face.

"You're talking to your dog in the middle of town. You've got to get more friends."

Brady spotted his sister on the sidewalk outside Bland's Department Store, a shopping bag over one arm, the sun shining on her flippy dark hair and a grin on her petite face.

"Allison, hi. What's up?"

"I could ask you the same. Last year you bribed me and Jaylee into doing all the shopping for your home-makeover recipients."

"Yeah, well, I had a little time."

She scoffed. "Since when? Mom says you haven't slept eight hours in so long, she's worried about your driving."

"I'm catching up." He motioned toward the gifts. "Want to help me with the rest?"

Her eyes widened. "There are more?"

Brady frowned. He'd already purchased the art set and now a few extras today. Had he gone overboard?

Nah, no such thing at Christmas.

"Not many. A few." He opened the truck door. "Coming?"

Allison hopped in the cab, chattering about everything under the sun, but especially her fiancé and the wedding they'd put off until spring. When they stopped in front of the Texas Rose Boutique, she fell silent.

"What are you buying in here?"

"Already bought. Angela's wrapping them."

"You didn't answer my question. This is a women's store, not a toy store."

"Well, my mom and sisters and Abby need presents under the tree, too."

"Abby?" His sister's dark eyes studied him for several long seconds. "What's going on, Brady?"

"What do you mean, what's going on? Come on, sis. Give me a break. It's Christmas."

"Granted, you love Christmas, and you're a born rescuer especially this time of year."

"I am?"

Allison laughed. "We all see it, Brady, even if you don't. That's why Dad made you COO. When things go wrong, as they always do at some point on every job, Brady jumps in to fix the problem. Even Dawg is a rescue!"

"I never thought of myself like that." He'd figured dad put the managerial job on him so he could be at his throat all the time, not because he saw his strengths.

"The Christmas home makeover is your biggest rescue of the year. That's why you love it so much." Allison studied him and then shrugged. "But this year is different. *You're* different. More personal. Like Abby is more than the latest recipient of Operation Christmas Makeover. You aren't rescuing Abby anymore, you're caring for her."

"No—" He stopped, pondering. "Maybe."

His sister's eyes lit up. "I think you're falling in love with her."

"What? No." But even as he denied the truth, he thought his sister might be right. "She's…"

Allison's look seemed to know more than he did. "Special?"

"Well, yeah."

"We all think so, too, Brady. Even though she's quiet, she fits with us. We like her." Allison flashed her engagement diamond in the sunlight. "Falling in love is a good thing."

Brady blew out a breath. "It's only a couple of presents, Allison. Christmas gifts. Don't make a mountain out of it. I don't think I'm ready for…that."

Her dark eyebrows lifted. "Are you sure?"

Brady opened the door and stepped out into the cold sunlight, reeling with the thoughts and emotions shooting through his body.

Allison was right about one thing. Abby meant more to him than the average housing project. He felt good when he was with her. Energized. Happy.

Maybe he *was* falling in love.

And maybe that wasn't a bad thing.

Abby heard voices in the living room, one in particular, and the sound of Lila's giggle let her know Brady had come to visit his parents.

She refused to believe he'd come to see her, though the night of the parade had been wonderful. She'd had fun, laughed and shopped and grown a hot cocoa mustache to match her daughter's. When they'd arrived home, Brady had kissed her good-night with such sweetness she wanted to believe it meant something more than a casual date.

"You take things too seriously," she reminded herself. Hadn't she always? Men kissed women for no reason other than they'd had a nice time and they wanted to. She'd kissed boys in high school and didn't even remember their names! "Don't read too much into a good-night kiss."

Or any of the other things he did that made her feel important. Brady made everyone feel important. It was the Buchanon way.

She twirled a length of silver ribbon around a box wrapped in blue paper, secured a label on which she'd written "from Abby and Lila," and added the gift to the small stack on the end of her bed.

Resisting a fluff in the mirror, she scooped up the gifts and headed into the living room.

Brady crouched in the entry between two large poinsettias, a red-and-green wreath on the door at his back, his arms loaded with bags and boxes, talking to her daughter. "And this one is for your mom, but it's a secret surprise." He lowered his voice. "Can you hide it under the tree so she won't know?"

"Yes," Lila whispered, clearly intrigued by the shiny red box.

So was Abby.

"Brady, you shouldn't have done that."

"Oops. Busted." He stretched to his height and said, "She's sneaky. I didn't hear her coming."

"Because you were too busy conspiring with my innocent daughter." She perched a hand on her hip, amused…and attracted. He looked so appealing, like a big Celtic Santa in jeans and brown leather jacket.

"It's nothing much," he said with a shrug. "I was feeling Santa-ish and couldn't stop myself."

"You never can."

Amusement crinkled the corners of his eyes. "Is that a bad thing?"

Only to my heart.

"You're spoiling my daughter." *And I can't give her all this stuff next year. She has to learn that money doesn't grow on trees. Not for a woman who works at the local diner.* He scared her, this man who couldn't seem to understand her fear of his generosity.

"Ah, come on, Ab. It's Christmas. Don't be Scrooge."

Karen came in from the patio carrying a potted plant, her usually coifed hair wind ruffled. "I thought I heard your voice. Staying for dinner?"

"Can't. I'm working on Abby's house tonight." He went to the merrily blinking tree and dumped the stack of gifts next to a mound of others.

The house telephone rang and Karen answered. "For you, Abby. Someone returning your call."

Tension leaped up into her shoulders. She had calls in to several individuals who provided child care in their homes. None was a school, but each came well recommended as someone who cared about children.

With Christmas break only days away, her time was running out.

"Thanks." She took the cordless and stepped around the counter into the kitchen for privacy. "Hello."

Please, Lord. Let this be the right place.

Brady stewed all the way to Abby's almost complete home. He'd overheard her phone conversation. She was searching for a new babysitter for Lila. Huckleberry Play School had kicked her out.

When she'd come back into the living room, expression hangdog, he'd gone to her. "Why didn't you tell me?"

"Tell you what?" she'd hedged. She'd actually hedged. With *him*!

"I overheard, Abby. Why didn't you say something?"

She'd crossed her arms and lowered her voice so Lila wouldn't hear. "Because…it's not your problem."

His temper had flared like an emergency torch on a dark night. He hadn't said another word, but he'd thought plenty, and a few minutes later, he'd left before his temper got the best of him.

Now, he tromped down on the gas pedal, his fingers gripping the steering wheel tight enough to hurt.

Not his problem? How could he be there for her if she shut him out? Lila was important. *She* was important. Why did she always have to carry the weight of the world by herself?

He had a half a thought to call Christina, but she'd likely tell him the matter was not his business. Just as Abby had done.

The truck's speedometer shot to sixty. He eased off the pedal and whispered a prayer to get his anger under control.

Maybe Lila and Abby *weren't* his business. Maybe

he only imagined Abby had feelings for him beyond the building project. She was grateful, yes, but she'd never once made the overtures. All the effort had been on his part. He'd invited her to dinner at his house. He'd initiated the kisses, the date to the parade, the lunches at the diner. Even the Christmas gifts were purchased over her protests.

He thumped his forehead on the steering wheel. "Idiot. She's trying to get the message through your thick skull and you refused to see it."

Abby liked him. She appreciated his work on her home. But that was where the relationship ended. She didn't want him in her business. Or in her life, for that matter. People who cared about each other shared the ups as well as the downs. That's what family did.

Okay, so he wasn't family. He was only the home builder. End of story. He could deal with that, would have to deal with it, though the truth stung more than he'd have liked. He was a big boy. He could take rejection.

He pulled into the driveway of the new construction. His brothers were already there, bless them. Even Quinn's truck was parked outside, evidence that he'd been bitten by the Christmas spirit. Lila had gotten to the grouchy brother, too.

Lila. The little girl had touched the whole family with her valiant spirit and sunny disposition. They'd seen the rigorous exercise Abby put her through each day and the discomfort she endured without complaint. Even the one time she'd cried from the pain of a new exercise and Abby had cried with her, she'd said, "It's okay, Mommy."

Abby didn't know he'd overheard that conversation

or that he'd wanted to cry with them. The little girl had been through too much.

An idea came to him and he thought, "Why not?"

No matter how Abby felt about him, she wanted the best for her daughter, and so did he.

He fished out his cell phone and tapped in his mother's number.

By the time Abby arrived, his temper had cooled, he had a plan in place and was stirring the pink paint for Lila's princess room.

Nail guns popped in adjoining rooms and Quinn one-armed a roller up and down the front bathroom wall. Abby had chosen colors as quiet as her nature. In this case, sea-foam green.

"This is beautiful, Brady." Abby stood inside the door to Lila's room, where Brady worked alone. The princess room was his project and his only. He wanted to do this for Lila.

Three walls remained covered in gray drywall primer, but the east wall shone with fresh princess pink.

"Should I grab a roller and help in here or move on to another room?"

Brady put aside the roller and said, "I want to talk to you about something first."

She perched her fists on the hips of her worn work jeans, expression cautious. "You sound serious. Is everything okay?"

"I hope so." Brady wiped excess paint from his hands and pulled a sheet of paper from the pocket of his coveralls. Abby moved to his side to look.

"Let me be clear." His voice sounded cranky even to him. "I don't want to be involved where I'm not wanted. If you think I'm butting into your business, I'll back off."

At his tone, she looked up, worried. "I'm not sure what you mean. Are you mad at me about something?"

"No."

"Yes, you are." Her eyes searched his. "What did I do?" She touched his sleeve. "Tell me."

"You said Lila's day care wasn't my problem."

"It isn't," she said quietly.

She was the most frustrating woman on the planet. "What if I want it to be? What if my family and I *want* to help? Come on, Abby, work with me here."

She pulled back, frowning. "Why would you?"

After all they'd done together in the past few months, she didn't trust him. "Why can't you accept help at face value? Because people care about you!" He was getting riled again. "Do you always have to question everyone's motives?"

"Yes!"

Her response stunned him. He quieted. "Why?"

But he knew the answer. Her life had been a journey of disappointments, letdowns and rejection.

She glanced toward the pink wall, mouth pinched tight. "People don't do something for nothing."

"Maybe that's your experience, but it's not true. Not always. Stop expecting the worst out of everyone. Out of me. I'm not going to hurt you, Abby."

Brady saw her hesitation and watched her struggle with some inner fear. He waited her out, letting her battle it through. She gnawed her bottom lip, looked at her feet and then at him.

Finally, her shoulders relaxed. "You've been more than good to us, Brady. I'm sorry if I hurt your feelings. I didn't want to burden you with anything else."

"You're not a burden. You're—" He caught himself,

breathed in the scent of paint and drywall mud, and tried again. He was crazy about her. Didn't she understand? "I thought we were more than builder and client."

Okay, he was putting his heart out there for her to drill with a nail gun.

She stilled.

"Are we?" The words were soft and incredulous.

His voice tendered. "I don't go around kissing clients."

A subtle shift occurred, a chink in her high wall of distrust and pride. Her mouth tilted the slightest bit. "I'm glad to hear that."

He decided to throw caution to the wind.

"I spend extra time with you because I want to be in your company. What I do on my personal time has nothing to do with this building. It's you." Couldn't she see that she meant more to him than a few boards and a coat of paint? "If I'm way out of line here and you're not interested, now might be a good time to tell me."

Eyes deer-in-the-headlights wide, as if the admission scared her to death, she whispered, "I'm interested."

A smile bloomed in Brady's chest. Now they were getting somewhere.

"Good answer. Come here." He opened his arms and she walked into him. Cradling her gently, he asked, "Will you stop second-guessing everything I do for you?"

She tilted her face up. "I'll try."

All right. A step in the right direction.

"Then look at this schedule the family and I put together and be happy. Don't argue. Be happy."

She tipped back, dubious. "A schedule for what?"

"Lila. The family volunteered to look after her when you're at work."

"Are you serious?"

He flexed his arm in a quick squeeze and loosened his hold to show her the schedule.

"There you go again. Yes, I'm serious. Until you can find the perfect place for day care, the Buchanons will take charge of the princess. Easy peasy." He tapped the paper. "Everyone who could took a spot for the next month. After that, we'll start again."

"I can't believe this. She loves your family and feels secure with them. They understand her needs. This is… perfect, but you don't have time for—"

He put a hand over her mouth. "We'll make time. We love her, too, Ab. She's fun."

"She's also a lot of work."

"Aren't we all?"

At that, she smiled her wide, full-mouthed smile that turned his world brighter. "I can't believe you people are real. Sometimes, I think this is a dream. I don't know how to thank you or what to do to repay you. You're just so—so—"

Brady didn't know who moved first, but Abby had her hands on his face and was kissing him. *She* kissed *him*.

The popping nail guns faded away and he didn't notice or care that his hair was flecked with pink paint or that his brothers were mere steps away in the next rooms. For the moment, Abby was his world.

Chapter Fifteen

The days leading up to Christmas were the happiest Abby could ever remember. Embraced by the Buchanon family and courted by Brady, she lived in a dream world. Sometimes late at night, she'd awaken, heart pounding in panic that the dream would end and she'd come crashing to the ground, brokenhearted and alone again.

More than anything, she feared for Lila, who sparkled in the Buchanons' loving attention. If the romance ended, her little girl would face the kind of disappointment Abby never wanted her to feel. Rejection. The belief that she wasn't quite good enough.

But in the light of day as her beautiful home neared completion, and she and Brady spent hours together, Abby put aside her fears, determined to bask in every beautiful moment.

Overwhelmed with gratitude, she rose early to clean the Buchanons' house and do as much extra for them as she could squeeze in to her crowded day. Though Karen insisted it wasn't necessary, she wanted to. She needed to. She didn't have money for big gifts, but she knew how to work. When she'd tried to pay them for looking after Lila, they'd refused.

"Spend your money on things for the new house," Karen had said.

She'd never met anyone like them in her life. But the savings gave her money to buy Christmas gifts, and she enjoyed a marvelous day off shopping with Charla.

On Christmas Eve, she and Brady attended a peaceful, uplifting candlelight service, and then shared a late supper of finger foods and chicken gumbo at the Buchanons' afterward.

Understandably overexcited, Lila had trouble settling down for the night. Finally Abby said, "Time for bed, baby. Santa Claus won't come while you're awake."

"Will you wead me a story?" Lila's droopy eyes kept returning to the pile of gifts under the tree. Abby had let her open one, a pair of fleece candy-cane pajamas that she now wore.

"Sure." She lifted her bath-scented daughter into her arms.

Karen offered a book. "I used to read this to my kids every Christmas Eve."

"My favorite," Brady said. *"The Night before Christmas."*

"Mine, too." Something else they had in common. "I've read it to Lila every Christmas, but I think this is the first year she'll remember."

"You come, too, Bwady," Lila said. "Wead with me. Mommy's a good weader."

Smiling, Brady looked to Abby for confirmation, and with her heart skipping too many beats, she said, "Come on."

Once Lila was tucked into bed, Abby sat on the

edge next to her. Brady, his powerful body dwarfing the space, knelt at the headboard close to Lila.

As they took turns reading, Abby listened to his manly voice, realizing this was the first time in Lila's life a man had read her to sleep. For a few sweet seconds, while Lila's coffee-dark eyes adored Brady, Abby let the thoughts flow, pretending this was her family and Brady was Lila's father.

The vision in her head was so strong and poignant, it pierced her. Being with the Buchanons had shown her the things she'd missed and the things in life that really mattered. God. Family. Love. She wanted all of them...with Brady. Was she foolish to believe something so grand could happen? After this time with him, after hope and love and joy had buoyed up inside her, if Brady walked away, she didn't how she'd ever recover.

"'Happy Christmas to all, and to all a good night,'" Brady declared, and clapped the book shut. "Ready to say your prayers?"

Abby's heart clutched when Lila folded her tiny hands over her red-and-white pj's while Brady led her in a simple, heartfelt prayer. At the *amen* he leaned in and kissed her baby's forehead. "Sleep tight, princess."

"'Night, Bwady." Lila heaved a deep, sleepy breath. "Bwady?"

He exchanged an indulgent look with Abby, probably suspecting as she did that Lila was procrastinating going to sleep on this exciting night.

"What?"

"I wuv you."

Brady brushed Lila's dark hair back from her face, his hand dwarfing the tiny head, his too-handsome face serious. "I love you, too, princess."

Touched and troubled that her baby was getting in over her head exactly like her mama, Abby glanced away from the endearing sight. She kissed Lila good-night, and the adults left the room together, snapping off the light at the door.

In the dim, shadowy hall with Brady's arm brushing hers, she said, "I think I'll call it a night, too." She tiptoed up, hands on his broad, capable shoulders and kissed him lightly. "Good night, Brady."

His smile tilted the edges of his mouth. "Good night."

He didn't move, though. He remained in the wide hallway, close enough for his warm apple-cider scent to fill her senses.

He looked as if he wanted to say more but after three heartbeats, he turned and started down the hall. The need to be as brave and bold as her daughter throbbed in Abby's throat. She wanted to call out to him, call him back. Three words she longed to say, but fear and uncertainty held them captive.

When he disappeared around the corner, Abby whispered to the emptiness, "I love you, Brady."

Christmas morning was a madhouse.

Warm, cozy and crowded, the Buchanon home was redolent of tempting smells—cinnamon, turkey and apple spice with a side note of peppermint. And noise. Lots of happy noise.

Dawson, in his gentle baritone, read the Christmas story from the Bible while the gathered family drank eggnog, cocoa or coffee and rubbed the sleep from their eyes. The three children, still in pajamas, loitered beneath the tree and anxiously awaited the big moment when they could dive into the mound of gifts.

"Santa came, Mama. He came!" Lila's eyes were as wide as saucers.

He had, indeed. Abby knew the Buchanons were a little Christmas crazy but she hadn't imagined anything this extravagant. Saying "you shouldn't have" was about as useful as telling Brady to grow shorter.

Abby perched on the edge of the couch. Brady handed her a cup of eggnog. "Thanks, I love this stuff even if it's überfattening."

"You have nothing to worry about. Scoot." He crowded out his sister to sit beside Abby. Allison winked at him and snuggled her cowboy on the other side. Abby didn't mind a bit that they were jammed together like sardines.

When the moment finally arrived, Dan took his place beneath the tree to hand out gifts.

"Need a little help this year, Brady. The family keeps growing."

"Like the business," Dawson said.

"And we're thankful for both." Karen raised a mug as if in toast.

Brady set aside his half-finished eggnog and unwound himself from the couch to join his father.

"My right-hand man," Dan said, and they hugged in that smiling, back-patting way of men. "Couldn't get along without you, son."

"Merry Christmas, Dad."

Throughout the gift exchange, the two men laughed and teased in the affectionate Buchanon way. Their relationship bewildered Abby, but on this day the father and son were at peace. For Brady's sake, she prayed the truce continued.

While Bing Crosby dreamed of a white Christmas

from SiriusXM, paper and ribbons flew, and the recipients, especially the overexcited children, squealed in delight. Abby vacillated between pleasure at her daughter's joy and the painful awareness that Lila had never before had more than three small gifts under the tree. Her best, it seemed, had been inadequate, because today there were so many she couldn't keep count. She was more thankful than ever that she'd been able to buy each of the Buchanons a little something.

Her favorite part of the morning was watching the interactions between the family members. The love that flowed in the room was almost palpable. Even Brady and Dan seemed to truly care about each other, and the usually solemn Quinn teased his sisters and snitched tempting morsels from the kitchen.

This was the kind of family she'd once thought only existed on television or in books. Families that stuck together and helped each other, that loved and laughed even when they disagreed. They were big and loud and wonderful and she loved them. She deeply desired this kind of life for her daughter and, yes, for herself, too.

Heart full and amazed, Abby sat on the floor beside the fireplace, surrounded by mounds of colorful paper and gifts. Brady's Dawg curled against the hearth, asleep in all the commotion.

"You gonna open those presents or keep them till next year?" Brady knelt next to her, leaving his dad to hand out the stockings.

"I'm watching Lila. This is the first year she's really understood what was going on."

Enamored with the play kitchens from Brady, Lila and Amber had already started a game of "house" with the tea sets from Allison and the dolls from Karen and

Dan. Giggling and jabbering, Lila scooted her walker with ease from stove to stove and balanced her belly against the crossbar to "cook."

"Incredible kid." Brady watched Lila with a soft smile. "Amazing the way she adapts. Look at her."

Pride and love filled Abby's chest. "She finds a way, but really, Brady, you shouldn't have bought so much—"

He placed two fingers over her lips. "Don't say it. Anything goes on Christmas. Including your gifts. Open something before we think you don't like them."

"Oh." She hadn't thought of that. She simply hadn't wanted to look like a greedy, needy pig. "You haven't opened yours, either."

"Let's do it!" He ripped into his with the same abandon as the children. From her, he opened a bottle of men's Eternity.

"How did you know this is my favorite?" He unscrewed the lid and sniffed.

"I like the way it smells on you."

"Yeah?" He seemed pleased by that. He slapped a little on his face and leaned close. "What do you think?"

What did she think? She thought he was gorgeous and wonderful, cologne or not.

She sniffed his cheek with melodramatic exaggeration. "I think I have great taste in cologne."

"Wait till you open yours. You'll laugh."

Abby took her time, treasured every ribbon, which she set aside in an empty box, admired the pretty paper and then delighted in each gift inside. A scarf, a wallet, a CD, things for her new house, a sweater, and from Brady, a perfume set she'd fallen in love with on one of their window-shopping adventures. She had spritzed her wrist and neck, and the rest of the evening he'd told her how good she smelled.

She didn't laugh that they'd given each other cologne. It made her feel closer to him.

Abby closed her eyes and held the bottle to her nose. "I love this. Thank you."

"Put some on." His quiet rumble was temptingly close.

She did. The light floral-and-sandalwood fragrance filled the air and her senses.

Lila looked up from her play. "Mommy smells yummy, right, Bwady?"

"Yes, she does." When Abby only smiled in return, he said, "I suspect your Christmas is usually quieter. Feeling overwhelmed yet?"

"A little, but in a good way. Thank you for the gift. For...all of this." How did she express the depth and breadth of her emotions to a man who'd always had this kind of Christmas?

"What do you say we take a run over to your house?"

"Now?"

"I want to show you something." He stood and pulled her up by both hands. "Lila's having a blast with Amber, and dinner isn't until two."

"But I'm helping your mom with the meal."

"Mom," he called to where his mother leaned on the bar talking to Charity. They were waiting for a Skype call from Charity's husband, a career military pilot. "Can you spare Abby for a few minutes?"

"Of course."

"We won't be gone long," Abby said, feeling a little guilty about running out on the work, though they'd done most of the dinner preparations last night.

"Take your time. It's Christmas."

"Okay, then, if you're sure. Let me get my coat." She whirled her new scarf around her neck and kissed her daughter goodbye. Entranced by toys, candy and a playmate, Lila hardly noticed Abby was leaving.

When they arrived at the house, now almost complete and looking new and inviting beneath the cold, clear Christmas sky, Brady handed her a small goldwrapped box. Inside was a key ring bearing her name and a set of keys.

"Is this—?" She glanced toward the red entry door.

"It is." He withdrew a packet of papers from inside his jacket and handed them to her. "Merry Christmas, Abby." Grinning, he spread his arms dramatically. "Welcome to your new home. The outside still needs a few finishing touches, but the inside is ready to go."

"But how is that possible? Two days ago—"

"A few guys and gals did a little overtime." He lifted a shoulder as if what they'd done was no big deal. "Maybe a lot of overtime."

"They worked on Christmas Eve? For me?"

"They wanted you to take possession today, a Christmas present from me and the crew."

"I don't know what to say." Her hand trembled as she put the key in the lock and opened the door. She'd been inside dozens of times but today was different. Today the home was hers.

They stepped into the smell of new wood, fresh paint and lemon cleaner.

All evidence of construction that had been here as recently as two days ago had disappeared. The paint cans, two-by-sixes and drop cloths were gone. Electrical outlets were covered, knobs were in place on the cabinets and doors, and every room had been immaculately cleaned, windows polished to a shine and wood trim rubbed with oil. Even a few pieces of furniture now graced the rooms.

"Oh, Brady," she breathed, gazing around her home. Her beautiful, beautiful home. Tears of joy prickled the backs of her eyelids. "Unbelievable."

Abby slid her palms along the cold granite countertops, turned the nickel faucets on and off, peeked in the stainless-steel refrigerator.

"Empty," Brady said, and they both laughed for no reason except pleasure.

They roamed the living room, tested the thermostat and gazed out the sparkling-clean dining room windows toward a backyard bare of plants except for two leafless red maples that had survived the bulldozer. In spring, grass would grow again. She could plant flowers. Karen had already offered starts from her gorgeous backyard.

This was perfect.

Inside Lila's room, Abby spun in a circle, heart spilling over, beside herself with happiness. To accommodate Lila's walker, the room was intentionally sleek and streamlined, but on the wall above a pink-and-white canopied bed, some artistic hand had painted a crown and the words, *Princess Lila*. Gauzy curtains draped the windows, which were framed in castle-turret wallpaper. It was the kind of room every little girl dreamed of.

"This is… I don't even have words. She will be so happy."

Brady's eyes sparkled. "What about her mom?"

"I love it. You know I do."

"Good. Good." He moved to the window and pushed aside a pink curtain.

Abby ran her fingers lightly over the girly white bed-side table, admiring the pink lamp. "I thought you'd want a reporter present when you turned over the keys. For publicity."

"She'll wait until the remaining furniture is in and the exterior is complete." He looked at her over one very broad shoulder. "I wanted today to be the two of us. No audience. No TV. No other family. And definitely not client and builder. Just Brady and Abby. You and me. Alone."

Abby's breath caught at the hushed tone in his voice.

He turned to face her, placing his hands on the windowsill behind him. For a sweet, aching moment their gazes locked until Abby looked down at the pink crystals dangling from the lamp. She was as wishful as a fairy tale.

Brady stirred, and she felt him move toward her, the giant of a man who moved with athletic grace. Abby's pulse thrummed with wild hope and terrible fear. Not of Brady but of her own needy heart and past mistakes.

He took hold of her shoulders with gentle hands and stood as quiet as a stone until she looked up and babbled, "You've worked so hard and done so much, I—"

He cut her off with a shake of his head, saying, "I'd do it all over again in a heartbeat. You're a special woman, Abby Webster."

Her mouth curved. "You're a special man. Just look at this fabulous place. No one else could have done what you did. No one would have wanted to."

"This isn't about the house. Or me. I'm talking about you, the woman who works too hard and champions her special child, who bought gifts for my family when I know you need the money." When she started to deny the truth, he put a finger over her lips and stopped her. "I know about the hours you and Lila volunteer on the hospital children's wing—I was there, remember? And about the time a mother and her five kids stayed with you to escape an abusive relationship."

"Where did you learn about that?"

"This is Gabriel's Crossing. People talk. But that's beside the point."

"What is the point?"

He cupped her cheek, smile tender. "The point is, I love you."

The admission was both beautiful and scary. She nodded, the words she wanted to say thick in her throat.

A battle raged inside Abby's chest as she fought against past experiences. Warren had said he loved her, too. But when times turned hard, so did his heart. Exactly like the other people in her past. Love was conditional.

Intellectually, Abby knew Warren and Brady were as different as fire and water, but the vulnerable part of her was afraid. The scared child who'd been shuffled from foster home to foster home, the awkward misfit who was prey to cruel gibes in school and the jilted pregnant fiancée still lived and ached inside the independent woman. She wanted Brady with all her heart but the coward inside held back.

Yet, Brady had put no conditions on this house or her. He'd given her a place to live with his family, a babysitting service and the best Christmas ever. Was that love?

No, that couldn't be right. He'd given home makeovers to other people, as well. Love had to be…more.

"Hey," Brady said softly. "Are you going to leave me hanging?"

She shook her head, throat dry as chalk. "Of course not. I—"

"Don't say it if you don't mean it."

Head down, she moistened dry lips and murmured, "I do."

He tipped her chin up, blue, blue eyes questioning.

She nodded. "Yes."

The brilliance of his smile was worth everything. He hugged her to him, his heart pounding and pounding in her ear. Her own heart pounded, too.

Even in the midst of joy, an earthquake shook her insides and the voice in her head shouted a warning. Love was temporary. Love exacted a painful price.

She pushed the voice down, down, down and clasped tightly to the hope that this time love meant forever.

Chapter Sixteen

The week following Christmas Abby began moving her stored belongings into the new home a little at a time. After business hours, Brady and his brothers did the heavy lifting, and if she and Brady spent too much time grinning at each other instead of working, she couldn't help it. She loved him desperately.

By New Year's Eve, the bulk of the donated furniture had arrived. Abby had spent most of her day off arranging and rearranging for the sheer thrill of it.

"You and Lila could sleep here tonight if you wanted," Brady said as he plunked a cardboard box on the countertop.

She shook her head. "I want to start the year off in my new home. Tomorrow, New Year's Day, Lila and I will bring over our things from your parents' house and settle in. It's…symbolic. A new year, a new start, a new house."

"Can't argue with sentiment." He dragged open the box flaps and lifted out a plate. "Where do these go?"

"Dishwasher. They've been in storage long enough to get dirty."

"A guy would wipe them on his jeans and stick them in the cabinet."

She laughed. "You would not."

"Probably not. Mom would hurt me."

"So would I." Plates clinked as they unboxed the dishes. The set was small and inexpensive, but she liked the clean white design.

As they loaded the dishwasher together, he said, "We still on for tonight?"

"Absolutely. Can't wait." She inspected a teacup for chips. "I usually spend New Year's Eve at home with Lila. We watch a movie, eat some popcorn and she falls asleep long, long before the ball drops. Mostly, I do, too."

He laughed. "I've done that a few times myself. But not tonight. I want to take my lady on the town."

His lady. Brady's easy acceptance of their new relationship made her feel vulnerable. How long would one of the town's most eligible bachelors be interested in ordinary Abby from the diner? Would she still be his lady this time next year? Or even next week after she and Lila were moved in and no longer a Christmas project?

Abby fought off the negative thoughts. Since Christmas Day they'd driven her crazy. Twice, she'd had a nightmare. She'd been in a crowd of smiling, talking, happy people but none of them could see her. She'd been invisible. She'd seen Brady standing tall above the crowd. Happy and relieved, she waved and called out. His eyes met hers, but when she ran to embrace him, he'd turned away and left her alone, invisible again.

The Old Red Barn was a popular restaurant and events venue that specialized in music, steaks and New Year's Eve.

"Ever attended one of their New Year's Eve parties?" Brady asked as he held her elbow and guided her from the quickly filling gravel parking lot through the darkness to the brightly lit building.

"No."

"Me, either."

"Really?" She'd imagined him as a man who always had a date and never missed a party.

"I've been here for dinner but not on New Year's Eve. The steaks are great. Shrimp's good. Lobster rocks the world."

"I've never had lobster," she admitted.

"Want to try it?"

Abby grimaced. "It looks creepy."

He laughed. "Looks are deceiving. Except for yours. You look gorgeous tonight."

Abby had pressed the one dress she saved for special occasions, mostly funerals and weddings, a simple black sheath with a blue cardigan and black heels. The temperature hovered around freezing and a stiff north wind blew in another arctic front, but there was no way she'd wear the puffy red jacket on a New Year's Eve date no matter how cold she got. She refused to shiver.

"You look nice, too." *Really nice.* In a suit and tie, her Celtic warrior was a dream.

Inside the restaurant, quiet music played and candlelight lit the room in a golden, shadowy glow. The atmosphere felt romantic and elegant, though all that would change when the live band kicked off at nine and the party really began.

Brady gave his name to the hostess, who responded with a very warm smile and led them to a cozy table. With a flirtatious tilt of her head, the hostess glanced at Brady from beneath her eyelashes. "Is this suitable, Mr. Buchanon?"

"Great."

Abby tried not to be jealous. Brady was with her, but obviously other women, including the young hostess, noticed his good looks and Buchanon clout.

After she was seated, Abby said, "I feel a little guilty eating anywhere except the Buttered Biscuit."

"It's not open."

"Good point. Jan and Dave are off on their cruise."

"See? Even they're eating somewhere else. So, what sounds good? You going for that lobster?"

She'd make a fool of herself trying to eat something served in a shell. She looked over the menu. "Maybe the grilled salmon with lemon-infused quinoa. That sounds pretty fancy for a woman who serves burgers and meat loaf."

"I'm not a fancy kind of guy. I'm going for the herb-crusted beef tenderloin and garlic mashed."

"Sounds fancy to me."

"Steak and potatoes. Can't get more basic than that."

The waitress reappeared with their drinks and took their orders.

"I thought we might see some of your family here tonight."

"Still could. Nightlife in Gabriel's Crossing is limited, even on New Year's Eve."

"Allison said she and Jake were going to a friend's party. A Mexican fiesta, I think."

"And Mom and Dad were having some business friends over. The twins had dates but I didn't ask where they were going, and Jaylee had plans with friends. A concert, I think, down in Paris."

"It was nice of Charity to invite Lila to spend the night."

"She was staying home with the kids anyway and thought having Lila over would be fun for Amber. I heard rumors about popcorn, movies and a bubble-blowing contest."

Lila would love every minute of the sleepover even if she'd be cranky as a bear tomorrow from staying up too late.

"That accounts for everyone except Quinn," Abby said. "I hope he isn't alone."

Brady frowned. "He probably is. He didn't used to be a loner but after the shooting, he withdrew from everything. When he finished college he took a job with a big firm in Dallas and moved away from all of us. Infuriated Dad."

"I'm sure."

"Yeah. By the time he moved home again, we thought he'd put the accident behind him."

"But he hasn't?"

"If anything he's gotten worse. He bought an old hunting cabin down on the river, and he'd rather be there than anywhere."

"Does he have a girlfriend?"

"Quinn? No. He'd scare a nice girl away."

"Was he always so reclusive and…?"

"Negative?" He smoothed the napkin onto his lap. "I forget you weren't around then. No, he wasn't. He was Mr. Big Man on Campus, the favorite son with the golden arm who was going to be a huge star in the NFL. He had an agent, a contract offer, the works. Everyone loved Quinn and he loved them, too." He fiddled with his fork. "All that changed with the accident."

"But he and Jake seem cordial when the family gets together."

"They are. The brothers had it in for Jake for a lot of years, but Allison loved him and we finally realized that forgiveness is better for everyone."

"Quinn forgave Jake for permanently damaging his arm?"

"He says he has. Sometimes I wonder if Quinn blames himself now that he doesn't have Jake to blame anymore."

"You worry about him."

"He's my brother. I love him. And, yeah, something is wrong, so I worry."

To hear a man talk so freely about love for his family touched her. "And you want to fix it."

He huffed softly. "You sound like Allison. She says I want to rescue everyone."

Did that include her?

The soft murmur of voices and gentle laughter filtered across the restaurant as waitstaff moved in quiet efficiency. The smell of steak and fresh, hot bread made Abby's mouth water while somewhere in the distance outside the restaurant a siren wailed.

The canned music kicked into Harry Connick Jr. crooning "Stardust."

"Are we still in Texas?" Brady joked.

"I think it's romantic."

He pumped his eyebrows. "Then I hope they play old Harry all night."

"I doubt that's going to happen since Boogie Salad takes the stage at nine."

Brady's eyes danced. "Crazy name for a band, but Boogie Salad is pretty good."

"You've heard them before?"

"YouTube. Checked them out before I made the reservation. They're a party band. Fun and energetic. They play a little bit of everything. Whatever the crowd wants."

Harry's smooth voice eased into "The Way You Look Tonight."

"Oh," Abby said, and sighed. "This is beautiful. His voice melts around the words."

"Melts? Should I be jealous?"

"No more than me."

"What does that mean?"

Abby blushed, the heat rushing up the back of her neck like warm water. "The hostess and the waitress were both flirting."

"Were they?"

She made a scoffing noise. "You know they were."

"You're the only one I'm interested in, Abby." His expression turned serious as he laced his fingers with hers atop the table. "I've never seen your hair down before."

"No?" Her hand went to the long waves that fell around her shoulders.

"It's beautiful." Above the flicker of a single candle, his blue eyes glowed with a soft, tender emotion, an emotion she felt, too. "Don't laugh, but I've had this crazy itch to take down your ponytail for a long time."

She didn't laugh. She couldn't. Her throat was too full. At the thought of Brady's wide fingers in her hair, a tingle raced over her skin. Tonight she felt like Cinderella at the ball, madly in love with her Prince Charming.

Please don't let the clock strike midnight.

"Abby," he started, lifting one of her fingers and then another. He sounded so serious.

"Yes?" Her pulse stuttered against her collarbone.

His cell phone interrupted. He leaned back in his chair and groaned. "This better not be work. Excuse me."

Abby sat back, too, sipped at her water and listened while Brady spoke into the receiver. He frowned. "What?"

When his eyes flicked to hers, she knew something was wrong.

Very slowly, she set her glass on the table. Condensation dampened her hands. She wiped the moisture on her napkin, aware that she was suddenly afraid and didn't know why.

Brady ended the call and stood with an abruptness that alarmed her.

"Brady?" She rose, too, fumbling for her handbag at her feet.

"We have to go." His face was set in harsh lines that no amount of candlelight could soften.

Fear prickled the hair on her arms. "What's wrong?"

He took her elbow.

"Brady, tell me. Is it Lila?" A mother's fear stole her breath. She froze, refusing to move until he told her. "Is she all right?"

"Yes. Lila's fine."

Relief made her knees shake. Brady propelled her toward the door. "It's your house."

Something in his voice was terrible. He tossed money at the hostess and opened the exit door. A blast of frigid wind nearly knocked them down.

Alarm sounded in Abby's head. "My house?"

"It's on fire."

Sirens ripped the night in high-pitched cries of alarm as Brady raced from one side of town to the other. Abby hovered against the passenger door, her face stark in the dashboard lights, her posture rigid, arms crossed.

Brady could relate. A tight knot had his empty belly in a stranglehold.

"It'll be okay."

Abby turned her head. She no more believed the words than he did.

He bit down on his jaw. He'd make it be okay.

Abby gasped and leaned forward, palms braced on the dashboard. "Brady. Look. Oh, no."

He saw. Flames as high as the moon turned the night into day and obliterated the stars. And he and Abby weren't even in the neighborhood yet.

His belly sank lower, sick. Nauseated. *God, how could this happen?* To her, of all people.

He turned on First Street and accelerated hard down the empty pavement. In seconds, the truck bumped over the railroad tracks and into Abby's neighborhood.

The smell of smoke seeped into the cab. Abby made a small noise of distress and Brady wanted badly to be holding her instead of driving. She looked so alone huddled against the window.

He screeched to a halt a half a block away, Cedar Corner blocked by the fire engine, a rescue truck, police and a handful of gawkers.

They got out and ran toward the house, but Brady didn't have to be up close and personal to know they were too late.

The north wind whipped the flames into an inferno. Sparks shot hundreds of feet into the air, and the awful sound of hungry fire crackled and chewed through wood. The porch awning shuddered and a firefighter shouted.

Bunker-geared figures pulled back, massive hoses aimed toward the flames but impotent in the wind.

"What happened, Jason?" Brady said to the fire chief, the first uniformed person he encountered.

"Don't know yet and won't know much until the fire settles down. This one of yours?"

"I built it. It's Abby's new house."

The chief, face flickering gray and red in the flames, looked at Abby. "You're Brady's Christmas makeover?"

She nodded numbly, arms crossed tight and lips trembling.

Brady looped an arm around her. She was like a statue, stiff and unyielding, but he held fast. She wasn't a makeover.

"I'm sorry, ma'am. By the time my men arrived, the roof was involved and the garage was gone."

Brady heard what the chief wasn't saying. If the roof was gone, the rest of the house didn't have much chance.

"Let me know what you discover on the cause."

"Will do." The man spoke into his radio and moved away.

Abby's body quivered in the cold and from shock, too, he imagined. "It's too cold out here and neither of us is dressed for this kind of weather. You don't even have a coat. Come on."

"They can't save my house, can they?"

"No."

Her stiff resolve crumbled then. She turned to him, shattered, shaking, and the tears flowed down her smoke-smudged cheeks. "Oh, Brady. All your hard work for nothing."

She walked into his chest and held him as if he had the most to lose. As if he was the one who mattered.

"I'm so sorry, sweetheart. So sorry." He crushed her to him and gave comfort where he could. He smoothed her long, beautiful hair, the hair he'd wanted to touch for so long. But not like this. Never like this.

Her body quaked and he knew she was crying silent, brokenhearted sobs. Secret sobs she kept to herself. They sliced him to the core.

The news media arrived to film the destruction and interview the fire chief. Brady was grateful that they hadn't come to him. Abby didn't need a camera in her face.

Car doors slammed, and flames crackled and popped. The fire engine's pump hummed, loud enough to drown out speech. The front of the house gave way; fire ate into the wood until walls collapsed in a gust.

Heat mixed with frigid wind reached them in swirls. Brady unbuttoned his suit jacket and guided Abby's arms inside, against his body. "We should go."

She shook her head. "I can't. I can't."

Everything she owned except for the few items at his parents' home was inside the burning house, and he couldn't go in and get them for her.

They stood in the heat and cold, light and dark, huddled together watching the flames devour her dreams. One by one, except for Charity who'd blessedly remained at home with the children, his family arrived and stood silently with them as Abby's dream home burned to rubble.

Chapter Seventeen

New Year's Day didn't begin the way Brady had intended. Running on fumes, his eyes as red as embers and the smell of smoke still in his lungs, he staggered into his mother's kitchen at eleven.

"Did you sleep at all?" She slid a cup of coffee onto the bar.

"A few hours." He'd gone home, gone to bed, but sleep had been elusive. "Every time I closed my eyes, I saw Abby's house burning." And her face. He'd seen her devastated expression over and over. Even now, it tormented him.

"I don't think Abby slept much, either."

"How could this happen, Mom?" He stared morosely into the steaming coffee. "We've never had a fire. What could have gone wrong?"

His father entered the kitchen, his Buchanon Built cap and jacket a sign he'd been out and about. He reached for a coffee cup. "I'll tell you how it happened."

At his crisp tone, Brady swiveled on the bar chair. "Did you hear something?"

"The fire marshal arrives later, but Jason thinks the fire started in the garage near the hot-water tank."

"The tank? It was working fine when I checked it."

"*Near* the tank, Brady. Pay attention." Dan's tone hardened. "Someone messed up."

Brady was already shaking his head. "I don't think so, Dad. I was the last person in that house yesterday afternoon. And even before I let Abby start moving her things in, I had personally checked everything from plumbing to electrical plugs."

"You personally checked? Did you? Are you positive? Or were you more focused on Abby than on your job?"

Brady stiffened, temper crawling up the back of his neck. "What are you implying?"

"I don't imply. You know me better than that." Dan poked a finger in his direction. "Your negligence caused the fire."

"Dan!" Karen came around the end of the bar to face her husband. "You don't know that."

"Fires don't just happen, Karen. Someone causes them, especially in new construction. Someone didn't do his job correctly. A loose wire in an outlet. Lacquer thinner or paint rags left behind. An overloaded plug. Fire is preventable. This was Brady's project. His responsibility."

"That doesn't mean he was negligent."

"No?" Dan slammed his hand down on the bar. "It does to me."

Anger warred with the overwhelming sense that his father was right. Abby's house was his from ground up. He'd been in on every single element of the construction. If something had gone wrong, the fault was his. He *had* stored lacquer thinner cans in the garage.

Even if he had an excuse, he knew better. Spontaneous combustion from rags or cans was real and a hot water tank, even across the room, could possibly spark and ignite the fumes.

"I'll make it right, Dad."

"I hope you had sense enough to have the house well insured."

Anger boiled up higher. He pushed it down. This was his fault, not his dad's. "I'll talk to the insurance adjuster today and start plans for the rebuild right away."

"Rebuild? We don't have time for a rebuild now."

He jolted, stunned. "We have to. Abby—"

Dan's voice rose. "You don't *have* to do anything on this house. It's a freebie, remember? No one is paying us a dime to rebuild."

Brady pushed his cold coffee aside. "Don't go there, Dad."

"You've strained us to the limit on this project already. The rebuild will have to wait."

Abby cried all the way to work. Exhausted, heartsick and guilt ridden, she didn't know what to do.

She'd heard the battle between father and son. The yelling.

The word *freebie* rolled over and over in her mind. Charity case. Freebie. They were the same thing. Both made her feel less than human. A weight, a nuisance, in the way.

After a full week of peace between Brady and his dad, they were at each other's throats again. Because of the house. Because of her.

She parked the car in back of the diner and patted makeup under her eyes before going inside.

"Oh, Abby, sugar." Charla enveloped her in a hug the moment she walked in the back door of the diner. "I heard about your house. You look a wreck. Go home."

Home? She had no home.

Tears bubbled up again. "I wish I'd never agreed to the makeover." Her old house hadn't been much but at least she'd had one.

"Oh, sugar, don't say that. Brady will rebuild. You'll see."

No, he wouldn't. He couldn't. Not now.

"I can't continue to impose on the Buchanons until that happens." Not after what she'd overheard this morning. Dan didn't want her there. She was a burden. A *freebie*. And her presence caused problems for the man she was supposed to love.

"You're a mess. Go home. Get some sleep. Everything looks better after a solid eight."

"But you'll be shorthanded."

"Business is slow anyway. Everyone is still eating leftovers and recovering from hangovers. We can handle things without you." She gave Abby a little push. "With your hands shaking like that, you'd probably break every dish in the place."

Abby tried to smile. "You're the best."

"Remember that on my birthday." Charla shooed her. "Go on now."

Abby left but instead of driving to the Buchanon house, she drove to the Fairview Apartments not far from her former home on Cedar Corner. Located across the tracks on the poor side of town, Fairview was a far cry from the Buchanon home, but the tiny units were cheap, furnished and move-in ready, and she'd lived in far worse. They'd do for now.

She filled out an application, paid the deposit and after being assured by the manager than she could move in right away, drove to a day-care center near the elementary school, frustrated to find it closed for the holidays. Enrolling Lila would have to wait until tomorrow. By the time she'd finished her errands, she felt in control of her life again. And immeasurably sad.

Telling Karen of her plans proved harder than she'd expected.

"Why, Abby? Is something wrong?"

"I've imposed long enough and with the new house destroyed—" She bit her lip, fighting tears. She would not cry anymore today. Crying was useless.

"We love having you and Lila here. You can stay as long as you need."

"I've already rented an apartment and decided on a new day care for Lila." Rainbow Day Care always had openings but was not her idea of the best facility for her daughter. The cost, however, was less than she'd paid at Huckleberry and they accepted toddlers in pull-up diapers. She'd talked to them before, but now she'd do more than talk. Rainbow would work until she could find something better or until, please Lord, Lila had successful toilet training.

"This seems so sudden." Karen's frown was puzzled.

"I don't know how to thank you for all you've done. You and your family made me feel—"

"Like family?"

The pesky tears threatened. "Yes."

Karen drew her into a hug. "You *are* family, Abby."

Since coming to know the Buchanons she'd been hugged more than she had been in all her life. And she loved it. But as much as she loved living in this house, she wasn't family. Not really. Though Karen was kind to say so.

Before she forgot the very good reasons she had to leave, Abby packed her meager belongings into the car, thankful that these things had been spared, and drove away.

She was glad Lila remained at Charity's, protected from the impact of last night, but as soon as she'd unloaded her car at the apartment, the time with Charity would end, too. They had imposed enough.

When she arrived at the apartment, Brady was already there. His tall, wide body blocked the front door. Arms crossed, a scowl on his face, he demanded, "What are you doing?"

He looked wonderful and awful at the same time. His blue eyes bloodshot, fatigue hung him on him like a baggy sweatshirt. She longed to hold and comfort him the way he'd done for her last night. He'd been her rock. Without Brady, she would have collapsed in a heap on the frozen ground.

She set the cardboard box of cleaning supplies on the concrete outside the door. "Your mother must have called you."

"She did. Did you think she'd let you move into this ratty place without asking me if I'd done something to upset you?" He uncrossed his arms and stood over her, his beloved face a mix of anger and hurt. "Have I?"

"No. No, Brady." She resisted the need to put a reassuring hand on his broad chest. "You've been wonderful."

"Then what's the deal?"

"I just thought—" She yanked in a breath, trying to decide the best thing to say. Should she admit to hearing the quarrel? Admit she knew she'd become a burden? "I'm cold out here. Can we go inside?"

He let out an exasperated huff, took the key and pushed open the door. The interior smelled stale and old. Age clung to the saggy furniture and yellowed walls.

"This is a pit. You're not staying here."

"We are. I just need to do some cleaning first."

His frown deepened as he blinked around the tiny space. "Where's Lila?"

"Still at Charity's house. I'm going after her as soon as I have the apartment ready."

"This is stupid."

"Brady, please. You'll need months, maybe longer, to rebuild my house. I can't live with your folks for a year."

"What makes you think—" The light came on behind his eyes. "You overheard Dad and me, didn't you?"

She began unloading the cleaning supplies on the single kitchen counter. The gold flecks had nearly faded away on the ancient white Formica.

"Yes."

"Okay, so you know I messed up somewhere and caused the fire. It's my fault. My responsibility. But I'll fix it. It's what I do."

"I don't blame you." She plunked disinfectant cleaner next to the sink. "Don't think that."

"Then what? Talk to me, Abby."

"Your dad is right." She turned her back to fill the sink with water but mostly to keep from looking him in the eyes. She'd crumble if she did. "Maybe we should— step back, let things cool down for a while."

"Step back?" He came up beside her. "What are you talking about? Step back from what?"

She fanned one hand in a helpless gesture. "Everything."

"From the house? From each other?"

If he kept looking at her like that, she'd change her mind, and she couldn't let that happen. She owed him this much.

All she'd done was cause problems for the man she loved more than she'd believed possible. She was no good for him. If stepping away would bring peace between him and his father, and take the load off his shoulders, she loved him enough to do it.

Heart pounding in her throat with enough force to choke her, she swallowed hard and said, "Yes."

Failure ate a hole in a man. Losing Abby had gutted him.

His worst fear had happened. Because of the fire, he'd failed Abby and Lila, failed his father and the business, and he'd even failed himself.

Three days later, he still didn't understand why Abby had turned on him, but no amount of conversation seemed to shake her resolve. She used words like *needing space* and *stepping back* that all sounded like *get lost* to him.

Worse, she'd said Dad was right. Even though she claimed not to blame Brady, she did, exactly like Dad.

He'd thought she loved him. In fact, he'd been sure of it until she'd shown him the door of her pitiful apartment. He hated seeing her live there. If he'd had his mind on his business, if he'd done his job as he should have, she wouldn't be in that situation.

He'd toyed with the idea of placing a mobile home on her property in place of the house, but Dad would go bal-

listic on that idea. Brady understood. They were builders. He could and would rebuild Abby's dream home.
The hours might kill him, but he was determined to get
Abby out of the Fairview Apartments as soon as possible. The only thing fair about the view at that place was
the exit sign leading out.

With the January cold seeping into his bones, he
walked along the yellow tape encircling the charred re-
mains of Abby's house. The fire marshal had released
the scene this morning. Brady still waited on the official
report, but he could now begin the salvaging process.
Not that there was much left to salvage.

An engine roar drew his attention to the street. His
brother parked at the curb and slammed out of the Buchanon Built truck.

Hands in his coat pockets, Dawson sauntered toward
him, boots padding on soil still soft from water and fire
trucks. "What's up, bro?"

"Cleanup time."

"No word yet from the fire marshal?"

"None. But we both know I messed up somewhere."

"Maybe. Maybe not. Mistakes happen, Brady. Don't
beat yourself up."

"Never happened to me before. I've never even had
a leaky pipe."

"Yeah, well." Dawson stared around at the pile of
rubble and ashes. One wobbly wall remained standing
but would have to come down. "Need some help?"

"You're supposed to be on the Taylor site."

"Sawyer's there. He can handle the work for a while."

"You don't pull off jobs without a reason. What's
going on?"

"I'm concerned about you. One renegade, moody brother is too many."

"Got a lot on my mind."

"What's the deal with Abby?"

He wished people would stop asking him that. "I don't know."

"Things were looking pretty sweet and then bam!" Dawson's fist hit the palm of his hand. "You're not a couple anymore."

"Yeah." Brady rubbed a hand over the back of his neck. "I guess she wasn't as serious as I'd thought."

Dawson made a rude noise in the back of his throat. "You're kidding, right? The woman's crazy in love with you. Maybe too much."

Brady frowned. "You been sniffing paint fumes or something? You're not making sense."

"I talked to her at the Buttered Biscuit."

"About me?"

"Look at it this way, Brady. Remember how reluctant she was to be part of the home makeover in the first place?"

"Yeah. But she got past that."

"Did she?"

Brady started to say yes again but stopped as the memory of her words came back to him. "She thinks nothing good ever lasts."

"Exactly. Think about her background. Her whole life has been temporary. I think she's a prime example of a self-fulfilling prophecy."

Brady rolled his eyes. "Dr. Dawson, general psychology and advice to the lovelorn. You've missed your calling, boy."

"Laugh if you want to but I'm the one Abby's talking to. She said something about letting you go so you could get back to your life and stop worrying about her and Lila."

Brady's scowl turned to disbelief. "She didn't say that."

"She did. I think she dumped you to keep you from dumping her. As crazy and confused as that sounds, Abby thinks she's not worthy of you. I also think she backed off to protect you."

"Protect me?" His brother had a loose screw. At six-six and two-fifty, he didn't need protection. "From what?"

"Yourself. Her. Dad. She was really upset that you and Dad had fought about her house."

"She told you all this?"

"Sort of. I read between the lines."

Brady's head whirled with his brother's advice. Could Dawson be right?

His cell buzzed. Annoyed at the interruption, he yanked the device from his pocket and barked, "Buchanon."

"Mr. Buchanon, Sherry Adams with the fire investigator's office."

Brady shook himself to refocus. Getting Abby off his mind wasn't easy, but this was the call he'd been waiting for.

To Dawson, he mouthed, *Fire marshal.*

"Yes, ma'am," he said into the phone. "What have you got?"

The woman rattled off a report, but one word stood out to Brady. "Accelerant?" He glanced toward his brother, who looked every bit as stunned as he felt. "You mean someone deliberately set this fire?"

"The vandals have struck again," Dawson murmured.

After a few more moments of conversation, Brady ended the call, fuming. Between clenched teeth, he ground out, "Arson. Some worthless piece of pond scum torched Abby's house."

He should probably feel vindicated but he didn't. He was furious.

"How?" Dawson asked.

"Lacquer thinners stored in the garage. The supplier was scheduled to pick up the leftovers but hadn't yet because of the holidays. I suspected they were the cause but blamed myself for leaving them in the garage. Spontaneous combustion and all that."

"But?"

"But the fire wasn't spontaneous. The arsonist used the lacquer thinner to soak Abby's cardboard moving boxes and left a clear trail to the hot water heater."

"And all it took was a spark."

"On a night as cold as New Year's Eve, a fire was only a matter of time."

Dawson nodded thoughtfully. "The only good news in all this is that the monkey's off your back, if that makes any difference."

"It doesn't. Dad won't care. He only sees the time we've lost."

"*You've* lost. Not Dad or the business. You've kept up with the other work."

Brady rubbed a hand over his face. His nose was cold but his blood still boiled. "If I find the creep who did this—"

"Let the police do their jobs. We have enough work to do." Dawson clapped him on the shoulder. "I'm out of here. You going to call Dad about the report?"

"Later."

"What about Abby?"

Brady shook his head. "I don't know. Maybe."

Dawson's eyes, as blue as his own, studied him. "You'll think about what I said?"

Brady couldn't think of anything else.

Chapter Eighteen

Later that afternoon, Brady sat in his office at Buchanon Built Construction. At least once each day, he stopped in to check messages, go through mail Jaylee stacked on his desk and check on Quinn. Not that his brother knew his intent.

Bone weary, he rubbed a hand over the muscle aches in the back of his neck. Dawson's advice rattled around in his head along with the news of the arsonist.

The door opened and his father stepped inside. Without preamble, he held up a plastic-sleeved paper and said, "Found this in the newspaper box outside Abby's house."

Brady frowned. The newspaper box on the curb was far enough away not to burn, but he was sure it had been empty the last time he'd been to the site. "What is it?"

Dan put the sleeve on Brady's desk. "Our arsonist left a note."

Brady took up the paper and read aloud, "Are you sorry yet?" He glanced up at his father's worried face. The vandalism had escalated to a whole new level. "Sorry about what? This sounds personal, Dad."

"I thought so, too, but I've racked my brain and come up empty."

"Does Leroy know about this?"

"I'm headed over there now, but I wanted to talk to you first." Dan shifted, his work boots scrubbing the concrete. "I should have suspected the vandals from the outset instead of blaming you."

Was this an apology? From the man who was never wrong? Brady thought of a snappy comeback, an in-your-face reply, but wrestled it down. Fighting fire with fire had burned them both too many times. Today, he was too tired to fight. Tired and heartsick.

"Things happen in the heat of the moment."

"Yeah, well, sometimes you're too easy on your old man."

"Dad, could I ask you something? Man-to-man?"

Dan cocked his head, curious. Brady rarely asked for advice, particularly from his dad. "Anytime."

"If Mom left you, what would you do?"

"Go after her and do anything she wanted to get her back." Dan dragged a chair close to the desk and sat. Brady saw that he, too, was worn from the ongoing drama. Deep grooves bracketed his mouth and new lines bisected his forehead. "You're thinking about Abby?"

"I love her, Dad, and I don't know what I did wrong."

"Nothing, probably. Women are tender and Abby's had a lot of hurts. Maybe she's scared."

"That's what Dawson says."

"Yeah, well, Dawson's intuitive like his mother."

"But what do I do?"

"You and me, we're alike. We're both blockheads sometimes and can't see the forest for the trees."

"Is that supposed to make me feel better?"

Dan barked a laugh. "I've been a blockhead about Abby's house. Your mom and me, we like those two Webster girls. Miss 'em, too. That little one, she kind of eases into a man's heart. Let's get that house rebuilt."

"But you were against rebuilding. 'Give the girl the insurance money and let it go,' if I recall."

"Like I said, blockhead." He picked up the arsonist's note. "Better get this over to Leroy." He went to the door but turned back to face Brady. "First time I saw your mother, I knew she was my future. If Abby's yours, don't be a blockhead."

Moments after his father departed, Brady grabbed his work overalls from the hanger. He still didn't know what to do about Abby, but with his father's blessing, he knew what to do about her house.

The heater in her old car warmed up slowly. Abby huddled inside her coat and frowned at the silvery, overcast sky. Sleet and snow was forecast for the Texoma area. Not much, but enough to freeze pipes and make the roads slick.

She drove from the Buttered Biscuit, thoughtful. According to local gossip, Brady was working at the destroyed house. Alone. It would be dark soon. He needed to go home and rest. He was going to make himself sick.

She bit her bottom lip, guilt stricken that she'd become such a burden to him.

She wanted him to let the makeover go, to make peace with his father by forgetting about freebie Abby and her house. She would survive. She always had. She was strong and independent.

Her car bumped across the railroad tracks with a

shudder. The heater finally kicked in with enough heat to clear the fog on her windshield.

As she pulled onto her street, she saw Brady's truck parked at the curb.

She parked behind him and got out, bunching her coat collar around her ears. The cold stung her eyes.

One lone man shifted through the rubble of her belongings, his russet hair and work clothes gray with soot. When he saw her, Brady straightened and lifted a hand. "Hi."

She heard the reserve in his voice and knew she'd hurt him. He didn't understand she'd done it for his well-being.

"Hi." She stood not five feet from him, every cell in her body screaming to run into his arms. He was exhausted and dirty and as steadfast as the sun. The love she bore him engulfed her in giant, rolling waves.

She closed her eyes, fighting the emotion. If she loved him enough, she'd set him free. Wasn't that a proverb or something?

She shoved her hands deep in her pockets to keep them off him, aching to wipe away the soot and worry from his face.

"Are you okay?" he asked.

She'd hurt him but he still cared enough to ask. "No. Are you?"

He stepped toward her. Broken glass crunched beneath his boot. "Be careful out here. You could get hurt."

"So could you. Give this up, Brady." *Let go of the project, so I can turn loose of this crazy, wild hope that I could ever be good enough for you.* Biting her lip, she glanced toward the neighbor's house.

"I never quit, Abby." His voice was tender. "I don't walk away. I don't let go. Don't you know that by now?"

She brought her gaze back to the beloved face. What she saw in his anguished blue eyes shook her resolve. Conviction. Concern. Love.

As steadfast as his faith, Brady had never let her down. Even though others had and even though she'd clearly hurt him, Brady, like the Lord she'd come to know through him, was still here for her.

"All I've done since we met is cause problems for you and your family."

"Not true. Problems are always around. You make them easier to bear."

She did?

"I'm in love with you, Abby. Can't you get it through your head? I need you. You need me. That's the way it's supposed to be between a man and woman. We're going through some rough times. Let's go through them together."

Knees shaking, mouth dry, she took a step. Brady took two and they were face-to-face, standing in ash and debris. His gaze searched hers, but he waited. The ball, she knew, was in her court.

"I won't ever give up, Abby. You're worth anything."

She? Awkward Abby was worth anything to big, beautiful Brady Buchanon?

Suddenly, she was no longer afraid. Not of him. Not of her past or the losses that made her shy away from commitment. Brady had proved himself over and over, and she'd been too self-focused to believe him.

"I love you, Brady. I didn't want to leave. I was just so afraid—"

"You don't have to be afraid anymore."

And she knew he spoke the truth. He'd never given her reason to distrust. Not once.

"No one ever stayed."

He grasped her upper arms, his gaze holding hers. "I will. And I need to know you'll do the same. Please. Don't leave me again."

She'd hurt him and yet he loved her. Awe swelled in her throat, choking off words. With a nod, her heart in her eyes and love about to burst from her chest, she stepped into the perfect fit of his arms. She clutched him to her, holding to what he offered. Holding to love.

There in the cold mist with dusk descending, surrounded by her broken dreams, new dreams were born.

And for the first time in her life, Abby understood what love really meant.

Epilogue

On a May evening when the purple sage was blooming and spring was scenting the air with green and sunshine, Abby and Lila attended a wedding on the arm of Brady Buchanon. After more than a year of waiting, Jake Hamilton and Allison Buchanon had finally tied the knot.

"They look so in love," Abby murmured to Brady, who sat beside her at the outdoor reception—a barbecue with all the fixings on the grounds of Jake's ranch. Up front, at the reception table, a photographer snapped photos of the happy bride and groom.

Dozens ambled beneath the tent and down to the pond, its grassy green banks mowed to golf-course perfection for this special occasion. The wedding had been intimate, but the reception included half the town.

"I feel weird seeing my little sister married, but it's time. She's loved Jake since she was fourteen."

"That long?"

"When a Buchanon falls," he said, smiling into her eyes, "he sticks."

"Is that a fact?" she asked, flirting with the man she'd come to love and trust with all her heart.

"Mmm-hmm." He nuzzled her ear. "Fact." Below the table he squeezed her hand.

Lila, on her opposite side, gnawed corn on the cob and basked in attention from the adored Buchanon family.

Abby could hardly believe the past six months. Amazingly, with his father's blessing and help, Brady had rebuilt her house. Because of the fire, sympathetic volunteers had turned out en masse, both to help with construction and to replace the lost furniture. Insurance, which she hadn't expected to be significant, covered much of the cost. The arsonist hadn't been caught and security cameras now guarded new construction sites.

After a month in her dream home, she was still rearranging furniture for the fun of it and adding Lila's framed angels to the walls. But the best part of the past months was Brady. She woke up each morning thanking God for this man in her life who accepted and loved her and Lila, faults and all.

"Want to take a walk down by the pond?" he asked, reaching for her empty plate.

"After eating those barbecue ribs I need to walk to Dallas!" she joked. "But this is a good start. Lila, do you want to go with us to the pond."

Across from them, the twins exchanged looks. Sawyer said, "She's still munching corn. You two lovebirds go ahead. We'll keep an eye on the princess."

Brady discarded their plates and, taking her hand, led the way across the green grass. She felt strong and secure with Brady in a way she'd never been before. She was different now. The future didn't scare her anymore. Getting close to others made her stronger, not more vulnerable.

Brady was different, too. He and his father had reached some sort of understanding. They still butted heads but eventually one of them would say, "Block-head." They'd both laugh and walk away.

"The redbuds are gorgeous," she said, admiring the clouds of fuchsia blooms growing wild around the glassy pond.

Frogs plopped into the water with small splashes that spun out in concentric circles. Butterflies dipped and danced among the wildflowers. A dragonfly, iridescent wings green in the sunlight, buzzed overhead.

"Look at us." Brady indicated the water's mirrored reflection. Their shadowy counterparts stood side by side, hands joined. Her head came to his chin.

"We're a fit," she said.

"More than a fit, Abby." He turned toward her, eyes sincere. His voice dropped lower. "No one has ever matched me the way you do."

Her mouth curved. "I feel the same."

"It's beautiful here, isn't it?"

His change of topics puzzled her. She tilted her head. "Gorgeous."

"Do you like it? Really like it?"

She gazed around, smiling. "I love it."

"What about me? You love me, too?"

Her smile disappeared. Her breath caught. "You know I do. With all my being."

"A perfect place. A wedding. Beautiful flowers." Still holding her hand, he slipped to one knee. "The woman I want to spend the rest of my life with."

"Oh." Tears spurted at the back of her eyes. Her heart leaped, banging at her ribs.

"I love you, Abby. You're my other half, the one I've

waited for. Marry me. Today, tomorrow, whenever you say. Just say you will."

"Oh. Oh." Overwhelmed, she couldn't get the words out. Finally, shaking with happiness, she managed, "I will," and fell into his arms.

She didn't care about her heels or the dress or the fact that her knees would be grass stained. All that mattered was the love of her life. She took his face in her shaking hands and stared into those beautiful eyes, eyes that someday their children might share, and when her heart could be no fuller, she kissed him.

A camera flashed. Applause and celebratory whoops broke over the pond. A voice said, "It's about time."

Abby turned in Brady's arms, surprised to find she and Brady were no longer alone. Dan held a bouncing, clapping Lila in his arms. Karen stood at his side with her daughters and sons, Sawyer, Dawson and Quinn stacked next to each other like an offensive line for the Dallas Cowboys. The bride and groom were there, too, grinning, as thrilled for Brady and Abby as for themselves.

"Mama! Bwady!" Lila reached out, wiggling her little hands. Brady swooped her into his arms, holding her between them. Abby's heart swelled with such joy and love, she thought she would burst.

Then Brady touched his forehead to Lila's and said, "What do you think, Princess? Will you be my little girl?"

Lila twisted her pretty mouth in serious thought. "Foreber?"

"Foreber and eber."

A sunny smile broke over the tiny face. She took his

cheeks between her chubby hands and said with a sigh, "I thought you'd never ask."

While everyone laughed, Abby soaked up the beauty of the moment and in her heart agreed with her daughter. She and Lila and Brady, together, a family, the thing she'd been waiting for foreber.

She gazed around at the gathered group, a circle of family. Brady's family…and at long last, Abby's family, too.

* * * * *

HER CHRISTMAS FAMILY WISH

Lois Richer

This book is dedicated to my nephew Drew, who is on the way to discovering his future. God bless you, Drew.

Whatever your hands find to do,
do it with your might.
—*Ecclesiastes* 9:10

Chapter One

"That little boy would be a good brother, wouldn't he, Mommy?"

Wyatt Wright stifled his groan. Not another one. He'd been in this grocery story almost twenty minutes, and he'd put only three things from his list into his basket, thanks to his son's many female admirers. At least, that's how he preferred to think of the women who used Cade to open a conversation with him.

Only this time Cade's fan sounded like a little kid.

"He's a cutie all ri—" A woman's light, cheery voice paused. "Uh-oh."

Intrigued by the way warning overtook her amusement, Wyatt did something he'd vowed not to. He looked directly at the stranger and spoke to her.

"Is something wrong?"

She peered at Cade. "Your son is about to be sick."

Clear gray eyes set in a heart-shaped face met his, empty of the coy look he often saw in the ladies who were—how did he say it without sounding conceited?—looking to make his acquaintance. And yet Wyatt didn't get the impression that he was the attraction here, given the coolly polite smile that lifted this woman's pink lips. Still, he couldn't help but admire her flaxen hair as it tumbled to her shoulders in an attractive disarray of curls. She wore a pale blue sundress, probably in deference to the heat of a late-October evening in Tucson, that flirted around her tanned legs.

Cade was sick? That was an opening gambit he hadn't heard before. Of course she was wrong. Wyatt had been eighteen-month-old Cade's sole parent for over a year. He knew all about—

"Look out!" the pretty stranger warned.

Wyatt turned in time to see his usually grinning boy grimace before spewing a sour mouthful all over his daddy's favorite T-shirt.

"Sorry. I tried to warn you." The slender stranger was quite tall, only a few inches shorter than Wyatt's own six-foot height. She dug into her large shoulder bag, pulled out a packet of wipes and extracted several. "Poor baby. But your tummy feels better now, doesn't it?"

Wyatt blinked twice before realizing her tender tone was for Cade. Gently she wiped the disgusting mess from his son's face and shirtfront, then tucked the used wipes into a plastic bag which she grabbed from a roll at the nearby produce stand. After removing more clean wipes, she reached toward Wyatt. He stepped back just in time to stop her from cleaning him up, too.

"Oh. Sorry." She blushed very prettily, then stuffed the wipes into his hand. "I guess you can do that yourself. Moms get used to cleaning up spills. But I suppose dads do, too, right?"

Entranced by the melodic sound of her light laugh, Wyatt couldn't find his voice. After a minute her smile faded. She shrugged, then bent to look at Cade.

"Hope you feel better, sweet boy." Cade grinned at her, his feet churning. She glanced at Wyatt. "You've got a real charmer here." Then she turned and reached for her daughter's hand. "Come on, Gracie."

Wyatt hid his smile when the little girl planted her feet and stubbornly refused to move.

"This man would make a good daddy for us, Mommy," the blue-eyed sprite mused, her silvery-gold head tilted as she assessed Wyatt.

That was so *not* funny. Wyatt suppressed his overwhelming desire to bolt.

"Then he—" Gracie continued jerking a thumb at Cade "—could be my brother. I'd really like to have a brother," she added, her head tilted to one side thoughtfully. Then she frowned. "'Cept I don't want him to spit on me."

Wyatt cleared his throat, intending to voice a firm yet delicate refusal that would end the child's ludicrous notion real fast, before her mother latched on to it. Instead he got sidetracked by the lady's burst of laughter.

"You used to spit up exactly the same way, Gracie." The mom chuckled when her daughter wrinkled her nose in disgust. "But we don't need a daddy," she said in a firm voice. "We're fine just the way we are, you and me. Don't you like our family?"

Instead of rushing her child away from a touchy subject, as Wyatt had seen other parents do, the mother waited for a response. He admired her serenity and total focus on her child and made a mental note to practice the same kind of patience with Cade when he got older so he'd be the best father a kid could have. He'd do whatever it took to be a better father to his son than his own father had ever been.

"Our family's nice," Gracie agreed. "But I want a daddy. And a brother. Melissa and Courtney have brothers and daddies," she said, her chin thrust up.

"So you've told me, many times." A resigned sigh colored the mother's response. "But I'm sure there are other kids in your kindergarten class who don't. Each family is different, Gracie. One isn't better or worse than another, just different." She smoothed the child's rumpled curls. "We need to get our ice cream now so we can go to Wranglers Ranch."

Wranglers Ranch? That was the place that sponsored camps for troubled kids. Months earlier the owner, Tanner Johns, had left a message on Wyatt's answering machine asking him if he was interested in taking on a full-time vet position there. Wyatt, his hands full caring for Cade, hadn't responded. Though he kept running into Tanner at church, the rancher had never pressed him for a reply, simply offered friendship. Wyatt figured Wranglers' ministry must be growing because of a mention at last week's church service about a youth group outing to the ranch.

"And—" Gracie dragged out the word, giving him and Cade another once-over before blowing out a heartfelt sigh. "Now that Beth and Davy live at Wranglers Ranch, they have a daddy, too. I'm the only one who doesn't."

The pathos in her mournful words reached in and squeezed Wyatt's heart, until he caught the mother's grimace as she rolled her eyes at him.

"Oh, that's not the worst of my shortcomings," she explained with a teasing chuckle. "Last week Gracie was the *only one* in her kindergarten class not allowed to stay up late to watch a TV show." She raised her eyebrows in a pseudo-severe look. "As you must know, single parenthood isn't for the faint of heart." She fluttered her fingers. "We have to go. Bye."

Wyatt nodded bemusedly until her gaze dropped to his shirt.

"You, uh, might want to get that off before it dries," she advised quietly. Then she took Gracie's hand and firmly drew her toward the freezer section.

Wyatt grimaced and used the wad of wipes she'd handed him to clean up the mess as best he could.

"Thanks a lot," he said to his son who was now happily blowing bubbles.

Wyatt quickly gathered the rest of the items on his list and hurried through the checkout determined to avoid another encounter with more of Cade's admirers. But in the parking lot he noticed the same woman buckling her little girl into a car seat. Pure impulse and an innate curiosity he should have suppressed sent Wyatt walking briskly toward them.

"How did you know?" he asked abruptly.

The woman jerked in surprise, bumping her head on the car before she ducked out.

"Ow!" She raised a slim arm to rub the top of her head. "Sorry?" Her eyebrows drew together as she frowned at him.

"How did you know Cade was going to be sick?" Wyatt repeated.

"Years of pediatric nursing and a child of my own," she explained with a shrug. "It's the kind of look I learned to interpret fast and clean up faster." She checked out his shirt. "Good job. Did you feed him something new for lunch?"

"A couple of brussels sprouts," he admitted. "He seemed okay with them."

"Ew! I'm afraid I'd have the same reaction as he did. Not my favorite vegetable." She shrugged at Wyatt's frown. "Well, sorry, but it's not."

"Rounded nutrition is the best thing for kids," he repeated, quoting verbatim from the baby book he used as his parenting mentor.

The woman opened her lips to say something but was interrupted.

"What's that boy's name?" Gracie asked, poking her head forward.

"He's Cade. I'm Wyatt. Wyatt Wright," he said, shocked that he was voluntarily giving his name to a child and her mother—a single woman, to boot. But there was something about this woman that drew him. Because she was attractive? Compelling? Intriguing?

All of the above.

"We're Ellie and Gracie Grant. But I already know who you are, Wyatt." Ellie laughed at his surprise. "I've seen you at church. In fact, you're the current hot topic."

"I am?" He frowned at her. "Why?"

"Mmm." She tapped her forefinger against her lips. "How can I put this delicately? Let's just say there are a lot of single ladies at our church who feel you've been a widower too long, that you need a good woman to help you with this little guy."

Aghast, Wyatt stood frozen as Ellie chucked Cade under the chin. Cade's giggle was Wyatt's favorite sound because it made him feel like he wasn't the awful failure his own father had been.

He wasn't sure how to reply, though he wanted to ask Ellie if she was one of *those* ladies from church. Not that it mattered. Wyatt doubted that even knowing she was would end the zip of electricity curling up his spine.

"Don't worry, Wyatt." That thread of laughter lilted through Ellie's voice. She winked at him. "You're safe with me."

"I am?" Wyatt gulped down a rush of disappointment. Hey! Shouldn't he be feeling relief?

"Yep, very safe." Ellie checked that Gracie was secure, then carefully closed the car door, maybe so her daughter couldn't overhear? "Despite Gracie's comments, I am not on the hunt for a husband. Raising Gracie takes all my focus. I'm not interested in romance," she said airily, though he heard a bit of an edge to the words.

Wyatt didn't have time to ask why a gorgeous woman like her wouldn't want love in her life because she walked around the car and pulled open the front door. She tossed him a funny, almost sad smile, then climbed inside and drove away.

"Well," he said to Cade as he pushed the grocery cart toward his car. "That was interesting. But don't do the sick part again, okay? It makes us both smell bad. Got it?"

Cade crowed his agreement as if he knew that the encounter with that remarkable woman and her daughter had made his daddy's day brighter.

While Wyatt fastened Cade in his seat, then loaded the groceries, his thoughts replayed his interaction with the mother-daughter duo. He'd liked them both, but he especially liked Ellie's forthrightness.

Wait a minute!

"Focus on parenthood," he ordered his wayward brain. "You're a single dad with a veterinarian practice that barely supports you and a ranch that needs tons of work and money."

It's up to you, Wyatt, to use your business to follow in my footsteps and make the Wright name stand out in this town. His father's last words brought the same rush of irritation and burst of inferiority that they had the day Bernard Wright had said them ten years ago.

Wyatt glanced in the mirror at his son.

"Can't focus on that right now, Dad," he muttered as he drove home. "Taryn's gone. I'm the only one Cade has. I have to be here for him." *The way I wasn't there for Taryn.*

A tinder of unforgiveness flamed anew at the memory of his wife's needless death. Yes, the underage teens who hit her were guilty. But so was Wyatt. Taryn shouldn't have been driving that night. Wyatt had promised her that morning that he'd pick up diapers and formula for Cade by lunchtime, but he'd forgotten. Later he'd promised Taryn he'd do it on his way home from a call, but he'd forgotten again. After dinner and another promise that he'd make a run to the grocery store when he'd finished his coffee, he'd fallen asleep with Cade on his chest, failing to remember his promise. So Taryn had let him sleep and gone herself.

His wife had been killed. Because of him.

Familiar guilt gnawed at Wyatt as he pulled into his driveway. He'd made promises he hadn't kept, disappointed his wife and, worse, left her alone day after day to fulfill dreams for the ranch they'd planned to restore together while he pursued the goal of making his veterinary business number one in Tucson. Wyatt had failed his wife miserably.

And why? Because he couldn't forget that deathbed promise to his father. He'd worked eighteen hours a day, taken on every client who called, hoping he could somehow prove himself worthy of the prestigious Wright name. But that time had been stolen from Taryn. Wasn't it silly that even now, alone, a single parent and almost thirty years old, Wyatt still couldn't shed his long-buried need to prove himself worthy of his father's love?

Losing Taryn had taught him one hard lesson. Don't make promises you can't keep. His father had taught him the other. Never make Cade feel he had to earn his daddy's love.

Wyatt carried his now-sleeping child into the house and settled him before retrieving his groceries and storing them. He would still make his father proud; it was just going to take a little longer. Because now Cade came first, before his practice, before the ranch, before the promise to his father, before anything.

Ellie's sweet laugh filled Wyatt's head, and for a moment he wished— No! He ruthlessly pushed her lovely face from his mind and started on the laundry. There was no way he'd let another woman in his life and risk failing her the way he had Taryn.

No way at all.

"He was a nice daddy, wasn't he, Mommy?" Gracie chirped from the backseat. "I liked Cade, too." She paused. Ellie saw her wrinkle her nose. "'Cept when he got sick. That was gross."

"Gross? Where did you hear that?" Ellie asked, one eyebrow raised.

"Melissa. Can I play with the horses at Wranglers Ranch?" Gracie asked in a quick change of topic.

"I don't think so, honey. The horses are probably ready to sleep now." Ellie hoped so, because she was too tired to deal with a wiggling, shrieking Gracie astride a horse.

She drove toward Wranglers Ranch, smiling as she remembered Wranglers' slogan. *You're always welcome here*. She did feel at home there, and she loved her job as camp nurse.

"I thought you wanted to play with Beth and Davy?" she reminded Gracie, lest her daughter get fixated on dreams of horse riding.

"I *do* want to play with them. And invite them to my birthday party." Gracie's forehead furrowed as she fell into thought. "How many days is it until my birthday, Mommy?"

"You'll be six in about three more weeks, right after Thanksgiving." Ellie bit her lip as worry about that birthday party built inside her. "Did you think of something you'd specially like for your birthday, honey?"

After Gracie's birth, Ellie had started a day care to enable her to stay home with her child. But outgoing, curious Gracie now needed more, and so did her mother. So late in the summer Ellie had closed the day care and enrolled Gracie in kindergarten. That's why she'd taken the job at Wranglers Ranch—so she could still be with kids. Ellie loved kids.

Tanner Johns had told her that the government had awarded him a big new contract to work with troubled youth, with one caveat—Wranglers Ranch must have a nurse on the premises when their youth groups attended. Tanner had offered Ellie the job one day after church, and since she was eager to return to the profession she'd originally left to care for her sick sister, Ellie gladly accepted. She'd started working at Wranglers in mid-September and never regretted her choice.

"I already told you what I want for my birthday, 'member?" A glance in the rearview mirror revealed Gracie's arms firmly crossed over her small chest. "I want a daddy."

"Honey, I can't give you a daddy for your birthday. Or at all," Ellie said for what seemed the hundredth time. "I've told you that before."

"But why?" Gracie's bottom lip jutted out.

"Because." Ellie stifled her exasperation. How long would the child keep constantly asking for a father? What was she doing wrong that Gracie wasn't happy with *her*? "Nobody can give daddies for birthdays, sweetheart."

"For Christmas, then? That's far away. That's lots of time to get him," Gracie wheedled.

"I can't get you a daddy for Christmas either," Ellie replied in her firmest voice.

"But I need one!" Gracie burst into tears.

Ellie heaved a sigh, wishing there was some way to meet and marry the perfect man who would give her daughter her dream.

You tried love. Look how that turned out. Gracie would have been left out in the cold.

Gracie sniffed and Ellie winced. Never did she feel more helpless, less capable of being a parent than when her daughter wept.

God? I'm new at this praying stuff. Will You help me? I don't know what to say. I don't want to break Gracie's heart, but I know now that marriage isn't part of Your plan for me.

"Honey, things like daddies and mommies and baby brothers or sisters are up to God." Ellie didn't know how else to put it. "I guess He thinks that we're doing okay together, just the two of us."

"I'm gonna keep praying." Gracie's chin thrust out. "Because we *need* a daddy."

"Gracie, you know I love you very much," Ellie said helplessly, "that I couldn't love you more."

"I know." Gracie watched as they drove through the gates on to Wranglers Ranch. "But I want a daddy to love me, too."

"But, honey—"

"I'm going to ask God to give us Cade and his daddy," Gracie said with resolute firmness.

"You can't!" Aghast, Ellie braked in front of the ranch house a little too hard as she scoured her brain for some way to dissuade Gracie. Only her daughter wasn't listening.

"I can, too, pray, Mommy. I can pray to God for anything. That's what Pastor Jeff said." Gracie's chin thrust out in unyielding determination. "And I'm going to pray for that."

"But—but—" Exasperated, Ellie fell silent. After all, hadn't she taken Gracie to church hoping she'd start learning more about *her Father*? Oh, dear.

"Hey, there's Beth, and she's holding a baby bunny." In a flash Gracie forgot about daddies, snapped off her seat belt and bolted out of the car. She was running across the yard before Ellie could stop her. "When did they come, Beth?" she shouted in her most excited voice. "Can I hold one?"

"You don't look happy." Tanner Johns, her boss, pulled open her car door, waiting until Ellie had climbed out before he asked, "What's the matter?"

"What else? Gracie. She won't give up on getting a father. And now she's found a candidate." Ellie grimaced, though she couldn't deny Gracie's choice was very handsome.

"Who's the chosen guy?" Tanner took the ice cream from her as they strolled to his front door.

"Someone we met at the grocery store tonight. You

probably know him." Ellie preceded Tanner into the house and waited for that speculative glint to appear in her friend Sophie's eyes as Tanner explained the gist of the conversation to his wife.

"Yes, who is Gracie's choice for a daddy?" Sophie asked with a smile as she turned from speaking to their friend Moses.

"Wyatt Wright." Ellie sighed. "Gracie says she's going to pray God will give her Wyatt for a dad and his son, Cade, for her brother."

"We all know Wyatt," Tanner said. "He's the veterinarian I've been hoping would take on Wranglers Ranch as a client. But I get the impression he doesn't feel he can handle our business right now."

"He seems like a great parent, though he missed the signs that Cade was about to be sick." Ellie made a face. "Wyatt fed him brussels sprouts," she told Sophie, who laughed.

"Maybe he's still learning about kids," Tanner defended. "But Wyatt is an expert on horses. The man has a first-rate reputation. About two years ago his practice was the most sought after in Tucson, but then his wife died shortly after Cade was born." He shook his head. "Whenever we talk at church Wyatt's totally focused on being a dad."

Moses was an elderly Native American who'd cared for and nurtured the abused horses that Wranglers Ranch took in and had lived here long before Tanner had taken over. Now he nodded his head in agreement.

"The Double M tried to hire him, too." Moses had a soft spot for anyone who loved horses as much as he did. "Heard Wyatt told them no, said he had to focus on his son and that work came second."

"Nice if you can afford it," Ellie murmured, thinking of her own years when Gracie was a baby and how she'd struggled to manage on her shoestring budget.

"Wyatt's a good-looking man, don't you think, Ellie?" Sophie's gaze trapped her.

"Yes, he's very handsome," Ellie managed to say while her brain mocked her tepid appreciation of that very attractive man. "But I'm not interested."

"Why not? He certainly seems to be the focus of the ladies' groups at church." Sophie scooped the ice cream Ellie had brought onto steaming slices of her fresh peach pie. "Moses, didn't you tell me Lucy Marten asked Wyatt to dinner last week?" She glanced at the old man, one eyebrow arched. "What's the news on that?"

"Heard he turned her down like he does all those females. Anyone can see they're just itching to get their hands on him. Prize catch, a guy like that." Moses grinned as he held out a hand to take his pie. "Thank you, Sophie." He lifted a forkful to his lips, then closed his eyes as he savored the dessert. "Excellent," he proclaimed a moment later. "No wonder we always have kids showing up here to eat. With cooking like this on offer, why wouldn't they?"

"You're very sweet, Moses." When Sophie patted his cheek Ellie could almost hear the crusty old man's gruff demeanor crumble. Then the children arrived and demanded some pie. As they devoured it, Sophie asked Ellie if Gracie could play with her kids, Beth and Davy, for a while longer.

"Yeah, why don't you stay, Ellie?" Tanner offered. He winked. "We can talk about Wyatt some more if you like."

"No need. I told you I'm not interested." Ellie pretended an airiness she didn't feel. "But since it's Friday and there's no school tomorrow, I guess we could stay awhile." She chuckled at Gracie's whoop of excitement as all three kids scampered into Beth's room to play with the amazing dollhouse Tanner had given her last Christmas.

"Hard to believe it will soon be that time again," he marveled with a fond look at Sophie. "What do you want this Christmas?" he asked as her hand slid into his.

"I have everything I want," she murmured.

"Good answer." Tanner leaned over to press a kiss against her cheek. "This has been a wonderful year for Wranglers Ranch and us."

"Your dream that this ranch would be a haven for homeless and needy kids is coming true with every child we reach." Sophie hugged his side. "We're blessed to have such wonderful helpers like Moses and Ellie and all the hands."

"Now if I could just find a way to persuade Wyatt to come on staff," Tanner murmured before he held out his plate for seconds.

Sophie dished up another piece of pie then turned to Ellie. "Maybe you could talk to Wyatt for us, tell him how much we'd love to have him working here on the ranch."

"Me?" Ellie shook her head. "I barely know the man."

"That's easily rectified," Sophie pointed out.

"Don't go there, Sophie," Ellie warned. "I'm glad you and Tanner found each other and that you're happy together. But I learned the hard way that romance isn't for me."

"But—" Sophie stopped when Ellie shook her head.

"I made a bad mistake when I let myself fall in love with Eddie. If I'd known him as well as I thought, I'd have known he'd change after he inherited that money, that he wouldn't want to be saddled with being a father to Gracie." A wiggle of pain still festered inside. "But I didn't really know him because I was too busy thinking that my silly dream of a big, happy family was finally coming true."

"Nothing silly about that dream, girlie," Moses piped up. "God gave us families."

"I know. And I have Gracie. That's enough." She saw Sophie was about to speak and shook her head. "Listen, when I got involved with Eddie I took my focus off parenting Gracie, and she almost paid for it. We were only a few weeks away from getting married when he suggested I put her in boarding school." The memory still made her flinch. "I don't need to repeat my mistakes. God's given me the job of raising my daughter and I'll focus on that. I guess I'm like Wyatt in that way. My child comes first."

Later, as Ellie drove home with Gracie sleeping in the backseat, her brain revived a mental image of Wyatt Wright. He was good-looking, interesting and seemed to be a great parent, but he wasn't for her.

Gracie was just going to have to ask God for something else, because Ellie had no intention of including Wyatt, or his very cute son, in their lives. Her broken engagement had proven that being a single mom had to be her number-one priority. Maybe someday, when Gracie was grown up and on her own, maybe then Ellie could consider a relationship.

Maybe.

But not now.

Chapter Two

"You're making a lot of noise for a kid who's been fed, watered and changed."

In the year since Taryn's death Wyatt had grown comfortable speaking to Cade as if he understood everything. What he doubted he'd ever get used to was the volume of noise a small child could generate.

"You'll give me a bad reputation as a dad," he complained as he drove into Wranglers Ranch.

While Cade, red-faced and bellowing, continued his vocal outrage, Wyatt parked beside the visitors sign and exited the noisy truck with a sigh of relief.

"Nothing wrong with his lungs, is there?" Tanner appeared and held out a hand. "Nice to see you again, Wyatt."

"You, too, Tanner." He shook hands then picked up Cade. "He's in a bad mood because he wouldn't settle for his nap." He offered a soother, but Cade knocked it from his hand.

"Got a temper, too." Tanner laughed as he bent and picked it up.

"I'm sorry about this," he said as Cade launched into

another earsplitting roar. "I did warn you I couldn't get a sitter." Wyatt jiggled the grumpy child in a futile hope that he'd relax and perhaps drift off to sleep. "Maybe you should get another vet."

"Don't want anyone else," Tanner said firmly. "You have the best reputation around these parts when it comes to horses, Wyatt. I want *your* opinion."

"Okay. On what?"

"Two animals I'm considering buying." Tanner winced as Cade amped up his protests. "Come on. We'll take him to Sophie. She'll know what to do."

Wyatt desperately hoped so. He'd been through Cade's overtired days before, and though his son eventually relaxed and fell asleep, the experience always left *him* drained.

But his hopes were dashed when he heard someone say, "I'm sorry, Tanner, but Sophie went shopping. She's catering that barbecue tonight, remember?"

Wyatt turned and saw her. The woman from the grocery store.

Though Ellie smiled as she approached the Wranglers' boss, Wyatt thought her face tensed when her gaze moved to him. "Hello, again," she said in a pleasant tone.

"Hi. Sorry about the racket." He shifted Cade from one hip to the other. "How's Gracie?"

"She's fine. May I take him?" Ellie held out her hands with a smile. "Hello there, little man," she said in that lilting voice he hadn't been able to forget. "What's your issue?"

Cade stopped midscreech to stare at her. Then he grinned and clapped his hands.

"Traitor." The word slipped out without thinking.

Embarrassed, Wyatt caught Ellie's grin. "He missed his nap."

"And he's been taking it out on you." She laughed and nodded. "Been there. Why don't you leave him with me? I'll rock him on the porch for a few minutes, and he'll soon nod off." She studied Cade's now-drooping eyes. "See? I doubt he'll be awake long."

"Maybe," Wyatt said doubtfully. "But that's too much of an imposition. This is your workplace." He held out his hands. "I'll just take him home. Maybe I can make it back another time, if you really want my advice," he said to Tanner.

"Please, leave him. I'd enjoy the break. The morning's been a little monotonous." Ellie winked at Tanner. "No kids have fallen off their horse or skinned a knee, so I've been a bit bored."

"Our guests do not *fall off*," Tanner protested indignantly.

"Sorry. Of course they don't. It's all to do with gravity." Ellie winked at Wyatt. "Seriously, we'll be fine. I'll call Tanner if I need you."

Wyatt hesitated, watching her face soften as she swayed back and forth with Cade. His son's eyes were almost closed, his thumb in his mouth. "You're sure?" he murmured.

"Positive." Ellie began to hum softly while maintaining the same swaying movements. A tiny smile flirted with her lips. "Walk away now," she sing-songed, never losing a beat in her lullaby.

Since Taryn's death Wyatt had trusted his son to only two sitters and then only after a complete vetting by him and Tucson's premier child care agency. Yet somehow he felt utterly confident in Ellie's abilities with Cade.

Maybe it was because he'd seen her with Gracie and knew her to be a loving parent. Or maybe it was the way she so confidently held Cade that he immediately relaxed in her arms.

"You can trust Ellie," Tanner added.

"I know." Wyatt set down the diaper bag he held. "Here's his stuff."

Ellie's gaze met his, a knowing look in her gray eyes. "I promise he'll be all right."

Of course he would. Because, thanks to Ellie, Cade was already sleeping.

"I'll be back in about an hour," he said.

"We'll be here." Ellie's smile lent encouragement as he went on his way.

As it turned out, Wyatt's inspection of Tanner's horses went slowly, thorough as it was.

"These mares appear healthy and well cared for. They should be fine to breed." Wyatt stretched his back, his examination finally complete. "I'll run the blood samples anyway, but I doubt there's an issue." He frowned, noting a larger, older stallion in the paddock beyond. "Him I'm not so sure about. Where'd you get him?"

"He was left here late last night." Tanner's lips tightened. "I'm guessing he's been kept inside a barn or something for a long time, because I'm pretty sure he's got thrush on his feet."

"That's not a common ailment here in the desert." Wyatt climbed the fence and walked closer for a better look, barely aware that Tanner followed. "He seems lame... Did you notice he doesn't flex his foot?" He spoke soothingly while he lifted the horse's leg and probed the tender heel and frog area.

"Yeah, I noticed. Lack of flexing usually means his hooves didn't get cleaned much." Tanner's voice was low and gruff. "Which certainly seems to be the case."

"It's hard to understand cruelty to animals," Wyatt agreed softly. "You're doing the right thing. Keep him in the fresh air, get him to walk around, and watch what happens."

"Can I call you if it doesn't clear up?"

"Of course. Meanwhile, keep his heels trimmed back." Wyatt swept his hand across the horse's flanks after releasing his foot. "He could stand some extra oats, too."

"He's getting them," Tanner said with a nod. "Don't worry, Wyatt. My foreman, Lefty, Moses and I are all keeping a close eye on this guy. He won't suffer at Wranglers."

"You've got some great stock here, the kind I'd like to add to my own ranch someday." Wyatt surveyed the other horses with their shiny coats in the surrounding paddocks. Someday, he promised himself as he closed the gate. Then he wondered if he could keep that promise.

"You're anxious to get back to Cade." Tanner wasn't asking a question.

Wyatt nodded. "I used to be a workaholic, but after Taryn died, I vowed I'd always put Cade first." Self-conscious about revealing that, Wyatt kept his head bent as he cleaned his boots on the grass.

"A good thing for all fathers to remember," Tanner agreed. "But doing your job isn't ignoring Cade. He's not suffering. He's probably still sleeping, in fact. And he's got an amazing caregiver in Ellie. She's really fantastic with kids. She used to have lists of people begging to get their kids into her day care."

"It was nice of her to watch him for me." So Ellie had run a day care. Was that how she'd known Cade was going to be sick that day in the store? "I thought she was a nurse."

"She is. But when Gracie was born, Ellie wanted to stay home with her. So she set up a day care in her house." Tanner made a face. "Believe me, there were a lot of unhappy folks last August when she closed down Fiddlesticks—that was the name of her day care."

"If it was successful, why would she do that?" He had no business asking anything about Wranglers' nurse, but Wyatt was curious.

"Gracie was ready for school. Ellie figured it was a good time to get back to nursing." He grinned. "Sophie and I have been blessed having her here at Wranglers. The kids just adore her. Cade will, too. You'll see."

Privately Wyatt doubted his son would be around Ellie Grant enough to get to that stage, but he simply nodded and kept his opinions to himself, anxious to see how his son had fared.

"He's still asleep," Ellie said meeting them at the patio door. "I've just made some coffee and put a tray out here. Want some?"

"Sounds good. I see Sophie's car. I'll just go see if she needs help," Tanner said. "You two go ahead."

Somewhat self-consciously Wyatt followed Ellie to the table under a lacy mesquite tree where she'd set a plate of cookies, a carafe and three mugs. Cade lay nearby in the shade in a makeshift bed in an old wash-tub, eyes closed, breathing deeply.

"He's still sleeping." Wyatt was somewhat surprised to realize two hours had passed.

"Of course." Ellie smiled, her eyes lighting up as she glanced at the little boy. "He wore himself out yelling, I guess. Gracie used to do that. Drove me bonkers sometimes. She'd get so tired out that she couldn't seem to relax and let sleep come. I was usually so exhausted that when she finally crashed I did, too."

"Except when you had to open your day care," he added. "Tanner said you had a long client list."

"I did. It was fun if exhausting. I was ready for a change. Especially after—" She checked herself as a fleeting frown washed over her face, then regrouped and shrugged. "I was pretty nervous about letting Gracie start school."

"Why?" He sipped the coffee she'd poured.

"Until then I'd been in total control of Gracie's world." Her lips tilted in a wry smile. "The thought of allowing someone else to take over and not be there to see she was all right caused me some sleepless nights."

"So how did you handle it?" he asked.

"With Sophie's help." Ellie grinned. "I'd consulted her about some catering, she led me to the Lord, and she's been mentoring me ever since. She suggested I needed to start trusting that God cares as much and even more about Gracie than I do, so now I'm trying to trust Him. Since I'm a control freak where Gracie's concerned it's not easy, but I'm learning."

"Was Sophie catering something for your day care?" he asked as he selected one of Sophie's homemade cookies from the plate Ellie held out.

"Uh, no." Ellie hesitated. To Wyatt she looked sort of embarrassed. "Something personal, but it turned out that I didn't need her services after all." Her diffidence surprised him.

"She sure has a good reputation as a caterer. Well deserved, judging by these cookies." He savored the lemon flavor. "I've heard about her success all over Tucson." Wyatt glanced around. "Just like I've heard about Tanner's success with this place."

"Sophie's amazing, and Wranglers Ranch is a fantastic ministry. I am so happy to be part of it," Ellie enthused. "And Gracie loves school, so God took care of that worry, too." She studied him, her head tilted to one side. "How do you manage work and Cade?"

"Mostly I don't," Wyatt admitted. "My wife died about a year ago. Since then work has come a distant second."

"I'm sure." She touched his hand fleetingly. "I'm sorry, Wyatt."

"Thanks. Anyway, I'm Cade's only parent now, so I've been trying to be sure I'm there when he needs me." He made a face. "Only thing is, toddlers don't have much downtime. And that makes it hard to build up my veterinarian practice."

"And you must do that—build it up?" Ellie's eyebrows lifted as she waited.

"Yes. It's very important to me." He wasn't going to tell her why, though he could see the question lurking in her eyes. "But it's difficult. Just yesterday I agreed to be at a client's place in the morning, but then Cade bumped his head on the coffee table. After that he wouldn't settle down, so I had to cancel." He made a face. "Doesn't make for a good working relationship with your clients or help your reputation when you have to withdraw from a call."

"No, I don't suppose it does." Ellie frowned. "Couldn't you hire a caregiver to come in?"

"I do sometimes," he said, feeling defensive. "But she wasn't available yesterday morning when I called."

"I can see that would be a problem. What about scheduling specific work hours? You could hire a caregiver from, say, eight to noon. While they watched Cade you could work, knowing you'd be available for him later."

"Actually I did try that once when Cade was younger. It didn't work." Wyatt reconsidered. "Maybe it's time to try it again. Thanks." The agency would be relieved if he had regular hours to offer their nannies instead of always calling at the last minute.

"Now, since I've helped you, would you be willing to help me out?" she asked with a cheeky grin.

"Uh, with what?" he asked. Depending on what she wanted, he might have to refuse her. He wasn't getting involved.

"I had this idea that Wranglers should sponsor a Thanksgiving Day dinner for kids who don't have any place to go." Ellie huffed out a sigh that lifted the spiky bangs across her forehead. "Of course Sophie will do the food, but she and Tanner asked me to set up some kind of decorations and, well..." She made a face. "I'm not exactly artistic. The most art I've ever done is kids' crafts at my day care."

"Why not go with that?" Wyatt shrugged. "Wranglers is a kids' camp, after all."

"How exactly would that work?" Ellie stared at him as if he had all the answers.

And that was so far from the truth that Wyatt wanted to laugh. He had the answers to exactly nothing in his own life. How could he possibly help anyone else?

"Come on, tell me what you were thinking," she pressed.

He tried to vocalize the vision that had fluttered inside his head. "I guess I always associate Thanksgiving with harvest, you know, a time to count your blessings like the Pilgrims did. So maybe bales of hay scattered around, a few pumpkins on top, a sheaf of wheat if you could find anyone to make it—that kind of thing."

"Sounds good," she said with a nod. "And easy. Sophie wants to have an evening meal outside so we'd need lights of some kind. I'd thought candles on the tables, but I suspect that's out because of the fire risk."

"There are lots of solar lanterns available. Or battery lights. You could even put some inside hollowed-out gourds and set those inside tipped-over bushel baskets. I've seen that done before." Wyatt felt silly throwing out these ideas about decorating, especially given the state of his ramshackle ranch. "Or you could string some lights in the trees. Maybe even leave them up for Christmas?"

"I love lights at Christmas." Ellie's eyes sparkled, her excitement obvious. "So, will you help me do it?"

"Uh, no. I mean, I can't. I, er, I'm busy with Cade," he stammered. Though he liked Ellie's enthusiasm, admired the way she threw herself into things, he pulled out the excuse he always used to escape involvement. He wasn't ever getting involved again anyway, so it was better to maintain his distance.

"Cade can sleep here while we work, as well as he can sleep at home." As Ellie called him out her face got a shrewd look. "In exchange for helping me with the decorating I could babysit for you once or twice. Gracie would love that."

This man would make a good daddy for us, Mommy.

Gracie's words reverberated in his head, and he knew he had to get out of this arrangement.

"I appreciate the offer, Ellie, but I don't think it would work." he said quickly and swallowed his coffee in a gulp. "I'd better get going. I've got chores to do at my ranch."

"You have a ranch?" Ellie's face had lost some of its excitement as she rose gracefully and walked with him toward Cade.

"It hardly deserves the term ranch, but I'm working on improving that," Wyatt told her, then grinned. "In my *spare* time."

Ellie smiled back before glancing at Cade. "He'll probably wake soon."

"Which is why I need to get home. He always wakes up hungry." Wyatt gently scooped the sleeping boy into his arms, relishing the baby powder smell of his son and the warm weight of him against his chest. "Thank you, Ellie. I appreciate all your help."

"You're welcome. It was my pleasure." She brushed one fingertip against Cade's cheek. "Bye, sweetie. I hope I see you again soon. You, too," she added, glancing at Wyatt.

He made a noncommittal response, feeling her gaze on him as he hurried to his truck. Funny how much he wanted to stay and enjoy her company. Ellie's warm personality, quick laughter and generous nature chased away the gloom and cares that had weighed him down for so long. Talking to Tanner and then sharing coffee with Ellie had, for a little while, brought Wyatt back into the adult world, a place where he didn't feel quite so incompetent.

As he drove home, Wyatt decided that today's excursion proved that both he and Cade could benefit from more time among others. Right now he only had that on Sunday mornings when he took his son to church. But keeping an eighteen-month-old toddler amused and happy didn't allow much opportunity for Wyatt to hear the sermon, let alone interact with adults later. But at least the Sunday morning outing gave them both a break from their routine.

Maybe Ellie was right. Maybe there was a way Wyatt could manage to get more work done. After all, Cade slept in the afternoons. It was unlikely he'd know if his daddy was there or not, but even if he did, wouldn't Cade benefit from contact with more people? People like Ellie? Wyatt grinned. He had a hunch there wasn't anyone else quite like Ellie.

Wyatt pulled into his yard and carried a wakening Cade into the house, mindful that he was thinking an awful lot about Ellie Grant. Just as well he'd refused to help her with that Thanksgiving thing at Wranglers.

He admired her plucky spirit and generous outlook. But no way could he allow admiration to turn into anything else. Wyatt would not allow a relationship to grow between them. He failed at relationships. Failed his father and failed Taryn.

What he could not do was fail Cade.

The following day, after she'd finished work at Wranglers, Ellie bundled Gracie in the car and drove to Wyatt's ranch. All day she'd vacillated between compunction about invading his personal space when he'd made it clear he wanted nothing more to do with her and a silly female yen to hold Cade again.

Okay, *and* to see his good-looking father. It had been

so nice to just talk to a male friend yesterday, one who wasn't her boss. She hadn't had that since Eddie had been part of her life.

"Hey, cut that out. Wyatt's a nice guy, but he's nothing to you," she reminded herself.

"What did you say, Mommy?" Gracie poked her head out from the book she'd been trying to read. A book about daddies, of course.

"Oh, just talking to myself, honey." Ellie gave herself a stern, though silent lecture about controlling her interest in the vet. Since the day they'd met Wyatt in the grocery store she'd repeatedly told her daughter that he could not be her father.

Well, neither can he be anyone special to you, Ellie Grant. But still, here you are driving onto his ranch on the faintest of pretexts...

"Is this where my new daddy lives?"

Her heart sinking, Ellie began, "Gracie, I've told you—"

"Look! Dogs, Mommy. Lots and lots of dogs." If there was one thing Gracie wanted almost as badly as she wanted a daddy, it was a dog. She clapped her hands in delight as Ellie parked near the house and several animals swarmed around the car, yapping excitedly.

"Don't open your door," she cautioned her daughter. "They might not be friendly. Wait."

When no one appeared, she tapped the horn. A moment later Wyatt poked his head around the corner of a dilapidated structure that might once have been a barn. He waved, disappeared for a moment, then began walking slowly toward them with Cade clinging to one hand, toddling along. As they came nearer, he gathered up the boy and shooed most of the dogs into a pen before shoving in a wooden stick to hold the loosened gate closed. But he left an adult German shepherd and a small puppy out. The shepherd went to lie down under a tree, but the puppy followed on Wyatt's heels to Ellie's car.

"Hey," he said when she rolled down her window. A question feathered across his face, but all he said was, "Welcome."

"Thanks." Seeing Gracie already had the door open and was exiting the car, Ellie followed her. "I'm sure you're busy, so I won't hold you up."

"No, it's good you came. I didn't realize the dogs had gotten out of the pen. That Irish setter is like a Houdini at escaping." He shook his head ruefully. "It's a good thing they're wearing collars for the electric fence."

"I think Gracie's already in love with this little one." Ellie smiled as a whirl of brown puppy raced circles around the little girl's sneakers, to her delight.

"Puppies. Their energy makes me feel old." Wyatt shook his head as the dog continued chasing his tail. "I was about to take a break. Want to join me for coffee?" He shifted Cade, who was sniffing and crying, to his other hip.

"Thank you. Oh, and I'm returning this." She lifted Cade's newly laundered blanket from the rear seat and held it out. "You left it behind yesterday."

He took the blanket, then shot her a confused look. "He has more than one blanket, Ellie. You didn't have to make a special trip. But thank you."

"I thought it might be his special *blankie*. Gracie would bawl for hours whenever hers went missing." Cade yelped and held out his arms to Ellie, jerking to be free of his father's hold. "He remembers me," she said with a chuckle, inordinately pleased. "May I take him?"

"Sure." Wyatt handed over his son, then led the way into his adobe ranch house.

"I see he's got a cold," she said. "They're the worst in little kids, aren't they?"

"Nope. They're the worst for adults. He was up most of last night with a fever." Wyatt shook his head. "He can't seem to settle much, poor little guy." He touched Cade's forehead. "Still cool."

"That's what we want. You have a lovely home." Ellie glanced around, trying not to appear too nosey but surprised at how show-homey it was beginning to look, even though parts were under construction. "The light is spectacular in here."

And everything is so perfectly planned, as if a professional designed this open concept layout.

"Thanks. One of the ladies from church asked to sit Cade last week. That's when I installed those French doors. They make a big difference."

Wyatt tossed his Stetson on a peg by the door, set the coffee brewer going, then glanced at Gracie who had flopped down on the floor and was cuddling the puppy she'd carried inside. "That's Mr. Fudge." He hunkered down beside her to scratch the dog's ears. "He's a chocolate lab."

"I like chocolate lots," Gracie told him. "But I really love dogs, 'specially baby dogs." She bent her head so her face was snuggled against Mr. Fudge's fur. "Mommy, can I have Mr. Fudge for my birthday?"

Ellie blushed as she remembered Gracie's request for a certain birthday gift of a daddy. But as she sat with Cade perched on her knee, her attention was diverted when the boy grabbed her beaded necklace and began chattering to himself in an unknown language. It felt so good to hold him, as right as it had yesterday.

Ellie knew that somehow she would have to rid herself of the yearning to cuddle another baby just as she needed to shed her lifelong dream to cherish a big family. Because it wasn't going to happen. So she tightened her grip on the little boy, determined to enjoy it while she could.

"Can I have this dog, Mommy?" Gracie pleaded. She lifted the squirming bundle in her arms and struggled to her feet, carrying the dog so Ellie could have a closer inspection. "See? Isn't he sweet?"

"He's very sweet, honey." Ellie touched her fingertips to the dog's ear, marveling at the silky skin. Aware of Wyatt's scrutiny she shook her head. "But I'm sorry, we can't get a dog. They don't allow them in the city complex where we live."

It was so hard to refuse her sweet daughter something as simple as a puppy. At Gracie's age Ellie's parents had given her a puppy of her own to cherish. If only…

Thankfully Wyatt intervened.

"I'm sorry, Gracie, but Mr. Fudge belongs to someone else. He's just here for a visit." He touched her bright head as he smiled. "His owners are coming to get him tomorrow morning."

"Well, I'm gonna pray we have to move into a new house so I can get a dog just like Mr. Fudge," Gracie announced. After shooting a stubborn look at Ellie she flopped down onto the floor and continued to play with the pup.

"Here, let me put Cade in his high chair." Wyatt scooped the little boy who'd begun to fuss from her arms.

"Oh, but I can hold—" Ellie's protest died with Wyatt's laughter.

"Believe me, you don't want to hold Cade when he's eating a cookie." He tied a bib around the boy and handed him a treat. "He makes a horrible mess."

I wouldn't mind. Ellie didn't say that. Instead she smiled politely, accepted the cup of coffee and the chocolate cookies he offered.

"All the dogs—your clinic is here at the ranch?" she asked.

"Yes, but mostly I just board animals here and go out to the calls." Wyatt shrugged. "I give shots here, if they're due. It keeps my name out there for prospective clients."

"So, out there, by the barn—" Ellie suddenly caught on. "You were working?"

"Trying to do a few much-needed repairs." Wyatt took two cookies for himself and bit into one. "Today wasn't optimum with Cade feeling off."

"How can you work with him nearby?" she blurted, unable to stop the question.

"I made him a tree swing." Wyatt chuckled when Cade dropped his cookie and began crowing with delight, arms swinging wildly. "Whoops, I said the word s-w-i-n-g. That's one he knows, and he loves riding in it." He held out another biscuit, and Cade soon forgot the topic. "I managed to get the hay changed and the stock fed during his sporadic rides. That's pretty good considering how he's feeling."

"Can I play with Mr. Fudge outside?" Gracie asked.

"Sure." Wyatt led her to the French doors, then glanced at Ellie. "The yard is fenced. Is it okay?"

"Yes, but don't go outside the fence, Gracie." She was

thankful Wyatt didn't open the door until Gracie promised, doubly grateful when he slid the screen across so she could see and hear her daughter.

"I could—" Ellie began, but his phone interrupted her offer.

"Excuse me." Wyatt set down the washcloth he'd been wetting under the kitchen tap and answered the call. "No, that doesn't sound good," he agreed with a frown. He asked a few more questions, obviously about a sick animal, then said, "It could be contagious, but I can't tell for sure without seeing him, and I'm afraid I can't get away right now."

Ellie waved her hand to catch his attention.

"Hang on a moment, will you, Mark?" He put his hand over the receiver, a question on his face. "Yes?"

"Why don't you go do your job? I'll stay with Cade. I had nothing special planned for this evening anyway," she added, then thought how pathetic that sounded.

"I couldn't ask you to do that, Ellie." Wyatt shook his head.

"You're not asking. I'm offering. And I'd really enjoy spending some more time with this little guy." She dabbed Cade's cheek, and he sneezed. Seeing Wyatt's dubious look, she insisted. "Actually I was hoping you'd let us stay long enough to work on Gracie's school project."

"Oh?" he frowned.

"She's got to collect some pinecones for art class. I noticed you have tons scattered along your driveway. We could collect them and take Cade for a walk." She nodded when he just kept looking at her. "Go ahead. Take the call. It sounds serious."

"It could be." Wyatt had an obvious internal debate

with himself, but it was equally obvious that he wanted to go. Finally, he nodded just once, then said into the phone, "Okay, Mark, I'm on my way."

Ellie smiled as he hung up. "Now, where's the stroller?"

"On the porch. You're sure about this?" He paused in the act of reaching for his hat. "You're not just trying to make me feel better or something?"

"Trust me, seeing your lovely ranch does not make me feel pity for you. Jealousy maybe. Look." She pointed outside to her daughter, suddenly a little too aware of the handsome vet standing beside her. Gracie ran around the yard with the puppy following. "I haven't heard her laugh like that for ages."

"Glad I could help." Wyatt slapped on his hat. "She must have her father's eyes," he said when the child looked up.

"No. Gracie has her mother's eyes." Ellie shook her head when he blinked in surprise. "I'll explain later. Go."

"I don't know how long I'll be." His worried gaze rested on Cade.

"We'll be here." She smiled when he looked at her. "I'm a nurse, Wyatt. I *can* take care of him."

"Of course. Thank you, Ellie," he said. He kissed Cade's head, then hurried out the door. A moment later his truck roared and he took off, a plume of red dust following.

"Mommy? Where did Cade's daddy go?" Gracie frowned, the puppy forgotten for the moment.

"Wyatt is a doctor for animals. He went to help them. He'll be back in a little while. Meanwhile, let's put the puppy in the pen and go for a walk to find those pinecones you need for school."

"Is Cade coming?" her daughter asked.

"Of course. Cade likes looking for pinecones," Ellie said as she went to take the child out of his high chair.

"How do you know?" Gracie's head tilted to one side, giving her the look of a curious bird. "Did his daddy tell you?"

"No. It's just one of those things mommies know."

As she picked up the baby and turned, her gaze fell on a huge portrait above the sofa. She walked over to study it.

Wyatt's wedding picture. He looked young and very happy, his dark eyes shining. The woman beside him was petite, her black hair upswept in a chic style. Even in the photo her love was obvious as her gaze locked with her new husband's. She wore a fancy, fluffy gown that looked very expensive. *Taryn & Wyatt* was engraved on a small silver plate along with a date.

Today's date.

Ellie gulped. Why had she come here today of all days, on their wedding anniversary? She was an interloper. Cade began protesting, and she glanced down, suddenly aware that this child was hers, Taryn's. She should be here comforting him, caring for him, sharing him with Wyatt.

"Come on, Gracie," she called suddenly. "Walk time."

Please, help me, Ellie prayed as she walked the children down the tree-covered lane, pausing here and there so Gracie could collect her cones. *I get carried away sometimes by my dream, by wanting what I can't have. Please, help me find a new dream, Your dream.*

Just before the spot where the lane joined the highway, Ellie paused and turned, the ranch spread out before her. It was a home for a family, but it could never be her home or her family. That dream had died the day she'd told her fiancé she would never be separated from her young child.

On that day Ellie had also realized that the dream she'd carried in her heart since childhood, a dream to be a mom to the kind of loving family her parents had given her and her sister, Karen, was just that—a dream. Her parents were gone, Karen was gone. All that was left of the Grant family was Ellie and Gracie.

And that had to be enough.

Chapter Three

Gracie has her mother's eyes.

With his animal patients well on the road to recovery, Wyatt's mind was free to puzzle over Ellie's words as he drove home. Wasn't *Ellie* Gracie's mother?

He pulled into his ranch, surprised by the warm glow he felt at seeing the house lights on as if to welcome him. He stood outside and paused a moment. In the twilight nothing looked amiss, as if this was a well-run hobby ranch instead of a work in progress. Still, Wyatt doubted his father would approve.

Inside the back door he inhaled the savory aroma of simmering beef. His stomach growled in response. Ellie walked toward him, a welcoming smile on her face.

"Hi. How'd things go?"

"Fine. The animal is recovering nicely." He liked the way she'd bundled her silvery curls on the top of her head, leaving her pretty face and wide smile free for him to admire. "Everything okay here?"

"All quiet on the western front," she said. "Cade zonked out a while ago."

"I'll just go check on him." Wyatt washed first, then

entered Cade's room, smiling at the sight of his boy curled up and snoring. His heart squeezed almost painfully tight as he smoothed a hand against Cade's dark head. "I love you, son," he murmured. He drew the blanket tighter, his heart welling with thankfulness that God had entrusted this small being to him. "Sleep well."

"I hope you don't mind that I put Gracie on the bed in your spare room," Ellie said when he returned to the kitchen. "I thought that way we wouldn't disturb her, and you can eat in peace."

"Very thoughtful, thanks. Speaking of eating… What is that tantalizing smell?"

"Oh, just some stew I made from that beef you had in the fridge." She lifted a dish from the oven. "I hope that's okay?"

"Yes, but—it's very kind of you to go to all this trouble." He licked his lips, slightly embarrassed when he realized Ellie was watching him. As her gaze held his he felt the intimacy in the room ramp up.

"I'm guessing you're hungry." Ellie's wide smile brought a sparkle to her gray eyes like sunshine glinting off a granite rock.

"Starving." He took out a plate and Ellie filled it with beef, potatoes and green beans.

"I made some biscuits, too." She set them beside his plate.

"Biscuits?" He licked his lips. "I haven't had those for ages."

"Go ahead and eat. I'll make some tea," she said and immediately set the kettle to boil. "Do you cook?" She sat at the end of the breakfast bar, not far enough to break the friendly feeling but enough to give Wyatt some room.

"Oh, yes. My father was a firm believer that his kid should know how to fend for himself." He scooped up some stew. No way was he going to spoil this meal by talking about his unhappy childhood. But Ellie had other ideas.

"Your mom didn't mind you in her kitchen?" She rose as the kettle boiled.

"I never knew her." He smeared butter on the feathery light biscuits and watched it melt before taking a bite. "These are fantastic. Everything is. Thank you."

"I'm glad you're enjoying it." Ellie put the teapot and two cups on the counter. "Tanner told me your father was a well-known lawyer."

Which meant they'd been talking about him. Wyatt didn't like that, but he didn't have time to dwell on it because Ellie was speaking again.

"You never had any desire to follow in his footsteps?"

"None. My first love has always been animals." No point in elaborating or discussing the many reasons why he hoped he'd never become like his father.

"I saw how much you care for animals."

Her comment shocked him. He stared at her, thinking that the flush of color on her cheeks suited her.

"I was walking Cade the other day when I saw you with that abused horse at Wranglers," she mumbled, her head tilted down. After a moment she looked directly at him. "He was filthy and mangy, and yet you touched him so gently, as if he was the most precious animal. You're a wonderful vet."

"Well, I try," he sputtered, a little surprised by the fervor of her words. Uncomfortable with her praise, he changed the subject. "Does that mean my son didn't settle as easily as you claimed?"

"He was restless, needed some fresh air." She shrugged. "He was fine."

"I see. Well, thank you for that. And for babysitting tonight and for supper."

"Oh." A furrow formed on her wide forehead as she moved to the fridge and pulled out a bowl. "I almost forgot. Rice pudding?"

"My favorite." Wyatt spooned some onto his almost clean plate, slightly unnerved by how intimate it suddenly seemed in the dim room with two sleeping children next door. How was he going to let her know he wasn't interested in getting better acquainted? Although if he was honest with himself, he *was* curious about Ellie Grant.

He ate the pudding. "Delicious."

"Good." He saw her gaze swivel to focus on his wedding portrait. "Your wife was a very beautiful woman. Was she also a veterinarian?"

"Taryn?" Wyatt laughed as he scooped out a second helping of the pudding. "She was an interior designer. We were polar opposites. I'm country and she's—she was," he corrected automatically, "definitely city. The ranch was going to be our compromise. Only—" He bent his head.

"I'm so sorry for your loss, Wyatt." Somehow the generous compassion in Ellie's soft voice soothed his lingering hurt. "May I ask how she died?"

"A bunch of kids were joyriding and broadsided her car. The driver was underage and shouldn't even have been behind the wheel." As it always did, anger flared toward the teen. "He claimed it wasn't his fault, but it was." Wyatt stared at his hands, guilt welling inside. "It was also my fault."

Irritated that he hadn't yet found relief from the guilt of that awful day, Wyatt rose and loaded the dishwasher. He was fully aware that Ellie was watching every move with her all-seeing eyes, waiting. There was nothing else to do but explain. He poured two cups of tea and passed one to her.

"Taryn was out that night because of me. She should have been here, at home, with Cade. Instead she was running my errands." He stopped to clear the rasp from his throat. "My son will spend every Christmas without his mother because I didn't keep my promise." He didn't want to talk about the past anymore, so he turned the tables. "Why did you say Gracie has her mother's eyes?"

"Because she does." Ellie sipped her tea nonchalantly. She must have realized he didn't understand, because she suddenly set the cup down and smiled. "Sorry. I forget sometimes that people don't know our history. Biologically Gracie is my niece. My sister, Karen, was her mother. She died after Gracie was born and I adopted her a bit later."

So Ellie, too, carried pain. Wyatt sat down on a stool to listen, curious about the arrangement.

"Karen was married to Kurt. She was four months pregnant when he was killed in an accident at work. Kurt was in construction. He was on the job site one day trying to secure everything in a windstorm when a structure collapsed and killed him." Ellie sighed, her eyes tear-filled. "It was so hard for Karen to go on, but the pregnancy gave her courage. Then one day she phoned me in Chicago. She'd just found out she had brain cancer, and she'd decided to refuse all treatment in order to keep Gracie safe. I flew down to be with her. She died three months after Gracie's birth."

"Ellie, I'm so sorry." Wyatt reached out to touch her hand where it lay on the counter.

"So am I." Ellie glanced at his hand, then eased hers away. "Karen would have made an amazing mother. I'm just her stand-in. I promised her I'd do my best to be Gracie's mom but—" She shook her head as tears rolled down her cheeks. "I think I'm failing."

"How can you say that?" Uncomfortable with her tears but hearing the worry in her tone, he tried to reassure her. "Gracie's a great kid. I think you've done amazingly well with her."

"Then why isn't it enough? Why does she keep searching for a father?" Ellie asked, her voice breaking. "I love her so much. I've tried to give her everything she needs, but I can't give her a father!" She dashed away her tears, the gray irises darkening to slate. "There is no man in my life."

"Because?"

"Because that's the way it has to be." Ellie's cheeks bore dots of hot pink. "I was engaged, but that ended and I realized that God doesn't want me to have a romantic relationship. He wants me to focus on being Gracie's mom."

"Maybe it was the breakup with your fiancé that triggered Gracie's sudden interest in finding a daddy?" Wyatt privately thought her ex-fiancé must be an idiot to have let this woman go. "Maybe her hopes were dashed because she thought she was going to have a father like the other kids, and then she didn't get him."

"I don't think that's it," Ellie said slowly. "Because looking back, I realize Gracie never called Eddie Daddy. She always called him by name. When I explained we weren't getting married, she seemed okay with it. And she hasn't seemed upset about it since then. She was very excited about starting school. That's all she talked about."

"Well, maybe Eddie gave Gracie a sense of, I don't know, security? Maybe his male perspective is something she needs?" he said. "Is there someone else in your life who could take his place as a father figure?"

"But that's what I'm saying. Eddie wasn't a father figure in Gracie's world," Ellie protested.

"Maybe he was, and you didn't realize it." But even as he said it Wyatt found it hard to believe that Ellie could have missed something so important to her daughter. He'd seen just how caring and protective of Gracie she was. "Maybe there's someone you could ask to act as a male role model for her?"

"No." Ellie's voice was firm and unhesitating. "Tanner and Pastor Jeff are the only influential males in her life right now, and their lives are full with their own kids."

"Well, I'm no psychologist but…" Wyatt felt uncomfortable giving advice, but clearly Ellie wanted his opinion, and after all she'd done for him tonight, he could hardly throw up his hands and give up. "My guess is Gracie wants a closer bond with a man. Why? Maybe to show him off to her new school friends, maybe to have him take an interest in her that others haven't, or maybe she wants someone special that she can confide in."

"Why can't she confide in me?" Ellie said with a belligerent glare. "I am her mother."

"Did you tell your mother everything? Weren't there some times when you wanted to share with someone else?" In his own life Wyatt had never shared his hopes and dreams with his father. He'd often wished he could, but knowing he'd be mocked had kept him silent.

"What does a little girl of five have to confide?" she asked.

"I have no clue." Wyatt felt like he was digging his way out of a quagmire. "But maybe Gracie thinks you wouldn't understand or that you'd try to dissuade her if she bared her heart. Or maybe she just needs perspective from another person."

"Which means I'm not enough." She looked so desolate that Wyatt hurried to reassure her.

"It doesn't mean that at all. It just means that she's growing up, expanding her world." He was speaking off the cuff, praying he said the right thing, because he had no clue how little girls' minds worked. "I don't think this is about you, Ellie. It's about her."

"But what do I do? She prays every night for God to give her a daddy. And now that she's met Cade, she's added a brother to her Christmas list." Ellie threw up her hands. "I can't make her understand," she wailed. "Sophie keeps telling me to pray about it and I am, but I'm not getting an answer and I need one because I don't know what I'm supposed to do."

"'If any man lack wisdom, let him ask of God.'" Wyatt shrugged. "I read that this morning. I guess you have to keep on God's case, asking Him to show you how to proceed."

"I guess." Ellie sighed. "Gracie's going to be heartbroken when a daddy doesn't appear at Christmas."

"Maybe I could talk to her a little, sound her out on what's behind her request." Wait a minute! What was he doing? He didn't want to get involved.

"I don't know if that's a good idea, Wyatt, though I

thank you." Ellie nibbled on her lower lip. "Gracie's already fixated on you as the daddy of her dreams. Maybe you'd only make it worse, make her believe you really are moving into her life."

"I'd make sure she understands that I'm her friend, but I can't be her daddy." Wyatt had a lot more to say on the subject, including a warning to Ellie not to get the wrong impression about his offer. But he couldn't say it because the phone rang. "It's after hours. Let the machine pick up," he said when Ellie glanced from the phone to him.

"Wyatt, this is Jim Harder at the Triple T. I've been trying to reach you for days. You promised you'd do those inoculations this week, and I'm still waiting. I can't run a ranch like this. Call me tonight with a time to get it done in the next two days, or I'm looking for somebody else. I'd rather have you, but your hours are too erratic. I need a vet who gets here."

In the dead quiet of the room Wyatt stared at the answering machine, ashamed that Ellie had heard but frustrated because he knew he was about to lose his most understanding client. Cade was sick. How could Wyatt have left him with some nanny and walked away? But he also needed the work the Triple T offered. They had the biggest herd around. The income from that call alone could pay off some of Wyatt's bills.

"What are you going to do?" Ellie whispered.

"I don't know." He raked a hand through his hair, trying to come up with a plan. "I guess I could do the inoculations in bunches. It would take me a few days, but I could do it. But Cade's sick with this cold—" He shook his head. "I just don't know."

She studied him for several moments, saying nothing, dealing with her own private thoughts.

"We both need to pray for wisdom, I guess," she sighed after a few moments had passed. "Right now I have to get Gracie home. Thanks for letting me cry on your shoulder, Wyatt."

"I thought it was the other way around." He followed her into the bedroom, watching as she lifted a sleeping Gracie into her arms.

"She's too heavy for you," he said. "Let me take her." He didn't wait for Ellie's permission but instead scooped Gracie from her arms into his, smiling when the child's eyes fluttered open.

"Hi, Daddy," she murmured, then fell back asleep.

Wyatt met Ellie's gaze without saying anything. He followed Ellie out to her car and set Gracie in her car seat, then drew back so Ellie could fasten the seat belt, his mind working furiously.

"Listen," he blurted when she emerged from the car and had closed the door. "I have an idea. What if I spend some time with Gracie, just to clear up this daddy notion of hers?"

"In exchange for what?" Ellie's eyes searched his face.

"For you watching Cade for a few hours."

The look on her face told him she was about to reject his idea, so he rushed on. "I'll arrange for a nanny to come every morning as you suggested and handle office calls then. But I have to spend time working my ranch. If you could watch Cade for a couple of hours in the evening, I could get a lot done. Then maybe I'd be able to see more clients here."

"But the evenings, before bedtime, those are special daddy moments you shouldn't miss with Cade," she protested.

"Something has to give, Ellie." He hated admitting that. "I have to work *and* keep up our home."

"I know." She glanced down at Gracie, then back to him. Her lips tightened as if she wrestled with a decision, then she nodded. "What if I come over after I finish work at Wranglers Ranch? Gracie's finished school by then. We could stay with Cade, maybe make dinner, and then you'd be free to bathe him and put him to bed. Would that work?"

"It would." Wyatt slowly nodded while every brain cell in his head screamed a warning.

"I have just one condition," Ellie added, her voice deadly serious.

"Name it." Then he'd tell her his condition.

"You have to agree that this is simply an arrangement between friends and nothing more. I'm not looking for a father for Gracie or a relationship for myself. I need you to be clear on that, Wyatt. Strictly friends."

"Agreed," he said with a nod, relief swelling. "I don't want any romantic entanglements either. I want help with Cade, and I promise to do my best to help Gracie." He grinned at her and thrust out his hand. "Deal, *friend*?"

Ellie took her time but finally she shook hands with him. "Deal, friend."

Wyatt stood there, in the dimness of twilight, holding her soft hand, staring into her lovely face, and wondered if he was making a mistake.

"I have to go." Ellie pulled her hand free and got into her car. She started it, then rolled down the window. "Beginning tomorrow?"

"Sounds good. We'll be here." He waved as she drove

away until the twinkle of her red taillights had disappeared. Then he walked inside his house and checked on Cade.

Satisfied his son was sleeping peacefully Wyatt returned to the living room and let his gaze rest on his wedding photo. The same old lump of bitterness toward the youth who had caused Taryn's death burned inside his gut. If not for that kid his wife would be here and Wyatt's world would be fine.

Only it wasn't fine because he'd kept breaking his promises.

"That's not going to happen again," he told her, his shoulders going back. "I'm focusing on Cade first. Everything else comes second. I promi—"

Wyatt stopped himself from saying it. No more promises. Turning away he lifted a sleeping Mr. Fudge from his recliner and, after a quick trip outside, locked him in the laundry room to stay safe overnight.

As he walked past the kitchen to his office to work on his accounts, Wyatt caught a whiff of Ellie's spicy fragrance. He sat down at his desk thinking of her. She was a focused, determined woman, and she cared deeply for her daughter. She would be an amazing caregiver for Cade, and Wyatt was certain she had no designs on him.

But what was he going to do about Gracie and her "daddy" quest?

Chapter Four

Wyatt's ranch was gorgeous.

While Gracie played with Cade in the sandbox, Ellie gazed at the ever changing horizon, mesmerized by the rosy hues of the November sunset above the craggy mountain peaks. For three evenings she'd watched this view and it was never the same.

Immersed in the display, she jumped when Wyatt asked, "Looking for something?"

"If I was, I found it. You have the most glorious sunset view I've ever seen." She tried to ignore the flutter of nerves his presence always brought.

"I do have that." He stood beside her, watching as the golden sun sank from view. "God's handiwork is pretty amazing."

"It is," she agreed, then snapped out of her daydream. "Are you finished already?" She checked her watch, surprised to find she'd been out here more than half an hour.

"I doubt I'll ever be finished on this place," Wyatt admitted in a dry tone. "But I'm finished for tonight." He lifted one shoulder and winced.

"Are you overdoing it?" Ellie asked as she shepherded the kids inside.

"No. I've just grown weak and out of shape since Cade came along." He grinned as he swung the boy in his arms and carried him inside to the bathroom. "Cleanup time. You, too, Gracie," he called over one shoulder.

"I'm coming." Gracie obediently trotted along behind him.

"And don't cheap out on the soap either," Wyatt warned. "I'm going to smell your hands when you're finished, and I only want to smell soap."

"Did your mommy used to smell your hands?"

Uh-oh. In the kitchen, Ellie froze at her daughter's question and the sudden silence that ensued.

"Supper's ready," she called, hoping to end Gracie's inquisitiveness and relieve Wyatt from the necessity of answering. To her surprise the three emerged with big grins. "What happened?" she asked in confusion.

"Cade splashed water all over the floor. We nearly floated away," Wyatt said as he set his son in his high chair. "And, no, Gracie. My mom didn't tell me that. Actually I didn't have a mom while I was growing up."

While Ellie set the serving dishes on the table she tried to decipher Wyatt's tone. She saw no distress on his handsome face.

"You didn't have a mom?" Gracie's eyes showed her shock. "How come? Did she die?"

"I don't know." Cade frowned as he fiddled with his cutlery. "Maybe. My father would never discuss her."

"So you didn't have a real fam'ly neither." Gracie frowned. "Just like me."

"Gracie, our family is real," Ellie began.

But Wyatt interrupted. "You and your mom are a family, Gracie. A very nice one, too." He smiled at her. "You don't know how blessed you are to have such a wonderful mommy."

"Yes, but—"

"Time to say grace," Ellie interrupted before her daughter got started on what was becoming her *daddy* theme song. "Hands together." She tucked her chin into her neck to hide her smile when Cade clasped his chubby hands together and closed his eyes.

"Thank You, God, for food, friends and family," Wyatt said. "Bless the hands that made this meal. Amen."

"Amen." When Ellie lifted her head she found him studying her in a curious way. She touched her fingers to her hair thinking she must have forgotten to comb it. "What are you staring at?" she asked, discomfited by his attention.

"You. Thank you very much for your help." Wyatt accepted the bowl she handed him, but his gaze returned to her. "I don't know how I'd have achieved so much without your help. I've got the kennels fully finished and the runs completely fenced now. Finally."

"That should help your business."

"It should," he agreed as he served Cade and Gracie. "But what I really want is to take in injured wild animals, treat them and give them a place to heal."

"Like Beth's rabbits?" Gracie asked with a full mouth. Catching her mother's warning look she gulped before continuing. "My teacher told us about some zoo animals that escaped. Are you gonna get lions here?"

"No lions." Wyatt chuckled. "I'm not sure what kind of animals I'll get, Gracie. So far that's just a dream."

"You have dreams?" she asked, surprised.

"Everybody has dreams, kiddo. Things we want to do or see or places we want to go, maybe people we want to meet. Even me." He smiled at her and took a bite of his food.

"I want you to be my daddy. That's my dream."

Ellie wanted to groan. How could she deal with this? Nothing, not discouragement, explanations nor anything she'd tried so far, had worked.

"Gracie, honey, you are a very sweet girl," Wyatt said softly. "But I don't think I can be your daddy." He laid down his utensils so his complete focus was on her.

"You hafta. I've been praying so hard." Gracie frowned.

"I know you have. And I know God hears you. But sometimes God can't give us what we pray for, even though we really, really want it."

"Why not?" Gracie's bottom lip thrust out, and her face scrunched up in a frown.

Ellie waited for Wyatt to explain, content for now, to leave this to him. After all, that was their bargain, wasn't it?

"Because sometimes what we want isn't good for us," Wyatt said.

"Huh?" Gracie was clearly puzzled.

"Well, think of it this way. God is a father, right? Our Father."

"Yeah." Gracie nodded.

"I'm a father, too. I'm Cade's father." He shot his son such a proud look that Ellie caught her breath at the love shining in his eyes.

"When he gets a little older and starts asking me for

things, do you think I should give him everything he asks for?"

"I dunno," Gracie replied. But Ellie could see that Wyatt's message was getting through as her daughter suddenly concentrated on her meal.

"Sure you do." Wyatt handed Cade half a roll. "If he asked for something to eat, do you think I'd give him that?"

"Yes." Gracie nodded without hesitation.

"What if Cade asked me for candy?" Wyatt said next.

"Candy tastes good. Cade likes choc'lat." Gracie grinned at the little boy. "Me, too."

"So it'd be okay if I gave Cade chocolate every time he asked for it?" Now Wyatt nonchalantly chewed on his salad.

Ellie wanted to cheer at his strategy. First her daughter nodded vigorously, then paused.

"Maybe not every time," Gracie said finally.

"But why not? You said Cade likes chocolate, and eating it makes him happy. I sure want my boy to be happy."

"He'll get sick." Gracie made a face. "I ate too much candy at Melissa's birthday, and I got a tummy ache. It hurt a lot."

"And I don't want Cade to get sick. I sure don't want him to hurt." Wyatt paused and held her gaze to make sure she heard him. "So sometimes when Cade asks me for candy I will have to say no. Because that's what's best for him, and as his daddy, I always want what's best for my child. Because I love him. Right, Gracie?"

Ellie's glance met Wyatt's. He smiled encouragement, but she couldn't return his smile. This was too important. Gracie *had* to understand that he was not going to be her father. That no one was.

"So even if Cade keeps asking me over and over, I can't give him what he wants." Wyatt's tone was so tender as he added, "Because I love him."

"But I didn't ask God for candy," Gracie protested. "I want a daddy. You."

"I know, honey. But it works the very same way." Wyatt leaned in so he could look directly into her eyes. "Getting you a daddy—that's up to God. God's your Father, and He loves you very much. If He wants you to have a daddy, then when He's ready, He'll make it happen. But *you* can't make it happen, Gracie."

Ellie held her breath, waiting to see how Gracie accepted this. Her daughter went on eating, and Ellie wondered if she'd finally give up her daddy quest.

Then Gracie looked up at Wyatt. "You mean I shouldn't pray for a daddy. But my Sunday school teacher said we should always tell God what we want."

"You should always pray, Gracie." Wyatt's face was very serious. "Even if your mom can't give you every single thing you ask for, you talk to her about other things, don't you?"

"Yeah." Gracie nodded.

"Well, that's how it is with God. We tell Him all about what's in our hearts, and He listens because He loves us." Wyatt lifted his gaze to Ellie as if asking her what else he could say.

Ellie scrambled for something to add, but Gracie preempted her.

"Pastor Jeff was talking at church one time about a woman in the Bible who kept asking Jesus to make her better even after He didn't do it right away." She focused on Wyatt with intensity. "Pastor Jeff said Jesus healed her, and maybe it was 'cause He just wanted her to stop asking. So that's what I'm gonna do. I'm gonna keep asking God for you for my daddy."

Ellie sagged in her seat. She'd been so sure—

"Maybe He'll do it just to stop me askin'," she said thoughtfully and finished the food left on her plate. "Are we havin' dessert?"

Aware that Wyatt had pushed away his unfinished plate after a resigned sigh, Ellie rose and served dishes of pecan pie.

"I bought it from a roadside market on the way over here. I hope they make a good pie," she said.

"They certainly do," Wyatt said after he'd tasted a bite. "Thank you very much, Ellie. I haven't had pie in a long time."

"I have ice cream for Cade," she said. A moment later she handed the little boy a cone which he grabbed and bit into. A surprised look filled his face as the cold hit, then he squealed, laughed and took another bite.

"I guess that means he likes it." Wyatt grinned at her, and for the life of her Ellie couldn't stop herself from grinning back at him like some kind of coconspirator. But wasn't that exactly what they were?

"I guess it's back to washing hands and faces," Wyatt said when everyone had finished their dessert. "Come on, Gracie, you, too. You can't get in your mom's car looking like that."

"Why not?" she asked as she followed him to clean up.

"What if a policeman stopped you?" Wyatt's booming laugh filled the house. "He'd have to give your mom a ticket for having a daughter with such a grubby face."

He was so good with Gracie that it was a shame he couldn't be— No!

Ellie stopped that thought dead in the water. That was ridiculous. She didn't want any romantic entanglements. She had all she could do working at Wranglers, babysitting Cade and caring for Gracie.

But as Wyatt waved her off and she drove home, Ellie couldn't help the silly little picture that filled her mind of a family having a picnic around Wyatt's big fire pit.

"Not your family," she chided her wayward brain.

"Are you talking to yourself again, Mommy?" Gracie asked.

"I guess so."

"If you're talking to you, who am I gonna talk to?" Gracie crossed her arms over her chest with a sigh. "I guess I hafta talk to God some more about gettin' me my daddy."

"Me, too," Ellie agreed gloomily under her breath.

She'd also have to talk to Wyatt again. Because nice as his try was, it hadn't deterred Gracie in the least.

Wyatt wasn't exactly sure what a pre-Thanksgiving-evening get-together at Wranglers Ranch included, but he'd come because Tanner had asked him to and because he wanted the company. Somehow he'd never imagined there would be people rushing around the place like whirling dervishes.

He walked with his son at his side to where Ellie was balancing on a stump, holding up a rope for Tanner who had climbed a eucalyptus tree and was clinging to it with one arm stretched out, trying to reach the rope to tie it on the branch.

"What's going on?" Wyatt asked, then glanced down when something tugged his pant leg.

"We're helpin' Mommy get ready for the giving

thanks day decoratin'." Gracie lifted a paper pumpkin for him to admire. "Can you please hang this up, Daddy?"

"Gracie Grant," her mother warned, cheeks flushed bright pink as she teetered on her perch. "We've talked about this. You may call him Wyatt or Mr. Wright. You may not call him Daddy."

"But he is going to be—"

"Not another word or you'll be having a time-out while everyone else celebrates tomorrow." Ellie glared at her daughter until Gracie sighed and nodded. Ellie's smile reappeared. "Good. And it's called Thanksgiving."

"But that's what I said, isn't it?" Gracie looked so confused Wyatt's heart melted.

"It's a really nice pumpkin," he said to cheer her up.

Her face came alive. "Thank you, Da—Mr.—um, thanks."

"Hand me your pumpkin, honey." Ellie sent Wyatt a warning look that made him stifle his amusement. "Tanner will hang it up for you." Once hung, the orange ball fluttered in the breeze. "Doesn't it look nice up there?"

"Yup." Gracie dashed off to find Beth.

"See why I'm no good at decorating? I did not know pumpkins hung from trees," Wyatt said, tongue in cheek. Cade flopped onto his bottom to play with his ball, so he held out a hand. "Get down from there, Ellie. Tanner and I will take care of the rest of the hanging."

"It's only a little stump," Ellie protested, clasping his hand for support as she descended.

"Who'd be left to treat the sick and injured if the nurse got hurt?" Wyatt thought how perfectly her hand fit in his, until she pulled it away.

"I was fine, you know." She scooped Cade from the

ground and pressed a kiss against his cheek. "But I won't argue if it means I get to hold this little guy."

Wyatt spent the next hour following her decorating directions, and he didn't mind helping one bit because Ellie made everything fun. He hauled bales and arranged them to Ellie's specifications. Moses brought a bunch of old lanterns, buckets and other antiques, and under Ellie's supervision Wyatt set up displays. That turned into a fiasco so Ellie took over. Then Sophie produced six boxes of tiny white twinkle lights which Wyatt and Tanner strung above the patio.

When the last table centerpiece of pinecones, cinnamon sticks and battery-operated candles were in place Tanner called a halt.

"That's enough. Remember, we'll have to take it all down tomorrow," he groaned, rubbing his back.

"Not the lights. They can stay until after Christmas." Ellie's smile made Wyatt feel like he was a part of the Wranglers' group. "Thank you, everyone. I think the kids will love it."

"Time for a snack," Sophie called. They all gathered around the outdoor kitchen to enjoy mugs of cocoa and fudge brownies.

"Your reputation is well deserved," Wyatt praised Sophie when he took his third treat. "These are delicious."

"Oh, I didn't make those. Ellie did." Sophie grinned at her friend. "And I agree. I'm thinking of offering her a second job as baker for my catering business."

"Maybe you could teach me to make them," he said to Ellie.

"Sure. They're simple. It's my sister Karen's recipe. She was a chocoholic." For a moment a shadow passed over her eyes, then she brightened and tickled

Cade under the chin. "Did you get any in your mouth?" she teased, wiping his chocolate-covered cheeks with a napkin.

"I did." Gracie grinned, showing brown-stained teeth. "Can me and Beth take some to the rabbits?"

Four adults all said "No!" at the same time.

Wyatt squatted down to Gracie's level. "Chocolate is very bad for the rabbits' tummies, Gracie. It makes them really sick."

"Dogs, too?" she asked with a frown glancing at Sophie and Tanner's dog. One hand poked out from behind her back. On her palm lay a mashed square of brownie. "I was gonna give this to Sheba."

"Dogs, too," he said with a firm nod.

"Oh." Gracie looked at the mashed dessert for a moment, then dumped it into his hand. "Okay." She bounded away, calling Beth and Davy to come play catch.

"Oh, dear." Ellie's eyes twinkled with amusement. She giggled at the face Wyatt made when he couldn't dislodge the sticky mess into a napkin. "Since you have to go inside to wash, you might as well take Cade." She lifted the boy and handed him over to Wyatt.

"What? No wipes to clean us up?" he teased, enjoying the way her face suffused with color.

"I don't have my bag handy," she said, glaring at him. "And you'd better get going before he plasters your shirt with chocolate."

"More laundry." With a sigh Wyatt headed inside for wash-up duty.

When he emerged the entire group was gathered around the glowing fire pit on the patio. Only the twinkle lights and the flickering flames provided light on the patio, just enough for Wyatt to see an empty space beside Ellie. He took it and cuddled an already dozing Cade on his knee, warmed by the sweet smile she gave him when he brushed against her shoulder.

That was the thing about Ellie. She always made you feel better, and it didn't have a thing to do with her nursing skills. She simply radiated warmth and inclusion, and she went overboard trying to make sure no one was left out. Hence the surfeit of decorations, an exuberant, over-the-top gesture meant purely to give joy to kids who'd visit the ranch for Thanksgiving.

"We always have stories around the campfire," Beth explained to Gracie. "What's the story tonight?" she asked Tanner.

"It's about giving thanks," he said and began. "A very long time ago there were ten lepers. Leprosy is a very bad disease," he explained to the children. "It's painful and it's contagious."

"That means other people could get it from them," Ellie interjected, then shrugged when Wyatt grinned at her. "I can't help it. I'm a nurse. I like medical clarity."

Tanner grinned at her, then paused until he had everyone's attention again. "So the people who had leprosy had to stay away from everyone, even their families, so they didn't pass it on to others." Tanner's voice was low, and the kids had to lean in to hear. "Whenever the lepers walked past, someone would yell 'Unclean,' so that everyone would step out of the way, so that they didn't catch it, too."

"What a lonely way to live." Ellie's murmur was so low Wyatt doubted anyone else heard. "The pain of leprosy would be as bad as losing your loved ones."

Wyatt knew from the emotion in her voice that she'd gone through those hard lonely times herself after her sister's death. Maybe she still was. Was that why Ellie worked so hard at everything she took on? Because she was trying to stay busy? Just as he was?

"So when these ten lepers heard about Jesus healing people, they decided they wanted to see Him. They didn't have medicine, so there was no other way for them to get well." Tanner spoke slowly, ensuring the enraptured children hung on every word. "So they asked Jesus to heal them. And He did."

"He made them all better. That was good," Beth said.

"Yes, it was." Tanner's smile lingered on his adopted daughter a moment before his voice dropped to a serious note. "There was just one thing wrong. Only one of the lepers came back to say thank you. Only one out of ten that Jesus made better." Tanner let them think about that for a minute. "That's why Thanksgiving Day is so important. Because it reminds us to be thankful for what God has given us. What are you thankful for?"

"Skateboards," Davy called out.

"Bunnies," was Beth's answer.

And so it went around the group. Until it came to Wyatt. He looked down at Cade, sleeping peacefully in his arms. Too often he forgot to count his blessings.

"Him," he whispered through the lump in his throat. He lifted his head and glanced around. "And all of you."

"That's what I'm thankful for, too," Ellie said softly. "Gracie, Wranglers Ranch and friends. You've all made a tremendous difference in my life this past year."

The only person who hadn't spoken was Gracie. Wyatt thought she'd fallen asleep until Tanner asked, "What are you thankful for, Gracie?"

"I can't say it." She peeked through her lashes at her mother, then quickly looked away.

"Sure you can. Tell us, sweetheart," Ellie encouraged.

Wyatt didn't think she'd answer. Then all at once Gracie inhaled and spoke, a hint of defiance in her voice.

"I'm thankful that God is going to give me my daddy, even if you don't think so," she said with a glare at her mother. Then, bursting into tears, she jumped up and ran into the darkness.

"Gracie!" Ellie rose, but noting the tight angry look in her eyes Wyatt decided to intervene.

"Here." He shifted Cade into her arms. "Let me go. I'll talk to her."

"But I'm her mother—" When Ellie hesitated Wyatt touched her arm.

"You're upset and so is she. Let me go." He leaned forward to whisper in her ear. "That's our deal, right? For me to help her with this fixation."

The sweet scent of jasmine filled his nostrils. In a flash that fragrance of Ellie's perfume started a video in his brain of a hundred different images of her caring for others. Now it was his turn to help her.

"Please?" he murmured. Her gaze met his, flames flickering in their depths until finally she nodded.

"Just be—"

"I'll be very gentle with her," he promised and squeezed her hand.

"I know you will. It's just—she's all I have." She squeezed back, smiled, then released his fingers.

Wyatt walked away, knowing he had to do his best. For Ellie. Because she always did her best for others. So he found Gracie, in the bunny pen of course, and let her cry on his shoulder as she poured out her deepest desire.

"I want you for my daddy," she wailed through her

tears. Hearing the longing in her words was like having her little hand reach in and squeeze his heart.

Wyatt had no idea how to help her, so he simply held her while he silently prayed for wisdom. When she'd finally calmed down, he took a deep breath and began to speak.

"Gracie, sweetie, hush and listen to me now." She sniffed and rubbed her eyes but paid attention. "Your mom and I have tried to tell you that I can't be your daddy. But you won't stop thinking about it all the time. It's like you have a sore on your finger, and you won't let it heal. That's what is hurting you. I think you need to forget about having a daddy, for a little while."

"But—"

Wyatt put a finger across her lips and shook his head. Finally, Gracie slumped, signaling her willingness to listen. In the gentlest words possible he used every argument he could come up with, short of telling her he had no intention of taking on the care and upbringing of another child.

He hoped he'd finally convinced her to let go of him as her daddy. In fact, he was certain he had because he asked her three times if she understood, and each time Gracie nodded soberly.

"Okay, then. Good." Wyatt wondered why he didn't feel relief that she wouldn't be counting on him anymore, but he brushed away the wayward thought and hugged her as Ellie called her daughter's name. "We're coming," he replied, then turned back to Gracie. "Is everything good with us?"

"Uh-huh." She swung his hand as they walked over the path. "I heard what you said."

"And?" He saw Ellie coming but wanted Gracie's

compliance before her mother arrived. "What do you think?"

"I think God can do lots of things, 'specially things adults don't believe." She let go of his hand and smiled. "You don't have to worry. God *is* gonna make you my daddy. I just gotta wait." Then she skipped past her mother and onto the patio where she announced, "I'm thankful God answers my prayers."

Ellie glared at him.

"What on earth did you say to my daughter, Wyatt?" she demanded in a whisper. "I don't want her believing that you are going to be her father."

"Neither do I," he sputtered indignantly. "I tried to tell her that, but she just won't listen." Then the funny side of it hit him, and he burst out laughing. "You have to admire her faith, though. It's a lot stronger than mine."

"That's your response to this...catastrophe?" Ellie handed him Cade, her eyes steely as she stood under the twinkle lights. "I'm not sure this agreement of ours is working out, not if it's adding to Gracie's hope that we are somehow going to become a family."

He sobered immediately. "What are you saying, Ellie?"

"I'm saying that I don't think I should come over and stay with Cade anymore." She gazed mournfully at his sleeping child, then sighed. "I'm sorry."

Stunned by the loss he felt at just the thought of not seeing Ellie each afternoon, Wyatt reeled.

"I have to do what's best for Gracie," Ellie said. "She's my primary concern."

"Of course, but—" Wyatt touched her arm. "I don't think you not caring for Cade is going to change her mind, Ellie. In fact, I think the only way to dissuade her is to prove to her that we are friends, but that we're *only* friends. When she sees there's nothing more, she'll give up."

"Are you sure?" she asked dubiously.

Wyatt wasn't sure at all. But the past few weeks Ellie had been coming to his ranch had been some of the best he'd had in the past year. He felt happier knowing he was accomplishing some of his postponed goals, practicing his vocation, all the while knowing Cade was in good hands. Lately, thanks to Ellie, both of the Wright men were happier. Wyatt had even managed to brood less about Ted, the boy who'd killed Taryn.

"Don't you like caring for Cade?" he asked, appealing to her motherly side.

"You know I do. But Gracie—" She frowned, watching as her daughter and Beth played hopscotch on the patio.

"I have an idea about Gracie," he said. "Something that just might change her mind about having me for a father."

"What is it?"

"Wait and see." Cade shifted, and Wyatt checked his watch. "I better get home. See you tomorrow."

As he walked away Ellie called his name.

Wyatt paused, turned and studied her face.

"Don't hurt her," she begged.

"Letting go of her dream might hurt Gracie for a little while, Ellie." How lovely she looked in the cascade of light from overhead. "But I promise I won't deliberately do anything to harm her." *Promise? Another promise?*

"Okay." After a very long pause she nodded. "Partner."

Wyatt left, wondering as he drove home why he suddenly felt disheartened. He certainly didn't want more than friendship with Ellie.

Or did he?

Chapter Five

"Ellie Grant, you're like a cat on a hot tin roof." Sophie edged around her to set down a pan of rolls fresh from the oven. "Waiting for Wyatt?" she asked, tongue in cheek.

"Sort of." Ellie blushed at the insinuation on her friend's face. "Not like that. I've told you before that I'm not interested in a romantic relationship."

"Yes, you did *say* that." Sophie slid two more pans into the oven. "But whenever Wyatt's around, you light up like a Christmas tree." She frowned. "Speaking of which, I wanted to ask Tanner to get that big spruce by the entry gates decorated before our dinner today."

"Sophie." Ellie snapped her fingers to get her friend's attention. "Wyatt and I are not having a romantic relationship. We're simply helping with each other's children."

"Right." Sophie tried to hide her smile, but Ellie saw it nonetheless.

"It's true," she insisted, ignoring the curious looks of Sophie's two helpers. "But I am anxious to see him today because he said last night that he has a plan to get Gracie to change her mind about him as her father. I want to know what his plan is."

"Of course. And that's why you keep checking the clock every ten seconds." Sophie chuckled. "Well, check no more, my friend. I believe that's his truck rumbling into view."

"Really?" Ellie raced to the window and peered outside. "He's here?"

"Yup. I can sure see how it's all about Gracie." Sophie's amused grin stretched from ear to ear. "Now, scoot! Go talk to him, so we can get some work done in here," she ordered.

"Yes, ma'am." Ellie scooted out the door and across the yard, feeling like a giddy schoolgirl as she waited for Wyatt to park his truck. "Hi," she said when he stepped down.

"Hi, yourself." His lazy smile did funny things to her stomach where butterflies were already dancing a jig. "How's it going?"

"Well, since I was just shooed out of the kitchen I thought I'd let Cade entertain me." She had to move, to break free of this odd rush of nerves, so she walked around the truck to the other side and released the little boy from his car seat. "Hey, you," she said, loving the way he reached for her.

"Is there something I should help with before the kids arrive?" Wyatt grabbed Cade's bag from the truck.

"I'm not sure. But be warned that if you go into the kitchen, Sophie's going to ask you to decorate that big tree by the gate." She laughed when he panned a look of terror. "It wouldn't be that bad."

"We all know how useless I am at decorating. We hardly need more proof after last night."

"Let's just say that you're better at pretty much anything to do with animals." She tried to hide her amusement but couldn't at the memory of him arranging gourds and pumpkins that would not stay put. "You have to admit it was funny how they kept rolling all over."

"Hilarious." He leaned back on the fence rail to study her. "You look pretty. Relaxed, ready to handle whatever crops up."

"Well, thank you." She felt inordinately pleased by the compliment. "What could crop up?"

"I have no idea." He winked. "That's what scares me."

"Let's go find Tanner and see what he'd like us to help with." More disturbed by this man than she wanted to admit to herself, Ellie headed toward the tack room with Cade walking beside her.

"Where's Gracie?" Wyatt ambled on her other side, his Stetson pushed to the back of his head.

"With Beth and the bunnies, of course." She wanted to contain her curiosity, but the question had been bugging her all night. "What's your plan, Wyatt?"

"Watch." He shot her a grin, then moved nearer the bunny pen and peered inside. "Hey, girls," he called. "How're those baby bunnies doing?"

"Good. Want to come see them?" Beth called. Gracie remained silent, watching.

"Sure." Wyatt wore a poker face as he looked at Ellie. "You may want to go back to the house or busy yourself with something else. I have work to do here." He took Cade and handed her his bag. "And this guy's going to help me."

"But—" She stared at him, unable to believe he was asking her to leave.

"See you later, Ellie," Wyatt said loudly, waving before he opened the gate and went inside the rabbit pen.

Frustrated that she wasn't to be included, Ellie considered going to check her supplies.

Only she couldn't leave. So instead she found a spot by the side of an outbuilding where she could surreptitiously watch Wyatt, Gracie and Cade without being seen. Beth left when Tanner called her away, so Ellie leaned in, trying to hear what Wyatt was saying to her daughter; but she was unable to catch it because of the noise of arriving guests. Minutes later Wyatt was leading Gracie and Cade out of the paddock, so apparently their "talk" was over. Not wanting to be caught, Ellie took her time returning to the house.

"Where've you been?" Wyatt asked when she stepped onto the patio. He looked hot and tired and more frustrated than she'd ever seen him.

"Is something wrong? Where's Gracie?" Ellie didn't like the look of the red spots in his cheeks or the way his eyes narrowed to mere slits. "Wyatt, is there something I should know?"

"Not really. Oh, wait. There is one little thing," he said sarcastically. "Your daughter is now telling every single kid at Wranglers Ranch that I've been showing her how to babysit Cade so that when we get married—" He shook his head in disgust, then dragged a hand through his hair.

"When we what?" She could only gape at him.

"When we get *married* so I can be her *daddy*, and after we *have more kids*," he enunciated clearly and precisely, "then she'll be able to look after them. Because that's what *big sisters do*." His groan sounded heartfelt. "How could a plan go so wrong?"

Words failed Ellie. The only thing she could do was sit down.

And pray he was joking.

For the first time all day Wyatt finally relaxed. With a little help here and there, the animals on Wranglers Ranch had survived an afternoon among tons of kids. He'd done his job. Now, seated beside Ellie with Gracie on her far side, at a table laden with delicious food, surrounded by laughing, happy kids, he exhaled the frustrations of the day and closed his eyes as Tanner said grace.

"Father, we thank You for Your blessings to us, for health, for friends and most of all for sending Your son to be our Savior. We can never repay the debt we owe You. All we can say is thank You. So thank You, Father. Amen."

Friends. Was that what he'd been missing since Taryn's death? People who cheered you and supported you. *And forgave you.*

"Rolls?" Ellie handed him the basket without meeting his gaze.

"Thanks." Wyatt took two and passed on the rest. And so it went. Ellie passed him the potatoes, the gravy, the stuffing and the turkey, all without comment. Apparently she wasn't yet over her anger. "I didn't do it on purpose," he finally whispered in her ear, liking the feel of the silken strands against his skin. "It just didn't go right, that's all."

"Really?" He'd never realized gray eyes could look so glacial. *"It didn't go right?"* Her voice brimmed with mockery.

"Ellie, I—"

She turned her shoulder and began speaking to the

boy across the table from her, her face suddenly bright and animated, though her body language screamed anger.

"Fine. I'll talk to you." Frustrated, he turned to his son, but Cade's interest was captured by a young girl who tickled and teased him as she helped him eat his dinner. Wyatt had never felt so alone among so many people.

Every time he looked at Ellie, she made an excuse to leave the table. She laughed, she joked, and she constantly smiled—at everyone but him. As Wyatt fed Cade the last bite of his pumpkin pie, he decided it was time to go home.

"Can you take a look at something before you go?" Tanner asked when he'd thanked his host.

"If you need me to." Wyatt wished he'd used the confusion of clearing the tables and kids departing to leave. He felt discouraged and defeated, and he did not want to run into Gracie or her mother again.

"Let's leave Cade with Ellie," Tanner suggested, but Wyatt balked.

"She's busy," he refused quickly. "I'd rather take him along."

"Okay." Tanner gave him a long look, then led the way toward the east paddock where several mares were grazing. "See the chestnut mare over there?"

"It's pretty dark out here, Tanner." Wyatt squinted, trying to figure out what was so important. "And I'm too far away to tell much anyway. It would be better if I come back tomorrow to examine her."

"Oh, I don't think you need to worry about her. I just wanted to show her off." A funny little smile tipped the side of his mouth. "She's pregnant. And so are we."

"We?" It took a moment for Wyatt to get it. "You mean you and Sophie? Wow. Congratulations." He held out his hand and shook Tanner's. "That's great, man."

"Yeah, it is. I can hardly wait to see my son or daughter." Tanner's face shone in the moonlight. "That mare's just one more reason why I'd like to have you at Wranglers full-time, Wyatt. So you could watch her progress, not just check on her now and then."

"I can't, Tanner. I'd like to, but I'm not ready to give up on trying to build my practice," Wyatt refused. "Not yet anyway."

"It's not going well?" The rancher led him to an old wrought-iron bench, and they sat together on it. Thankfully, Cade had fallen asleep in his arms.

"I thought I was making progress, thanks to Ellie helping out with Cade." Wyatt pressed his lips together. "Her being there really made a difference. I could get things done, spend a little longer on a call if I had to without worrying about Cade."

"So, what's the problem?" Tanner frowned.

"Gracie." Wyatt wasn't exactly sure where to begin, so he just spilled his guts. "I had this idea that if Gracie knew that it isn't all a bed of roses to have a little brother, then maybe she'd rethink this idea of me being her father."

"You thought you could talk Gracie out of her daddy goal?" Tanner huffed a laugh, then apologized. "Sorry. It's just that the strength of that child's faith in God answering her prayers often makes me feel like a wimp."

"I know the feeling." Wyatt sighed. "Anyway I messed up."

"I heard a rumor that you and Ellie are getting married and having kids." Tanner was trying not to laugh.

"Obviously, Gracie didn't quite get my point," Wyatt mumbled, utterly embarrassed. "And Ellie's really mad. She isn't going to come out to my place anymore. She thinks that might help get Gracie's mind off—uh, me."

"You think she's right?" Tanner studied Wyatt's face, then nodded. "Me, neither. That little girl isn't going to let go of her dream so easily." He paused before softly asking, "You don't want to make that sweet child's deepest longing come true?"

"No." Wyatt glared at Tanner. "My wife's dead because I didn't keep my promise to her. Now I have a kid to raise on my own. That's all I can handle, Tanner. I'm sure not making any more promises that I'll end up breaking. Besides, Ellie and I are just—"

He didn't finish that sentence, because it wasn't true anymore. He was pretty sure they weren't friends any longer.

"Ellie will come around. You'll see," Tanner insisted. "She's just frustrated at not being able to control Gracie."

"She can join the club." Wyatt rose. "I need to get this guy home. Thanks a lot for the party. It was fun."

"I'm sorry we had to put you to work, but I sure am grateful you spotted Abigail's lame leg. That splint you put on her should help." Tanner walked with him toward his truck, waited while he buckled Cade into his seat. "If you need help, call me, Wyatt. And send me a bill for today. You deserve to be paid for all your help."

"It was no trouble, and I did get two pieces of pie." He shook hands with the chuckling rancher then drove away.

Just before he turned the corner he saw Ellie standing beside the big tree she'd said Sophie wanted to have decorated before Christmas. She didn't wave. In fact, she made no indication that she'd even noticed him. But

Wyatt knew she had. Just as he always noticed when she was near.

Maybe it's better if she stays away. Maybe I'm getting too interested in her and Gracie.

Wyatt figured the next little while was going to be lonely until he got used to not seeing Ellie's smiling face every day. He'd have to pray harder that God would send him someone to help with Cade because one thing hadn't changed. He still hadn't fulfilled the promise to his father to make his veterinary practice the best in the city.

Thing was, Wyatt wasn't sure he even wanted to.

Ellie stood in the little log cabin that now served as her nursing station, unabashedly listening to Tanner talking on his phone outside.

"I'm going over to Wyatt's, Sophie. I haven't seen him for two days, and he doesn't answer his phone. I'm wondering if something's wrong. He was pretty down when he left Thanksgiving night."

The words caused a rush of shame so intense that she missed the rest of the conversation. She desperately regretted her chilly attitude to Wyatt that night. He'd only been trying to help her, after all. It was just that she'd been so utterly embarrassed by Gracie's declarations and certain they wouldn't have happened if he hadn't caused it.

Totally unfair. She realized that now. Gracie was going to believe what Gracie believed until someone other than her mother or Wyatt proved her wrong. But it was hard to eat crow, to apologize to him and take back her words about watching Cade.

She stepped outside the door and hailed Tanner.

"I heard you say you're on your way to Wyatt's. If

there's anything I can do, will you let me know?" She saw her boss's eyebrow arch in surprise, but he simply nodded. "Thanks."

She watched him drive away, a prayer in her heart for the man she couldn't get out of her mind. She'd treated Wyatt shabbily. He'd no doubt been just as embarrassed as she.

"I goofed, God," she mumbled as she dusted the office while waiting for Gracie to arrive on the bus. "And I should have known better. I'm not *that* new a Christian."

Gracie's appearance and jubilant explanation about her day at school took center stage, and for a few moments Ellie forgot to worry. Until her phone rang and Tanner said, "Ellie, can you get over here right away? Wyatt and Cade are both sick as dogs. I need you to check them out while I see to his stock."

"On my way." She ushered Gracie into her car seat as she explained where they were going.

Once they were at the Wright house, Cade's wails demanded her attention. So did Wyatt. He sat on a kitchen chair, haggard, pale and disheveled.

"Thanks for coming," he rasped. "I don't know what's wrong with him. Since I can't seem to stand without getting dizzy I'm scared to pick him up."

"Why didn't you call me?" she reprimanded, then closed her lips. She knew why. "Let's take his temperature." Ellie did a quick check of the little boy, then said, "I think it's the flu, but I want a doctor to see him. You need to see one, too."

"I don't think I can make it to a doctor's office," Wyatt mumbled. "I feel really weak."

"You have to. They won't attend to Cade without you present." She found a soda cracker and gave it to Cade to chew on while she felt Wyatt's forehead. "You're burning up. What have you taken?"

"Nothing. I wanted to be here for Cade." He looked so miserable she stifled her reprimand that he wasn't much use to his son in this condition.

"We're going to the doctor," she said firmly and made a quick phone call to a doctor she knew who would see them immediately. "Gracie, you come and sit in the car with Cade. Then I'll come and help Wyatt."

"I don't need help—" He tried to rise and flopped back down in his chair.

"Of course you don't." Ellie phoned Tanner and asked him to leave the stock he was tending and come help her. She switched Cade's car seat into her car and buckled both him and Gracie in. By then Tanner was escorting Wyatt out of the house and into her car. "We'll be fine," she assured him. "But can you be here when we get back?"

"Of course." He waved them off.

Ellie drove as quickly as she could with Cade's screams filling the car.

"Sorry," Wyatt muttered before he nodded off. By the look of him it was the first sleep he'd had in a while.

At the doctor's office a passerby helped Wyatt inside. Half an hour later they were on their way back to Wyatt's, medication in hand.

"I'm sorry." His dark eyes looked directly at her, lines of tiredness fanning out around them. "You shouldn't have had to rescue us."

"Don't be silly. Now relax. When we get home, you'll take two of those pills and go to bed," she ordered. "Gracie and I will look after Cade."

"There aren't many groceries," he muttered weakly. "And I—"

"Wyatt?"

"Yes?"

"Let me handle it." Ellie pulled into his yard and turned to look at him. "Okay?"

"Like I have a choice?" A grin flirted with his mouth before Tanner appeared to help him into the house.

"Okay, Gracie, it's time for us to get to work." Ellie carried Cade inside and, after setting some soup to warm, gave him a bath with Gracie's help. Her daughter's tender ministrations to the unhappy child touched Ellie's heart. "You'd make a great nurse, sweetheart."

"I don't want to be a nurse. I want to be a mish'nary." Gracie hummed as she showed Cade how his rubber duck could swim.

"You'll be a success at that, too," Ellie murmured. Once Cade was dressed again, she fed him a little of the soup and the medicine he'd been prescribed to settle his stomach. Then, sitting on Wyatt's porch, she rocked the little boy to sleep with Gracie nearby, playing in the sandbox as the sun slid under the horizon. "Good night, little one," she whispered, placing a kiss on his forehead.

"He's out?" Tanner stood in the doorway watching.

"For now. His fever seems to be down a bit. I think he'll rest." She carried Cade to his room and tucked him in, then returned to ask, "How's Wyatt?"

"Fussing about all the things he should be doing." Tanner frowned. "He doesn't look good."

"The doctor said he let himself get dehydrated. He needs fluids, but I didn't see much juice in the cabinets. Can you pick up some groceries?" she asked.

"Sure. Got a list?" A few minutes later he was gone.

Ellie made up a tray for Wyatt in case he was hungry. She knocked on his door, but he didn't answer. She listened closely and thought she heard him muttering, so she peeked inside. He lay sprawled on the bed in his clothes, thrashing his head from side to side.

"His fault, not just mine," he groaned. "Ted shouldn't have been driving. He killed her. He killed Taryn. He has to pay, just like I do."

"It's okay, Wyatt," she said softly. "Everything is fine." She touched his shoulder gently, hoping to draw him out of the dream. "You're fine."

"No." He grabbed her hand and held on, his face ragged with misery, his delirium obvious. "He must be punished," he rasped.

"Leave it with God, Wyatt. It's not your burden, it's His. Forget about it now." She didn't understand exactly what was wrong but because he didn't relax she tried another approach. "Taryn's safe now. She's okay. Ted can't hurt her."

"He did, though. He should pay. God knows he should pay. I have. I've paid dearly." He kept repeating that over and over until he finally fell asleep.

Ellie tiptoed out of the room and returned to the kitchen, her mind whirling with questions. At the top of the list: How was Wyatt to blame for his wife's death?

Chapter Six

Wyatt wasn't sure what day it was or why he was still in bed when the sun was shining. All he knew was that he had to make sure Cade was all right.

But when he tried to get up, his legs wouldn't support him, and he collapsed back on his mattress.

"Everything's fine, Wyatt. Relax."

"Ellie?" He tried to clear his raspy hoarse throat, watching as she walked from the doorway toward him. "What are you doing here?"

"Looking after you and Cade. He's fine, by the way." She smiled as she set a tray on his nightstand. "Do you feel like something to eat?"

"I'm starved. And I want a cup of coffee," he said, then frowned as a thousand questions filled his head. "Why do I need looking after?"

"You don't remember getting sick?" She waited for him to think about it, then said, "Tanner found you and Cade sick with the flu. We took you to the doctor. That was four days ago."

"Four days?" He stared at her. "I've got to get up. My stock—"

"—are fine thanks to Tanner and some folks from the church." Ellie snapped the covers around him in the crisp efficient way nurses did. "You're weak. Why don't you just relax for a bit, see if you can handle some toast and tea, then we'll talk about you getting up. Okay?"

She gave him a *strictly business* smile. Wyatt didn't like it nearly as well as the smile she always lavished on Cade.

"But I've got things to do," he protested.

"Yes, like care for your son." Ellie stared straight at him. "And you can't do that if you aren't well. Correct?"

"Fine." He reached for a piece of toast. "But I am getting up today."

"You'll have to," she shot back. "Because you're getting crumbs in that bed." The door swished closed behind her.

Wyatt chewed on the toast thoughtfully. Four days? Was that why lifting a bit of bread felt like he was hoisting a calf for branding? He managed to eat a portion, but chewing wore him out. Every single muscle in his body ached as if a bull had gored him. He leaned back against the headboard and sipped his tea. Things must be bad if he was drinking tea—and liking it.

He must have dozed off but wasn't sure how much time had passed when Ellie returned. She raised an eyebrow at the toast he'd left but lifted the tray without saying anything.

"Can I see Cade? Please?" he asked.

"Yes, of course. You must be worried about him. I'll bring him in but not for long because he's fighting his own bug. Though he is much better today." She left and returned moments later, holding Cade by the hand.

"Dada."

The sound was music to Wyatt's ears. Ellie chuckled when the little boy crowed with delight and tried to scramble onto the bed. Wyatt dearly wanted to pull his son into his arms but figured he'd embarrass himself if he tried to lift Cade.

Ellie must have noticed, because she scooped up Cade and plopped him down beside Wyatt.

"There's your daddy." The loving tenderness of her voice surprised him by its intensity. Wyatt figured he'd have to think about it later. For now, he cuddled his son next to him.

"I love you, Cade."

"You two have a little visit. I have some chores to do. Call if you need me," she said, then hurried out the door.

He was surprised by her hasty exit. Had he done something wrong? Then Cade tugged on his shirt sleeve, and Wyatt forgot everything but the joy this little boy had brought to his life.

"How are you doing?" Ellie peeked around the door a while later. "Need a break?"

"No. He's asleep. We're good." Wyatt waited until her gaze lifted to him. "Thank you, Ellie. For everything. I don't know how I'd have managed without your help."

"God would have sent someone," she said with a shrug. "He doesn't abandon His children."

"How's Gracie?" he asked, even as he wondered if that was a safe subject.

"Mad at me." Ellie sighed, then inclined her head toward Cade. "Enjoy every moment of this stage," she advised.

"Because of the terrible twos you mean?" He saw weariness around her eyes and wished he wasn't part of the cause.

"They're nothing compared to the trying sixes. Call when you need me." She chucked Cade on the cheek, then left.

Six? Gracie must have had a birthday. But what kind of a party could she have had with her mom stuck here watching him and Cade? Wyatt figured he'd have some making up to do with the little girl once he got vertical again.

All he could do now was snuggle a sleepy Cade by his side and do exactly as his nurse had instructed.

He could learn a lot from Ellie, Wyatt decided before sleep took over.

"When do I get to have my birthday party, Mommy?"

Same old question, same old answer.

"I don't know, honey. Soon." Ellie felt bad, but she'd been so busy taking care of Cade and Wyatt that there hadn't been time for a party. She set a plate of freshly baked cookies and a glass of milk on the counter. "Cade's having an after-school gingerbread man cookie. Want one?"

"Cade doesn't go to school." Gracie hooted with laughter. "I do." She wiggled on to the kitchen stool and, after much deliberation, picked up a cookie. "Do I have to wait till Christmas for my birthday party?" she complained in a grumpy tone. "Teacher said Christmas is only three weeks away."

"Would it be so bad to have a Christmas birthday?" Ellie asked.

"Well, me and Jesus would have a birthday on the same day." Gracie mused. Then her frown reappeared. "But I wouldn't get as many presents."

"Is that what Christmas and birthdays are about?" Ellie resisted the urge to lecture Gracie. She wanted her to figure out the meaning of Christmas on her own. "Gifts?"

"No." Gracie crunched on her cookie. "But they're very important."

"I see." Ellie continued icing the gingerbread cookies, surprised that Gracie didn't offer to help. Clearly her daughter was seriously contemplating the subject.

"Don't you like getting gifts, Mommy?" Gracie asked after she'd crunched her way through the cookie's arms and legs. "I think you do, because you laughed and smiled that time when Eddie took you for a birthday supper and gave you that big book."

"That wasn't because he gave me a gift, sweetie." Since Gracie had never spoken much about Eddie, Ellie's radar zipped to high alert. "I was happy because he did something special just for me. It meant a lot to me because I cared about him."

"And now you don't?" Those big blue eyes riveted on her, waiting for an answer.

While she considered her reply, Ellie lifted two sheets of golden cookies from the oven and set them to cool.

Making her mother's gingerbread cookies was a childhood Christmas tradition both Ellie and Karen had treasured. She would carry on the same tradition with Gracie again this year at their home, but these cookies were for Wyatt. Ellie wanted to make his Christmas more enjoyable, though she didn't want to think about why that seemed so important.

"You can tell me why you and Eddie never got married." Gracie propped her head on her palms and sighed. "I'm not a baby like Cade, Mommy."

"Yes, I know." Babies were so much easier to deal with. "Uh, Eddie is still my friend, Gracie, but in a different way. I couldn't marry him."

Gracie reached for another cookie. "Last one," she promised, correctly reading the look on her mother's puckered brow. "But *why* couldn't you marry him?"

"Because I realized I didn't love him enough." *Not enough to put you in a boarding school.* As if traveling the world could compare with raising Gracie. "I told you all this," she reminded her daughter.

"No, Mommy." Grace shook her head, her icing-covered face solemn. "You only said we weren't gonna be a fam'ly." She finished her milk. "I wanted to ask why, but you were so sad so I didn't." She climbed off the stool. "But now you're happier," she said before she headed for the bathroom to wash up.

Ellie tried to puzzle out what Gracie meant.

"Is she right? Are you happier now?" Wyatt leaned against the doorjamb, his face pale.

"Come and sit down before you fall down." Ellie was prepared to rush over to lend a shoulder, but Wyatt made it on his own. His hair was damp. "You took a shower?"

"I needed one. Don't fuss." He picked up a cookie and took a bite.

"A nurse does not *fuss*," she said in a stern tone. "And a cookie is hardly the first thing you should be putting in your empty stomach."

"I'd put coffee in there if you made some. Please?" He grinned at her. "And you're dodging my question."

"Which was?" She avoided his scrutiny by turning to the coffeemaker.

"Are you happier now?" Wyatt wiped off his son's face and hands and lifted him down from his high chair. "Now that you're not with this Eddie person anymore?"

"Wyatt, that's kind of personal." Ellie tried to regain her composure while she poured a cup of coffee and set it in front of him.

"You've seen me at my worst. Cared for my sick kid. What's a little more personal stuff between friends?"

"Uh—" Ellie looked around for a way to escape.

"I think Mommy would be more happier if she put me in the wooden school." Gracie came in and flopped on to the floor to play blocks with Cade.

Aghast, Ellie stared at her daughter. She'd been so careful, trying to ensure Gracie would never know she'd been the reason for the breakup with Eddie. Well, part of the reason.

"Wooden school?" Wyatt's gaze shifted from Gracie to Ellie. "What's that?"

"It's school for kids who can't live at home 'cause their moms aren't there." Gracie sounded nonchalant. "I asked my Sunday school teacher."

"Boarding school," Ellie explained for Wyatt's benefit. "I wish you'd told me you overheard that, Gracie."

"I couldn't tell you. You'd have cried more. I don't like it when you cry, Mommy." She looked at Ellie, her face utterly serious. "But I *could* go there. Then you and Eddie could get married."

"Gracie, honey, Eddie and I don't want to get married."

"He might want to if I went to the wooden school." It was obvious she'd thought about this a lot. "If I went there you could ask him. You'd hafta say please," she warned. Then her bottom lip began to tremble. "'Cept I'd really miss Melissa. An' Wranglers Ranch." She gulped. "An' you," she whispered as a big shiny tear dribbled down her cheek.

"Oh, darling." Ellie swallowed the lump in her throat as she rushed across the room and knelt to hug her precious little girl close to her heart. She didn't have to worry. Gracie knew all about giving gifts. And she'd just given her mom a priceless one. "It's very kind of you to offer, but I don't want to marry Eddie."

"Sure?" Gracie sniffed.

"Positive." Ellie swiped away her tears, her heart brimming with love. "I keep telling you, darling. You and I are a family. We always will be, even when you grow up and get married and have your own children."

Gracie's smile blazed with relief, but a moment later her eyes turned troubled. "I can't get married," she wailed. "I don't got no daddy."

"What does having a father have to do with getting married?" Wyatt asked.

"Miss Carter, she's my teacher," Gracie explained with a sniff. "She said her daddy is going to walk her into the church when she gets married. She said all daddies do that. But I don't got a daddy to walk me, so I can't never get married." Fresh tears poured from her eyes.

Ellie leaned back on her heels and glared at Wyatt, whose peals of laughter filled the room.

"Gracie, honey, you have a very long time before you have to think about marriage. Let's not worry about that now."

Gracie sniffed as she considered this. "'Kay," she finally agreed. She brushed away her tears and began gathering blocks. "Cade, you an' me are gonna build a church where people get married. Only not Mommy and Eddie."

Sighing, Ellie rose and rescued the last of her cookies from the oven.

"Escaped that by the skin of your teeth, Ellie Grant." Wyatt's eyes crinkled with his smile. "But don't think I don't expect an answer. About your happiness," he whispered with a check over one shoulder to be sure Gracie didn't overhear. "Or lack thereof."

"Did you know there are certain kinds of poison you can add to food which are totally undetectable?" Ellie methodically stirred the pot of soup on the stove. "The person who eats it never even knows it's their last meal." She glanced at Wyatt over one shoulder. "Totally oblivious."

She hid her smile at his gaping stare and calmly set out four bowls and four spoons to go along with her freshly baked bread.

"Supper's in an hour," she said brightly. "If you're strong enough to watch the kids for a bit, I think I'll go for a walk."

When Wyatt finally managed a nod, Ellie left, inhaling deeply as she strode down the drive.

Wasn't it funny that the thought of marrying Eddie no longer held any attraction? He was part of the past, a part she could forget and not mourn.

What wasn't funny was that she'd begun to have silly dreams about living here, on Wyatt's ranch, watching the spectacular sunsets with him, seeing him raise his son, listening to that full-bodied laugh.

"God, I'm really trying to manage Gracie on my own, to keep us strong as a family and find contentment in the life You want for me," she whispered as she strolled among the lacy mesquite trees. "But I think I'm getting too fond of Cade." *And Wyatt.* "It sure would be nice if You could heal Wyatt so Gracie and I can get back to our own lives."

Ellie really meant that. But she had a hunch that from now on, being a single mom wasn't going to be quite as fulfilling as it once had been.

"You have to be on your best behavior tonight," Wyatt told his son two evenings later. "No spilling, no yelling. There will be ladies present. Okay?"

Cade gave him a baleful look. "Dada. Meem." Meem was Cade's word for more.

"No more juice right now," Wyatt told him. "We have to get going." He sniffed, then made a detour to change his son. "One of these days, when you're a little older, you and I are going to have a heart-to-heart about how to attract girls. This isn't it."

Cade blew a raspberry.

"That won't impress them either. And you'll only be able to get by on those baby-face good looks for so long, kid. Trust me, it's not easy when you get older."

Wyatt paused. Was that what he was doing, trying to impress Ellie? A surge of guilt rose as he glanced at his wedding picture and Taryn. No, he wasn't looking to get involved again. No way. It was just that Ellie—

He shoved the thought away, did one more check to be sure he had everything, then he headed out the door. He was just pulling up at Ellie's place when his phone rang.

"Hey, Wyatt. Where are you?"

"Hey, Tanner. At Ellie's. We should be there in ten minutes. Everything ready?"

"And waiting," came Tanner's response. Then he hung up.

Ellie and her daughter were waiting outside, so Wyatt jumped out to help Gracie into the backseat beside Cade. When she was buckled in he moved to the passenger side and held Ellie's door, closing it once she was inside.

"What's going on, Wyatt?" she asked after fastening her seat belt. "Where are we going?"

"You'll see." She tried to probe further, but he avoided her questions. "Here we are," he said a few minutes later as they drove through the gates to Wranglers Ranch.

"Mommy, my name is on that sign. What does the

rest say?" Gracie asked, pointing to a banner attached to the fence and lit up by the yard light.

"It says *Happy Birthday, Gracie*," Wyatt told her. "I hope you don't mind, but since you couldn't have a birthday party because Cade and I were sick and keeping your mom busy, I made you one. This is your birthday party." He pulled in and parked, laughing out loud at her squeal of surprise when a clown appeared and opened her door. "Happy birthday, Gracie."

The clown lifted Gracie down from the truck, then he produced a crown and set it on her head. He bowed in front of her, then blew on a whistle. Suddenly lights, thousands of them, blinked to life on a huge Christmas tree. The clown took Gracie's hand, and as he led her toward the tree, candy canes glowed to life, lighting up a path.

"Shall we?" Wyatt asked Ellie. He was a bit worried by her silence. But when he opened the door, and the interior lights clicked on, he saw she was crying. "I blew it, didn't I?" he said, utterly devastated by those tears.

"Are you kidding me? You are the most amazing man…" Ellie dashed away her tears, leaned over and kissed him hard and fast. Then she jerked away, flushed a bright Christmas red and clapped a hand over her mouth. A second later she recovered enough to say, "This is the nicest thing you could have done for her. Thank you, Wyatt."

"You're welcome." He grinned and quashed the desire to return her kiss. Friends, that's all they were. "Shall we join the party?" At her nod he unbuckled Cade, and they joined Gracie.

"Come on," she called with a frantic wave. "Mr. Clown says we hafta follow the candy canes."

As they walked through what he hoped looked like an enchanted forest where even the cacti had been dressed for the event, Wyatt couldn't help watching Ellie's reaction. She was as much a kid as Gracie, her head twisting from one side to the other to take it all in. She stopped short at one point and gazed upward.

"Snowflakes," she whispered. "How perfect."

"Perfect?" He was puzzled by the comment. "In Tucson?"

"Perfect for me." Ellie tilted her head, as if she was waiting for one of the white plastic snowflakes to fall so she could catch it on her tongue. "I was born and raised in North Dakota. We always had snow at Christmas. It's the one thing I still miss." She looked at him. "And you managed to re-create it in the desert."

"With some help." He steered Cade back on to the path. "It's the least I could do for making Gracie miss her birthday."

"And you said you couldn't decorate." Ellie made a face at him. "How long did it take you to make all these snowflakes?"

"I can't decorate, and I didn't make them. Taryn kept the snowflakes from some hospital fund-raising gig she did once. They were sitting in boxes in the garage so... Tanner helped me put them up."

"They're beautiful. Oh, look!" Ellie grabbed his hand, her face every bit as excited as Gracie's when she spied the blow-up snowman. "It's so cute." She stopped short when a group of kids began to sing "Happy Birthday" to Gracie.

Wyatt stood beside Ellie, enjoying the myriad expressions that flickered across her face. "I hope it's okay that

I invited her whole class. I didn't want to leave out anyone. Her teacher helped."

"You invited twenty-two kids to Wranglers Ranch and Tanner let you?" she said.

"Actually he suggested it. He also hired the bus to bring them here. Apparently the parents will pick them up at eight o'clock." Wyatt smothered a surge of pleasure at Ellie's surprise and obvious enjoyment as she mingled among the kids.

"It's amazing," she breathed when she returned from circulating. "A bouncy castle. A clown and those little ponies—where did they come from?"

"I mentioned to Tanner that one of my clients is selling his place. His buyer doesn't want the miniatures, so now they have a new home on Wranglers Ranch." Wyatt smiled as Gracie climbed on one with Lefty's help. "Tanner thinks they'll be perfect for the smaller kids to ride. I checked them over. They're all healthy."

Ellie watched as the kids went squealing from one activity to the next. When she finally turned to face him, there was a look on her face that Wyatt couldn't decipher.

"Tanner was right," she murmured.

"About?" he prodded.

"You working for Wranglers Ranch. Look how this place has blossomed since you started. Tanner told me you caught two infections another vet missed." She studied him, her face serious. "Your suggestions are amazing. You should come on board full-time."

"Tanner's asked me, but I have my practice to run." Cade dragged at his hand, wanting to go to the horses. So, with one of Wranglers' hands holding the reins, Wyatt lifted his son on to the smallest horse and walked beside it. "Look at him," he crowed with pride. "A true cowboy through and through."

"I suppose you'll be entering Cade in the rodeo in February," Ellie teased a few minutes later. "Seriously though Wyatt, why don't you think about working here?"

"I'm committed to building my own business." She didn't have to know he'd lost another client this week.

"A laudable goal for sure," she said quietly.

"But?" Since Cade was drooping Wyatt lifted him off the horse and carried him to the drinks table. "You don't think I can do it?"

"Of course you can do it," Ellie said firmly. "It's more a question of do you want to? Full-time work here would give you more regular hours. You could spend evenings and weekends with this guy, mostly uninterrupted." She tickled Cade and laughed when he giggled. "He won't nap in the afternoon forever."

"I know but—" Wyatt wanted her to understand, but he wasn't sure he wanted to explain why he needed to build his business. "I must have my own business, Ellie."

"Okay. So why can't part of your business be as the on-call vet for Wranglers? I know Tanner has asked you several times." Her eyes held his, waiting for his response. "Don't you like working here?"

"I love it." He was embarrassed by how fast that response slipped out. "It's a fantastic place to work. Tanner knows his stuff, and he treats his animals well. He takes my suggestions seriously, and I'm very proud to be associated with his work with the kids that come here." He grinned. "Plus, he's a great spiritual mentor, and I need that."

"So what's the problem?"

"I guess I could agree to be his on-call vet." He

shrugged. "That's basically what I'm doing now anyway, and so far it's working well. I don't mind the extra income either."

"That's good to hear. I'm sure he'll be pleased." It looked like she was, too. "We'll enjoy whatever time you can spend here. You'll be a great asset to Wranglers."

Wyatt was about to thank her when he noticed her attention had turned to Gracie. As Ellie moved closer he followed, noting her frown as they both overheard Gracie tell another child how she'd prayed for a special birthday party.

"And God answered." She glanced around with a happy grin. "Isn't it great? He'll answer my other prayers, too," she added, her attention now focused on Wyatt. "I know it."

Seeing that Ellie was about to have words with her daughter, Wyatt stepped in. "Gracie, are you ready for your cake?" He hoped the fairy-tale cake Sophie was setting on the table would divert her attention.

Wyatt moved behind Ellie, breathing in her fragrance as a light breeze tossed stands of her hair across his face. Standing there contentedly as he watched Gracie blow out the candles, he couldn't help but marvel at the little girl's faith. She had implicit trust in God to answer her prayers. Ellie seemed the same. Both of them expected God to be there for them.

Wyatt wanted to share that trust. Longed to.

But how can God give you your dreams when you still blame that boy for Taryn's death? When you can't trust Him with that?

They were sobering questions. Ones he didn't have the answers to. Yet.

Chapter Seven

"Mommy?"

"Yes, honey?" Relieved that Gracie's star was finally perched atop their Christmas tree, Ellie carefully lifted her daughter down.

Getting the star in place on Monday morning before work and school wasn't exactly the way she'd planned to finish the weekend job of decorating their tree but at least it was one less thing on her list. With only two and a half weeks left before Christmas, that list seemed endless.

"Can we go to... Cade's house after school today?"

Ellie gathered her daughter's backpack and ushered her out to the car. "Wyatt told me at your party that he has a sitter for Cade in the afternoons now. We don't need to go there anymore."

Ellie knew she should be grateful for that freedom because every second of her day was filled with things to do. Only she missed those visits. A lot. And not just because of Cade.

"But I *need* to go to Cade's house to see him and his daddy," she insisted.

"Why?" Might as well get it out in the open, Ellie decided in resignation.

"To find out what to get them for Christmas." Gracie said it as if Ellie should have known. "We haven't got them a gift yet."

"I wasn't thinking we would." Ellie didn't have the resources to *buy* that many gifts. "Anyway, Cade couldn't tell you, and I'm sure Wyatt won't either."

"I'm not going to *ask* them." Gracie looked at her askance. "I'm just going to see what they need."

"Oh." Ellie coughed to cover her mirth.

"'Sides, Da—" Gracie peeked at her, then quickly adjusted to say, "—*he's* going to let me help him with a hurt owl."

"Wyatt. His name is Wyatt. Or Mr. Wright." Exasperated, Ellie pulled into the school lot. "When did he say that?"

"At church. Yesterday." Gracie grinned. "I liked helping him with the animals."

As if she'd done it more than twice.

"We can't go today," Ellie insisted. "I have too much to do before Christmas."

"When then?" Gracie stared at her, waiting for an answer Ellie didn't have.

"I don't know. We'll see. Now off you go so you aren't late." She pulled into the drop-off zone, leaned back and kissed her cheek. "Bye, sweetie."

"Can I go tomorrow?" Gracie asked as she exited the car.

"We'll talk about it later." *When the answer would still be no.*

Gracie's over-the-top-birthday party on Friday night, a camp at Wranglers Ranch on Saturday, which he'd helped with, and yesterday when he'd sat beside her in church—Ellie had been seeing entirely too much of Wyatt Wright lately.

Not that she wasn't grateful to him. She was. That party had been an incredibly kind and generous gesture to a little girl.

But lately it seemed Wyatt was at Wranglers Ranch every day, which meant she talked to him every day and admired him working with the animals *every day*. She'd lectured herself a hundred times about it and still couldn't shake this silly schoolgirl crush on him. It seemed like her no-romance rule was in danger of being breached, and that wasn't going to happen. She wouldn't, couldn't let it.

By the time she arrived at the ranch she was ten minutes late, and Tanner was waiting in her tiny log house/office.

"I'm sorry I'm late," she apologized.

Ignoring her apology, he blurted, "Sophie's sick." The miserable look on his face said it all. "Nothing I do helps."

"Morning sickness," she guessed. "I'll go make her some peppermint tea."

"Thank you, Ellie." Tanner's sunny smile reappeared. "I knew you'd know what to do. And if Wyatt comes looking for me, tell him I'm in the north quarter trying to figure out how that coyote got in."

"Any damage?" There must have been if Wyatt had been called.

"It bit one of the pregnant mares, which means a tetanus shot and probably some antibiotics." He made a face. "Lefty's tracking the coyote in case it's sick."

"Okay, I'll tell Wyatt." Ellie walked to the main house trying not to skip as she went. What in the world was wrong with her that thoughts of Wyatt made her act like Gracie?

After reading herself the riot act, she took Sophie the tea she'd brewed, her heart saddened by the mom-to-be's stricken look as she lay in bed, her face whiter than her sheets.

"Drink this," Ellie said handing her the cup. "And munch on those crackers."

"I'm a nuisance," Sophie groaned. "And I'm so tired."

"It will pass. Drink the tea." Ellie waited until she'd taken a sip. "You don't have any catering jobs today, do you?"

"Nothing till the weekend. Thank You, Lord." Sophie lay back on the pillows. "I'd forgotten all about morning sickness."

"And you will again when this baby's born," Ellie promised. "Rest now."

In the kitchen she cleaned up the counters, turned on the dishwasher and started a slow-cooker meal for Sophie and Tanner's lunch. She was about to leave when she saw Wyatt drive up.

Settle down, she told her dancing stomach. *It's only Wyatt.*

Only Wyatt. Right. Mocking herself, Ellie stepped outside and closed the door behind her. She set a little Do Not Disturb sign on the step.

"Good morning." He glanced from the sign to her, a question in his eyes.

"Morning sickness. She'll sleep for a while." Ellie couldn't help studying Wyatt with an approving glance. He looked fresh and ready to take on the day, his usually bristled jaw clean, revealing his sharp chin and full lips. He must iron his shirts to get them so crisp. And where in Tucson did they sell jeans that fit like that?

"Ellie?"

"Sorry." She tried to hide her blush. "Uh, Tanner said you could find him in the north quarter."

"Hunting for the coyote, I expect." He frowned when she kept standing there. "Is anything wrong?"

"No." She scanned her fuzzy brain for something to explain her fog. "Just that, well, I was wondering…" This was going to sound so awkward, especially since yesterday she'd refused his lunch offer because she'd been trying to distance herself. "Is there a good time when I could bring Gracie over to your place?"

Surprise widened his eyes.

"She wants to help you with an owl." Relieved when understanding dawned, she added, "And find out what to get you and Cade for Christmas."

"Oh, that's not necessary."

"I'm afraid it is to her," Ellie told him. "Can we walk and talk?" He nodded, so she led the way to her office. "Gracie has this thing about Christmas gifts."

"Thing?" Wyatt arched an eyebrow.

"She's been making a list of gifts she wants to give," she explained. "In fact now she wants to give one to each of the friends she's made here at the ranch."

"But surely you can't afford that." Wyatt blinked. "What I mean is—"

"I know what you mean, and you're right that I can't buy that many gifts." She smiled. "Fortunately we're making decorated gingerbread people. A little bag of cookies for each friend."

"That's a lot of work." He stopped outside the door.

"Especially since my place is so small. The kitchen is dinky and the oven even smaller. I was going to ask Sophie to use the kitchen here until I found out how much Christmas catering she has booked. I don't want to add to her stress."

"You tell Gracie those cookies would make a great gift for Cade and me, too." Wyatt grinned.

"Uh, I don't think cookies will cut it with Gracie, though you could try suggesting it."

"But I don't want her to spend her money on us."

"Wyatt, you should know by now that there's no point in telling me to stop Gracie," Ellie said with asperity. "It's like telling a horse not to eat grass."

Wyatt's laughter reached to the top of the Palo Verde tree outside her door. "Don't I know it." He sobered. "What does Gracie want for Christmas?"

"I think you already know that answer," she said, keeping her face expressionless.

"She's still harping on about a daddy for Christmas?" Her nod made Wyatt groan. "I was hoping we'd moved past that by now."

"You wish." Ellie needed to prepare for a new class of troubled kids who'd been court-mandated to spend time at Wranglers. Tanner's successful equine assisted rehabilitation program was getting high marks from those who worked with kids at risk. Still, she stood there studying the handsome veterinarian.

"You have quite a daughter." Wyatt's gaze held hers for so long Ellie wondered if she was the only one that felt the air simmering between them. Eventually he said, "I better stop gabbing and go find Tanner. See you, Ellie." He waved, then walked away.

Ellie forced herself to enter her office knowing he'd saddle up and ride cross-country to find Tanner, which was quicker and easier than driving the rugged foothills.

It took every bit of self-control she had, but she refused to go to the window and watch him ride off.

She couldn't help it if her brain noted the sound of his horse trotting away, or that she couldn't focus until she heard the same trot signalling his return. She was going to have to do something about this ridiculous fixation on Wyatt Wright.

Before it got out of control.

Wyatt ended his call and shoved his phone into his pocket while trying to stifle the guilt that always rose whenever he left Cade with a sitter. But Tanner had offered him an afternoon's work, and he couldn't turn it down. Besides, according to the sitter, Cade was having a ball in the sandbox.

"Kids who've had encounters with the justice system are sometimes desperate to vent, and they take it out on the animals. I'd appreciate it if you could stay today, Wyatt, just in case something crops up," Tanner had said earlier, so Wyatt had agreed to stay until the class was finished.

Now he stood beside Ellie outside the tack room, watching as a bunch of trying-to-be-tough teens fumbled and bumbled with the equipment they'd been given to groom their horses.

"Who exactly are these kids?" he asked sotto voce.

"Kids who've had some kind of brush with the law. Not hardened criminals, which is why they're here," she explained. "Tanner's program has had a lot of success breaking down the barriers that troubled kids usually have."

Wyatt immediately thought of the kid he knew only as Ted, the boy he blamed for Taryn's death, and felt a surge of anger. He sure hoped no judge sent that kid here to play with horses as punishment.

"Have you given any more thought to Tanner's offer of full-time employment?" Ellie asked.

"You mean because I'm around Wranglers so much?" He chuckled at her sheepish face. "It's very attractive but—"

"You still feel you have to build your own business." She frowned. "You *are* here a lot."

Brutal, but it was the truth. "I can't accept Tanner's offer."

"Why? Can you tell me?" Ellie's kind eyes studied him. It was the compassion Wyatt saw there that drew his response.

"I made a promise to my dad before he died that I would make mine the best veterinarian business in Tucson, worthy of the Wright name." He saw her lips purse. "What?"

"It's none of my business, of course, but I don't think it's fair for parents to put those kinds of restrictions on their kids. What parent can know the future choices their kid will have to make?" Ellie sounded annoyed.

"What did your parents do?" he asked curiously.

"They told us that it didn't matter to them what career we chose. They said they'd be proud of us as long as we were the best that we could be." Ellie nodded. "I think that's what every parent should want for their child."

Wyatt thought about that for a moment, about how sensible it sounded. "You had a good childhood, didn't you, Ellie?"

"The best." Her face transformed into pure happiness. "We never had much money. Dad farmed. Mom helped him and took in sewing for people. But they always had time for us, and we had so much fun together." Her face sobered. "My parents gave my sister and me things money can't buy, like boundless love, joy and encouragement. They're both gone now, but we never doubted we were loved. That's what I want for Gracie." She sighed. "And that's what I can't seem to instill in her."

"Why do you say that?" Wyatt hated that sound of defeat. "Gracie knows you love her."

"But it's not enough. She's still trying to find security by finding a daddy," Ellie said, her pain obvious. "I'm doing something wrong."

Wyatt didn't have time to dispute that because Tanner waved him over to help with one of the kids, a barely-teenage boy named Albert. Seeing the kid's embarrassment and shyness, Wyatt joked as he demonstrated how to untangle the reins so the horse could move its head more freely. As he did he tried to ease Albert's obvious nervousness. But all the while Wyatt couldn't forget Ellie's face when she'd spoken of her parents, because that was exactly how he wanted Cade to feel about him.

By the time the class left, Wyatt was glad to share the coffee and snacks Sophie offered. Clearly much recovered, she was baking Christmas goodies. Tanner stayed to talk to her while Wyatt and Ellie went to the patio for their coffee break.

"That boy you were working with. Albert? Did you notice the marks on his arms?" Ellie sat, her troubled tone drawing Wyatt's attention. "When he bent to treat his horse's hooves, his shirt bagged, and I saw bruises all over his chest. And he winced when one of the other kids slung their arm over his shoulder."

Tears filled her eyes and rolled down her cheeks. Her pain clenched his insides.

"Ellie!" he exclaimed. "What's wrong?"

"Those marks—I've seen them before. Lots of times in the pediatric wards." She bit her bottom lip. "Albert avoided answering my questions about how he got those marks. He said he's fine, his home life is fine. Everything is fine."

"You don't believe him?"

She shook her head. "I think Albert is being abused." She looked as though the words had been pulled from her lips, her face heart-wrenchingly sad.

"Did you tell Tanner?"

She sniffed, then nodded.

"And?"

"He said I should call his social worker and ask her to investigate. So I did." Ellie burst into fresh tears. "It's horrible to think about, isn't it? That sweet, gentle kid being used as someone's punching bag. I hated these cases when I worked pediatrics."

Unable to bear seeing this caring woman so broken up, Wyatt moved to sit beside her and drew her into his arms.

"It's okay," he soothed. "You did the right thing. Now things will get better for him. They'll investigate, find the truth and move Albert somewhere safe," he said, trying to comfort her. But Ellie slowly shook her head from side to side. "It won't get better for him?"

"It doesn't always. Adults in these situations can be devious." She drew away. Funny how empty his arms felt without her in them. "You don't believe me, but I've heard it before. Trust me, the story will be something like this, 'Albert needed discipline and struggled when we tried to get him to obey, so we had to restrain him.' It's always a variation like that."

"And you're worried?" he guessed.

"Wyatt, I saw the marks at the back of his neck. I'm positive they were bruises from thumb prints." Her voice lowered. "There is no good explanation for that. What if they hurt him more seriously?"

"The social worker's been warned," he said as he tried to put it all together. "She'll be on the lookout now."

"I may have made it worse by reporting it." Her face whitened even more.

"Ellie, you had to. Given your suspicions you couldn't have done nothing. Could you?" He brushed her silky curls off her face to peer into her eyes. Slowly she shook her head.

"No. I had to tell."

"So now there's nothing more you can do." Some tiny glimmer in her eyes made Wyatt add, "Is there?"

"I don't know." She didn't look at him, stared instead at her hands clenched in her lap. "Maybe."

"What do you mean?" Wyatt had a hunch he wasn't going to like this.

"Albert's group is scheduled to return twice more this week, Wednesday and Friday." Ellie's shoulders went back. "I'm going to keep a close eye on him, and if I see further signs of abuse, I—"

"What?" Dread tiptoed up his back. "What are you thinking?"

"I might visit him at home." She stared directly into his eyes, her resolve firm.

"Ellie," he warned, his admiration for her rivaling his concern. "You can't just waltz—"

"Mommy doesn't know how to waltz, do you, Mommy?" Gracie stood behind them. When they twisted to face her, she frowned. "Did you make my mommy cry?" she demanded of Wyatt, her gaze frosty.

"No!" Wyatt didn't get a chance to explain.

"Of course he didn't. And you know it's rude to eavesdrop, Gracie." Ellie rose, straightened her shirt and brushed a hand across her cheeks. "I was just sad about something, and Wyatt was—er, helping me feel better."

"You know, that's exactly what I was going to tell her." Sophie stood in the doorway of the house, a big grin spread across her face. She winked at Wyatt, then said, "Gracie, honey, I saw you get off the bus. Beth will be here soon. Do you want to come and taste one of my star cookies while you wait?"

"Sure." Gracie dropped her backpack and loped toward Sophie.

"I'd better get back to work. I need to clean my office," Ellie said, speaking quickly as if she was embarrassed by Sophie's teasing.

"Yeah, that kid who cut his hand on the curry brush made a mess waving all over the place." Wyatt grinned. "I never knew anyone could cut their hand on a curry brush."

"He did seem a little accident-prone, didn't he?"

"Maybe that's what happened to this Albert kid?" he suggested.

"I have no doubt that someone will suggest that," she said quietly.

"Promise me something, Ellie." If you couldn't beat the Grant women, you could only join them. Wyatt exhaled. "If you do decide to go to this Albert's place, will you let me know, so I can go with you?"

"You? Why?" She looked stunned.

"Because I don't want you to walk into a situation where you could get hurt," he said gruffly.

"You think his relatives would try to hurt me?" Clearly that hadn't occurred to her.

"That's the thing. You don't know. Neither do I. If it's as bad as you think, anything could happen." He held her gaze. "So you'll tell me, right? And we'll go together."

She studied him for a long time before she finally nodded. A smile lifted her lips. "Thank you, Wyatt."

"You're welcome. Now I've got to get home." He turned and almost tripped over Gracie who was crunching on a cookie with vivid red icing spread across her face.

"Can I go with you?" she asked, her mouth full.

"What? Why?" Gracie's sudden reappearance left Wyatt feeling slightly off-kilter.

"To help with the owl, remember?" She licked her lips and rubbed her messy hands on her jeans. "And I want to see that old billy goat with the bad leg. An'…"

She trailed away on a nonstop sentence that included almost every animal on his ranch.

"I can't go there today, Gracie," Ellie said. "Tanner wants to talk to me."

"I want to talk to Wyatt, too." Tanner stepped up to them and smiled at Gracie. "Beth's bus is here. Can you play with her while I talk to your mom?"

"'Kay." She pinned Wyatt with a warning look. "I want to see the owl," she said firmly, then left.

"You know, Tanner, you and Gracie need to stop creeping up on people," Wyatt complained when she'd left. "It makes me nervous."

"Must be your guilty conscience." Tanner sniggered at the menacing look Wyatt shot him. "I had a phone call today from your favorite organization, Ellie."

"Make-A-Wish Arizona? So they did call." She grinned, then explained to Wyatt. "They're a group I volunteer with. They've been trying to arrange Christmas wishes for some of their terminally sick kids."

"Ellie suggested Wranglers Ranch could help with that." Tanner scratched his chin. "They want to bring four children the day before Christmas Eve."

"Why do you need me?" Wyatt asked.

"Because these specific children probably can't ride our horses as other kids do. Of course, there'll be attendants for them, all that kind of thing," Tanner explained. "But apparently they'll need modifications and adaptations, and I'd like your input. They also want assurances that someone will be on hand to guarantee the horses are safe and that Ellie's here to deal with any potential incident."

"Understandably, they are very big on safety." Ellie said.

Tanner nodded. "I really want to do this. If Wranglers Ranch can bring some Christmas joy to children who are fighting for their lives, then we ought to do it."

"So…?" Wyatt glanced from him to Ellie, noting that the shadows were gone, and her gray eyes now sparkled with anticipation.

"Wyatt, I want to hire you for the next two and a half weeks to work with five specific animals that the children may ride," Tanner said. "I don't want even a risk of a problem with my animals, because if this works out, I'd like to do it more often."

"We can get their doctors' suggestions as to what's needed, because some kids will need adaptations of the saddles." Ellie's earnest voice begged Wyatt to agree. "We'll have to make sure everything complies if we're going to make this Christmas special for them."

"I also want some contacts from you, Wyatt." Tanner pulled out a notepad and pen. "I loved the way Wranglers Ranch added to Gracie's birthday party. I'd like to try and re-create it for two other 'Wish' kids who may visit." He paused, then lifted an eyebrow. "So, what do you say? Can you give us the time?"

Should he? Wyatt knew he needed to distance himself from the lovely Ellie, not spend more time with her. But he couldn't say no to suffering kids. What were a couple of weeks of his time? If it were Cade...

"I'm in," he promised.

"Good. We'll start preparations tomorrow." Tanner tapped his pen. "Now, what's the phone number of that clown you hired for Gracie's party? He was great."

Wyatt answered, but his attention wasn't on Tanner, it was on Ellie. She worked with young kids in Sunday school. She worked with troubled kids and school groups, and now she'd be there for sick kids who came here to Wranglers Ranch. She was determined to go out of her way for this kid named Albert whom she'd only met once. She'd cared for Cade, and she also had a daughter who needed her. Ellie gave and she gave and she gave.

For all of those reasons, and a hundred more that he wasn't going to enumerate right now, Wyatt really liked this woman. And he was determined to keep his promise to be here to help with the Make-A-Wish kids.

But then you'll have to back away, because you don't keep your promises. You haven't even kept the one you made your dad ten years ago. Do not let this woman or her precocious daughter get under your skin, because you will disappoint her, just as you disappointed Taryn.

Later, as Wyatt drove home with Gracie singing to Cade about owls, he caught himself anticipating dinner with Ellie, and he wondered if that mental warning hadn't come just a bit too late.

Chapter Eight

"I feel sorry for him." Two evenings later Ellie felt like she'd lost her Christmas spirit.

Wyatt sat at his kitchen table beside Gracie who was cutting out Christmas cookies for her gifts. It had been so decent of him to offer her his kitchen with its double ovens to work in. Ellie knew she should be happy that Gracie's cookie list was getting finished and yet…

"You feel sorry for who?"

"Albert. He didn't look much better today, did he?" Ellie plopped three silver candy beads down the front of a gingerbread boy. "I wonder if it's my fault."

"Did you do something bad, Mommy?" Gracie frowned at the star she'd mashed.

"I'm not sure yet." Ellie wished she hadn't mentioned it with little ears listening. "Can I help you, honey?" When her daughter nodded, Ellie took the cutter from her hand, reformed the last bits of dough and quickly pressed out the star.

"It will look pretty with this blue sugar on it," Gracie said.

"Very nice," Ellie approved. "Now we're finished for

tonight, so you go wash up. Quietly because, remember, Cade's sleeping. As soon as these are baked, we need to get you home to bed, too."

Gracie did an exaggerated tiptoe to the bathroom, making Wyatt smile.

"She didn't argue. She must be tired." Ellie moved quickly to clean up and then started the dishwasher. "Thank you so much for letting Gracie help you with the animals and for allowing me to use your house as my workshop," she said over one shoulder as she removed two more cookie sheets from the oven. "This baking is going a lot faster than I ever imagined."

"How many more batches do you need?" Wyatt asked, snitching one of the cookies for a taste test.

"Maybe three more." She grinned at his surprised face. "Gracie's list is huge."

"But—"

"I know it's overkill," Ellie defended. "But I want to encourage her giving spirit. I like that she's thought about these kids, thought about how many of them might not receive much for Christmas, especially something homemade. She's trying, in her way, to make it special for them. I don't want to crush that."

"And Albert?" Wyatt arched one eyebrow when she didn't immediately respond.

"I'm wondering if my speaking up made his life worse." She took a sip of the coffee she'd made earlier. "I'm going to visit his home."

"Ellie, I don't think—" Wyatt stopped speaking when Gracie returned. A muscle in his jaw flickered, but all he said was, "When?"

"Maybe on the weekend." She slid the cooled cookies into a big tin she'd brought and snapped on the lid.

"Sweetheart, do you think you can put this tin inside the cooler I left on the doorstep?"

"Sure." Holding the tin as if it was pure gold, Gracie walked out of the room.

"I'm not keen on kids who've been in trouble with the law spending time at Wranglers," Wyatt muttered. "Seems like they get off too easily."

"Tanner's programs are for troubled kids, not necessarily those mandated to attend by the courts." Ellie frowned. "You're thinking of the boy who was involved in Taryn's accident, aren't you?" She could see from his expression that she'd guessed right. "What do you know about him?"

"Not much." His tone was sour. "I never heard any details in the press, but then again, he was a juvenile."

"You were burying Taryn and busy with Cade. I doubt you had much time to watch the news for details," she soothed.

"At the time I didn't think much about it." He crunched hard on the rest of his cookie. "A police officer said there was a group of kids who'd been driving illegally and mentioned the driver's name once. Ted. That's all I know about him."

"Ah, that's who Ted is," she murmured.

"You know him?" Wyatt asked in surprise.

"No." Ellie wondered if she should have said anything. But Wyatt's stare had to be answered. "You spoke of him when you were sick. I think you must have been dreaming."

"About the night Taryn died." He stared at his hands. "It happens sometimes." Then his voice dropped. "Probably because I can't get rid of my guilt. Or the anger toward this Ted for what he did."

"If you're still dreaming about him, the anger is eating at you." She sensed the anger had festered since the accident. "I'm sorry for you, Wyatt. But I also feel sorry for him. It must be horrible to carry such a burden. Can't you free yourself by forgiving him?"

"No," he refused in a hard tone.

"It's not my business, and maybe you think I should be quiet, but I have to say this. Christians are commanded to forgive. I think it's mostly so we don't harbor ill will that eats at us." She studied him with a troubled look. "Besides, God has forgiven us for so much. How can we not forgive others? Sooner or later you have to let it go, Wyatt."

"He has to pay," Wyatt insisted in an irritated voice. "We all do."

"Maybe. But when will Ted, or you," she added, "have paid enough?"

Wyatt got suddenly quiet, so she forced a smile at Gracie who had returned. "Gather up your coloring things and put them in your backpack. These are the last pans. We just have to wait for them to cool a bit, then we'll head home."

Ellie noticed Gracie covertly studying Wyatt as she packed her things. After a time her daughter asked, "What are you getting Cade for Christmas?"

"Gracie, that's—"

"I don't know." Wyatt looked at her warily. "Why?"

"'Cause I know the perfect thing." Gracie grinned. "Cade would love a puppy."

"I see. Why do you think that, Gracie?" Wyatt lifted her onto his knee. "Is that what you want for Christmas?"

His tender voice brought a lump to Ellie's throat,

which grew when Gracie cupped a hand on his cheek and shook her head.

"You don't like puppies?" Wyatt asked.

"I love 'em." Gracie's fervor was hard to miss.

"But a puppy isn't what you want for Christmas?" Wyatt pressed.

Gracie shook her head. After a sideways look at Ellie, she leaned close to Wyatt and whispered in his ear. Ellie didn't have to hear a word to know what she said. Her guess was confirmed by Wyatt's heartfelt sigh of resignation.

Ellie sighed, too, but silently. She packaged the rest of the cookies in a box. Clearly it was time, past time, to leave.

"Thank you very much for lending us your kitchen, Wyatt." She held the box under one arm and stretched her other hand out to Gracie. "Time to go, sweetie."

Gracie flung her arms around Wyatt's neck and squeezed hard. Ellie could hardly breathe when her daughter tilted her head and flickered her eyelashes against his cheek.

"That's a butterfly kiss," she said with a giggle, then she slid off his knee.

"Thank you, Gracie." He walked them to the door and said, "Good night," in a soft voice. His thoughtful gaze slid from her to Ellie. "Sweet dreams," he murmured.

Ellie fluttered a hand, unable to say anything in the intimacy of the moonlight. She was too aware of Wyatt standing on the step, watching as she drove away.

"He's nice, isn't he, Mommy?"

Nice? What an insipid word to describe such a dynamic man.

"Mommy?"

Though Ellie nodded her agreement with Gracie's sentiment she privately thought the Grant women were entirely too smitten with Wyatt Wright.

"Glad you could come over, Wyatt." Tanner looked up from the tack he was sorting. "We'll sure be glad to have your help with those boys again this afternoon."

"No problem." Wyatt felt reluctant at the thought of working again with Albert, the kid Ellie was so worried about. Yet he couldn't very well refuse to help when Tanner had phoned today.

So far this one ranch was keeping his office afloat, but Wyatt's practice was a long way from the shining business his father had wished for.

"I should have asked you earlier," Tanner said with an apologetic look. "Would you be willing to have a reference check done? I'm required to get them for anyone at Wranglers Ranch who works with the kids."

"No problem. When Taryn did some design work for a government building a few years ago she made friends with a social worker who persuaded us to take the foster parent training so we could be emergency foster parents." Wyatt remembered the time fondly. "We took the whole course."

"I didn't know that." Tanner grinned. "I'm guessing they didn't teach potty training."

"I wish." Wyatt grimaced. "Cade's about ready for that, I suppose." He shuddered at the thought of training his headstrong son. "I think that's when Taryn decided she wanted a baby. It was funny, because up until then she never talked a lot about kids; but after we had those kids to stay, she couldn't talk about anything else but having her own and raising them on the ranch." He sobered suddenly, remembering that she would never mother Cade. "Anyway, the agency did a check on us back then. It's probably still in police files."

"Thanks, Wyatt," Tanner said quietly.

He shrugged. "No biggie. I'm going to take a quick look at that lame pony before your kids get here. If you still intend to use her for the Make-a-Wish ride, we can't wait for the swelling to go down by itself."

Wyatt left the tack room and headed for the pasture where the pony stood munching on hay. He completed his examination and was returning to the house when he saw Ellie speaking to Albert. The boy looked uncomfortable. Figuring Ellie might need help, Wyatt veered their way.

"Albert," he said, nodding at the boy, who wouldn't meet his gaze. "Ellie. What's up?"

"I was just telling Albert I'd be in his neighborhood this weekend, and I wondered if he'd like to go for a soda or some ice cream with Gracie and me."

Ellie was trying hard to carry off nonchalance, but Wyatt heard the intensity behind her words. She was worried about Albert. Whether his concern was unfounded or not, he wasn't about to let Ellie go alone.

"Cade and I could use an outing. Can we come along?" he asked. "In fact, why don't we make it lunch? I'll spring for burgers."

"Do you like burgers, Albert?" Ellie asked.

"I used to love my grandmother's burgers." Albert suddenly fell silent.

"A grandmother's food is always special." Ellie smiled that sweet, gentle look that coaxed confidences. "I'd love to meet her."

"She died." Albert turned and walked away.

Ellie started toward him, but Wyatt held her arm.

"Let him go," he said softly. "He's embarrassed for you to see him cry."

"How do you know?" Ellie stared at him, her forehead pleated in a dark look.

"I was a kid his age once. I remember what it was like." Wyatt didn't want to go into the past, but he'd said too much.

"It's hardly the same. You had your home and your dad."

"Yeah." *Let it go, Ellie.*

"Tanner's beckoning." Ellie walked by his side silently for a moment, then asked, "Did you ever find out about your mother?"

"No. I did ask some of my dad's friends, but they didn't seem to know anything. Guess I'll never know now." He'd told himself a hundred times that it didn't matter, but it did. The lack of knowledge about her was like a bruised bone that wouldn't heal. It just kept aching and aching.

"I think you should hire someone to find the truth. Then you'd know." Ellie studied him for a moment, then shrugged. "Of course, maybe you'd rather not find out about her."

"Why would you think that?" Stunned by the comment, he stared at her.

"Well, it seems like you're not putting much effort into finding her." Ellie held up her hands, palms facing him. "Sorry. It's none of my business."

But she had a point. He should discover what he could and then finally put the matter to rest. He made up his mind then and there to contact a private detective. Maybe he wouldn't like what he learned, but wasn't that better than not knowing? Besides, he owed it to Cade to learn their entire family history.

Ellie had a point on another subject, too. Forgiveness for Ted. Her words had troubled Wyatt ever since she'd said them. *God has forgiven us for so much. How can we not forgive others?* He needed to be forgiven for so many mistakes he'd made.

But Wyatt couldn't dwell on that now, because Tanner again assigned him and Ellie to work with Albert and another boy, Jason. Ellie's knowledge of horses and riding surprised Wyatt until he recalled that she'd been raised on a farm. Several times she left him alone with the two boys to treat superficial scrapes of other guests. While Jason seemed comfortable with riding, Albert acted nervous about controlling his horse.

"Jonah here wants to know what you expect of him," Wyatt explained. "He's been broken to ride, so if you don't tell him what he's supposed to do, it makes him feel like he's doing something wrong. You have to pull on the reins to get him to respond."

"But it might hurt him," Albert worried. "That thing in his mouth will cut him."

"No, the bit is for Jonah's protection. It helps him understand what you want him to do." Wyatt strove to reassure him, relieved that Lefty had taken over with Jason. "Climb on and try again," he urged Albert. "Remember, Jonah's trying to do what you want."

As he encouraged Albert to pay attention to his horse, he couldn't help but wonder what the kid had done to end up in this program. A kid who was so worried about hurting his horse and spoke with obvious love about his grandmother hardly seemed the troubled-teen type.

A short time later Tanner called a halt to the trail ride,

and Wyatt was more than ready for a coffee break. As the kids devoured the snack Sophie had prepared, Wyatt cradled his coffee and thought about how he could adapt the equipment for the Make-A-Wish child whose file Tanner had given him that morning.

"Cookie for your thoughts?" Ellie sat down beside him and handed him a huge oatmeal cookie.

"Not sure they're worth it, but thanks." He munched on the treat, suddenly very aware of the strong bond forming between him and Wranglers Ranch's nurse.

"What were you frowning about?"

"The Make-A-Wish thing." He shook his head. "I can't figure out how we can manage for that little girl they added at the last minute."

"Esther." Ellie sighed. "I know. I've been struggling with the same issue, but I just can't bring myself to say no. There has to be a way for her to ride, doesn't there? This might be the last time she's well enough to live her dream."

That's what Wyatt liked so much about Ellie Grant. Giving up wasn't even in her vocabulary, especially not when it came to kids.

"Wyatt?" She nudged him back to the present with her elbow.

He looked up to see Albert standing in front of them, looking uncomfortable. "Hey, Albert. Good work today."

"Thanks." The boy exhaled as if he was about to take a giant leap of faith, then looked straight at Ellie. "I was thinking. About the weekend. I maybe could go for an ice cream with you. If you still want to."

"Oh, I still want to, Albert," Ellie assured him.

He nodded when the bus driver called him to come. "Uh, thanks. Thanks a lot."

"See you Saturday." Ellie watched him leave, but when the bus had driven away she thumped the table with her fist. Wyatt blinked and saw the glitter of tears on her lashes.

"Hey, what's wrong?"

"Didn't you notice the marks around his wrist?" she asked, her eyes glinting with anger. "They're new, so the abuse or bullying or whatever it is hasn't stopped. But it will. I'm going to make sure of that."

"Okay, then, so we'll take Albert out for lunch on Saturday," Wyatt said mildly. "I'll pick you up when?"

"You're really coming?"

"There is no way you're going alone. And Tanner agrees with me." Wyatt thought Ellie would argue, but she didn't. Instead she exhaled a sigh of relief.

"Oh. Good. I was hating the idea of going by myself."

"But you would have, wouldn't you?" he said, knowing the answer. "He matters that much to you?"

"Every kid matters, Wyatt." Ellie sipped her coffee. "I couldn't forgive myself if something happened to Albert because I was too scared to act."

"Ellie Grant, you are, quite simply, amazing."

"No, I'm not. I'm just a mom who doesn't want a kid to get hurt." Her cheeks were flushed as red as he'd ever seen them.

"You're a great big softie." He rose and held out a hand. "Come with me."

Ellie frowned but finally placed her hand in his, allowing him to draw her up. "Where?"

"To the ponies. I need your opinion about something. And Gracie's help."

"Gracie?" Ellie walked beside him, obviously curious, but after a couple of steps she drew her hand away.

Wyatt wished she hadn't. He liked holding Ellie's hand, sharing things with her. He'd never known anyone with such a big heart. And Gracie had grown on him, too. She yearned for a father to love her in the same heart-aching way he'd yearned for his father to love him.

Be careful. You can't get too close. You can't afford to fail another woman. Your job is to father Cade, remember?

His guilt wouldn't let him forget. But as he explained his idea to modify the saddle and harness to Ellie and then Gracie when she arrived, Wyatt realized Gracie didn't care about his failures or shortcomings. All she wanted was a daddy who would love her. And he intended to do that, but as her friend. Somehow he'd have to make her understand he couldn't be more than that.

Chapter Nine

"So you've brought over some of Tanner's rescued horses." On Saturday morning Ellie studied the scruffy-looking animals surrounding Wyatt inside his pasture and thought how happy he looked among them. "To stay?"

"Temporarily. I know they're not the most handsome beasts, yet," he said. "But with some pampering, they soon will be." He smoothed his palm over the withers of the nearest stallion who quivered under his touch. "You'll be amazed by what they look like in a month."

"I don't understand why you're spending so much time worrying about your practice." Ellie smiled as he fondled the ears of a mare who bore obvious signs of malnourishment. "Caring for animals is obviously what you love most about being a vet, so why won't you accept Tanner's offer of full-time employment?"

"You wouldn't understand." He opened the gate and left the paddock, his face mirroring his inner struggle.

"Try me." She walked with him toward the house, enjoying Cade's laughter as they swung him between them with Gracie egging them on.

"I told you. Growing my practice, making it the best in the city, that was the last thing I promised my father before he died." He stopped and stared into the distance. "I promised that I'd make him proud, Ellie. That's a promise I cannot break."

"You don't think just being who you are would make him proud?" Cade tugged his hands free, then headed for the sandbox. She nodded when Gracie asked to join him.

Ellie walked with Wyatt to the patio table and sat while he poured them each a glass of lemonade. She lifted her face into the sun, loving the warm caress of it, especially after hearing numerous reports of a blizzard in North Dakota. Today she did not miss the cold or the snow that were part of her childhood, but, oh, she missed her family.

She frowned at Wyatt's smartly pressed shirt and perfectly fitting jeans, then glanced at herself. She'd chosen to dress down for the visit to Albert, choosing worn jeans, a plain shirt and her favorite battered sandals in hopes that she wouldn't stand out against Albert's usually threadbare clothes. But Wyatt's appearance gave her second thoughts. Either the man didn't own a pair of tattered jeans or he'd chosen not to wear them. As usual, he looked great. And he'd shaved.

A memory of his bristled face against hers when he'd kissed her burst to life. Her skin prickled, her heart started thumping, and her brain screamed *again, again* so loudly she could barely hear the mourning doves cooing in the gravel path.

Focus, Ellie.

She cleared her throat, took a deep breath and returned to the subject at hand.

"Wyatt, you're a well-respected veterinarian who's

been asked to join the staff of a thriving ranch that's doing good work in the community. What's not to be proud of?"

"Working at Wranglers—that's not the kind of thing Dad would have admired." His face stiffened into a mask that warned her not to press any further. "He was more into status and wealth."

"Okay, but you're not your father."

"No, I definitely am not." Wyatt's emphatic response enhanced her curiosity about his troubled relationship with his father.

"So you have to do what fulfills *you*." Ellie whispered a silent prayer for a way to help him.

"I made a deathbed promise to my father, Ellie. I can't just break it. Remember the verse that says to honor your parents?"

"But you've done that. You've tried to make your business what he wanted." She sensed this part was very important to clearly state. "You honored your father as best you could when he was alive, right?"

"Well, yes…" His voice trailed away.

"Think about this." Ellie searched for the most appropriate words to help him reevaluate. "Is continuing to handle all the minutiae of running an office because of a sense of duty to your father—who is no longer here to see it, I might add—how you really want to fill your life?"

"I'd rather work with animals than do books or send out bills any day. Who wouldn't?" His quick response showed that he'd asked himself the question before. The way Wyatt now plunged a hand through his hair revealed his confusion with the answer. That rumpled hair also added immensely to his good looks. "But I did make the promise."

"That was what—ten years ago?" Ellie made a face. "Isn't it time for a new perspective?"

"What perspective?" He looked at her, his brow puckered.

"You are an amazing vet, Wyatt." Ellie drew a deep breath of courage, then leaned forward until her face was mere inches from his, determined to make him see what she saw. "You love working with animals, and it shows every time you handle one."

"Thank you." Her flattery embarrassed him, but Ellie would have none of that.

"Don't thank me because it's true. Animal medicine is your God-given gift." An idea formed. "Have you ever read that sign Tanner has hanging above the door of the barn?"

"'Fan into flame the gift that is within you,'" he recited with a nod.

"Right. So if God has given you such an incredible gift with animals, isn't your job to fan it, as in to do the most with that gift that you can?" She let the question hang for a moment.

"It's not that easy, Ellie."

"Isn't it?" She loved the way he kept his focus on her when she spoke to him, as if at this moment she and what she had to say were the most important things in his world. "As I see it there's only one question to ask, and you must answer honestly."

"I'll try," he promised.

"So the 64,000-dollar question is this—where does your heart lie? In building your own practice into the biggest in Tucson or in working directly with the animals?" Ellie waited for him to think it through.

"When you put it like that—" He sighed. "It doesn't help."

"There's another verse in the Bible that might. Ecclesiastes 9, verse 10 says, 'Whatever your hand finds to do, do it with your might.'"

"Interesting." He nodded, but she knew he was wondering where this was headed.

"Whenever I see you working with the animals I think of that verse," Ellie admitted.

"Why?" Wyatt blinked in confusion.

"Because you never settle for half measures. You put your whole heart into treating an animal. You don't doubt what you're doing or second-guess your decisions. You especially don't consider whether or not you'll make someone proud." She heard the fervor in her voice but couldn't stem it. "You treat needy animals because you can't bear to see them suffer when you can stop it, and because it's what you love to do. Because that's where your heart is. Correct?"

"I guess." He shrugged.

"So tell me, Wyatt." She met his stare unflinchingly. "Can you put that same devotion, that same pride and compassion into making your practice the biggest one in Tucson?"

"I don't know." He fell into thought, only speaking again after several moments had passed. "Yes, I enjoy working at Wranglers Ranch. I especially enjoy having Tanner as a spiritual mentor." He winked. "And I'm enjoying Gracie's stubbornly determined spirit more every day. She doesn't give up on us no matter how often we use her as a guinea pig to figure out preparations for the Make-a-Wish kids."

"You're digressing," Ellie pointed out.

"Yes, a bit," he admitted. "I need time to think things through. But about Gracie—she's so willing to help. It's a great quality in anyone but especially nice in a kid."

"I notice you left me out of that admiration society." Ellie felt the sting deep inside and chided herself for it. Why did Wyatt's opinion of her matter so much?

"Not true. In fact, you're at the top of my People-I-Most-Appreciate list." Wyatt's eyes twinkled. "I like how you challenge me to do more with my faith, Ellie."

"Ah, you're talking about this morning and how I roped you into helping with the church kids' Christmas program."

He nodded, not even pretending to hide his grin.

"Well, you did agree to meet me at the church," she defended. "And since you were there already, who else would I bug about figuring out how to get their angel to hover over the manger?"

"Yeah," he said with a chuckle. "You go with that excuse." His face grew pensive as he swirled his lemonade before taking a drink. "But actually I meant how you challenged me to forgive Ted."

"I challenged you? How?"

"I forgot your exact words." Wyatt stared directly at her. "The part that lodged in my brain was that if I expect God's forgiveness for the messes I've made in my life, I owe others some forgiveness, too."

"I don't think I said anything of the kind, but it is a precept that's worth remembering. 'Do unto others,' right?" Ellie had a hunch that if he could break free of the blame, he'd find it much easier to move ahead with his life. "The one thing I too often forget is that God loves us, warts and all. He sees into the depths of our hearts, knows our worst secret and loves us in spite of it."

"I have a lot to be forgiven for," Wyatt mumbled.

"I believe we all do." She liked his humility so much.

"You don't understand." He sighed. "I wish I could undo the past. I made so many mistakes in my marriage, broke so many promises to Taryn."

Wyatt's admission forced the realization that she'd never had this kind of conversation with Eddie. He'd never been this open with her about his past or his mistakes. In fact, he'd hated to discuss anything truly personal. Further proof that their marriage could not have worked. *Thank You, God that You saved me from that failure.*

Wyatt wasn't like Eddie, but it was now clearer than ever that, despite her feelings for him, there could be nothing between them. God had given her the job of raising Gracie. The older her daughter got, the more attention and love she would need. Ellie couldn't get sidetracked by her own wants. Often God called people to sacrifice, especially moms. Wincing at the pain of that, she tuned back in to what Wyatt was saying.

"I never loved my father the way I should have." His chin rested on his chest, his lowered voice revealing his shame. "I still feel like I failed him. I'm sure not the best parent for Cade. I make mistakes, get frustrated…"

"Wyatt." She placed her hand on his arm to draw his attention, cherishing the intimacy of these confidences he shared with her. When he lifted his head to look at her with his deep, dark gaze she smiled. "Welcome to the human race."

He rolled his eyes.

"I'm serious. I haven't been a Christian for very long, and there's much I have to learn," Ellie admitted. "But the one thing Sophie *has* drummed into me is that none of us is perfect, but God loves us anyway, and the important thing is that we keep trying to do His will."

"And forgiving Ted is His will." He nodded. "Got it. So that's not in question. What is in question is whether or not I can do it." He stared at Cade. "Every time I think about Ted, I get furious. He took Cade's mother. How do I forgive that, Ellie?"

There was so much pain in Wyatt's face that it took Ellie's breath away. She longed to wrap her arms around him and comfort him. But she couldn't do that. Wyatt had made it clear long ago that he did not want a romantic relationship. And neither did she, despite the overwhelming attraction she felt for him. Yet she had to help him. Somehow.

"No answers?" he said, managing a weak smile.

"I don't know how you find forgiveness, Wyatt," she admitted. "But God does. I think you'll have to ask Him to show you, because I'm pretty sure forgiveness is your only way out of the pain."

Ellie left Wyatt with his private thoughts, stepping away. She'd never known anyone like him, and she wanted to know more. In that moment she regretted her promise to Albert. Of course she still wanted to see where the boy lived and with whom, only not today. Not now when Wyatt was finally opening up to her. If only...

"I guess we'd better get going." Wyatt rose, collected their glasses and carried them inside. A few moments later he returned with a light jacket for Cade.

He walked over and swung the boy into his arms, gently shaking him to free the excess sand from his clothes. "I probably should bathe him."

"Why bother?" Ellie called Gracie to come. "You're the only one who looks model-perfect. Besides, I have some wipes." With her hand midway into her backpack to reach for the package, she stopped at his shout of laughter.

"Of course you do," Wyatt guffawed. "Shades of other messy meetings." He winked at her, then held out a hand. "Okay, give me some and let's mop 'em up."

He made cleaning the children's hands and faces into a game, and by the time they were finished, both Gracie and Cade were giggling. On that happy note they set out for the address Albert had given them.

"It's a rough-looking section of town," Wyatt muttered as they searched for the right house number. "I don't like the way those two guys on the corner are watching us."

Neither did Ellie, but there was nothing to do but keep going.

"There's Albert." Ellie waved at him. When Wyatt had parked, she opened her door and climbed out of the truck. "Hi. Ready to go?"

"I guess." The boy glanced behind him hesitantly, then left the front step to walk toward them.

"I tried to call and ask permission from your mom for you to come with us, but I couldn't get an answer at the number you gave me. Is there someone else I should speak to?" Ellie noted the curtain twitch in the front window.

"My mom doesn't live here." Albert climbed into the truck. "This is my uncle's place."

Ellie was about to say she'd ask his permission, but Albert assured her that it was fine for him to go and that no one but his older cousin was at home anyway.

"Your cousin knows you'll be with us?" After Albert nodded Ellie debated a moment longer, then gave up when Wyatt urged her to get into the truck.

But as they drove toward the restaurant, Ellie had second thoughts. She should have put this outing off until she'd been able to contact Albert's guardian. But her need to know, to help him or at least get him away for a time, had overtaken good sense. All she could do now was apologize to whomever was at his house when they returned and hope the person she believed was maltreating him realized that she and Wyatt were looking out for Albert.

Within minutes they were seated in a booth in the restaurant. Gracie soon had their guest talking freely and laughing at Cade's antics. They all ordered, except for Albert who wouldn't choose anything.

"I don't need to eat," he kept saying, though it was obvious from his rapt attention to other guests' meals that he was hungry.

"It's been a while since breakfast time, right?" Wyatt guessed. "Order another, or lunch if you'd rather. I had kind of a late start to the day and missed my breakfast so I'm famished."

"So am I." Ellie grinned at him, enjoying the camaraderie.

"I didn't know you were married," Albert said, his glance moving back and forth between them.

"We're not married!" Too aware of Wyatt's shoulder rubbing hers, Ellie shifted away, then felt suddenly bereft of the contact. Why had she chosen this booth instead of a roomy table where they wouldn't have to sit so close? "I drove out to Wyatt's ranch this morning so we could come together in his truck because my car is too small for all of us. Now what will you have to eat?"

Gracie finally persuaded Albert to match her pancake order.

All during the meal Ellie used every tactic she could think of to coax Albert to talk about himself, but he offered little response. Only with Gracie and Cade did he seem perfectly comfortable, again mentioning his late grandmother.

Ellie reached across to pat his hand. "It's good you had some family you could come to." She'd said that deliberately, ignoring Wyatt's nudge under the table while she watched Albert, trying to gauge his reaction.

"I guess." Albert didn't look at her, and Ellie grew more worried.

"I thought after breakfast we might take a drive out to the Sonoran Desert Museum." Wyatt wiped the sticky pancake syrup off Cade's face. "I haven't been there in a while. I wouldn't mind seeing the raptor flights again."

"Would you like to go, Albert?" Ellie asked.

"Doesn't matter to me," he said, showing no emotion.

"Maybe we should stop by your place and make sure it's okay with your uncle," Wyatt offered with a meaningful glance at Ellie.

"He won't care."

It wasn't the words; it was the way Albert said them that bothered Ellie. As if it didn't matter to him that his own uncle didn't care where Albert went or what he did.

"I'll try calling him again." Ellie pulled out her phone and dialed, but there was no response. "I guess there's still no one home."

Did Albert look relieved? She wasn't sure. She kept close watch on him as they walked the paths at the Desert Museum, noting his interest in the animal displays, especially the javelina pigs.

"Okay, let's keep going," Wyatt urged after a prolonged viewing. "There's a lot more to see."

Ellie wondered how silly and schoolgirlish it was to like the way he kept them together, to enjoy his hand on her back as he shepherded her past some youths that were roughhousing. Was it wrong to revel in his arm looping through hers and tugging her in a different direction than she'd intended? Well, if it was, so be it. Because Ellie was delighting in this day more with every passing moment.

Until she read the sign that said what lay ahead.

"Reptiles?" she hissed in Wyatt's ear, squeezing his arm.

"Of course." He flashed her his Hollywood smile. "That's my favorite exhibit. Why?"

"Oh, no reason." She forced her fingers to unclench and waged combat on every nerve that screamed *no way*.

In the dim underground display where the others ogled reptiles wriggling and writhing, the truth crawled up Ellie's skittering nerves and smacked her in the heart.

She was willing to be here, even to endure snakes, to be with Wyatt Wright.

Because she was in love with him?

Wyatt wasn't exactly sure where or when it happened, but somewhere along the way the fun of their trip to the Desert Museum lost its enjoyment for Ellie.

No matter how he explained the features of the different animals, he couldn't hold Ellie's attention. Albert and Gracie were avid pupils while he enthused about toads, turtles and tree frogs, but when they neared the rattlesnake display he noted Ellie shy away, keeping a good distance between herself and the glass.

Because she was terrified, he suddenly realized and wished he'd noted her aversion earlier. What a good sport she was to stay there and let everyone else appreciate what she hated. He wanted her to have fun today. He had to do something.

"I'm thirsty," he announced. "Let's go to the restaurant. Ellie?"

Stirring as if from a fog she nodded. "C-coffee sounds g-good," she stammered and immediately headed for the exit.

Wyatt felt a tug on his pant leg and glanced down. Gracie motioned to him to bend over.

"Mommy doesn't like snakes," she whispered in his ear. "But don't tell her I tol' you. 'Kay?"

"Our secret," Wyatt agreed and glanced at Albert, who nodded.

"Girls are usually scared of snakes," the boy said as if he possessed much worldly knowledge about the female of the species.

Wyatt hid a grin as he followed them out. He found Ellie waiting far down the path, as if she couldn't get enough distance between herself and the reptile enclosure.

"Albert was just telling me that girls often don't like snakes," he said to Ellie. He winked at Albert. "Was your grandmother one of those girls?"

"Yeah. Gran hated snakes." A smile lit up Albert's thin face. Was this the first time the boy had been able to share his memories of that woman? "If Gran thought there was a snake nearby, she'd get out this big old garden boot, and she wouldn't let go of it until the snake was dead or gone. She even took that boot to bed once. Kept it on the pillow right next to her head."

Gracie hooted with laughter. Wyatt joined in. Even Cade gurgled with amusement. Only Ellie seemed to think such an action was perfectly logical.

As they walked up the path to the café, Gracie pestered Albert for more stories about his grandmother, and

Albert obliged, apparently enjoying sharing his memories, especially about her cooking.

The restaurant was very busy so Wyatt suggested they quickly choose a table on the deck outside before everything was filled up.

"Sitting in the shade up here and savoring this amazing view of the valley is the perfect accompaniment to iced coffee." Wyatt handed Ellie Cade. "What would the rest of you like?"

"Iced tea for me, please." Ellie tickled Cade. "Maybe milk for this guy?"

"Ice cream?" Gracie asked Ellie.

Ellie wrinkled her nose. "Milk?" she suggested. Cade swung his arms wildly, as if to disagree.

"Ice cream's like milk," Albert said thoughtfully. "Only thicker and colder."

"An' lots better to eat," Gracie agreed. She turned to Wyatt. "Me an' Albert an' Cade would like ice cream, please."

She did not, Wyatt noted as he hid a smile, check with her mother. But when Cade started bellowing as if he agreed with Gracie he howled with laughter. After a moment Ellie joined in. Her lovely musical laugh echoed across the balcony, turning many heads. He knew exactly what the people who studied them were thinking; here was a family truly enjoying their day at the museum.

And for some strange reason Wyatt didn't mind them thinking that. Because, in some weird kind of way, maybe they were—a family of stragglers who'd banded together to have some fun. That's what Ellie did, he realized. She brought people together and helped them laugh.

That's exactly what she'd done for him.

While Ellie stayed at the table with Cade, Wyatt took Gracie and Albert inside to help carry the ice cream. While they waited he glanced out the window and found he couldn't look away from the vision of Ellie playing with his son. She was so pretty, a real natural at motherhood with her generous, nurturing spirit. Ellie was the kind of woman most men dreamed of having for a wife.

Whoa!

Wyatt forcibly reined in his thoughts. Forgiving Ted, that made sense. He needed to get past that hurdle to fully live his Christian faith.

But starting another relationship, even with someone as great as Ellie, was something Wyatt could not allow himself to consider. Too many broken promises blocked that path, too many memories of how he'd failed.

So for the rest of the afternoon Wyatt worked hard to stop the myriad images of Ellie from engraving in his head. And failed. Ellie laughing as she tried to photograph a darting roadrunner, smiling when a bee kept buzzing Wyatt, teasing Cade out of his grumpiness and making everyone's day a little happier. His brain captured and stored a thousand images of sweet, generous, earnest Ellie.

After they'd shared a barbecue dinner at his ranch, after they'd driven Albert home and Ellie had left, after he'd put Cade to bed, poured himself a fresh lemonade and sat on his patio—when the world had fallen silent around him—Wyatt let those images play like a recording that he couldn't erase. Didn't want to.

Because Ellie Grant was a very special woman.

Chapter Ten

"He said what?" Ellie couldn't believe the words she just heard. Maybe she was in a Monday morning fog.

"This morning Wyatt told Tanner he accepted his offer of full-time employment at Wranglers Ranch." Sophie hugged her in a burst of exuberance. "Isn't it wonderful? A true answer to our prayers."

"Wonderful," Ellie repeated, feeling dazed. When Sophie left she passed the morning preparing for Albert's group to visit this afternoon while her mind repeated one question. What in the world had happened to change Wyatt's mind about breaking the promise to his father?

She'd seen him at church yesterday, and he hadn't said a word. She'd sat beside him at the Christmas potluck afterward, and he hadn't mentioned closing his office. She'd gone back to his ranch to do another batch of baking yesterday afternoon, with Albert lending a hand decorating the cookies, and still Wyatt hadn't said anything. Though she repeatedly searched her brain, Ellie found nothing to suggest that Wyatt had been considering this action.

She had tons of questions to ask the handsome veterinarian, but Wyatt never appeared.

"He asked for the morning off to make some phone calls about his practice." Tanner answered her question about his whereabouts when she joined him and Sophie for lunch on the patio. "He'll be here for the class after lunch."

"What about Cade?" She blushed at Tanner and Sophie's shared glances of amusement.

"Cade will have a sitter every morning and every other afternoon. If I have to call Wyatt in, I told him to bring Cade along, and we'd figure out something." He kept a straight face as he asked, "Is there a problem if I ask you to care for him?"

"Of course not."

"Truth be told, you'd relish the opportunity to hold that little guy in your arms again, wouldn't you?" Sophie teased.

"So I like kids." Ellie concentrated on eating.

"Cade's a cutie, all right." Tanner swallowed the last of his coffee and rose. "Say, did you ever get to speak to Albert's uncle?"

"No." Ellie frowned. "His house looked dark when we dropped Albert off last night, as if no one was home. But he insisted his cousin would be around, and I had to get Gracie home—"

"You don't have to apologize, Ellie. It's not your job, or Wyatt's, to care for Albert, but it does raise some questions about the folks whose job it is." Tanner kissed Sophie goodbye. "I'll be sorting out tack," he said, giving her a long look, as if he couldn't bear to be far from her side.

Ellie's heart ached for someone to look at her with

that same gaze of adoration. But that was silly to hope for when she knew what God expected. With a sigh she buried herself in her work until she heard the bus rolling in. Then she pasted a smile on her face and went out to greet the kids.

She managed to keep her mind off Wyatt while the boys demonstrated their ability to curry their animals. Then they were learning how to trot their mounts when Wyatt appeared on the other side of Albert's horse. Ellie couldn't control her racing heart or the silly smile she knew she wore.

"I hear you'll be joining our staff. Welcome." She pretended her smile was purely professional. "I think you'll enjoy it here."

"News travels fast." He stopped Albert to point out his loose cinch, then grinned at her. "I already enjoy it here."

"Good." *Don't read anything into his friendliness, Ellie. He's one of the nice guys—to everyone.*

"I took more of your advice last night." He offered his encouragement as Albert tightened the cinch, then nervously climbed on the horse and nudged it to move.

"My advice?" Ellie gulped when Wyatt swiveled to look at her. "What was that?"

Wyatt leaned forward and whispered, "I asked God to help me forgive Ted."

"Great." She noticed the way he glanced around at the group and saw how the corners of his mouth tightened.

"I think that's going to take some doing, though, because as I look around, I don't feel compassion for most of these kids."

"You need a different filter." Ellie grinned. "It's something Pastor Jeff said in his sermon a few weeks ago. When it's hard for us to do as God instructs us, Jeff suggested we put on a 'God filter' that strips away all the things we see as so good about ourselves and see what God sees."

"Which is?"

"The view that we are no better than the next guy, that we need forgiveness just as much as he does, and maybe more."

There was no time to talk for the rest of the lesson as Ellie was called on to treat a boy who'd caught his foot in a stirrup when dismounting. But that didn't stop her from silently praying for Wyatt as she worked.

She escorted the boy to the gate and remained, smiling and waving as the kids loaded onto the bus. Albert had a window seat, and after a moment's hesitation, he waved back at her, his smile faint but still there.

When the group was gone, the staff gathered for a coffee break on the patio where Tanner made a little speech welcoming Wyatt to their group. Ellie forced herself to keep her applause mild, but inside she was jumping with joy because she'd now see Wyatt almost every day.

Foolish, her brain chided. She wanted to ignore it, but Gracie's arrival off the bus reminded her of her duty.

Ellie was more than ready to put some distance between herself and the ranch so she could sort out her feelings for Wyatt. But her daughter, it seemed, was not.

"We hafta go to Cade's place," Gracie said as she tossed her backpack into the car.

"Oh, honey, not tonight. I've got so much to do to get ready for Christmas." Ellie knew from the jut of Gracie's chin that reason wasn't going to work. "Why do you need to go there?"

"I hafta do something Melissa said to do 'bout my gift for Cade." Gracie frowned darkly. "An' I can't tell you what 'cause it's a secret."

"What's a secret?" Wyatt asked after stepping out from a stand of sycamores. He listened carefully to what Gracie said, wrinkled his nose and shot Ellie a questioning look.

"She won't tell me." Ellie shrugged, wishing she could control the rush of joy that filled her every time he appeared.

"I don't think today is a very good time, Gracie."

Something about Wyatt's voice got Ellie's attention. She surreptitiously studied him, wondering what had happened to turn his eyes so dark and turbulent.

"Oh." Gracie deflated. There was no other description to fully convey the way her chest slumped, her shoulders dipped, and her lips drooped. "But Christmas isn't very far away," she pleaded.

"Exactly nine days," Ellie added almost but not quite under her breath.

"And you've got things to do." Wyatt nodded. "So do I. Maybe another time, Gracie." He turned to walk away. To Ellie's eyes he also looked deflated. And maybe a little cross?

"You stay here, honey," she ordered Gracie. "I need to talk to Wyatt in private."

"Please, Mommy, please get him to let us come. Please?" Gracie begged, hope sparkling in her blue eyes just the way Karen's had when she and Ellie were young.

"I don't think so. Now, stay here," she directed.

"An' pray. That's what I'll do." Gracie flopped down on a stump and clasped her hands.

Shaking her head, Ellie walked up to Wyatt. "Is something wrong? You seem—"

She wasn't prepared when he whirled to face her, fury evident in his body language.

"He's coming here."

"Who?" Ellie had never seen him this angry.

"Ted." He glared at the phone he still held in his hand. "I just had a phone call from a friend who learned that Ted was never charged with Taryn's accident."

"I'm so sorry." She knew how much he'd been counting on Ted's punishment to make him feel that his wife's needless death would be avenged.

"That's not the worst of it." Wyatt's jaw flexed. "Apparently he has some youth sponsor from the church, a do-gooder who wants to be sure that poor Ted doesn't suffer any negative effects from his brush with the law, so he's enrolled him in a program here, at Wranglers. Isn't that rich? Ted gets to ride horses while Cade goes without his mother."

"I don't know what to say." Ellie could hardly stand to watch his pain. "I'm so sorry you have to go through this."

"I don't have to." His jaw clenched again as he turned to peer into the brush. "I'm going to resign. I should never have taken the job here anyway."

"But you don't have clients." Suddenly she knew not seeing Wyatt every day would be far worse than enduring the pain of seeing him, loving him and not being able to do anything about it. "You can't quit."

"I can't be here when he comes, can't watch him gloating over his escape from justice," he said in a cracked voice.

"Oh, Wyatt." Ellie couldn't help it. She stepped forward and drew him into her arms, hurting because he hurt and desperate to assuage his pain.

As Wyatt's arms slid around her waist and he drew her near, his breath brushed her ear. For a moment it was pure bliss to be so close, to be the one he leaned on, the one he turned to for support. But even as those thoughts filled her head, Ellie knew it couldn't last.

So she eased away, breaking contact with him, though it was so hard not to let that embrace go on and on. But that wasn't what either of them needed right now.

"Tell me what you're thinking," she urged.

"That I let myself get too consumed with work and Cade. I keep making the same old mistake over and over." A sigh came from deep within him. "I should have done something, insisted the police find more evidence. Something, anything, because now Ted's going to get away with what he did."

"Wait a minute." Ellie squeezed her eyes closed to think. When she opened them Wyatt was staring at her, a frown on his face. "Who said Ted did anything wrong?"

"The police?" Wyatt's confusion was obvious. "He was arrested. He was found at the scene. I don't know what you're saying, Ellie."

"I'm saying you don't know the reason he wasn't charged." She had to get him to refocus. "You don't know anything about Ted, not for sure."

"I know what the cops told me." Wyatt stared at her as if she'd somehow betrayed him.

"That was how long ago? The night Taryn died?" she asked quietly and waited for his nod. "You lost your wife, Wyatt. You were grieving, you had a baby to care for, a funeral to plan, a life to put back together. Two lives. That was more than enough for you to handle. It was the duty of the police and the courts to find out who was to blame and to punish them."

"Which they have not done." He was clearly unable to reconcile his anger and guilt.

"How do you know?" She touched his arm, trying to make him reconsider. "You're angry and upset. All this time, since that awful night, you've blamed Ted for ruining your life. You haven't been able to forgive him, you said."

"No, but I thought that if I tried hard, if I was willing to let go of everything…" He exhaled. "But I can't."

"Can I say something?" She saw his nod but hesitated. "You won't want to hear me, Wyatt. It will hurt, and you've had a bellyful of hurt already. But I think you need to consider who you can't forgive."

His head jerked up, and he gaped at her.

"What I mean is this. You've tried so hard to do the right thing, be the right son, to not repeat your father's mistakes. And yet your life got dumped on." She touched his arm, trying to soften words that couldn't be softened. "Are you really truly unable to forgive Ted?" she whispered. "Or is it God you can't forgive for letting Taryn die, for letting your perfect family be destroyed?"

The words hung in the air. How she wished she could take them back, could unsay them and never have to remember Wyatt's devastated eyes.

"No, Ellie. That's not it." He glared at her, his face rigid and unyielding. "Taryn died because I didn't keep my promise to her. If I had, she'd still be alive." The harsh words hit her like ice pellets. "I have to live with that. But I'm not the only one to blame. Ted should pay for his part in her death, and now he won't. That's what I can't forgive. Or forget."

Then he turned and walked off. A moment later his truck roared away from the ranch.

"He doesn't want us, does he?" Gracie stood watching the red plumes of dust with tears rolling down her cheeks. "He's got Cade and he doesn't need anybody else in his family. He doesn't want to be my daddy."

Ellie consoled her daughter all the way home, then went to extreme lengths to cheer her up by letting her try on her angel costume for the concert. But later she sent a constant barrage of prayers heavenward. Not just prayers for Gracie, but for a man, a generous, kind veterinarian caught in a maelstrom of pain, anger and bitter regret.

Please, please, don't let me love him.

What a futile prayer. Wyatt Wright was embedded in her heart.

At first Wyatt held off on giving his resignation, because he was too embarrassed to cancel on Tanner when he had such huge expectations for the Make-A-Wish kids. He went to work, did his job and pretended everything was normal. And he avoided Ellie.

If only it was so easy to avoid her voice in his head.

Is it God you can't forgive for letting Taryn die?

Somewhere in those words he thought he heard a ring of truth, but unable to handle more than his new job, his son and his needy ranch, Wyatt blocked them out in exactly the same way he blocked out the memory of Ellie holding him, trying to comfort him. Ellie the nurturer.

He was successful at avoiding her for one day. Then she tracked him to the farthest quarter of Wranglers Ranch on a horse she could barely sit.

"I have something to tell you, and you've no alternative but to listen to me." Her hair was a halo of mussed curls, her face glowed with perspiration, and she kept rubbing one hand as if it hurt. "This time you cannot run away."

"Who said I was running?" he asked, then gave up because there was absolutely no point in lying to Ellie. She homed in on truth like hummingbirds to nectar.

"Now, listen to me, Wyatt, because this is important." She dismounted then sat down on a bale, her eyes locking on him. "Albert is Ted."

"What?" He couldn't figure out what she meant.

"His real name is Albert, but his relatives call him Ted. That's the name you heard the police use that night." She studied him as if trying to assess his reaction. "Well?" she demanded, frustrated by his lack of response. "Aren't you going to say anything?"

"How do you know this?" He fiddled with his gloves, trying not to stare at her and failing. She was so lovely, especially when that temper showed.

"He came to decorate cookies last night. That's when he told Gracie that his uncle had started calling him Ted because he said he was fat like a teddy bear."

Wyatt just sat there, trying hard to make sense of what she'd said.

"Do you want to hear the rest?" she demanded.

"Do I have a choice?" He watched a pucker form on her brow and nodded. "That's what I thought. Continue."

"When he was five, Albert's mother left him with his grandmother and never came back. His Gran was a wonderful woman who loved him and raised him right. But she died and that left eleven-year-old Albert—eleven, Wyatt," she emphasized in case he hadn't heard her the first time. "It left that poor kid at the mercy of his relatives whom, I might add, have a very disreputable reputation, according to a certain social worker I know."

"Ah, the hard luck story."

Her eyes narrowed in warning.

"Sorry," he apologized, though he wasn't in the least sorry. Ellie mad was really something to see. "Go on."

She studied him with a glower that said she wasn't sure he was serious, then shifted from the bale to the ground and continued.

"Yes, I will, because you need to hear this to understand who Ted is." She blew her bangs off her forehead.

"Okay then, go on." He looked at her and realized he'd missed her. This steamrollering nurse who didn't take no for an answer, didn't even hear it, truth be told.

"So here's this orphaned kid and, despite having to change his home and school and move into that drug-infested neighborhood where his sketchy, not to mention abusive, relatives live—" Her steely gray eyes dared him to argue with that assessment. "Despite losing the only mother he's ever known, our Ted manages to steer clear of trouble and keep up his excellent grades."

"A model citizen, in fact. Bravo." He was deliberately goading her, but he couldn't stop, couldn't make himself forget what Ted had done.

"He really is, Wyatt. And you know what? He had nothing to do with your wife's death." She must have seen his skepticism. "It's the truth, and there are many witnesses who back up his story, which is why he's innocent. He was only at the scene that night because his cousin—the driver of the car—called him for help. Because he was scared and he knew Ted would know what to do. Which was good because Ted called 911."

Ellie leaned back on her hands and studied him like a

hawk with prey, obviously waiting for his reaction. But Wyatt struggled to comprehend what she'd said.

"Don't you get it? Ted isn't guilty of Taryn's death." Her tone modulated. "He doesn't deserve your anger, Wyatt, and he doesn't need your forgiveness because he didn't do anything wrong."

"He was still there." The feeble excuse sounded pathetic even to him. But he'd blamed the kid for so long, blamed an innocent boy when the blame lay directly on himself.

"Let it go." Ellie shook her head. "It's not doing you any good to hang on to this ill will. Besides…"

He recognized that pause; it meant she had something else to say, something she thought he wouldn't like.

"Besides?"

"What if the situation was different, Wyatt? What if Cade was the kid someone was blaming for something that wasn't his fault?" Those gray eyes wouldn't let him ignore the truth. "Would you want them to treat Cade as unfairly as you're treating Ted?"

Trust Ellie to illustrate his stubbornness so perfectly.

"Okay, I get it. But it's going to take me a while." He heaved a sigh because the truth could no longer be disputed no matter how unpalatable it was. "I have to mentally mesh Albert and Ted, figure out how to deal with what I thought I knew. It won't happen overnight."

"I know." She rose, walked over to him and touched his arm. "It won't be easy, but you'll do it, Wyatt."

"How do you know that?" he demanded, frustrated by the idealized vision she seemed to have of him. Couldn't she tell how unsatisfied he was by this knowledge? Couldn't she see that Albert's—Ted's—innocence only made his own guilt seem worse?

"Because of who your Father is. God will heal your heart, if you let Him." Ellie's words triggered an awareness inside him. The hole Taryn's death had left in his heart *was* healing, thanks in part to Ellie's gentle comfort but also because of Gracie's unwavering love.

But if his faith was real, if he truly believed God was the master of his life, there was more to the story.

"What are you thinking, Wyatt? Please, tell me." Ellie stood before him now, her face troubled as she waited.

"It's just dawned on me." Wyatt could hardly wrap his brain around it. "Ted—Albert—I can't blame anyone because, in truth, Taryn's life was in God's hands. That's what she believed. He's who she trusted completely."

"Yes." Ellie smiled, but she still waited expectantly.

A flicker of something fresh, something joyful seemed to come alive inside him.

"Nothing happens unless God allows it. He knew she'd die that night and that it would be my fault for breaking my promise."

"Right." A huge grin spread across her face. "He knew, and He forgives you. Don't you think Taryn would, too, if she was here?"

"Yes." He had to admit it, because she had not been one to hold grudges. "She wouldn't have liked the way I've been."

"But she would have understood." Ellie pinned him with her gaze. "If Taryn were here right now, wouldn't she encourage you to reach out to Albert, to help him however you can? Isn't that the kind of woman your wife was, Wyatt?"

"Yes." He studied Ellie, suddenly thankful that she hadn't left him in his misery, blame and unforgiveness, so glad that she'd pushed and prodded and nudged him to the truth. "I've made a lot of mistakes," he murmured. "And I'll probably make more in the future."

"Of course you will." Ellie chuckled at his dour look. "Because you're human," she added with a wink. Her eyebrows arched. "And...?"

"And I promise I'll give Albert a chance." There he was, making promises again, but somehow Wyatt thought he might be able to keep this one with God and Ellie's help.

He was not prepared for Ellie's squeal of delight or for the way she launched herself into his arms. But he liked it.

"Oh, Wyatt, I'm so glad." Ellie's arms tightened around his neck as she hugged him. "Albert needs our help and—" Suddenly the words stopped. She shifted, easing back from him, her cheeks flushed. "I'm sorry, I wasn't thinking. I know we're not either of us looking for a relationship—"

Was that true?

His arms still around her waist, Wyatt held on and let himself bask in her sudden shyness. Holding Ellie like this—it felt right, as if she belonged there. He'd loved Taryn, but the hole her loss had left in his heart was healing now, thanks in part to Ellie's gentle nudges into the future and to Gracie's sturdy faith in God. And his heart—was Ellie in it?

"Wyatt, I should—"

"Ellie?" He cupped her silken cheek in his palm.

"Yes?" She gazed at him.

"Be quiet." Then he leaned in and kissed her.

And Ellie kissed him back.

Chapter Eleven

"My father would not have approved of all this Christmas fuss."

Ellie froze for a moment, wondering if she should offer some sort of platitude to ease the situation. She felt confused, giddy, wary and a thousand other emotions every time she was near Wyatt. Because of his kiss yesterday.

Wonderful though it had been to be enveloped in his arms, to share that tender moment with him, nothing had been the same since.

"Maybe your mom would've," Gracie said, not even glancing up from the snowman cookie she was frosting.

"Maybe she would have. I don't know." Wyatt helped Cade press another snowman out of the cookie dough, and Albert slipped it onto a baking sheet.

"Well, arn'cha gonna look for her?" Gracie demanded. "That's what I'd do if I lost my mommy."

"Smart cookie," Wyatt said, and they all shared a laugh.

"Wyatt has been looking, honey," Ellie said, and for the moment, that seemed to satisfy her daughter.

Ellie waited until Cade was asleep and she and Wyatt were having coffee on the patio while Gracie and Albert finished the cookie decorating, before she asked, "You haven't learned anything more about your mom?"

"The investigator says he has a lead he's checking out. We'll see," he said with a shrug. "Want to order a pizza for supper?"

"We could." A little thrill tiptoed across her brain at the prospect of spending more time with this amazing man. "On one condition."

"Name it." He grinned at her, and Ellie's heart flew sky high.

"That we get your Christmas tree up." Ellie wondered at his frown. "You need to celebrate Christmas, Wyatt. I don't think it's too early to teach Cade about Christ's birth."

"A tree, besides all the stuff you and Gracie have already added?" He nodded toward the house, to where she'd added pinecones on the table, homemade wreaths on the doors, paper cutouts on the windows. He grinned, though she saw several emotions skitter across his expressive face. Finally, he nodded. "Okay, we'll go get a tree as soon as Cade wakes up."

And that was how the five of them ended up eating pizza at the mall before they loaded up on ornaments and lights.

"Uh, do you know what excessive means?" Ellie asked as they stood in line at a checkout.

"You mean as in wasting an inordinate amount of money on glittery geegaws that will be garbage by next year?" He nodded. "Yes, I do know what excessive means, Ellie."

The way he said it, in a mocking tone, told her that

someone had once said those very words to him and that the memory was not a pleasant one. Ellie was guessing that person had been his father and that the teeming shopping cart in front of Wyatt was his way of exorcising the negatives of his youth.

"Oh, good." She grinned at him. "Albert, could you get another package of lights? One can never have too many lights."

Albert glanced from her to Wyatt, shrugged and left with Gracie in tow.

"Clearly that kid knows about excessive," Wyatt muttered. "Too bad nobody ever showered him with it."

"Maybe we can be the first," Ellie said.

"What do you mean?" Wyatt said.

"Ever heard of Christmas gifts?"

He groaned. "Another reason to shop?"

"Why not, when we're using your credit card?" Ellie couldn't stop her giggle.

"My father did not approve of credit cards," he said when they were on their way to his truck with the bulging cart.

"What did he approve of?" Ellie asked, only half serious.

"Not much. Not me, for sure."

"I'm sure that's not true. I'm sure he loved you in his own way." Except she wasn't sure. And now she'd begun wondering if the parenting worries she'd once heard Wyatt mention stemmed from fear that he'd somehow lose Cade's love as he'd lost his father's.

"We didn't get a tree," Ellie suddenly realized as they left the mall.

"We will. I know exactly the tree I want." Wyatt leaned forward, peering through the windshield as he drove. "It used to be right along… Yeah, here it is." He turned into a nursery lot that glowed with so much Christmas decor she thought she'd stepped into Las Vegas.

"Wow." Ellie gulped, her eyes wide. "This place gives new meaning to excessive."

He laughed and got out of the truck.

"Albert, can you give me a hand?" Wyatt's voice held a certain reserve when he spoke to the boy, but Ellie thought he was getting used to thinking of Albert as someone other than the enemy.

"Can I go, too?" Gracie said as she reached for her seat belt.

"Not this time." Wyatt winked at her. "It's a surprise."

Frustrated but also curious, Gracie kept watch until she saw the two males returning. "They didn't get anything," she said, disappointed.

"Don't judge by what you see," Albert told her. "Christmas is all about believing. Gran used to say nobody would believe God would send His son as a baby in a manger where animals were, but that's exactly what He did."

A little thrill wiggled inside Ellie when Wyatt smiled at her, delighted when he suggested prolonging the fun by treating them all to ice cream.

Back at his ranch Gracie squealed with excitement when she saw a conical shape sitting in a massive pot on the front step.

"It's a Christmas tree!"

"See, Gracie? You have to believe," Albert told her. "Wyatt had it delivered while we had ice cream." His chest puffed out a little. "I helped pick it out."

"Good job." Ellie applauded. "It's gorgeous and much better than a fake tree."

"Or cutting one down." Wyatt unlocked the door and waited for everyone to enter before he carried in the tree. "It's an Aleppo pine tree. I'll plant it when Christmas is over. In ten years I'll have a nice grove of trees. If it survives," he muttered as Cade yanked on a bough.

They immediately began to decorate it. Within minutes Ellie was doubled over in laughter.

"It's not funny," Wyatt growled as he lifted off the strand of lights Gracie had tossed on, and rearranged them more symmetrically.

"It's hilarious." She chuckled even harder watching his face as the kids hung ornaments willy-nilly. Like a robot on overdrive Wyatt unhooked and rehooked them, trying to keep up. "Give up. It's a Christmas tree, Wyatt. Not a work of art."

Ellie felt awful for saying that when his face got a stricken look, and he left to sit rigidly on the sofa.

"I'm sorry," she apologized. "It's your tree and your home. You should decorate it the way you want."

"Do you know what I was doing?" he whispered, his voice ragged. "I was doing exactly what my father did to me. In all my years of living with him I never managed to hang even one Christmas decoration the way he wanted. I was trying to decorate the tree as he wanted, and he's not even here to see."

Ellie couldn't stand seeing his pain, so she leaned over and threaded her fingers in his.

"So you'll change. Right?"

"Absolutely." He squeezed her fingers, then covered their clasped hands with his other one. "Thank you, Ellie."

"No." She shook her head as she pulled her hand free, desperate to move away before she did something rash—like kiss him again. "Thank *you* for making this such a fun time for them." She nodded toward the kids.

"For me, too," was all Wyatt said, but when she relaxed against the sofa, Wyatt's arm somehow crept behind her head and rested above her shoulders. And she liked it.

"Christmas is coming together, isn't it?" she said later after he'd put Cade to bed and Albert was sitting in a corner reading the Christmas story to Gracie. "What do you hope for Christmas, Wyatt?"

"Finding out about my mother would be the perfect gift." He grinned. "I might get it, too."

"Oh?"

"I just got a text. I'm getting a report about her tomorrow." When Wyatt turned his head, Ellie caught her breath at the hopeful yet wary look she saw there. "Can you pray about it?" he asked.

"Absolutely." For the second time that night she reached out and took his hand. And this time she hung on, tamping down her own feelings to offer support and encouragement to him. But inside she was whispering a totally different prayer than the one he requested.

This man has a place in my heart, God, and I know that's not Your will for me. So what am I supposed to do about it?

"Esau doesn't understand why he's wearing this strange harness, Gracie." Wyatt gazed down at her as she regarded the fidgeting pony. "That's why we need you to help him get used to it. Okay?"

"Yeah." Lately the little girl had seemed down, despite the fast approach of Christmas. Wyatt was pretty sure it had to do with him and his refusal to be the daddy she longed for, but he wasn't sure how to fix it other than the obvious solution, and he wasn't going to do that even though he'd grown very fond of Gracie.

"You're sad today." It felt like her tiny fist squeezed his heart when she bowed her head. "Can you tell me why?"

After a very long silence, Gracie lifted her head, her eyes locking with his. "Why doesn't God answer prayers?"

Nothing like an easy question.

"What makes you think He doesn't?"

She gave him a look of disdain.

"You mean about me being your daddy?"

She nodded glumly.

Wyatt frowned. "But that's not the only thing bothering you, is it?"

She shook her head.

"I'm no good at guessing. You have to tell me what's wrong, Gracie."

"It's not just my prayers." Her bottom lip trembled. "It's lots of people's."

"Like?" Wyatt had no clue how to deal with this, but some inner warning compelled him to keep her talking. "Who else doesn't get their prayers answered?"

"You."

Wyatt blinked in surprise. "Me?"

"Uh-huh." Gracie looped the horse's reins around the saddle's pommel. "You been prayin' to find your mommy, but God doesn't answer."

Her words and the sympathy in her gaze touched

his heart. What a dear, sweet child she was. Any father would be proud to call Gracie his.

"My mom has been gone a long time. Maybe God needs some time to find her," he explained. The day was almost over, and the investigator still hadn't called.

"God doesn't need time," Gracie scoffed. "He can do what He wants when He wants to."

"Then maybe I need time." Torn by anticipation that perhaps today he'd finally learn the truth about his mother and yet hesitant to have those years-long questions answered, Wyatt had a hunch Gracie would understand his issues. "Do you want to know a secret?"

Gracie's eyes widened as she slowly nodded.

"I'm a little bit scared to meet my mother." It felt good to admit that.

"Why?" Gracie's forehead pleated in a frown. "'Cause maybe she won't like you?"

"Something like that," he admitted, giving voice to what had hidden inside him for years. "Maybe that's why she went away, because she didn't like me."

"Nah. You're nice, so I don't think that's why." Gracie's staunch support made him chuckle. "'Sides, mommies always like their kids."

Wyatt didn't have the heart to tell her it wasn't always true, but he didn't have to because Gracie found her own answer.

"Maybe not." She frowned again. "Albert's mommy left him, and he's been prayin' a long time for her to come back." She heaved a giant sigh. "So why doesn't God answer our prayers?"

"There might be lots of reasons, and I doubt we'll ever know all of them." That answer was weak as water. Wyatt wanted desperately to reassure this sweet child so he hurried on. "I think the important thing is to keep talking to God and trusting that He'll do His best for us."

"I guess." Gracie's face looked only a little less glum.

"So can you try riding Esau again now?" he asked, feeling like he'd failed her. "Hold the reins as I showed you and lean back, just the way you think Esther would."

"But I don't even know her," Gracie complained.

"You'll meet her soon," he said, hoping he could keep his word.

"How's it going?" Ellie called from her stance by the fence rail. She gave Gracie an encouraging smile. "Looks good, sweetie."

"Can you stay here with her for a minute?" he asked her because he'd just figured out the problem. "I need to get Tanner, so he can see what I mean about an adjustment. I'll be back in a minute."

It took a little longer than that. By the time Wyatt returned, Albert had appeared and was trying to persuade Gracie to put her feet in the stirrups.

"It makes the horse feel better," he said as if he were a riding pro.

"But it makes *my* legs hurt," Gracie complained. "They don't fit."

"Exactly." Wyatt turned to Tanner. "See what I was saying?"

They mulled it over for a few moments, then came up with a solution.

"Am I done now?" Gracie finally asked. "'Cause I gotta go to the practice."

"Choir rehearsal for their concert," Ellie explained when Wyatt sent her a questioning look. "After that we're going caroling at a seniors' home. Want to come?"

"That's why I stayed after the class today," Albert explained. "I'm going, too."

"I'll go with you." Wyatt made the snap decision because there was still nothing from the investigator, and it was driving him nuts.

Ellie gave him a big smile. "Glad to have you." Her dazzling grin did funny things to Wyatt's midsection.

"I'll have to bring Cade—"

"I can look after him," Albert volunteered. His face got a little red when all eyes focused on him. "I like little kids," he said defensively. "And Cade's cute."

"Thanks, Albert." Wyatt felt a kindling of a connection with the boy. Now that he knew Albert better, he realized he wouldn't have been part of the joyriding bunch that killed Taryn. Something inside him yearned to befriend him, but he hesitated. What if he failed Albert?

"'S'cuse me," Gracie said in a loud voice, exasperation all over her face. "Can I get down *now*?"

"Yes." Wyatt hid his grin as he lifted her off Esau's back. "You've been a great help. Thank you, Gracie."

"Welcome." She smiled at him as if they shared a secret. And maybe they did.

Wyatt was about to leave with the horse when she tugged on his pant leg and motioned him to bend down. When he did Gracie stood on tiptoe, cupped her hand around his ear and whispered.

"Don't be scared no more. If I pray about finding your mom really hard, maybe God'll answer that prayer."

She was such a sweetheart. A lump lodged in Wyatt's throat, making it impossible for him to speak. So he simply nodded then, without thought, hugged her tightly. If only—

"I gotta go now," she whispered this time much louder, giving a slight wiggle to get free.

"So we'll meet you at the church?" Ellie studied the two of them with a confused look.

"After I get Cade, you mean? Okay." Wyatt had a hunch he was getting entirely too dependent on the lovely Ellie for company, but how could he not?

Ellie was the very spirit of Christmas, baking goodies, insisting he get a tree and helping decorate his house. He felt a rush of warmth inside him whenever he thought about the bighearted nurse who spread cheer wherever she went.

His life would be so boring without Ellie.

But he couldn't care for her as more than a friend, and even that was risky because he always ended up failing people.

Wyatt snapped himself out of that vein of thought, then noticed Albert standing just beyond the circle of their group, as if he felt left out. Wyatt knew exactly how that felt. He made a sudden decision.

"Want to come with me, Albert?"

A surprised look flickered across the boy's face before he gave a nod. "Sure."

"I'll meet you at my truck in five minutes, after I unsaddle Esau." Wyatt walked the horse toward the tack room. Lefty met him halfway and insisted he'd take care of Esau. Wyatt was almost to his truck when his phone rang.

The private investigator. Finally he'd know the truth about his mother.

"Albert, did something happen with Wyatt?" Ellie murmured as they waited for the vet to unbuckle his son from his car seat and join the choir that was to sing at the seniors' home. Earlier she'd met Wyatt at the church as they'd planned then spent the entire choir rehearsal trying to figure out what was wrong with him. "He seems...sad."

"He got a phone call before we left Wranglers Ranch," Albert said. "I think it was something about his mom."

Ellie sucked in her breath on a silent prayer that the news hadn't been bad. Wyatt so needed answers. Maybe if he—

"Sorry to hold you up for the caroling." He led Cade by the hand as he approached.

"The seniors are going to love him." Ellie helped the choir leaders shepherd the children inside to a large room.

Knowing their part, the kids assembled immediately, smiled at the seniors and, when given a chord, burst into a series of songs they were going to sing at their Christmas concert in a few days. She had to laugh when Wyatt set Cade down and the boy immediately headed for the Christmas tree with its glittering decorations. Wyatt, busy texting on his phone, didn't seem to notice Cade's disappearance, so Ellie scooped the child into her arms and took him to the back of the room where she gave him a toy truck to play with.

"Sorry." Wyatt's face was pale when he caught up. "I should have been paying more attention."

"No problem." Ellie couldn't ignore the trouble brewing in Wyatt's eyes as he gazed at his phone. "What's wrong?"

"Nothing." He quickly shoved the phone in his pocket.

"Haven't we gotten past the social niceties yet?" she said in a very quiet voice. "Please, tell me what's wrong."

"The investigator found my mother." He said the words without emotion.

"Isn't that good news?" But she could see from his haggard look that it wasn't. Fear snuck in and grabbed Ellie by the throat. "Wyatt?"

"My mother is in a care home," he said. "A care home for mentally unstable people. She's been there for nearly twenty-eight years, Ellie."

Oh, Lord. Help him. Please, help him. Heal his hurting heart.

When the silence between them stretched too long and she couldn't stand it anymore, she said, "It doesn't change who you are, Wyatt."

"Doesn't it?" His dark eyes seemed frozen.

"Of course not. She has an illness, and she's in a place where they can treat it. That's something to be thankful for." Ellie felt as if her words were bouncing off him but she didn't know what else to say to break his stony demeanor.

"Why didn't my father tell me?" The words seemed pulled out of him. "Why let me go on wondering, thinking she'd abandoned me?" His tortured words begged her for an answer. "If the dates are right I was barely two when she left. Maybe he couldn't have told me then, but why not later on when I asked about her?"

"He didn't tell you anything?" Her heart ached for him. If only she could ease this burden for the man she loved.

"When I was eighteen, just before I left for college, I asked him if he knew where my mother was or if she was dead." Wyatt lifted Cade and cradled him in his arms so the weary boy could rest his head on his daddy's shoulder. "He said she was never coming back, and that was the end of it. We never spoke of it again."

"I'm sorry." She placed her hand on his arm, wishing she could bear some of his pain. "Do you know where the care home is?"

"Right here in Tucson." His lips pressed in a tight line of anger. "Eventide Rest Home." He made a face. "Would you believe I made a call there recently to treat an injured cat? I was in the same place as my mother, and I never even knew it."

Anger and pain oozed through the words. But Ellie needed to help this man she loved see past the pain to the opportunity.

"You have to go see her," she said firmly. "Talk to her, find out what you can. Get your questions answered." As the choir neared the end of their final song, she asked, "Did your investigator say you could do that?"

"He didn't say." Wyatt frowned. "You think I should go there?"

"Don't you want to?" She couldn't believe he didn't.

"Yes, but—" He swallowed hard. "What if she isn't able to tell me anything?"

"Then you'll know." The children were bowing to their audience's applause. They only had seconds before they'd be interrupted. "Tomorrow, Wyatt. You go after work and get the answers you want. All right?"

Wyatt didn't answer until they were outside in the parking lot, the kids buckled in.

"I'd like to go tomorrow," he said for her ears alone. "And I'd be very grateful if you would come with me, Ellie, because I don't think I can do this alone."

"I'll go with you," she assured him. "And so will

God. He's known the truth all along. And now you'll learn it, too."

Cars pulled out of the parking lot as the rest of the choir left. Wyatt stared at her for so long that eventually they were the only ones left in the lot. Finally, he spoke.

"I've never known anyone quite like you, Ellie." His voice was low, deep. "You go way above and beyond, as if you can never give quite enough. You're like the song, making spirits bright wherever you go." He leaned forward and brushed his lips against hers and then suddenly, he deepened the kiss, showing her without words that he cared about her.

At least that's what she thought he was showing her.

Ellie kissed him back because she couldn't help herself. Wyatt was the man of her dreams. He held her heart in his hands, though he didn't know it.

You're not free to love him, her brain whispered. *You gave your life, your wants, your dreams and your future to God. And He's given you Gracie to care for. That has to be enough.*

The thought sobered her like a snowball in the face. Ellie drew back, breaking the kiss.

"Get some rest, Wyatt," she whispered. "Tomorrow's going to be a big day. Good night."

"Good night," he called just before she closed her car door.

"You were kissing my da— you were kissing *him*," Gracie accused. "Me 'n Albert saw you."

"Be quiet now, Gracie," Albert admonished softly. Then he looked at Ellie. "I could take the bus home."

"Be quiet, Albert," she said, unable to stem the spill of tears down her cheeks.

The ride to his home was utterly silent. When they

pulled up to the curb, a large man in a tattered T-shirt came barreling down the walk, yanked open the car door and dragged out a cringing Albert.

"You're late," he said in a furious voice. "I told you to be here at eight."

"I'm sorry, sir," Ellie apologized. "It's my fault we're late. I—" She caught her breath when the man turned on her, his eyes blazing hate.

"Leave, lady," he ordered with menace. "And don't come back." Then he looked at Albert. "Get into the house."

Ellie clearly saw fear in Albert's eyes. How she wished Wyatt was here. But just because he wasn't didn't mean she'd leave without trying to make Albert's life easier.

"Excuse me?" She cringed when the man wheeled around with a sneer. "You don't have to be so mean," she said in her firmest nurse voice. "He's just a boy."

"I'm the only thing standing between him and re-form school, so I'll talk to him any way I please. Butt out, lady." After another sneering glare the man stomped toward the house.

Ellie drove home with a terrible feeling that Albert was going to pay for her interference.

"Is that mean man going to hit Albert again?" Gracie asked in a voice brimming with fear.

Again?

"Did he hit Albert before?" Ellie asked as nonchalantly as she could.

"Lots of times, Albert said. Can't you stop it, Mommy?"

"I'm going to try," she promised grimly.

Later, once Gracie was in bed, she phoned Wyatt and asked for the number of his investigator.

"Why?"

Ellie admitted what had happened.

"I'm going to have him investigate Albert's uncle. Maybe then the boy won't have to live there."

"Where *will* he live?" Wyatt asked.

"I don't know. Somewhere where he's not terrified, I hope," she said staunchly.

"That's my Ellie. Spreading love and happiness wherever she can."

My Ellie? How she wanted to be!

Wyatt's chuckle didn't sound like he was making fun of her. It sounded tender. Maybe even affectionate.

"Isn't that what a Christian is supposed to do?" she finally asked, then quickly added, "See you tomorrow, Wyatt," before she hung up.

Ellie turned on the Christmas tree, switched on the electric fireplace and stared into the flickering light.

"I'm scared, God. I've let myself fall in love with Wyatt. Please, help me."

Ellie's Christmas list dangled on the fridge, but for once she didn't try to check off anything. For this one moment she sat silent, waiting for God to show her how to get over a very handsome vet to whom she'd given her heart.

Chapter Twelve

"Albert's scared stiff of his uncle. I can't just let that go." Ellie's passionate voice made him proud of having her for a friend.

"I wish you'd waited till I could be there." Wyatt grimaced as he drove toward the place where his mother lived. "But I'm glad you talked to the social worker and that she's laying down the law to his uncle." Because he guessed Ellie was already stretched thin in the finance department, Wyatt had instructed the investigator she'd hired to send him the bill.

"Why are you so quiet?" she asked moments later.

"I saw something this morning at Wranglers Ranch that really got to me." With school closed for Christmas break, the ranch was full of youngsters. But one in particular had drawn his attention today.

"I saw Albert," he said.

"So did I." Something about the way she said it made Wyatt glance at her. Her lips were pursed, and she was frowning. "He was clutching his side, but when I asked him about it, he said he'd bumped into something."

"Like maybe his uncle?" Wyatt inwardly fumed. "I

hope that social worker acts fast. He needs to be out of there if there's even a suspicion of abuse."

"I have way more than a suspicion." Ellie grimaced. "Anyway, you were saying?"

"Albert was talking to a kid in the corner of the tack room. Gracie was hiding around the corner outside. She had dirt on her face, and I think she'd been crying." Wyatt held the picture in his mind. "They were all quick to make an excuse and leave when they saw me, but— Ellie, I think Albert was defending Gracie."

"Defending her?" Ellie frowned at him. "From what?"

"Whom," Wyatt corrected. He wished now that he'd talked to Albert first before he worried Ellie. But it was too late for regrets. "I only overheard a little of what Albert said."

She poked his side when he didn't immediately speak. "What did you hear, Wyatt?"

"I thought I heard him say, 'We don't bully little kids at Wranglers Ranch.'" When Ellie didn't respond, he glanced at her.

"Gracie's had mud on her shirt a couple of times, and once she had a tear on her jeans, but she never said anybody was bullying her." Ellie sounded shocked.

"Maybe she didn't know that's what it was. But Albert did." He studied his hands on the wheel, trying to sort through his feelings. "Does he know because he's suffered the same thing?"

"I don't know." Ellie sighed as she stretched out her legs. "It's so hard being a single parent. You have to be constantly aware of every detail in your kid's life and if you miss one tiny thing—" She couldn't finish.

"We'll talk to them both when we get back," Wyatt promised. "We'll sort it out. Don't worry. I just thought you should know." He took the exit ramp toward Eventide Rest Home, trying to ignore the stir of uneasiness in his stomach.

He was going to see his mother, a woman he'd stopped hoping was alive.

He parked in the visitors' lot, then looked around. It was a typical one-level care facility spread out over an area with lovely winding paths and raised beds burgeoning with flowering pansies in a host of different colors. Brown wicker deer wearing big red bow ties stood here and there throughout the landscape, tiny lights covering them. At night it would look like they'd come to feed.

"I guess we should go in." He pulled his keys from the ignition. "My appointment with the administrator, Graham Parker, is in five minutes."

"Are you ready for this?" Ellie waited while he thought about it, then finally nodded.

Before they got out, she reached for his hand. Her warm capable fingers closed around his and gently squeezed, imparting comfort and solidarity, as if she knew he was a quaking mass of jelly inside. In his mind one question grew to gigantic proportions.

What if his mother wanted nothing to do with him?

As they walked up the path to the main door Wyatt wondered if he'd ever be able to forgive his father.

They went in and were ushered in to see the administrator.

"We didn't know Mrs. Wright had a son," Mr. Parker said, studying Wyatt from his seat behind a massive desk.

"I didn't know I had a mother," Wyatt shot back, frustrated by the man's need to chat. "May we please see her now? You understand if I'm impatient after all these years."

"Of course. But I must caution you. Your mother has days when things are crystal clear in her mind. Then she has times when she's terribly confused." The administrator narrowed his gaze. "If she becomes agitated, my staff will ask you to leave. Mrs. Wright's comfort is our primary concern."

"As it should be." Wyatt had to ask one more question. "How is her care paid for?"

"By an annuity. Her husband set it up. As I understand the terms, it will take care of everything she needs until she, er, doesn't need it anymore."

"I see." Anger burned at his father's actions. Why the secrecy?

"Are you ready?" Mr. Parker rose and walked to the door. "I'll take you."

"Maybe I should wait here, Wyatt." Ellie hung back. "This is a special moment between the two of you. You don't need me there."

"Yes, I do." He reached for her hand and clung to it. "I need you with me, Ellie." The words came from his heart, without forethought. But they were the truth.

He *did* need her. Ellie was the glue that held his days together. It was she who had brought back his joy in Christmas, her and Gracie. Maybe he was being selfish, but at the moment Wyatt couldn't imagine taking this next step without Ellie at his side.

As they walked down the hall, her hand in his was about the only thing that kept him from turning tail and getting out of there.

Mr. Parker stopped. "Here we are." After giving a quick rap on the door, he pushed it open and stepped inside. "Hello, Ruth. You have visitors today. This is Wyatt and Ellie."

Wyatt stood gazing at the woman seated in a soft blue upholstered rocker. Her hair was long and tied to the top of her head, sandy brown like his. Her eyes shone a dark brown—also like his—as she peered up at them through small gold-framed glasses. She was delicate-looking, as if one of Tucson's windstorms might pick her up and toss her away.

"Hello. Have you come to help me decorate the Christmas tree? It will soon be Christmas, you know." Her voice was soft and musical. She clasped her hands together and smiled. "I do so love Christmas, though some call my decorations geegaws."

Ellie's glance shifted from him to the paper chains covering the table in front of his mother. Wyatt knew she was recalling the time he'd used the same word when she'd been decorating his house. But he couldn't take his eyes off his mother.

"Please, do sit down." She glanced around. "I think the teapot's here somewhere."

"No tea for me, thank you, Ruth." Ellie sat across from his mother on the small footstool. "These are very lovely," she said fingering the chains. "You've done so many."

"I have a large tree to decorate." She frowned suddenly and peered at him. "Your name is Wyatt?" He nodded. "Oh, how wonderful." She smiled and leaned toward him to whisper, "I have a son named Wyatt, you know. He's such a sweet boy."

Wyatt moved behind Ellie and let his hands rest on her shoulders as he listened to his mother recall his birth and the first few months of his life. Ellie's hands covered his, lending him the strength to stay still and listen to his own history. But then his mother's memories grew vague, confused, and she began to ramble.

"I couldn't stay because I was ill," she whispered, peeking over one shoulder and then the other. "Everything kept going wrong, and he blamed me."

"You mean my father, Bernard, your husband?" Wyatt asked, speaking for the first time since they'd arrived.

"You mustn't say his name. That's the rule." She began rocking back and forth, repeating, "That's the rule."

"Ruth—uh—" Was he supposed to call her that? Wyatt didn't know, but there were so many things he wanted to ask her, so many blanks to fill in. He stepped forward, placed his hand on top of hers. "Can you tell me—"

"No. Can't tell." She reared away from him, crossed her arms in front of her and resumed rocking back and forth.

"I'm sorry, but Ruth can't visit anymore." A pleasant-faced woman stood in the open doorway. "You'll have to leave now."

"But I need to know—" Wyatt froze as his mother screamed.

"Can't tell. Can't ever tell. No. No," she shrieked.

"We have to make decorations, Ruth." Ellie quickly and carefully laid a paper chain in her lap, her tone calming. "Here's yours. What a lovely thing it is. See how it dances in the light. How shall we hang it on the tree? I know. We'll use ribbons. Bright red ribbons. And maybe we can add some silver bells."

As Wyatt watched, Ruth slowly relaxed, put her hands

down and was soon humming "Silent Night" along with Ellie as they rolled and taped foil bits.

"She's a great one, your wife," the attendant murmured to Wyatt. "Knows exactly what our Ruth needs to calm her."

Wyatt ignored the "wife" comment, though it caused a hundred pictures to flash through his mind. Ellie mothering Cade, coaxing his Christmas spirit by baking succulent treats, playing checkers with Albert and Gracie, laughing and smiling and making the world a better place for all of them.

"Don't worry, son." The attendant patted him on the back. "Next time you visit Ruth will have a better day. No good talking to her anymore now, though."

"But I need to ask—" He wasn't sure what. He only knew he couldn't leave yet. Not with all his questions unanswered.

"Ruth can't tell you any more today, Wyatt. She's worn herself out." Ellie moved beside him, whispering as they watched his mother's frail chest rise and fall. "She needs to sleep."

"Come back another time," the attendant said as she ushered them through the doorway. "Tomorrow." Then she closed the door behind them.

Speechless, Wyatt walked beside Ellie out of the building and over to his truck. Then he paused, tilted his face up and let the sun chase away the chill he'd felt the moment Ruth had become hysterical.

"Are you okay?" Ellie asked him.

"I don't know what I am, but I don't think okay applies." He checked his watch. "Do you have time for coffee?"

"I have all the time you need, Wyatt."

Her voice, the gentleness of her response, the tender way she slid his keys from his fingers and ushered him in to his own truck and then drove them to a café reminded Wyatt of the loving care a mother would give her child. It caused a feeling he'd craved but never known in his entire life, a feeling of acceptance, of understanding.

"Tell me what you're thinking," she said when they were seated in a booth and cradling steaming mugs of coffee.

"I don't know." He tried to list the emotions he recognized. "Shock, surprise, pain, yearning, love. Hate," he added bitterly.

"Hate for your father." When he nodded, she brushed her knuckles against his cheek. "You don't know why he did this, Wyatt. You don't know the details or what drove his decision to put her there."

"No, I don't. Because he never told me." He leaned into her touch, loving the way being with Ellie brought his world back on its axis. "Why? That's what I can't get past. Why did he do it, and why did he never tell me about her?"

"Can you face never knowing?" Her eyes caressed him as she spoke. "Can you love your mother in spite of what he did? Because I think that's the only choice you have. Love her and squeeze every moment of joy and happiness you can from the relationship."

"To make up for the past, you mean?" He loved the way her lips tipped up at the corner, the way her curls bounced when she shook her head and how her eyes chided him for looking for the easy way out.

"You can't make up for the past, Wyatt. It's long gone. All you have, all any of us have, is today, this moment." Her hand dropped from his face, leaving a chill. How he craved her touch. "That's why it's so important that we make today the very best we can."

"How am I supposed to do that, Ellie? Clearly she's incapable of giving me the answers I need." He half smiled, remembering. "Gracie had a good question the other day. She asked me why God didn't answer her prayer for a daddy. I gave her platitudes." He grimaced. "Now *I'm* asking why He didn't answer my prayers for my mom."

He expected comfort, sympathy, understanding. As usual Ellie surprised him.

"Get over it, Wyatt."

He blinked, stunned by her tough response.

"What difference would knowing make at this point?" Her gaze probed his as her voice softened. "We all want answers. Why didn't God heal my sister so she could raise her baby? But what difference does asking make? It only paralyzes us."

"So how did you handle your questions?" he demanded, slightly irritated.

"The same as you. I had tantrums for a while, demanded God explain Himself to me." She made a face. "Thing was, there was this bawling baby who needed a mom, and I was the one available, so finally I got down to the business of being her mom."

"It's not the same."

"Isn't it?" She leaned forward, her voice now oozing kindness. "You have your mother, a woman you claim to have wanted to know for years. Forget about your father, and seize this opportunity to get to know Ruth. God has given you your mom, Wyatt. What are you going to do with *that* answer?"

"You're really something, Ellie Grant," he said in amazement.

"Thank you. I think." She frowned as her phone pealed. "It's Tanner." She answered, then listened, cheeks paling a pasty white. "We'll check it out," she promised before she hung up.

"What's wrong?" Wyatt watched her gather her belongings and knew this was serious.

"Albert didn't show for this evening's dinner that Tanner's holding for his group. Apparently his uncle picked him up earlier and insisted he go home. Albert never came back, and nobody at his house is answering the phone." Fear whitened her face. "That dinner was a big deal to Albert. I can't believe he'd be a no-show without a word to anyone. Something's wrong, and I need to go to his place to find out what."

"Okay." Wyatt rose, tossed some money on the table and held out his hand. "Let's go. And this time, I'm driving."

"You have to," she murmured as they left the café. "I'm a mess of nerves. Why would his uncle prevent him from coming?"

Wyatt flung his arm around Ellie's shoulders and hugged her against his side as they walked to the truck. It felt wonderful to have a chance to comfort her this time. As they walked, Wyatt sent a prayer heavenward for Albert's safety.

"A very smart nurse told me to stop asking why and act instead. That's what we have to do now, Ellie. We need to be bold and seize this opportunity to help Albert. We need to trust God to show us what to do."

"Agreed." Ellie climbed in, then slid across the seat

so she was next to him. "Thank you for caring about him, Wyatt," she murmured.

They needed to leave, but Wyatt took a few seconds to enjoy her lovely face before he dipped his head and kissed her.

"We can do this, Ellie. You and I and God."

"Sounds like a great combination."

Chapter Thirteen

"Looking a little haggard there, Wyatt." Tanner bumped his veterinarian in the arm with a smirk. "Foster parenthood wearing you down already?"

"No, Albert's great. It's potty training Cade that's killing me." Wyatt chuckled. "You'll find out soon enough." He winked at Ellie. "Won't he?"

She nodded, though she thought Wyatt looked great. In fact, she let her eyes feast on him as the men talked.

"Don't know how you persuaded the social worker to let Albert come to your place," Tanner was saying, more serious now. "But I'm sure glad you did. I'm gathering from his broken arm and what Sophie's managed to pry out of him these last two days, he had it pretty rough at the uncle's."

"It wasn't a matter of persuading the social worker," Ellie explained. "Foster spaces are pretty full this time of year. Since Wyatt has previously fostered, he was a perfect candidate. And Albert loves it at his ranch."

"How long will he stay?" Tanner asked. "Hopefully, until after Christmas."

"He can't leave now," Ellie blurted. "He belongs with people who care about him."

"I had this thought—maybe it's a stupid one but uh—anyway I thought maybe I should petition the court to give me custody. I mean he's a good kid and…" Relieved to have finally blurted out his thoughts, Wyatt smiled at her surprise. "Albert's got a lot of potential."

"That's a great idea!" Ellie couldn't believe he was willing to do that. A phone call took Tanner away, but she remained seated on the patio across from Wyatt, eager to hear more about his plans to get involved in Albert's life.

"The kid's had some bad breaks. I think he could really make something of himself, and I'd like to help him. Have you seen how great he is with the horses?" he asked, his face animated. "He's sure got the touch."

"Oh, no." Ellie clapped a hand over her mouth in pretended horror. "Are you going to try to make him over as your father tried with you?" she teased.

"I'm never going to try to mold either Cade or Albert into something they don't want to be. They have to make their own choices." He winked. "I learned that much from my father."

"I'm glad." She slid her hand across the bench and slipped it in to his. "And I think it's wonderful that you're helping Albert. God will bless you." Why wasn't holding his hand enough for her? Why did she crave more from Wyatt than a smile or a shared laugh? Why couldn't she stop wanting his love?

"Your Christmas party's still on for tonight, right?" He waited for her nod. "Can I help?"

"Thanks, but I'll manage." But how she loved him for offering.

"That's not the point. I'm your friend, and I'd like to help."

Friend? Is that all?

"Thank you." She shrugged. "It's just a cookout for a few friends, nothing special."

"If it's done by Ellie Grant, it will be special." Wyatt's dark eyes held hers for a space of time that seemed to stretch forever. "Because you're special, Ellie. Especially to me." Then Wyatt leaned forward and kissed her.

It wasn't a dreamy kind of kiss. It was quick and fast, the briefest of caresses. But it still made her toes tingle and her heart race long after Wyatt had left.

"Are you dreaming of getting *who* you want for Christmas?" Sophie came outside and sank onto the bench across from Ellie.

"You mean 'what,'" Ellie corrected.

"No, I don't." Sophie snickered.

"You finished your catering job early," Ellie said, hoping to divert her attention.

"No digressing. Your love for Wyatt is as transparent as Gracie's so-called 'secret' giant cookie gift that I've been helping her make for Cade. Oh, don't do that," she pleaded when Ellie began to cry.

"I think of Wyatt all the time," Ellie sobbed, unable to stifle it any longer. "He's such a wonderful man. He's great with Gracie, and he's even going to apply for Albert's guardianship. What's not to love?" she wailed.

"Then, what's the problem?" Sophie asked. "Are you afraid he won't reciprocate if you tell him how you feel?"

"I can't tell him how I feel! You know I can't."

"I do?" Sophie frowned and shook her head. "No, Ellie, I don't know why you can't tell him your feelings.

Wyatt is a godly man who clearly cares about you. He wouldn't be kissing you so often if he didn't."

"He just sees me as a friend," she clarified with a sniff. "But it's not his feelings I'm talking about. It's mine. I can't love him. Or anyone," she added.

"I guess this pregnancy has really impaired my brain because I don't understand anything you're saying. Why can't you love Wyatt?"

Ellie heaved a sigh. "You told me I couldn't love him, remember?"

"Me? I don't think I said that." Sophie studied her. "Refresh my memory."

"After I became a Christian, and Eddie and I broke up, you said I shouldn't be sad about it, that God was protecting me, so I could be the kind of mother Gracie needs." Ellie could tell Sophie didn't yet understand. "You said that the breakup was part of God's plan for my life, to enable me to focus on Gracie. So that's why I can't love Wyatt, because God wants me to focus on raising my daughter."

"But not exclusively!" Sophie looked shocked. "I didn't mean you couldn't ever love anyone again." She touched Ellie's cheek, her face full of compassion. "Sweetie, you can't interpret one romantic mistake as God's refusal to give you a family. I'm so sorry if I led you to think that."

"You mean it's okay with God if I love Wyatt?" Ellie studied her friend with a heart full of hope.

"Well, I think you should ask Him about it, but I don't see why not." Sophie smiled a fleeting smile. "God is love, and I believe He wants us to love fully and from the heart. But a word of warning here. You need to remember that Wyatt has issues with the past."

"But—"

"Yes, I know you said he's coming to grips with some of them," Sophie agreed, "But I don't think he's resolved all of them. Do you?"

"No. So, what do I do? Try to maintain a friendship? Tell him how I feel and hope he feels the same? Wait?" Ellie was desperate for an answer.

"I don't have all the answers, honey. My best advice would be to keep praying for God's help. Ask Him to show you what to do with these feelings you have for Wyatt. Take your time, be sure you know where He's leading you, and then wait for Him to work it out."

"You're the best friend, and just like my sister, Karen, you always have great advice." Ellie dashed around the table to hug Sophie. "Thank you so much. And now I have to run. You're coming later, right?"

"Tanner and the kids and I wouldn't miss your party for the world, sister." Sophie hugged her back, then waved as Ellie raced to find Gracie.

All the way home her daughter sang Christmas carols while Ellie silently sang, *I love Wyatt Wright* to the same tunes.

Surely God would work it out. After all, Wyatt had kissed her in broad daylight.

Again.

Wyatt stood in the festively decorated backyard amid a score of laughing people, but he only had eyes for the hostess.

Ellie smiled when she saw him, then headed his way, threading her way through kids and adults with a word and a grin for each.

"Hi." She greeted him, then hunkered down to tickle Cade. "Hey, pumpkin."

Gracie raced over to ask if she and Beth could play with him.

"Sure," Wyatt agreed. "Just be careful he doesn't eat anything he shouldn't. Like brussels sprouts," he added when the kids had left.

Ellie burst out laughing. "That seems like a long time ago, doesn't it?"

"Eons," he agreed, unable to look away from her laughing face. He remembered he'd been a shell back then, only half-alive, unable to forgive, oblivious to the joy to be found in the world.

Ellie had changed him.

"You look deep in thought." She handed him a green-and-red punch-filled paper cup.

"I was thinking about what I was like before you and Gracie turned my world upside down." He smiled as wariness filled those lovely gray eyes. "I was a sad case back then."

"How are you doing now, Wyatt?"

"I'm good," he said, surprising himself with how true it was. "Ellie, I—" He was cut off when someone called her name. "Go ahead and circulate, Ellie. We can talk later."

"Promise?" She gazed at him in a way that made him gulp. All he could do was nod. "Okay. See you in a bit."

Wyatt spent a few moments speaking to Tanner and some other folks from church he knew, but his attention never moved far from Ellie. There was so much joy in her, so much pure delight in things he'd always found ordinary. And she never missed a detail to make someone's world special, especially his.

Wyatt had no idea how he ended up as her partner in a trivia game, but since he knew less than nothing about the answers, of course they lost.

"Punishment is to sing a duet," Sophie, the judge, declared. "How about 'The First Noel'?"

Wyatt detested the idea of standing in front of a bunch of people making an idiot of himself, but there was no way he was going to ruin Ellie's party.

"Are you up for this?" he murmured, hoping she'd say no.

"I am if you are," she said with a grin.

"Why couldn't you be a shy, quiet woman, Ellie Grant?" he groaned as she led him to the center of the group.

"Now, what's the fun in that?" she asked with a mischievous wink. "Ready?"

"As I'll ever be." Wyatt had heard Ellie's lovely voice in church so it was no hardship to sing with her. But it wasn't her voice that touched him, it was the words. When they sang the chorus, those familiar lyrics sank into his heart, reminding him of the true meaning of the story they were telling, the story of love. The story of the very first Christmas. A hush fell on the group so that even the kids gathered around, sitting on the ground to listen.

Noel, Noel, born is the King of Israel.

As their voices died away into the night, Wyatt got trapped in Ellie's gaze and something he glimpsed there—something like tenderness. Or maybe compassion.

Or perhaps—

"Okay, that's enough torture for one night," Ellie joked, easing out from under his arm.

Wyatt, still caught up in the magic of those moments when it seemed the two of them were alone together, couldn't even remember placing it on her shoulders.

"You've been holding out on our choir, Wyatt," Tanner called over the applause. "Now that we've heard you sing we'll expect you to join us."

"I don't know," Wyatt said automatically. "I have Cade——" He stopped short as he encountered Ellie's gaze. Wasn't it time to stop hiding and start participating in life?

"Everyone, come and eat," Ellie called as she moved away.

Her departure felt like a physical loss to Wyatt. He stood frozen in place as once again her yard resounded with happy people enjoying what she'd prepared. Ellie's bounty. Tons of food, masses of decorations and always laughter.

He wanted to be part of her world.

Permanently?

Wyatt studied her from a darkened corner of her yard, marveling that he was even considering the question. And yet, he was tired of being alone, of trying to manage. These past weeks of sharing with Ellie and Gracie had opened his eyes to joy, and it had been so long since he'd felt that.

He'd finally come to terms with the fact that he would never be the son his father wanted, and he couldn't spend the rest of his life trying to achieve something he didn't want.

But he could strive to be the son God wanted.

He wanted Ellie.

She'd swept into his world and prodded him back to life, despite his intention to remain aloof. Now he couldn't conceive of a day without her there to cheer and encourage him. She made him think of possibilities. He cared about Ellie Grant a great deal.

Cared about? Who was he kidding?

He loved Ellie.

The knowledge terrified him as much as it thrilled him. Relationships meant promises, and Wyatt was so lousy at keeping those. But he could learn from his past, couldn't he?

What about Gracie?

That little girl wanted a daddy so badly. Involvement with Ellie meant Wyatt better be fully committed, because Gracie needed and deserved a man who'd be there for her no matter what. He didn't think that was going to be a problem. He already loved her. But she would demand his total attention. She wanted a real daddy, not a fake or a halfway man. Wyatt suddenly realized he wanted to be that little girl's longed-for father.

But the real question was Ellie. She'd told him she wasn't interested in a relationship.

She'd also kissed him and seemed to like it when he kissed her.

Now he had to make a choice: embrace life and love with Ellie or remain on the sidelines of life. But doing the latter meant risking becoming hard and embittered like his father.

When Wyatt weighed not having Ellie and Gracie in his life permanently, there was no contest. He wanted them both. It might take a while to convince Ellie he'd make her a good husband, but that was okay. As far as Wyatt was concerned, he had all the time in the world.

"Hey, Wyatt? Can I talk to you for a minute?" Albert shuffled his feet nervously.

"Sure." Albert would make a great addition to their family. Wyatt didn't doubt Ellie would agree with that.

The boy was still quiet, but at least he was losing that nervous tenseness. "What's up?"

"I was thinking… Ellie has done a lot for me and—" Albert stopped, then started again. "I—uh, I want to give her something for Christmas."

"We can go shopping tomorrow," Wyatt promised.

"I don't have any money. Anyway I want to give her something from me, something that I put effort into."

"Okay." Wyatt wondered where this was going.

"Gracie and I were exploring the other day, and I saw some woodworking stuff in one of the sheds." He stopped, then blurted, "Can you show me how to make a wooden bowl for Ellie?"

"I haven't used my tools in a really long time." Wyatt thought of how his father had hated him working with his hands, and of how much he'd loved creating from wood. "It would be nice to share my hobby with someone." He smiled at Albert. "When do you want to start?"

"Tomorrow?"

"Right after supper," Wyatt said. "I've got something to do in the afternoon."

If Wyatt was going to move ahead with his life and loving Ellie, wasn't it about time he found out everything about his mother? Then maybe he could finally put the past behind him and embrace the future.

And then he'd tell Ellie he wanted to share that future with her.

Because he loved her.

Ellie was trying to be positive, but she couldn't quite understand Wyatt's urgency.

"Why do you need to visit her today?" she asked as he drove toward his mother's home.

"I need answers. But, first, I want to introduce her to Cade. I want him to meet his grandmother. I don't want him to spend his life asking questions about her."

She heard the underlying *As I did*.

"Good idea," she said, determined to be supportive. "I hope you brought a camera."

He nodded.

"I'm not sure she'll be able to answer your questions, though, Wyatt." She hated dashing his hopes.

"I'm not going to ask her many," he said as he turned into the parking lot. He shot her a grin full of confidence. "I'm going to talk to Mr. Parker. My investigator said he's been at Eventide for fifteen years, so he must have known my father."

"What if Mr. Parker doesn't have the answers?" Ellie was worried that Wyatt had too much vested in what he thought he'd learn today. "It might not go as you want," she cautioned.

"Ellie! Is that you with no faith?" he teased. He leaned across and tapped her on the nose. "'If God be for us, who can be against us?' Remember?"

She waited until he'd come around to open her door. He held out a hand, and she took it, unable to stop herself. How she loved this man.

"I'm sure your mother will be delighted to meet Cade." She watched as he lifted his son from the car seat, wet one fingertip and smoothed the small curl on the top of Cade's head. "What a handsome pair you make."

She clung to Wyatt's hand when the receptionist told them Mr. Parker would meet with them after they visited Wyatt's mother. She held his hand when Ruth sat holding Cade on her knee. After a few minutes, she began to call Cade Wyatt.

"Wyatt was such an active boy. I had to have three sets of eyes in my head," Ruth said. "He was so busy. He walked when he was seven months, and then it was running. Running everywhere, all the time. Such a sweet boy."

The way she, too, licked her finger and smoothed Cade's curl brought tears to Ellie's eyes. Wyatt's eyes grew damp as well when the frail woman pressed a kiss against Cade's cheek. But when the little boy began to wiggle and try to get down, Wyatt's mother seemed to fade.

Ellie took Cade to a corner of the room, so Wyatt could focus on Ruth's now faint words.

"Bernard was so busy. He seldom stayed home in the evening," she whispered. "I asked him to help me, and he always said yes, but he never had time or he forgot."

Ellie saw how deeply those words hit Wyatt. He, also, had been too busy and forgetful, and he'd spent months regretting it.

"Forgiven, Wyatt," she whispered just loud enough for him to hear. "You're forgiven."

He stared at her for a moment, then nodded, his eyes shining. A second later he clasped his hands around his mother's.

"You did very well," he told her gently. "You were a good mother."

"I tried to be." She frowned. "But then I got sick. I had to go away."

"Did Bernard send you away?" he asked carefully.

"No! He wasn't like that. It wasn't his fault." Ruth began rocking back and forth, clearly growing more agitated. "I had to leave." She gripped his hands fiercely and stared into his face. "I had to go because something bad happened. He didn't want me to go. But I *had* to leave."

Those were her last coherent words. Suddenly she began wailing, growing more distraught with Wyatt's attempts to calm her. A moment later the attendant showed up and asked them to leave.

"Ruth *had* to go," the attendant repeated just loudly enough for them to hear.

Wyatt immediately caught on. "Yes, of course she did. We understand."

"You see, Ruth, they understand. We all do. You had to leave, and that's the way it was. Come now, dear. We'll go have some tea." With an arm around her shoulder, the woman urged Ruth out of the room.

Wyatt watched his mother leave, his hands clenching and unclenching by his side. Finally Ellie went to him.

She wrapped her arms around him and held him. "Whatever happened back then, Ruth is all right. Your mother is fine, and she has great caregivers."

"I was the same kind of man he was." Wyatt's arms slid around her waist. He pressed his forehead against hers and spoke words that seemed to be dragged from him. "I never kept my promises, either. That's what my father taught me."

"And now your heavenly Father is teaching you a different way with Cade." She glided her fingers through his hair, loving the touch of its tight curls against her fingertips, loving the opportunity to be here, in his arms, sharing this most important moment with him. "You're not the same as your father. You're Wyatt, and you're a wonderful dad to Cade."

"I love you, Ellie Grant." Wyatt's words shocked her with their quiet intensity. Then he bent his head and kissed her the way Ellie had only ever dreamed of being kissed.

She kissed him back, pouring her heart and soul into

showing him, and then, lest he not have understood, she leaned back and said, "I love you, too, Wyatt. So much."

He touched his lips to her neck, a smile in his voice as he said, "I thought you didn't want a romantic relationship, Ellie."

"I didn't. Until you came." She kissed his jaw and the corner of his mouth and the end of his nose. "What about you?"

"I was never going to risk failing another person. I was going to focus totally on Cade." He grinned at her. "Until I fell in love with you."

"When was that?" she asked, savoring the wonderful words.

"The moment I saw you, I think." Then he kissed her again, and Ellie lost all rational thought until a squeal just outside the room separated both of them. "Where's Cade?"

"Right here." Graham Parker stood in the hall, holding Cade in his arms. "He runs fast," he said with a chuckle.

"I'm sorry." Ellie took him. "I should have been watching him more closely."

"No problem." He smiled, then looked at Wyatt. "Would you like to have that talk now?"

Wyatt nodded.

Ellie threaded her fingers in his as they walked to the administrator's office. At last Wyatt was going to get the answers he'd been waiting for.

Please, be with him now, she pleaded. *Please, please, let it be okay.*

But as soon as Mr. Parker began speaking, she knew it wouldn't be.

Chapter Fourteen

Wyatt sat in stunned silence as his questions were finally answered.

"I'm sorry to have to tell you, Mr. Wright," the administrator said as he leaned forward in his chair, "but your mother suffers from schizophrenia. She has for some time."

He felt as if a vise was clenching his heart, but he sat there, quiet and still as Mr. Parker continued.

"Mrs. Wright was brought here by her husband almost twenty-eight years ago."

"Why?" Wyatt squeezed the word out past the lump in his throat.

"I wasn't in charge then, you understand," the man said, his tone troubled. "But I checked the records for you. They indicate that she was brought in by her husband, at her request, after she left her son alone in an empty house to walk through the desert. Apparently she had some sort of break with reality. Since that day Mrs. Wright has not left our care."

"Surely she was treated?"

"Oh, yes. She's received ongoing treatment," Mr.

Parker assured him. He sighed. "It has not been—shall we say, totally successful."

"But when my father died—" He tried to order his thoughts, grateful when Ellie stepped in.

"Wyatt was never informed that his mother was alive or that she was here," she told the administrator. "Why was that?"

"Quite simply, and I'm sorry if this sounds hurtful, but your father didn't want you to know." He tented his fingers.

"Why?" Wyatt couldn't stop the words from exploding from him. "Why didn't he tell me? I could have visited, talked to her, helped her. Instead I've gone all these years without knowing my mother was even alive."

Fury built inside until he could no longer sit. He jumped to his feet. When Ellie rose, too, he waved her off.

"I need some time to process this. Can you watch Cade?"

"Of course." After giving him a loving look she left with Cade.

Wyatt wandered down the hall, drawn somehow back to Ruth's room. He stood outside the open door, listening to her voice, trying to make it sink into his brain that this was his mother, the woman who'd given him life, the one who should have been sharing his life.

Wyatt wasn't sure how long he remained there before it dawned on him that Ruth was speaking to someone. He peeked around the corner but saw no one else in the room. Puzzled, he stood there, listening.

"I can't, Bernard," she said in a mournful tone. "Don't you understand? I can't take care of a child, not even my own. I'm afraid that you'll leave me alone, and I'll do something wrong again. Help me, please. Don't make me stay." Her voice dropped to a whisper. "What if I hurt him?"

Hurt him—Wyatt? She'd run away to save him? Wyatt couldn't make the pieces come together.

Confused, he walked back to the administrator's office.

"May I interrupt again?" he asked.

"Of course. Whatever I can do to help you," Mr. Parker assured him.

"Can you tell me more about her disease?"

"Certainly. Schizophrenia is a long-term mental disorder of a type involving a breakdown in the relation between thought, emotion and behavior, leading to faulty perception, inappropriate actions and feelings, withdrawal from reality and personal relationships into fantasy and delusion, and a sense of mental fragmentation." The man frowned. "Of course there are treatments."

"Drugs." Wyatt grimaced.

"Antipsychotic medications," Mr. Parker corrected. "Your mother has been treated with a number of them in different combinations but with limited success. If you wish you could certainly make an appointment to speak to her doctor."

"Why don't you give me the short version?" Wyatt suggested.

"Well, according to her records, she seems to suffer side effects from most of them, so treating her is a delicate balance." He glanced at the file in front of him. "Ruth is also receiving ongoing psychotherapy."

"Which doesn't seem to be working much if she's still having these—what did you call them—breakdowns?" Wyatt exhaled and asked the question uppermost in his mind. "Is it genetic?"

"I'm not an authority—"

"Please, just tell me what you know," Wyatt pleaded.

Mr. Parker hesitated for several moments, then spoke very quietly.

"Schizophrenia has a strong hereditary component. Individuals with a first-degree relative such as a parent or sibling who has schizophrenia have a ten percent chance of developing the disorder, as opposed to the one percent chance of the general population." The administrator sighed. "I'm sorry."

Wyatt's insides froze.

"Son," Parker said softly. "Your father believed that was the main reason your mother insisted on leaving her home and you," Parker said.

Wyatt blinked back to reality. "Excuse me?"

"She wanted to protect you." Parker shrugged. "Your father made certain she would be taken care of here at Eventide."

"But he never let me see her or even know she was here." Wyatt couldn't get past that.

"He may have shared her fears that you would get hurt."

With that comment Wyatt's lonely childhood suddenly made sense. His father's strict demands were to make sure his son didn't go off on some tangent, didn't get sidetracked. He'd pushed Wyatt to become a lawyer to be grounded in facts, as he was. Mental disease would be abhorrent to socially conscious Bernard Wright.

"Of course treatment has changed a lot. Diagnosed earlier, success rates are much better. Many people who suffer with this disease are able to manage it with medication and return to work and a normal life." Mr. Parker studied him. "I don't think you—"

"Oh, you're in here." Ellie stood in the doorway. "Sorry to interrupt, but Cade's really hungry, Wyatt."

"Yes, we need to leave." He rose, thrust out a hand to the administrator. "Thank you for explaining. I'm sorry I took so much of your time."

"Not at all. I'll walk out with you." Mr. Parker plucked a wafer out of a red Christmas tin on his desk and handed it to Ellie. "This might help with your boy."

She took it and handed it to Cade who immediately stopped weeping and began eating the treat. "Thank you."

"It's a wonderful time of year to share with a child that age." Parker led the way outside, smiling as the landscape lighting clicked on. "Kids are so inspiring. For them Christmas means anything's possible."

Anything? Like not developing schizophrenia?

"May I say one thing more?" Mr. Parker asked. "Your mother's fears are probably unfounded. But at least you know the truth now, and with advance warning you can seek treatment."

Thanks for nothing.

Parker mussed Cade's hair, urged them to visit Ruth again, then wished them a Merry Christmas.

"Let's go." Wyatt walked back to the truck, replaying everything he'd learned.

The ride home was silent. Finally, he pulled up in front of Ellie's, and when he helped her out of the truck, she grabbed the front of his jacket and stood on her tiptoes to kiss him.

"You won't get schizophrenia just because your mother has it, Wyatt." Ellie's confidence came through the whispered words.

"How can you be so sure?"

"I love you, Wyatt. And I have faith that God has

something special planned for you." She touched his cheek, her eyes brimming with love.

He loved that about Ellie, that steely confidence in her heavenly Father. Truth was, he loved everything about her, from the top of her ruffled curls that never seemed to tame to her pink-tipped toenails peeking out from her sandals. She was as lovely inside as out.

But he couldn't offer her security, and therein lay his problem.

Yet neither could he walk away, not from sweet, loving Ellie.

Wyatt leaned forward and rested his lips on hers, trying to tell her without words how much he cared for her. Since the day they'd met, she'd been there for him, cheering him on, encouraging him to embrace life. He wordlessly tried to tell her how much her support, her love meant to him, infusing as much into the kiss as he could.

But Cade had woken and was not to be silenced. After several moments, Wyatt eased away.

"Thank you for coming with me," he said. He reached out and lifted one wiry curl away from her amazing eyes. "Thank you for everything, Ellie."

She stepped back, a troubled look filling her face.

"You're making this sound like goodbye," she whispered.

He smiled, squeezed her hand, then climbed back into his truck and drove away, glancing in his mirror just once to see her standing where he'd left her, staring after him.

Wyatt forced his gaze back on the road. As he drove home, his mind teemed with imaginings of leaving Cade alone as his mother left him, or worse, leaving Ellie to manage two children on her own.

No, he couldn't indulge his yearning to love Ellie and

be loved by her. Doing so could ruin her life. It was better for him to make preparations for Cade. Tomorrow he'd ask Tanner and Sophie if they'd be his son's godparents.

Wyatt fed Cade but had no appetite for his own meal. He tucked his son into bed, loving the way his chubby arms reached out for a hug and a kiss. How could his mother have given this up? How much love she'd had to walk away in an effort to protect him. And his father, too? Would Wyatt be able to do the same if the time came?

Wyatt returned to his living room and sat staring at the Christmas tree until Albert arrived on the church's youth group bus.

"Was it a good Christmas party?" he asked.

"The best."

"That's good." He wouldn't be able to adopt Albert now, not with the future so uncertain. But he'd wait until after Christmas to tell him that. Albert deserved a happy, peaceful Christmas.

"You seem down." Albert studied him. "I guess you don't want to work on Ellie's bowl tonight, do you?"

"No, this is a good time, if I can get my neighbor to babysit." Wyatt pushed away his dark thoughts and picked up the phone.

The older woman readily agreed and arrived less than five minutes later.

He and Albert went out to the shed where Albert chose a piece of cherry wood from the stack Wyatt had left to dry shortly after he and Taryn had bought the ranch.

"That'll make a great bowl," he said and began showing Albert how to use the tools to create his gift for Ellie.

When they'd done all they could for the night, they returned to the house. The sitter left, and Albert went to bed.

But Wyatt sat long into the night alternately praying for help and trying to make sense of the incomprehensible.

What if, even now, the genesis of this awful disease was growing inside his head, threatening to cloud his mind?

There was only one thing to do. He'd have to break off his connections with Ellie. It wasn't fair to let her keep thinking there could be something between them. Even the thought of not seeing her face every day, not hearing her laugh or working with her at Wranglers tore at him.

He loved her so much.

"Only two days until Christmas, shoppers." Gracie's shrill voice parodied the advertisement on the car radio in such a lackluster tone that Ellie's heart hurt.

"You don't seem very eager for Christmas to get here, honey." She glanced in the mirror and saw Gracie's frown. "Aren't you looking forward to Melissa's Christmas party this morning, or to giving out your cookie gifts this afternoon?"

"I guess." Gracie heaved a sigh that told the truth.

"Want to tell me what's wrong?"

"It's Wyatt."

Ellie was surprised at hearing her daughter actually call the rancher by name. What happened to Daddy?

"He's not the same anymore." Gracie frowned. "Yesterday he hardly said anything when I was ridin' the horse for the girl who's coming today. He looks sad."

"I'm sorry, sweetie." Ellie did not want to talk about Wyatt, not after the way he'd been shutting her out every time she came near him. She'd tried everything, but it was like talking to a wall. Wyatt couldn't hear her. He was shut down by fear.

"He doesn't look at you like he did, neither," Gracie mumbled.

"How did he look at me before?" Ellie asked eagerly. She'd told herself she'd only imagined him saying that he loved her because she'd wanted it to be true for so long.

"Before when he looked at you, he'd smile, like he was happy inside 'bout sumthin'." Gracie exhaled heavily. "Now I think he hurts."

Join the club.

But Ellie didn't say that. She'd prayed constantly for guidance, for words that could melt the ice of fear in him and free the heart she knew was aching. She'd also struggled to find the right words to explain his absence from their world to Gracie. But she couldn't find them.

"Have fun at the party, honey," she said as she pulled up in front of Melissa's. "They'll bring you back to Wranglers Ranch when it's over because I have to be there for the Make-a-Wish kids. Okay?"

"Yeah." Gracie unsnapped her seat belt but paused before she opened the door. "Mommy?"

"Yes, sweetie?" Ellie knew this was something important because Gracie hesitated so long before she spoke.

"God isn't going to give me a daddy, is He?" Her eyes were shiny, and she dashed a fist against them as if to stop the flow of tears. "I thought if I prayed really hard and tried to do good things that He would answer my prayer, but He isn't gonna."

So that's what was behind all the cookie gifts, Ellie realized. Gracie's sad face deepened her heartache. She got out of the car, opened Gracie's door and enfolded her child in her arms.

"Nobody can know God's plans, sweetie." She inhaled

the essence of this precious child. "We have to trust He'll work things out even if it's not the way we want."

"I know." Gracie kissed her cheek, sighed, then wiggled free. "I'll keep prayin', I guess."

"Yes. And, Gracie?" Ellie straightened her ponytail, then cupped her face in her hands. "I want you to remember that you do have a Father, God, and He loves you very much." Ellie hugged her once more. "Now throw away your sad face and have a good time with Melissa. Remember, it's Christmas."

"In two days, shoppers." Gracie giggled when her mother rolled her eyes, then dashed up the walk calling, "Bye, Mommy."

Ellie drove to Wranglers with her mind made up. She had to try once more to make Wyatt see sense. However, when she found him in the tack room with Tanner, she soon realized something had changed.

"Good morning," she greeted them both. "Big day today." Then she faced Wyatt. "When you have a minute, I'd like to talk to you."

"You can talk here if you like," Tanner said. He held out a hand to Wyatt. "I'll be sorry to see you go. I've appreciated your work with us. Thanks for staying today. God bless you." He walked away, leaving them alone.

"What does Tanner mean? Where are you going?" Icy fingers clutched at her heart.

"I gave him my notice. Today's my last day."

"Why?" She touched his sleeve while inside she begged God to change his mind. "I love you, Wyatt. Doesn't that mean anything to you?"

"It means everything." He eased away, his voice ragged. "I love you, too. But I won't saddle you with a future like I may have."

"You don't know—"

"I can't risk it, Ellie, not knowing I could end up in the same place as my mother. You'd have two kids to take care of alone." He shook his head, his voice sounding tortured as he continued. "I'll finish out today at Wranglers, but then I'm gone from here. I have to—"

"What?" she demanded angrily. "Prepare for a future where you lose your mind?" It hurt to see his pain. "Where's your faith, Wyatt? Where's your trust in God, your real Father?"

"I'm sorry." He touched her lips briefly with his, then walked away.

Heartbroken, Ellie stared after him for a long time, fighting back tears. Then she went to her office to prepare for their guests. In the ensuing hours she devoted herself to the sick children that visited the ranch, doing her utmost to make their time at Wranglers a dream come true. But each time she glimpsed Wyatt, each time his turbulent gaze met hers, each time her heart cried out for him, she sent a prayer for help heavenward.

That evening, after work, she treated Gracie to a meal out before they went to the church for the choir's Christmas cantata. In the darkened sanctuary, while her daughter announced the good news to shepherds in the fields, Ellie saw Wyatt with Cade and Albert in the back pew. She silently wept but made no attempt to speak to him.

This time she would wait for God to work things out. At least she'd learned that much.

Chapter Fifteen

Christmas Eve.

"We need to go shopping, guys," Wyatt told Cade and Albert.

"Good, because thanks to the allowance you gave me I can buy a gift for Gracie." Albert grinned and wiped Cade's face. "And this guy."

Gifts? Wyatt almost groaned, realizing he had nothing to put under the tree for either Albert or Cade. And what in the world could he possibly give to Gracie and her mom?

"I was thinking of groceries," he said. "Can't have Christmas without groceries." *Or Ellie.* "But we can hit the mall, too. I was also wondering if you'd mind watching Cade later while I visit my mother?"

"Sure." Albert asked in a much quieter voice, "Can we stop by Ellie's, too?"

"Of course." So after some grocery shopping and a mall stop, Wyatt pulled into the parking lot at Eventide. His mother seemed to recognize him, and after accepting a bouquet of flowers, she began a rambling series of memories revolving around his first Christmas. When she finished, Wyatt seized his opportunity.

"I brought you a Christmas gift, Mom," he said, using the word for the first time.

He pulled out the small tattered box that held a locket he'd purchased many years ago when he'd still believed his mom would someday come home. He handed it to her, feeling a bittersweet delight when she enthused over the gift. Inside he'd placed two pictures, one of him as a child and one of Cade.

After staring at those pictures for several moments, Ruth suddenly changed. She fidgeted and grew increasingly agitated as she muttered about having to leave. The attendant arrived, and Wyatt knew that was his cue to go. So he kissed her cheek, wished her a Merry Christmas, then collected Albert and Cade from the gathering room, realizing that he'd just spent the first Christmas he could remember with his mom.

Back in his truck, he closed his eyes while Albert buckled in Cade, praying for—what, he didn't know. Help, perhaps, to deal with his uncertain future.

"When will we go to Ellie's?" Albert asked after a long silence.

"I think she'll still be at work. Let's go home and give your bowl one last oiling before you give it to her." He couldn't see her yet, not like this, not while his emotions were so ragged.

But back at home, time didn't help, because everywhere Wyatt looked he saw Ellie's hand. The huge box of baking that now sat inside his porch could only be from her. The decorations that made his home look so festive. The tree she'd helped him decorate when he realized he was trying too hard to be his father's son. Even the bowl Albert carefully wrapped showed Ellie was tied into his life with bonds not easily broken.

Wyatt desperately wanted to run to her, to let her love him, to love her back. But one thing stopped him. Fear of the future. He could not, would not, saddle her with the responsibility of raising Cade, Gracie and maybe even Albert, alone. That was one promise he intended to keep, no matter how much it hurt.

"Wyatt?" Albert stood before him with two glasses of milk and a plate of Ellie's gingerbread cookies. "Cade's napping, so I thought—I wondered—did you always have happy Christmases like this?"

Happy?

"Not always." But Albert pressed, and finally Wyatt began recounting details. Somehow the pain from his past came pouring out.

When he eventually stopped, Albert remained silent for a long time, then said, "I think your father was hard on you because he was trying to protect you."

Taken aback, Wyatt frowned. "Why do you think that?"

"Isn't that what fathers do, what parents do, what everyone does? They protect the special people in their lives as best they can. Because they love them. That's what Gran did for me." Albert munched on another cookie before he continued. "That's what God as our Father does for us. That's what Ellie does. Even Gracie's trying to protect her mom by searching for a daddy who will love them."

Surprised by the depths of Albert's thinking, Wyatt could only listen.

"Learning about your mom made you realize how alone you are." Albert nodded sagely. "It was like that for me when Gran got sick. I knew she was going to die and that then I'd be all alone. I was so scared."

He marveled at Albert's wisdom, the poise he showed

in his words, and was reminded of a verse he'd read. *A child shall lead them.*"

"What did you do?"

Albert gulped his milk before he replied. "I remembered what she'd taught me, that God is always there, always protecting me, no matter what happens. When my uncle got mean I remembered a verse she'd taught me when I was little. I must have said 'I will not fear' a thousand times while I waited for God to protect me." Albert grinned, his milk mustache comical. "And here I am."

"It's not quite—"

"The same?" Albert finished. "Sure it is. Because that's what you're doing for Ellie and Gracie by pushing them away. You're trying to protect them. That's what love does. And you love them. Don't you?"

Those words gave Wyatt a glimpse of his future—sad and empty without Ellie and Gracie, brimming with joy with them in it.

Albert put down his milk. "I think you're protecting them the wrong way," he said.

"You do?" Intrigued, Wyatt looked up at the boy.

"Uh-huh." Albert studied him. "See, Christmas is all about love and giving. That's what God showed us when He gave the gift of His son at Christmas." He finished his cookie. "I think God was saying that with His love we can deal with anything."

Though Wyatt detested milk, he realized he'd drunk the entire glass as he mulled over Albert's words.

With God's love we can deal with anything.

Even schizophrenia?

That meant he'd have to trust God with the unknown. Trust God to help him share whatever future he could forge with Ellie and Gracie. But what was the alternative? Go it alone and miss out on really living, really loving? Throw away everything he wanted in his world?

Become like his father?

No.

It took every ounce of faith Wyatt could dredge up to make the decision.

Okay, God. I'm trusting You.

Overwhelming relief told him he'd made the right choice.

"Albert, I need to go shopping," he said as he jumped to his feet.

"Again?" Albert groaned, then rose. "Okay. But after that, can we go to Ellie's?"

"Absolutely." Wyatt's heart thrummed with anticipation as he drove to the mall. He left Albert pushing Cade in his stroller while he went inside a store and found two gifts that exactly met his needs.

Then they drove to Ellie's. He'd been so stupid to push her away. Ellie had said she loved him. After his colossal mistake, would she still?

"We'll stay in the car so you can have some privacy." Albert grinned. "Not that you'll get much with Gracie there."

Wyatt thanked him and walked to the door. Pushing out a ragged breath, he knocked.

He was prepared to plead his case with Ellie. He was not prepared for a little girl clad in a pair of red jeans and a white T-shirt wearing a green felt elf's hat that flopped over one eye to open the door.

"Hi, Gracie. Is your mommy here?" Boy, had he missed this kid.

"She's in the shower. Why? Are you gonna make her cry again?" Gracie glared at him.

"No, I, uh—" Wyatt had to do something fast to change this situation, or nothing would go as he wanted. "Actually I was hoping I could talk to you first."

"Why?" she demanded.

He knelt on one knee, right there at the door, and looked straight at her. "Because I was wondering…if your mom agrees to marry me, could I be your daddy?"

Gracie shoved back the hat, her blue eyes wide. She gaped at him then breathed, "Really?"

"Absolutely. If your mom agrees. Because I love her, and I want to marry her. That means I'd be marrying you, too." He took a breath. "But I make an awful lot of mistakes, and sometimes I break my promises and—"

"That's okay." She grinned. "Me an' Cade an' Albert will help you get better 'cause we love you."

"I love you, too, Gracie. So will you marry me?" he asked formally.

"Sure." She nodded, her happy smile stretching across her face.

"Thank you. I'm going to make you one promise that I'll never break. I'll always love you, Gracie. As long as I live." Wyatt lifted her hand, pressed a kiss in her palm, then slid a tiny ring with a topaz stone on to her finger. "This is to remind us of my promise to love you always."

"Wow." Gracie lifted her hand to stare at her ring. "Are we 'gaged?" she whispered.

Wyatt nodded and kissed her forehead. "We certainly are."

"Gracie?" Ellie's voice echoed from inside the house.

Wyatt put his finger to his lips. "But you have to keep it a secret until I ask your mom. Okay? Can you do it?" he begged.

"Sure." Gracie turned and yelled, "Mommy, Da—

somebody's here to see you." She winked at him. "'Cause I can't call you Daddy yet," she whispered.

"Gracie Grant, you know very well you are not to open the door—Oh." Ellie appeared, her hair a mass of damp curls. She wore an outfit matching Gracie's, except her hat bore a white fur band. "Hello," she said in her coolest voice.

"Gracie, may I talk to your mom alone?" Wyatt thought he'd never seen anyone so lovely as his Ellie. *Don't let me botch this, God.*

"'Kay." Grace shot him an outrageous wink, then raced away.

"Ellie, I—"

"Merry Christmas, Wyatt. I hope you, Cade and Albert have a happy day." Her cool gray eyes gave away nothing.

Wyatt immediately revamped his approach.

"Thank you for the baking you left. I have your gift here," he said and held out the black velvet ring box. When she didn't take it, he flipped it open to show her the diamond solitaire sitting inside. "Ellie, will you marry me?"

Ellie's gaping stare swiveled from the ring to him, back and forth, confusion filling her face. "Why?"

"Because I love you. I need you in my life." Wyatt's heart welled with emotion. "I have no idea whether or not I will end up as my mother. I have no guarantees to offer you except that, for as long as I breathe, I will love you and do my utmost to cherish you."

"But you said—"

Wyatt touched her cheek, unable to keep his hands away from her. This beautiful woman was what he wanted in his life. Her love meant his world would be whole, complete.

"I forgot, Ellie," he whispered. "I forgot that God is in

charge of my world, and He'll decide my future. I forgot that I need to trust that He will do His best for me." He took her hands in his and pressed the ring box into her palms. "What I finally realized today, thanks to Albert, is that any moment I have with you is more precious than years without you. Because I love you and that's a precious gift from God. So, will you marry me, Ellie Grant, and make Gracie's Christmas wish come true?"

"Yes," she said simply and with heartfelt emotion. She held out her hand for him to slide on her ring. "Because I love you, Wyatt. You are God's answer to me. I'll grab whatever time we have together to share with our kids and whomever else He brings into our paths. Because I love you."

His heart brimming with joy and thanksgiving, Wyatt embraced her. With slow deliberateness he kissed her, pledging his love to her for as long as he lived.

And Ellie kissed him back, at least until a voice came from behind Wyatt.

"Do you think Cade and I can come in now? He needs a diaper change."

Wyatt and Ellie glanced at Albert and burst out laughing.

"By rights, you should have to change him since you're going to be his brother," Wyatt teased.

"Hmm. Something to think about. Merry Christmas." Albert handed Ellie her bowl and Wyatt his son. "Where's Gracie?"

"In here," she called out. "Looking at the 'gagement ring my daddy gave me."

Ellie's eyebrows arched as she glanced at Wyatt.

"I hope you don't mind that I asked Gracie to marry me first," he said as he ushered her inside and closed the door. "And I should have mentioned something else."

"Oh?" In between sneaking glances at her ring, Ellie gave him a wary look.

"I don't know what will happen in the future, darling Ellie, but I intend to keep working at Wranglers Ranch as their staff veterinarian because that's where I belong."

"I know what will happen in the future," she said as she pressed a kiss against Cade's head and then Wyatt's cheek. "What will happen is that I will love you, and you will love me, and together we'll work at Wranglers, showing kids what God's love is all about. Right?"

"Lady, you are so right." Wyatt turned his head just the tiniest bit to kiss her again, thrilled by what his future held as long as she was by his side.

"Mommy, Albert wants me to open my gift. An' I want Cade to open his giant nutcracker cookie. 'Kay?"

"Wait till we're all there, sweetie. We'll open them together." Ellie nudged Wyatt toward the bathroom. "You can change Cade in there. After we open gifts, we're going to Wranglers. They're having a staff campfire, and I can't wait to share our news."

"Excellent idea. Christmas Eve together with friends. How can it get better?"

But as they sat around a campfire later, singing carols, Wyatt knew in the depths of his heart that it would get better. Because God so loved the world that He gave His only son.

That was the message he and Ellie and their family would help Wranglers Ranch spread.

He clung to his fiancée's hand, ready to face their future with God in charge.

* * * * *